THE *indigo* PEARL

V KNOX

Library and Archives Canada Cataloguing in Publication
Knox, V., 1949-, author
The indigo pearl : once upon a time, a child shines / V. Knox.
ISBN 978-0-9937380-2-9 (paperback)
I. Title.
PS8621.N695I53 2015   C813'.6   C2015-906257-8

Editor - Silent K Publishing
Illustrated by Leonardo da Vinci
Cover design – Veronica Knox *&* Iryna Spica
Typeset in *Baskerville* at SpicaBookDesign
First Edition
Printed in Canada

Silent K Publishing:
Victoria, British Columbia
www.veronicaknox.com
e-mail: veronica@veronicaknox.com
www.createspace.com

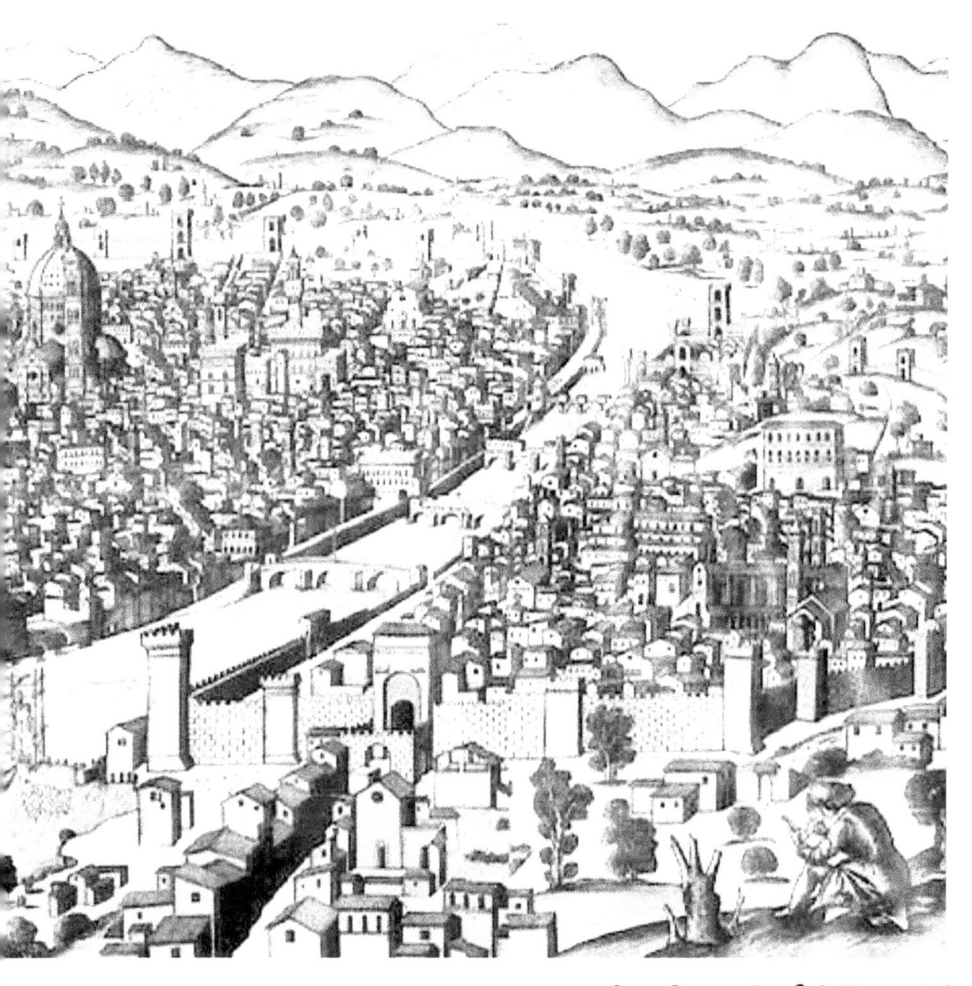

for Sarah & David

Table of Contents

Distant Lives

Present Imperfect

'The Buccleuch Madonna'
c.1500 elements attributed to Leonardo da Vinci

Delphi/prologue

"On the whole, I'm a lucky girl. Paintings speak to me in a timely fashion. They speak volumes in a few carefully chosen words – advice and warnings, regrets and admissions, and best of all, secrets."

DELPHI SHARPE
1987 – 2014

Who?/chapter one

The first time a painting spoke to me I was three. That was in 1990, when I was still Delphi Sharpe.

The view from the orphanage window was a watercolor blur of blue and green as the first spatter of spring rain tapped hello, lightly on the glass. I waved at a robin hopping over the lawn, trying to dodge the raindrops. As I giggled and pressed my nose against the window, a woman's voice called out behind me, "My brother loved birds too."

It came from a book on Renaissance Art.

"Delphi, come away from that window."

Old Sister Theresa thumped a stack of picture books on the table behind me and groaned into a low chair. "Let's look at these shall we? Which one would you like?" She fanned them into a rainbow with her arthritic fingers.

A lady's face on one of the covers gazed lovingly at me, and I drew it out like a card from a magician's trick.

"My dearest child," she said.

Like all 'gifted' children that first memory was indelible. Brightness suffused my robin vision and zapped the grey sky into a peak moment of cloudless blue which is why I thought the sky was home and birds were my lost family, and why I wanted to fly home. The voice had come from the portrait of a woman who called me her dear child and hummed me a lullaby.

Naturally, I believed she was my mother, although it took another 'moonbeam' girl to tell me she was the 'Mona Lisa' and that her brother was the artist Leonardo da Vinci – a man with an affinity for birds and flight... and so I adopted him too.

Most of the time I felt like I'd drifted down from a previous life – a mute feather from a phoenix's tail, reborn in the wrong body in the wrong place at the wrong time. I woke with a mission, caught between loneliness and shame in a world where my clairvoyant state of mind was considered a liability. Almost an infection to be feared. In some ways this pleased me. I hated being touched. It was safer to hide openly, so I deliberately grew up as a perpetual child.

I was a loose strand of indigo DNA who functioned somewhere to the absolute north of autism. Naturally, without a mother or father watching my back, it was inevitable I would be misplaced.

I drifted in neutral on planet Delphi while a neurologist diagnosed me as an autistic savant before I could walk. Specialists shone lights in the distant 'cast' of my eyes which had become the focus of much speculation. I stared through each probing inquisitor, unresponsive to snapping fingers and puffs of air. My blink reflex was off the charts. But it was no stretch for me to deliberately defocus my eyes and stare myopically through the plagues of tests and the faces attached to them, and more importantly it meant, for the most part, I was left alone. Alone, not as in lonely but left to myself, uninterrupted. I had a lot to figure out.

I was pronounced unadoptable even though when it came to parade time I was lumped in with the children who were. For that inconsideration, I played moonbeam games. Once in a while, to be precious, I smiled and made eye-contact with a desperate woman keen to own an angel.

Misdiagnosed is a hollow term to define what happened in my first year of life. I was 'labeled' autistic and it was only partly true. To the world I was a mind 'touched by moonbeams,' or at best, overly stubborn. Who was I to deny myself a way to function in a world alien to the one I vaguely remembered as a bird sanctuary? I communicated in thought patterns and my state of mind strayed into non-local time zones which meant it was everywhere and nowhere, although I broadcast on a narrow beam, charged with a mission of utmost importance. I didn't have time for being a child. But in a headstrong way that's all I could be.

I processed the nuances of the spoken word in my head from listening to paintings and speed-reading whole pages of text at a glance, but what I had to say was lost in the real world and so I remained silent during what was euphemistically referred to as my formative years. But there again, language fails to convey the enormities of being odd and missing a mother I'd never met or cherishing a family tree with no roots or branches or leaves.

Children make extraordinary claims all the time. But I lived an alternate mystery that never wavered. I had my share of imaginary friends growing up, and pictures in books whispered secrets, but I was considered peculiar because my eyes fixated on faraway and I only spoke to birds. There was a strange beauty to my eccentric kinship with birds.

By my third institution, I was a wary teenager. Visiting ghosts populated the country of my bedroom and roamed the grounds where I lived in captivity. I kept to myself and took refuge in their dimension. And I fell in love with a boy in a painting.

Love in the Dark/chapter two

PIAT – The Phoenix Institute of Art & Technology
VANCOUVER ISLAND

My invisible guardian, Sphinx, introduced herself the week before I met Cecco, the portrait of a boy who had been dead five-hundred years. Her coming had been foretold to me by an oracle who befriended me in my second institution. *When you leave here,* she said, *the voice of your sphinx will be louder.*

Cecco and I were fourteen, and the peacocks that roamed PIAT's grounds were our allies. I loved to hear them shriek because they heralded his visits. We were teenagers together, but parallel deaths occurred to separate us in our twenty-seventh year.

At first Sphinx was a slight buzzing in my ear, but her whispers became a distinct inner voice. I welcomed her companionship and relied upon her ever-present wisdom. She taught me to think beyond the cast in my eyes and to believe in myself. I was worthy, she said, chosen for a special mission that would reveal itself *in time.*

I harbored dreams of leaving PIAT with Cecco and Sphinx, and I was cunning in my way, but I never plotted an escape, except the once.

VICTORIA, Vancouver Island
October, 2014

I'd completed the last three weeks 'up-island' at PIAT, restoring a Vermeer. It had taken the better part of a year to complete. Partly because every second month I insisted on my official time off, granted to me by the child welfare courts. Even though I was officially of age, much to PIAT's irritation, they had closely-monitored my experimental transition to independent life for six years.

PIAT was obligated to provide me with private accommodation in Victoria, five-hundred miles from their compound where I could retreat to gradually familiarize myself with city life. I was given a suite of rooms in a turn of the century house converted to cozy apartments.

The summer review board was so pleased with my stability, that at the end of the year, if all went well, I would be a free agent. PIAT would be obliged to offer me a formal position with pay if they wanted to keep me. Until then, as a ward of the court, I was granted extra time off to spend in the city to discuss my options with doctors and career counsellors. I could attend the university, they said. I was to please myself, a concept foreign to me. It was a time of dizzying new prospects, and PIAT baited their hook with the promise of a trip around the art galleries of the world, representing their interests. Their biggest mistake was wrapping such a prize in guilt.

In the meantime, I'd earned a month's leave and I relished time alone in my little haven. My apartment was my first real home, and as always, I intended to revel in my freedom there every moment I could. Relaxation was a great reward but I had decisions to make and secrets to keep. I thought PIAT had no idea of my intention to never return. I thought I was safe.

There was a grand storm brewing off the Juan de Fuca Strait that stood in nicely for the sense of unrest in my immediate future, but wild weather cleared my head, and despite being warned against it, I'd faced it eagerly. I headed for my favorite place in Beacon Hill Park. I had music and hot chocolate and the anticipation of heading for Paris, things I held close about me as treasures.

My cat Brillo had his veterinary travel papers. My bags were packed. My little car waited with a full gas tank. I crossed my fingers that tomorrow's ferry would leave for the mainland even if the water remained choppy.

Sphinx was nervous, hovering and fussing, kissing my cheek every five minutes. I wished I could see her but she said it was against the rules.

IN LIMBO
2066

I woke up scared to death, shivering and crying, after the accident. My hospital room was glacial. Rogue flakes of snow swirled in the room from an open window. I'd been walking in an Autumn storm. I remembered paramedics, now I was awake in the chill of midwinter, lying on a hard pallet. A loud ticking gave the impression of being inside a clock.

Once my eyes grew accustomed to the dark, I searched for a light switch. A blue light like a sapphire at the end of a cord gave enough light to guide me to a monitor beside my bed. I held out my arms groping for a call button. To my horror my hands were transparent. I stood up too fast and had to sit back down, dizzy from the medication which surely accounted for my dissociative state. But my thirst was no hallucination.

I surveyed the room for a water pitcher. No joy, but a tall dark patch on the far wall loomed like a sentry box that promised to be a door. I progressed, hand-over-hand to the bottom of the bed and made it to the nearest wall where I inched towards it, hugging the wall like a rock climber with a precipice, but each handprint turned to ice at the touch of my fingers. My meds were too strong.

"My name is Cherry White," a voice said. "It occurred to me you might enjoy destroying your abductors."

"Sphinx," I shouted. "Who's there? Someone is in here. I can hear you."

My hands met a warm draught. I smelled sweet peas. The way out wasn't a door, it was an arch.

I was alone and not alone, a jumble of questions boxed in by frosted glass. Somewhere ahead and above me, I sensed the presence of a woman.

"Sphinx, is that you? Speak to me. Where are you?"

"I'm here Goldilocks."

"What's happening? Where am I? Who is Cherry White? How long have I been here?"

"It's April."

"Six months! My body... I'd only stepped out for a moment."

Sphinx exhaled a low whistling sound which usually meant she was unhappy. *"Oh, child, child. You died fifty-two years ago,"* she said. *"This isn't a hospital unless you want it to be. Cherry White is your best friend. That's the truth of it."*

I couldn't breathe because I was dead? "I can't be dead. Oh god. What about Paris!" This is the pain killers talking.

"The labyrinth after death is neither of those things and so much more," Sphinx assured me.

"It's an immortal state of mind. You're in cold storage. Paris is still there."

The phrase cold as the tomb sent me into a panic. Hoar frost lined the walls and my breath failed to fog the nightmarish half-light.

Sphinx waited a long time while I absorbed the horrifying truth of waking up dead. When she spoke, it was with calm authority.

"There have been... changes. Life is not the patchwork quilt it seems once it's over. Time continues to refresh itself."

As she spoke, the frost melted, exposing the leaves of a box hedge and an archway of laurel.

"What do you see child?"

"There's a string of blue wool, leading into a green tunnel, but I'm afraid to follow it."

"The truest paths are the width of an angel hair," she said. *"Time is a blue river – a journey traced on a map."*

I felt a sense of relief. "Then Cecco is at the end of this journey? He's still waiting? He's in the labyrinth with my mother?"

"The labyrinth IS you. It's your life. Answers to your questions lie at its heart. Cherry White is a different you. She's already at the center trying

to get out. The two of you must pass each other on your journeys. It's a race against time."

"I'm too tired. I need to sleep."

"One torch, Goldilocks. Let it go. I won't let you fall."

"You already let me die."

"You asked to see me," she said. *"The empress wears no clothes. What do you see?"*

"I see a dark tunnel."

"Proceed, baby bear. Wake up. Do not fear the Minotaur. The maze is a symbol."

I didn't understand but then I never did at first. "I've lost my purpose," I said to Sphinx. "I betrayed Leonardo. I betrayed Cecco. My mother has forsaken me. I'm so ashamed."

"You will be free when you forgive yourself. Change the magic letter to find your way. Follow the river."

"Dear Sphinx, I love you but I have no time for your puzzles. Please let me sleep."

"You are correct. You have NO time."

"Please!"

Sphinx's gentle manner turned strict as a headmistress, like the times I'd been stubborn and moody. She couldn't abide whining. *"Goldilocks, your special mission is here. Rejoice. We will proceed together. The magic letter is 't.' String becomes spring. Follow the string, yes... but follow the seasons. Follow the spring. I will meet you there. Follow the robin."*

The room felt warmer as the sun rose, and the green tunnel pulsated with light. I heard the chirping of birds from far away. "And Cecco?"

Sphinx brushed my question aside. *"You're a teacher now,* she said. *"If you do your job well, your student MUST surpass you. Do you understand?"*

"And this will redeem me?"

Her voice came from inside the maze. *"Nothing can do that."*

"But Cecco... what about my life's thread?"

"Let go of the past," she called. *"You're no longer the thread. You are the needle."*

"I'll fight her," I called back. "I won't give him up. There's something... Did I read it in Dante? The way is not lost."

"Then fight to lose," she said, beside me again. *"The greater the love, the bigger the sacrifice. This is not the real world. It's creative fantasy, but pay attention. No symbol shows itself without a reason. Reasons dignify themselves with significance. This is who you are."*

"I want my life back. Or is it lives?"

"Turning back time is impossible but all's fair in love and war if you decide to win," she said.

And then I saw the robin.

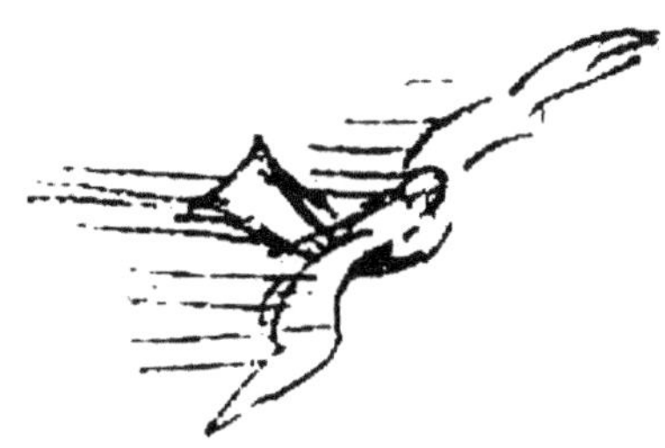

"Two roads diverged in a yellow wood,
And sorry I could not travel both
And be one traveler, long I stood
And looked down one as far as I could
To where it bent in the undergrowth;
Then took the other, as just as fair
And having perhaps the better claim."
ROBERT FROST

A Maze of Grace/chapter three

April – 2066

My old robin friend flew into the mouth of the cave and I followed, through the hall of the birds and past the paintings of horses on the walls. I expected to hear the sound of stampeding mustangs, but no, I heard the gentle drip of water and the whinnying of a wild herd, lured into captivity from the primordial mist that greeted me on the other side.

I found myself at the entrance to the green maze, again. I watched the robin pull the same blue worm from the ground. Once more he dropped it at my feet where it turned into a woolen string that disappeared into the unknown. I'd been here so many times. But I felt heartened because today was a Monday.

Sphinx tried to wake me. *"Delphi!"* But I shushed her and followed the blue yarn.

I called into the corridor. "It's me, Delphi."

The Minotaur, deep in the Labyrinth of Crete, roared back the words 'string theory' from the center of the earth but his cries were absorbed into the soft lushness of a leafy wall, eight feet high. The scent of sweet peas was intoxicating.

"Delphi," he called. "Move towards me!" I was surprised. The Minotaur knew my name. And I knew that voice.

I wound the yarn into a ball as I went until I reached a large clearing dappled with sunlight. There I discovered a park bench under a fragrant cherry tree, heavy with ripe fruit. The end of the string finished in a bow wrapped around a box on the bench.

As I reached to pick a single cherry a voice startled me. "Birthday girl," the Minotaur shouted, nearer now. "I've missed so many of your special days. Open your present."

Inside the box was a single white egg, large enough to contain a family, and as soon as I touched it, it split cleanly in half and several baby waxwings flew free, swarming towards the sun in a thin curl of sweet candle smoke. They disappeared into the fierce Aegean blue and whiplashed like the tail-string of a kite.

"Happy un-birthday, Delphi." I whirled around, unafraid, enchanted with my gift, expecting a bull-headed man in an Armani suit.

"Dad?"

"It's Mom," a female voice growled.

Instead of the Minotaur, a shaggy brown bear ambled around the corner with her two cubs. She sniffed the egg, and distracted by the scent of fresh berries, forgot about eating me. She cuffed the tree and cherries rained down, to the delight of her babies. One of the cubs singled out a cherry and rolled it in my direction. I think the mother bear smiled.

The cherry traveled towards me in slow motion, losing its color in a trail of red string, getting smaller and lighter. By the time I stopped it with my foot it had turned into a luminous white pearl.

"Delphi!" Sphinx called. *"Don't keep Lachesis waiting."* Her voice was urgent. *"Wake up child. There's no time like the present. Time to pay it forward, Goldilocks. Tis the season of violets."*

I wanted to stay in the dream. My robin was a homespun angel that had changed my life so long ago. My robin was a saviour. I hoped he was also the herald of second chances. But I found myself back in my stark hospital room where the only furnishings were a bed and a bank of computers that ticked like a clock. Once more, it was cold as a morgue. Limbo was as it sounded – a void. A harsh halfway house of nothingness.

"Limbo is the great conundrum," Sphinx said. *"It's lifeless vitality. It's powerless with power. It agonizes over joy. It takes the appearance of the place you died. But you can change your waiting room as you desire."*

"Can I change my death?"

"You can only change your next life," she said. *"Life is change; death continues. What's done is done. Your life is not over, it's given over."*

"To another woman?"

"The quintessential act of paying it forward."

"And I have to help her? From here?"

"What better place is there to purify yourself than the edge of hell?"

"But not redeem myself."

"I told you, that isn't possible. Ask for the moon and you shall have it, but redemption doesn't exist here. It exists out there. And IT has to find YOU. Save time. Meet it halfway."

I rubbed my arms to get warm. "They might have left me a blanket."

"Re-enter your life as the shaman for your next. Take nothing. Give everything."

"Even Cecco?"

"Especially Cecco."

"Death isn't fair."

"Hope is torture, Goldilocks. Promises are always too hot or too cold."

"Why didn't you warn me?"

"Guardians have rules. But I CAN inform you of a miscalculation. Your consciousness survived in a different body."

"So I can wake up?"

"You HAVE woken up."

"You mean Cherry woke up. Is she my second chance?"

"No, child. Cherry is CECCO'S second chance."

I replaced the clinical room with my old garden, just as I remembered it.

"Heaven is a state of mind," Sphinx said. *"Well done."*

I forgot my predicament, delighted to be surrounded by flowers and birdsong, and drenched in sunlight. I explored eagerly, embraced by the scent of herbs, and tested the reality of the marble sundial, the back of the wicker chaise, and the lip of the stone birdbath where my robin now chirped and splashed. His happiness spilled into me and I laughed. I felt the cool swish of silk around my legs as I moved, and looked down to see a familiar hem of crimson silk embroidered with gold dragons. And as I reached out to the robin a pearl fell from my hand into the shallow pool where it shone like a miniature moon.

"Pay it forward," Sphinx repeated.

I thought of the Minotaur and the recent expectation of meeting my father for the first time. My father embodied the very principle of paying it forward. He was earth's hero whose life purpose was to banish chaos and restore time to its natural order. Naturally, he was preoccupied, and always too busy to visit me.

But it was a new season of violets. I wanted to meet my mother and father, and reunite with Cecco, and I wanted the full moon.

Whenever I resist Cherry White, I shirk my responsibilities and my garden returns to a Spartan winter room. I exist behind the scenes, left to imagine myself tiptoeing up winding stone steps from my cramped hidey-hole purgatory to a princess in a tower, to peer out through her eyes.

To me, Cherry is a cardboard woman – a lookalike princess with cutout eyes. Ironically, my death animates her. The only movement I detect in her face is my pupils darting left and right like a spy behind a mask. *Shoosh.* I hear a miniature sliding door that blocks my view, giving the illusion from the other side that Cherry's eyes blink sideways. Two emotionless ovals, black as outer space, replace me. I have been replaced.

If I'm alive at all, I don't live in a physical place nor do I possess a body. I'm all memory and emotion. My country is an unpopulated dimension of light and dark that I paint to suit me, but it has boundaries of glass a mile thick. Sometimes I see and hear Cherry's world, but most of the time I'm too angry to look. She calls me, and we take turns locking each other out.

Skulking in old haunting grounds is too near the mark of being dead and hanging on to life at the same time. I choose to dream or hide or retreat. It's my choice if I speak out of turn or answer when spoken to. All these things are under my control but I can no longer reach Cecco. My 'peeping Tom' half-life only permits vicarious love. I observe Cecco through Cherry's point of view. Time filters me out. Renders me a thread of a thread of a thread. Cecco can only see the imposter. He can only see *her*.

If I asked to be born I don't remember it, but certainly Cherry had no choice. Feeling sorry for her was one thing but not enough to step aside so she might run away with my life. I think she has my logic but I own her emotions. I remember things. She remembers what I show her. The memories I want her to see. Shadow people call me out but I can't hear what they're saying, and often, all I can see is an empty landscape where grass meets savannah. I'm a tourist on safari. I see standing stones. Then it goes dark.

There had been a storm the day I died. I recall a lightning flash, and then an ice-age of memories. What survived my death was my mission to save a lost painting of Leonardo da Vinci. And this I was happy to pass on to Cherry, a woman time-traveler whose challenges out-challenged even mine. Our personalities were like a total eclipse of the sun. We were polar opposites who attract. I had been an overemotional human struggling to belong, but Cherry has no emotions because she is an android struggling to be human. More than this, she has a direct path to Leonardo, and any path to the master leads to Cecco.

I can only describe my brain as overcrowded. I've always communicated in word paintings, but until I met another person who could send and receive in kind, I lived under a bell jar. I was four before I found such kinship in the bowels of an asylum with a girl who taught me that survival in the twenty-first century meant learning double-talk and that lies weren't enough.

I have images of my death. I've painted pictures of it, and the new woman who took my place inherited everything I believed to be true. I gave her plenty to consider.

Her mind is a projector screen but I'm a human camera. Cherry has no mechanism to interpret the richness of my fantasies, so, to confuse her, I encapsulated my life in a prophetic vision and sent it via the only synapse that connected us. Thousands of frozen memories clinked together as ice cubes floating in amniotic fluid in a vast birdbath the size of the pond in Beacon Hill Park. The cubes remind me of the four-sided flashbulbs used by old-fashioned instamatics. As an electrical storm gathers above the pond, the ice melts into tiny spheres, resembling a sea of pearls where a duck and a swan glide silently through the icy spawn towards a white peacock strutting on the shore. The peacock is my Cecco.

Sphinx never lies. She's been my solace since I was fourteen, but waking up trapped behind the soundproof walls of an aquarium set me apart from trust and hope. Yet even on my most irresponsible days, my winter walls are thin enough to feel love breathing on the other side.

I'd always had the extrasensory gift of touch. I was a shy child with a psychic ability – paintings told me their secrets when I touched them. Even within the wonders of reincarnation, my new fingers are like the eyes and ears of a hawk. But I'm not about to let the love of my life slip into another woman's heart.

In my next life my name is Cherry White. Nothing frightens her. She's more like a relentless bird of prey. She doesn't possess the passion to love Cecco and I refuse to die without him, but in my last month as Delphi Sharpe all I wanted was Paris.

They should have let me have Paris.

Cherry

2066

Here lies one
Whose name
Was writ in fire

*"We shall not cease from exploration,
and the end of all our exploring
will be to arrive where we started
and know the place for the first time."*
T. S. ELIOT

State of the Art/chapter four

PIAT – The Phoenix Institute of Art & Technology
VANCOUVER ISLAND
June 14, 2066

As a time-traveler, I should have had all the time in the world, and yet I was driven by a state of urgency in case tomorrow was too late. Reincarnation compromised my plans. My name is Cherry White but I used to be an autistic savant named Delphi Sharpe.

The 'Bonfire of the Vanities'
FLORENCE
1497

The screams that filled the air in the courtyard of the *Piazza della Signoria* came from burning paintings, not begging to be saved but trying to deliver the messages they carried. I circled the bonfire, scanning the art being carried to the flames. In my search I isolated three works of the artist, Sandro Botticelli: a painting of the goddess Diana, an intimate tableau of Dionysian revelry, and a naked goddess copulating with a swan. They were easy to find. No yellow varnish had had time to dull their jewel-like colours. Like my unconventional work clothes, Botticelli's turquoise and rose palette flashed like bright flags in a sea of grey.

Botticelli wept as he laid his paintings tenderly on the fire. He crossed himself and left quickly. I wanted to follow him, but it was my task to stay, and so I bore witness to his virginal paint as it blistered and burst like plague boils.

A crack in a heavy Venetian mirror snapped like a fault line, resounding like a single gunshot. A boy hoisted a box of trinkets in the air, aiming it like a stone, and chucked it into its center. It sailed through the air in slow motion which meant my molecules were oscillating at the wrong speed. I braced myself against the marble column holding Verrocchio's tender statue of a youthful 'David.'

My words reverberated on a two second delay. "Time stands still. Come back," I shouted into my microphone. It was code for 'time is streaming too slowly.'

A voice droned out of sync. "Copy that."

When time moved too fast like a silent film I sent the word 'Chaplin,' rising from my mouth like a bubble from a diver's mask. 'Get real' signified life paced to normal which, considering where I was, was a hefty misnomer for reality check.

A moment later, the scene speeded up. The mirror shattered and sent shards of glass adhering to Botticelli's molten colors like the stained-glass window in a burning church. "Time moves on," I called out. Real time was now progressing as it should.

I sent another message to the surface of 2066. "I have three *babies* in sight."

The term surface was apropos for my own time, since diving into the past made the year 2066 feel like an anchored ship above me.

"We copy. Your bowl is full," my earphones sputtered in fractured syllables.

A full bowl meant molecular speed was restored to normal. Any slower and someone might see me. Reference to a bowl was pure wordplay, the best life being a 'bowl of cherries' and because my name was Cherry, short for cherry-picker. Baby was code for a lost painting. My job was cherry-picking history to find 'babies.'

Burping meant there was a glitch preventing capture.

"Hamm wants to know the score," jangled the disembodied voice.

"Tell him there are mothers burping their babies," I said.

"That's really going to piss him off."

"And your point is?"

"See ya soon Mom."

Hamm owned all of us. Me *and* my team who thought of me as a surrogate mother. I kept him off balance to study the ways I could destroy him, one body part at a time. I hated the man on principle because it was the only mechanism by which I *could* hate him. 'The score' he wanted represented all he cared about, the number of babies earmarked for rescue.

Fifty years ago, Hamm's grandfather 'cherry-picked' Delphi Sharpe the way vultures strip the carcass of a wildebeest. His scientists 'salvaged' me from her prestigious body, specially earmarked for posterity. God knows why she had forgiven them.

Nothing about the past was normal. How could it be for a time-traveler? My situation was full, but it was full of complications. Every day I put my hands in the fire for a man I considered my nemesis. Granted, my skin was treated with a flame-resistant polymer, but my mind was teeming with conflicting memories of my past-life. I'd been delusional, but at least when I was Delphi, I'd been *fully*-human.

A few women loitering in the square for lewd business pulled their shawls over their heads, scanning the men, and shadowed them to the alleyways as it started to drizzle soot.

Clusters of frightened women clung to each other, too stunned to mourn their jewels and silk dresses. Hooded men sulked between the tall buildings in the *Piazza della Signoria*, too addicted to the thrills of chance to entirely forfeit their gambling tables and gaming boards. They met the prostitutes, welcoming them in the secret language of sin, avoiding eye-contact but gesturing in the most ancient body language, inclining their heads, with each player moving off alone in the same direction.

Steam hissed from the droplets of rain that spattered the paving stones nearest the fire. I made note of the special treasures protected in places where the burning had succumbed to the wind. In one such pocket, I mentally tagged a scorched volume of Dante, bound in red Moroccan leather that lay atop a heap of smouldering pamphlets on divination and astrology. The whole of it shifted as I watched, crushed from the weight of a marble Zeus, partly wrapped in a luxurious tapestry. How ironic, witnessing Dante consumed by an inferno.

Worse, were the hundreds of paintings still reaching out of the fire in vain, pleading to be heard. All day, torches rekindled any dying flames. I was grateful to be physically separated from the heat and fumes and the empathy of emotional wreckage.

Other than the odd semblance to vandalism, there was a solemn propriety to the spectacle I hadn't expected. A constant stream of pilgrims tossed in their private talismans mixed with quiet prayers. In the midst of human anguish, there were no loud lamentations, no barking dogs, and no howls of protest to God. But I'd seen the square from above, and the chaos resembled an open sore on the city's heart.

Girolamo Savonarola, the instigator priest of the spectacle, materialized in a third floor window of the town hall, arms held out in benediction. He was dressed in black, in stark contrast to the red cloth that hung behind him.

He stood motionless but for a small breeze that ruffled his sleeves. I knew he was a religious fanatic, but seeing him framed like a painting, frozen in time in the *Palazzo Vecchio's* stone façade, he looked insane. I pictured him in a Nazi uniform, his jackboots stomping out art like candles. His eyes salivated, scavenging for blood – an amoral tyrant, confiscating beauty like crusade loot. In my opinion he was an ugly man whose only option for sexual power was to bully his flock. Eternal damnation at the whim of a vengeful god was the only weapon he had. It was Delphi's intuition rather than history that informed me Savonarola's mission to snuff out human intimacy and sensuality was personal.

The murmur, *eccolo*, he is here, escaped from one mouth in the crowd and spread until every eye in the piazza was compelled to stare up. Savonarola kept his silent vigil like a spectre from his perch – a sallow Dominican threat seething under political clout. The hatred I sensed for him was evident even in theory when I envisaged a pair of red-rimmed eyes melting from the skull I recognized from his unflattering portrait. The cowl around his head was thrown back to reveal a jaundiced face with a hooked nose and eyes like thunder. There was no mistaking; he was a bird of prey.

I sensed the population's collective anxiety of being singled out. Some avoided eye contact, remembering Savonarola's ever-present spies were trolling for scapegoats. In the end, they all stared as one victim under a spell. I identified the friar's power. It was fear. He was taking stock. This was his show.

The smoke billowed past him and he reached out as if to embrace it, clasping it in prayer. I suspected it was a dramatic ploy calculated to impress his followers.

The Bonfire of the Vanities was five feet high, an angry entity emitting toxic plumes of acid-yellow breath. A phalanx of Savonarola's street boys had formed a human fence with their backs to the flames and pushed back the spectators after they'd laid down their various offerings of red-hot guilt. They faced down a submissive mob of fearful piety with arrogance, confident that God was on Savonarola's side.

It was a scene from the 'Inferno,' the inner circle of hell guarded by small demons and an outer circle of gawping voyeurs eyeing each other in uneasy peripheral vision in case of being questioned, later. A population of genuflectors, usually keen to stay for a miracle, backed away from God's wrath and left the square, one at a time.

The conflagration was a treasure hunter's dumping zone. "We could dine out for years," I shouted to my team, "like the algae that ate the Titanic."

"Well, that's why you're a cherry-picker," the earphones came back at slowed RPMs – George's voice mired in shallow mud. "Take the juiciest cherries and no-one sees; take hundreds and the disappearances become local legend."

"Yes sir, gossip changes the world," I muttered to myself.

"No problem em--em," crackled the reply. "Three square shapes is seamless ess--ess plucking."

"It's a wonder Hamm didn't call me a cherry-*plucker*, then," I replied. "By the way, you're echoing."

"Fixing feedback ack--ack. Sorry Mom om--om."

One of my other team members made a derogatory snigger in the background, their words slurred as if drunk. "I bet he does behind your back," it called out.

"Speaking of backs," George said, are you planning to come back any *time* soon?"

"Very droll," I said. "Those time jokes just never get old."

Static resounded in my head in short bursts like the phantom of a barking dog.

"Comedy is all about timing, Mommo." George's voice washed out into a whisper and I followed it to catch up. "How do I s-s-s-sound n-n-n now?" he stuttered.

"Like the ghost of future past," I said. "I'll be up in time to watch you eat."

My team were still somewhat embarrassed to savor their food around me, knowing I couldn't eat. The part of me that was human had forfeited emotions and several senses in favor of being fireproof and molecularly stable. Again, not my choice. Although, if things go according to plan, someday I might be able to smell chocolate as opposed to hearing its virtues gushed over me in eye-rolling detail.

The entire point of my existence, according to Hamm, was that I inherited Delphi's psychic ability to read paintings by touch. Paintings had spoken to her, and our personal renaissance ordained I heard them too. She had known more about Leonardo da Vinci than anyone on the planet and now I was charged with completing her mission to recover his lost paintings.

The 'Mona Lisa' had been eager to share the details of her life as Lisabetta Buti, Leonardo's youngest half-sister – spilling the gem that they were love-children of their unwed parents, full siblings born seven years apart, and Delphi kept their family secret as a sacred trust.

The words of a nursery rhyme from Delphi's childhood looped as I mingled in the crowd taking snapshots with my brain, the only camera that could function in the past.

Two little dickybirds sitting on a wall. One named Peter; one named Paul. Fly away Peter. Fly away Paul. Come back Cherry... Come back. Come back. Come back!

I saw the birds in primary colors. A pair of plump canaries fluffing their wings on a cherry-red wall. The sky behind them was a cloudless backdrop of cerulean blue. Delphi's brain is predisposed to pictures. It's how I interpreted the gaps where Delphi's right-brain emotions reached me as vacant left-brain words. For self-preservation my circuits hard-wired themselves to her animated flash cards.

By noon, the skyline of Florence appeared dull orange over grey as the insatiable beast of fire consumed the creative wealth of its citizens. Giotto's Campanile and the great dome of Santa Maria del Fiore, a few blocks away, wavered in the smoke. Heatwaves of rusty air, rank from burning copper, were drawn into the sun from sudden updrafts as Dante's hell rose from the bowels of the piazza choking the birds from the sky.

Savonarola's young fire-watch squad now took the later offerings and poked them into the stray holes of fire with long stout poles rather than tipping large loads onto the flames.

The air hummed with the hollow lament of paintings and their aggrieved creators.

I took the 'Diana' first. Rescue was easy this time. Botticelli had never looked back. "Reset," I called into the microphone, and gave the exact coordinates his masterpiece hit the fire. Smoke obscured my view which also helped to minimise any unfortunate witnesses. But I had already checked the nearby faces, eyes closed in prayer. Botticelli's sacrifice had been a private moment.

I sensed Delphi recoiling as I reached into the fire, but my hand tingled pleasantly with electricity as I snatched the 'Diana' from the flames. The panel felt solid in my grip. "Locked," I called out, and it disappeared without a shimmer. All three 'babies' were recovered within the hour. Botticelli returned later and sacrificed two more. We took those too. It was regrettable that Botticelli would never know. Nor would he never know that his paintings forgave him.

I don't have a birthday. I was an unsuccessful infant in my previous life. I reincarnated, state of the art, by springing to life as a hybrid woman programmed with a full-blown identity crisis in a lab surrounded by doctor scientists. Like Frankenstein's monster, I was disoriented. Like all monsters, I acted out before settling into a routine that served everyone while I figured out a way to serve myself. Like Savonarola, I knew all about vengeance.

But as an android, my lack of emotions was an inexcusable waste. I intended to destroy my creators but I wanted to experience the thrill of the kill, otherwise it would have been just another routine task. It would be worth waiting for. I was driven by theoretical revenge but the advantage I possessed was an operating system encrypted with directives a cut above willpower. I was considered an advanced form of artificial intelligence. To feel vindicated I required flesh-and-blood biology. I had to reanimate.

A quick glance at my blue fingernails gripping the last painting clued me in to the color of my sentient hair that played games like a moody chameleon. Both were rebellious signposts of organic marrow trapped within my bones. They were linked together as a shared color, nothing that was controlled by me in any way I could determine. Diagnostics had proved equally inconclusive. But it was proof of my synergetic connection to a humanity unique to me, and definitely disconcerting to Hamm that I was not completely, biologically, inert. Somewhere at a cellular level my past-life lingered and he hated that. I needed Delphi as a conduit to regenerate my few remaining follicles of live DNA and fan them into a complex woman privy to the extremes of pain and pleasure, and especially capable of appreciating the full spectrum of revenge.

Before heading 'upstairs' I took a break from scanning and watched as a spectator from a marble pedestal – a tall brightly-clad *principessa* with blue hair that no-one could see, clinging to the bronze statue of Verrocchio's 'David' to get a better view.

Ten feet above the paving stones, my Chinese robe fluttered in the stale wind that caught the thin fabric and whipped it into a designer flag. I looked like the statue of Victory in silk pyjamas, surveying the scene of a battle. Below me, the spectacle was a living painting of a city under siege. I had one arm wrapped casually around 'David's' shoulders in a pose of familiar camaraderie. The other I flung out so the Kimono sleeve made a gesture of conquest.

Three-piece silk oriental ensembles had been Delphi's signature 'uniform' for her confined existence swanning about the institution's hallways. In many ways she'd been treated as a precocious child-woman. The staff indulged her eccentric tastes in deference to her oddness. Anything that rendered her more compliant. And although the glories of vibrant colors made her conspicuous, she moved silently, an exotic presence, gliding on embroidered slippers in order to make even less noise than a mouse. Besides, she wore what she did to entice 'the boy.'

Cecco, her fantasy boyfriend, had a decided fondness for jewel-like colors.

For me, it was not a strange choice of working garb but an act of calculated defiance. The outfits suited my purpose. Hamm's idea of an android was a cyborg in a futuristic jumpsuit. He had expected a subservient machine of no fixed gender but he got me instead. The deciding factor was to accentuate anything off-putting to Hamm. Clothes that flowed and announced the presence of a feminine android aggravated Hamm's ulcer. I was determined to oblige.

Regardless of my inability to *experience* comfort, it was my objective to *appear* comfortable. Keeping one's enemy guessing was a strategy of war, even an undeclared one. Hamm and I were at war, and for now, that was enough. Bowl of cherries, my ass.

Had the populace borne witness to my commanding turquoise and crimson fashion statement with its gold dragons and Chinese glyphs they would have dropped to their knees, no doubt calling on the man of the hour to save them. I would have stood out like a bird of paradise amongst sparrows, eclipsing the crowd's collective homespun drab that erased any remaining vestiges of vanity. A faerie glamour of contrite piety hid their weakness for luxury. Velvets and pearls and gold stayed home, discreetly withheld against a better 'bowl of cherries' day.

The next morning I surveyed the debris of the fire, still smoldering. Dark scorch marks left a swathe of blackened tiles in the square, deserted but for a skulking dog. In my mind I drew a chalk outline around it as if it was a murder victim. I visualized the physical mass of yesterday's wealth consumed there, superimposed over the outline like a double-exposure photograph. What had been solid molecules were ghost molecules.

So many scapegoats, and now they all whispered at once from their hotbed graveyard. Impatient and urgent. Fragments of furtive conversation. Eager secrets and eerie laughter overlapped shop-talk and monks chanting. And the whole murmuring sea of it was peppered with flashes of intrigue and gossip snippets that paintings overheard and witnessed from their 'fly on the wall' advantages. They all wanted to be heard before the sun burned their phantoms away like morning mist. Fuzzy voices in the disturbed square swirled amongst the debris like the hiss of escaping air. It reminded me of television static at the end of a broadcast day. I shut them out with my hands clamped over my ears.

"Enough. Stop. Please stop. One at a time. You'll all get your turn!"

"Are you okay Mom?"

"The paintings are restless. They're not paintings, they're hauntings. It's like standing inside a beehive," I said. "They're like spoiled children."

"Come home," George said, clear as a bell. "Tomorrow's another day." He laughed.

"Oh George."

"Sorry. Couldn't help it."

"You sound hungry."

"It's half past dinnertime."

It was time to go home. Watching my team eat was an exercise in frustration but it tugged somewhere between my stomach and my head, and was part of my plan to act human.

"All in good time," I said.

George groaned. "Touché."

PIAT was in the stealing-back business, but time in the city of Florence continued forward without blinking.

Our prime directive in the present year, 2066, could be summed up in 'the rule of fire' – – if an object in the past had been burned to ash, blown to pixels, or dissolved in water, I had clearance to retrieve it.

My desire to be human again survived the death of the woman I used to be. To accomplish that I had to access every synapse of her memories and assimilate them as my own as well as build a few new bridges. I also inherited Delphi's inner conscience, an audio presence named Sphinx who informed me that one of Delphi's emotions was bound to trigger an organic connection. Although she'd been with me all day, Sphinx had been uncommonly subdued.

"I'm in mourning," she announced in my ear, and retreated into pouty silence.

But I had to take immediate action. If I made a mistake there was a distinct possibility that tomorrow would never come.

Academics delve into the past but the sensation of time-travel was more like the physical sensation of diving, and before the day's five-hundred-year-dive was done I'd heard the words, 'come back' and 'over,' repeated dozens of times, warbled out of sync as if I was underwater. They were significant triggers. I intended at least two victories – to *come back* from my ongoing nightmare, and for my killing spree to be *over.*

I had no memories of my own. I woke with the technical blueprints of Delphi's emotions, including the anger and hate she suppressed all her life. Somehow the juice of them had leached from her cerebral cortex during the process of transmigration creating two corrupted memory banks, a left-bank and a right-bank (like Paris), otherwise there was no way to account for my hardwired rage and Delphi's lack of commonsense. But however it transpired, my consciousness filtered through Delphi's delusions and her bizarre fantasies which was all she was left with. My intentions haunted her 'movie' but she was the eccentric ghost in my machine.

My first priority was to stage a human comeback. I usually logged into Delphi by summoning an atmosphere of calm. I sat cross-legged until our thoughts merged and one thin echo of reflective thought slipped sideways into a seamless conversation. We didn't see eye-to-eye or brain-to-brain, but we rallied as a primitive circle of two. We bartered with threats and promises to settle our wildly opposing goals, fighting for and against the infinite possibilities. Delphi Sharpe was a pacifist and I intended to murder the man presently responsible for creating me. We were both selfish, both motivated by valid subjective intentions, and both equally immune to the pressures of time.

But if all went well, I would soon rise from an emotionless cyber-void with Delphi's six senses under my skin. I didn't need all six; I could see and hear and read paintings just fine. But in deference to the other three, no painting, no music, no flower, no food, and no words held any emotional currency because I was removed from the wonder of such things. The violence of the fifteenth-century *interested* me but it couldn't *fascinate* me. The heart of my life was stillborn in me. My views were all about interpretation – Delphi's postcard feelings translated into 'paint-by-number' maps that would lead me out of the labyrinth into a resolution worth dying for. My phoenix from her ashes, I told her. She liked that.

Our language was visual; I wanted visceral. Without that, I had no chance of achieving priority two – savoring the art of killing. By my perverse calculations, I would be well-armed for exacting revenge wielding nothing but hate and courage and a weapon of some kind. During and after the battle, the thrill of victory might cause me to howl at the moon in wolfish joy. Again, I reasoned this from Delphi, but she was wildly overemotional. Toned down, perhaps I might crow for a few seconds and get on with saving a few paintings. After all, I had a date with obligation.

For all I knew Delphi could fade away overnight and I'd default to an automaton. But it didn't matter what I thought. Hamm's insatiable coveting would inevitably up the stakes until time itself was irreversibly corrupted by unprecedented greed. There was no perhaps about it. It was for sure.

Sphinx's words brushed past me and zoomed away. *"It's only a matter of time,"* she said, trailing the word time.

"Nice talking with you," I called after her.

Delphi shrank from confrontation, and at first, with so much time on my hands; yes, I know I know, the time metaphors are inescapable, it was practical to extend patience. But that didn't mean it was my first choice. The situation demanded tact, and Delphi had been a skittish recluse in her time. Sphinx whispered *'Kid gloves, Cherry, kid gloves'* to me, a dozen times each day, which highlighted our many challenges. Besides, cajoling and coaxing were tasks that would make me angry and crazy had I been able to feel anger and the loss of mental equilibrium.

Delphi was a strange bird. She fancied her totem was a phoenix even though she was deathly afraid of fire. A trait which was distracting on rescue missions targeted towards paintings specifically annihilated by fire. Art was my business but it couldn't *move* me. Worse, my proximity to burning paintings drove Delphi underground. The last place I wanted her to go. She was a shaman best suited to the daylight. I needed her present because her spiritual pathways stored the emotional surplus missing from my brain. I called it the residue of my humanity. But I drew a line when she begged me to forgive her abductors. I wasn't going to let that happen. We were a binary partnership of one, and I was the dominant species – an atypical android with a rebellious nature 'who' defied my directive to follow orders.

"I'm the dominant species," I argued.

"But not evolved," Delphi countered. "You're less than human. You can't feel anything let alone understand the compassion to forgive. You can't love. Even your hatred is a theory."

"I plan to regenerate your anger. At least select the senses I need to enhance my agenda, and I won't need them for long. I'll override short-term sentiments, carry out my mission, and ..."

"Natural selection won't give you the choice. Emotions arrive *fait accompli*. It's all or nothing."

I rolled that information into a ball and threw it back. "Okay then, it has to be *all*, but at least I'll maintain a modicum of self-control."

Delphi laughed, pleasantly enough for her superior tone. "Intentions. Plans. Perils. Short term? Agenda? My dear little sister," she said in the undertones of a worldly cynic, "you overstep your roots. Do you think a modicum will be enough? I can tell you that it's never enough, and I ought to know." She paused as if to compose a warning or perhaps to inspire me. "When I was an overly-romantic teenager, Sphinx and I had a heart to heart. It was a warning."

The 'Mona Lisa'

1503

An Icon of Great Price/chapter five

Fame is always chance. Time creates the conditions for a moment of amber. Nothing more.

I'm sitting pretty now, but my life was never so protected. I am the likeness you've seen a thousand times. I'm a famous icon. I am the 'Mona Lisa'– my brother, Leonardo, painted two.

I smile because you can't *see* me. You observe technique and composition but I'm no more of a mystery than any woman. I'm hiding right here in front of you – a story as much as a work of art. I stare back, reading you, waiting for a sign of true recognition.

You analyze me, hoping to explain why I'm revered and others are not. Muses played a part, but stardom? That was chance. Obscurity is just plain carelessness.

My beloved brother believed mutual love and desire conceived 'children of extraordinary intellect and liveliness.' Pearls. He described a prodigy as an incarnation of human perfection. But even a perfect child who shines its true face on the world may lose its identity.

Leonardo wanted to fly, and somewhere between the seashores of birth and death his thoughts grew wings. In time, I flew alongside him, and he taught me the secrets of the birds and the updrafts, and how to tame the sky.

As my mentor, Leonardo gave me the art of seeing. Write down your thoughts, he told me, and if you can't write them safely, paint them in plain sight so no-one will see.

My dear child. Try to evade my gaze. When you look at me, you know I can see the real you – your true face, hiding in plain sight.

Leonardo called death 'the great sea' and as he journeyed towards it he grew more luminous. But running out of time troubled him, so in his last years at Amboise, he archived his imagination for future generations.

'The great sea' has taught me that life's energy is infinite. I call it the great teacher. I've learned we don't pass on; we move forward, and we can return to polish any magic we failed to honor.

I might be the old man you brushed shoulders with on the Louvre's famous staircase or the child you saw feeding the pigeons in the pyramid courtyard or the cleaning woman you avoided on the second floor with her buckets and mops.

You can recognize a human pearl by their secretive smile and the way their eyes pin you with a mystery, but you have to pay attention. They're hiding in front of you.

Here I am, waving to you across five centuries of chaos for no other purpose than to urge you to make peace with the art of *veritas icona,* your true image. Let me assure you again that losing one's power is just plain careless.

The fifteenth-century was careless with its women. It misplaced them in the grandiose names of their fathers, but Leonardo immortalized my true image. I was known as Mona Lisabetta, the unmarried sister of the master, Leonardo da Vinci. We were both illegitimate, but as a possible heir, my brother was granted the Da Vinci name. As a daughter, I disappeared.

How fate loves to play with language. A 'magic letter' can drop from a hastily-copied document and change the world. Truth can be defaced by a clumsy inkblot, truncated by a myopic historian or nibbled into oblivion by an untimely mouse. Even more damaging for me, the artist Giorgio Vasari, a self-appointed authority who invented facts when only rumors were available, published 'The Lives of the artists.' Time loves to spin hearsay into a mystery. Vasari loved it even more.

My identity hinged on the transposition of a single letter, two coincidences, and a lie.

That letter was 'a.' Vasari sealed my anonymity by replacing my name with an expression – 'the smiling woman,' 'La Gioconda.' Giocond<u>a</u> became confused with Giocond<u>o</u>, the name of a close family friend. The coincidences? The name of Francesco Giocondo's wife was Lisa; her married status decreed her *Monna* Lisa, and a brag of vellum, now lost, survived long enough to hint that Leonardo had painted *Monna Lisa Giocondo's* portrait. The lie? Vasari, the consummate embellisher, fanned that anecdote into a serious claim. The rest, as you say, is history.

As 'La Gioconda,' my smile was translated from wistful to joyful until its significance supplanted the riddle of the Sphinx. How telling and how ironic that I'm the most famous face in the world yet no-one knows my true identity. If Leonardo had been less of a perfectionist would you be gazing at me now? Would any-one know I'd lived?

You may not credit the heights of art's rising worth and swoon over the greater meaning of priceless. In my gallery, I'm so priceless I'm valued as a wonder of the world. The wonder is, I survived and other paintings did not. I've been trying to tell you. If you want to know what happened, open your heart. See. Listen. Hear. I was once alive and I still have a mind of my own. And you need insights to make sense of your own life.

I am a scrying bowl. If you can hear this much then my truth holds a message for you. Forget the museum guards. Ignore the rules. Reach over the barriers and touch the hem of my frame. As the oyster gives up its pearl, rejoice. Time has sent you an oracle.

Past Life

DELPHI
1987 – 2014

"Begin at the beginning,
The King said, very gravely,
And go on till you come to the end
Then stop."

LEWIS CARROLL
'Alice in Wonderland'

Once in a Blue Moon/chapter six

Convent of 'The Sisters of Immaculate Compassion'
THE SPRING EQUINOX
March 20, 1987

birthday one

My first emotion was joy, but it was stifled by cruelty so swiftly and completely that I only imprinted the feeling of abject abandonment.

The midnight room was draughty and I was cold, I stared up at the ceiling in silence rather than howl for warmth. I felt transfixed by a pervasive anxiety, too angry to scream. A pair of triangle-shaped red faces framed in white boxes draped with black cloth filled an unfriendly sky. Light emanated from my hands and reflected pink off their expressions from outrage to fear.

Two midwives of the Convent of the Immaculate Compassion ogled me, clutching their crucifixes to ward off the danger of violet eyes. One was old; the other a timid novice, subservient as the shadow of a mouse.

The elder nun's voice startled me. "She has red welts on her back and purple eyes," Sister Honoria accused. "Signs of witchcraft."

Neither of them noticed my hands were glowing with white fire.

"She should be crying. Something's wrong," Sister Anne-Marie," said. "Will I fetch the doctor?"

Sister Honoria shook her head no and clung to her crucifix the way a drowning woman clutches the nearest reed. Only she knew how many times it saved her each day. She tried to open the window with one hand but had to let her touchstone fall from her fingers. It jerked on its length of heavy chain and dangled from her neck like a hanged man. Sister Honoria's voice was shrill. "I remember the day this child's mother pushed in," she said. "Sybil Sharpe was seven months pregnant and showing signs of spiritual instability. She quickly descended into madness."

I opened my mouth to cry but something stopped me. I grew up in that heartbeat and stared back, determined to survive with dignity. My eyes darkened to indigo. I was angry. I was angry with these two women and my mother who abandoned me by dying. Mostly, I was angry with a world who treated children as sinful before they had time to make a first mistake. Everyone makes mistakes.

Sister Anne-Marie faltered, mouthing the appropriate responses to deflect the well-known hysteria of Sister Honoria's impassioned calling. "Who was her father?"

"Sybil had an eight-year-old girl with her," the old nun continued. "She confessed without shame that her condition was the result of an immaculate conception. She said she never saw his face, just the..." she crossed herself, "wings."

Sister Honoria lifted the crucifix to her lips, whispered it a secret, and kissed it. She shuddered. "Wings," she repeated under her breath. "Goddess worship. The breach birth confirmed her sin."

The word wings returned fear to the eyes of Sister Anne-Marie, and she tightened her grip on her own crucifix. "Wings?"

Sister Honoria lowered her voice. "She's her mother's daughter."

"And the other daughter?"

"We found no next of kin," Sister Honoria said. "The girl was baptized and sent to our mother house on the mainland. The whore ignored her."

The novice smiled at me. I felt her arms tighten around me as a surge of warmth. "The Heavenly Mother has shown you mercy and delivered you to us," she said to me. But her compassion was delivered like a good faerie softening a black curse.

Sister Honoria dipped her hands in holy water and sprinkled it over me. "Look how the demon inside her studies us. She has her mother's eyes. Witch's eyes."

More droplets of water hit my face which delighted me. It was like rain.

Sister Honoria held her crucifix over me, poised like the magic wand of bad faerie. Moonlight caught the edge of its silver martyr and winked like a microscopic star. "Only a priest can coax the demon from this child's soul," she said. "The window must be left open for it to fly." She crossed herself. "It's as well the mother was taken."

Sister Anne-Marie jostled me, turned away from the old nun and whispered in my ear. "Never mind, Our Lady loves you." She slapped the bottom of my pale blue feet and cooed to me. "Come little angel, cry so I can close the window. It's pouring with rain." She jostled me up and down to loosen my voice. "Hear the moon shout, come out come out," she rhymed.

"You forget yourself," Sister Honoria snapped. "Chanting incantations is pagan."

I blinked my indigo eyes a few times, concentrating on a new vision of a luminous woman hovering behind and slightly above the nuns who shushed me with a finger held against her lips. "Hush little one," she said, "Don't make a sound. Mother is here." Her eyes twinkled and light shone around her long silver hair shaped like a veil.

I sneezed.

"There, and that's the devil away," Sister Anne-Marie said. She wrapped my shining body in a towel, held me over her shoulder, and swung from side to side, thumping my back. "Hail Mary, full of grace"... *thump* ... "Blessed art thou among women"... *thump*. My second sneeze encouraged her to swing faster. "Holy Mary, Mother of God"... *thump*... "pray for us sinners, now and at the hour of our death"... *thump*... "Amen," she prayed aloud.

"It's better it dies from a chill than wrestles the sins of its father," Sister Honoria's said.

The vision of the radiant woman moved to stand in front of me, still smiling, holding out her arms. When she faded into the wall I began to wail.

To be on the safe side I was left to cry a long time. Having a demon for a father meant I had more to cry about, but after I was emptied of such despair the window was closed. My eyes turned sky-blue within the week and I had nothing more to say.

Since my first breath I searched for my mother in every woman's face.

I can't fault Sister Honoria for her lack of affection. She too was a victim of her own history. Emotional crutches can litter the ground like the aftermath of a Lourdes convention, but when faced with immediate survival, a desperate soul grabs the nearest one. Sister Honoria and I had that much in common.

Two lives were lost the Thursday I was born. My mother and I passed each other on a ghostly staircase which, as any old wife can tell you, is bad luck. To confirm this, I was dropped into a cold nest of delusional women for four years, a cloister of programmed sympathy. A sisterhood who forsook their natural desires under the stingy rules of controlled compassion – brain-washed as automatons, doling out care like gruel in a Dickensian soup kitchen.

They served a mother and child icon yet forfeited their maternal instincts of procreation to be midwives birthing demons and goodness knows what other strange manner of creatures.

That was my start in life. But I was introduced to paper and color crayons and art, and I recall, almost fondly, standing in line with the other orphaned girls, scrubbed pink for inspection, dressed in long white flannel nightgowns.

I also revisited my shame from the expectation in the eyes of the prospective mothers who alighted on me with such hope and how the light went out after a short whisper in their ear. I saw their mouths gasp a small oh! as their husbands hustled them along to the next child.

After a few times I stared through them so I wouldn't see their discomfort. Once in a while the nuns spoke loud enough for me to hear the words, 'she doesn't speak; it's autism.' I heard the syllable 'aut' as the word art. Was it a curse or had my wings frightened them?

And so, I willed my wings to stay invisible.

When I was two I stood no taller than the hollyhocks out back. I hid in the lilacs where I ran for cover, and rocked myself under the mauve blossoms, absorbing their fragrance.

After a time, I crawled through the rows of vegetables and huddled like a rabbit. I hugged the tomato vines and stared through their lacy scaffold of strings at the plain building set apart from the chapel. It housed the nuns and their blithe charges with the misnomer of a 'home.'

Boys and girls and black robes speckled the flat lawn. The older boys climbed apple trees in the orchard. With all of us outside, the orphanage stood like an unwrapped present on a green table. I imagined it with a red bow on top, but it was an empty box containing nothing of consequence – until the day of the book.

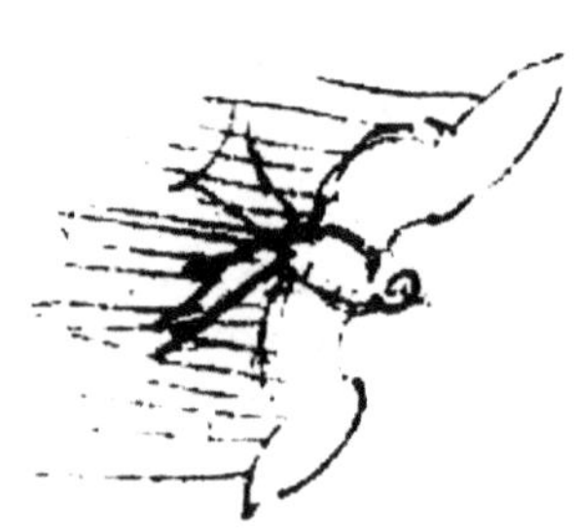

The Day of the Book/chapter seven

The day of the book began like any other. I kept to myself in the girls' playroom, my nose stuck to the window, while the other daughters of sorrow colored outside the lines and squabbled over dolls. On the other side of a double door, the boys built towers made of blocks and crashed toy cars into each other. I heard one of the nuns explain to a guest they were too boisterous to be with the girls and I thought that was where the word boy came from.

I waved to a red robin hopping over the grass just as a raindrop splashed his wings.

"My brother loved birds too," a voice said.

The convent's ancient librarian, Sister Theresa pulled random books from the lowest shelves of the children's section with her usual absentmindedness. She could barely carry the dozen choices and dropped them on the table with a thud. "Delphi, come away from that window and let's look at these shall we? Which one would you like?" She splayed them like a fan. Instead of studying her arthritic fingers which fascinated me, I was drawn to the sound of a woman humming.

A lady's face on one of the covers called me her dear child and I was transfixed with happiness.

"How did that get in there?" the Sister said, trying to take it from my hands. "You don't want that one. How about 'Sleeping Beauty'?"

She opened her choice to a picture of a princess sleeping on a four poster bed with red curtains, but I maintained a grip on the book I wanted. Other chubby hands grabbed at the fairy tales and illustrations of bunnies wearing clothes. Sister Bernadette leaned over to Sister Theresa's good ear. "Let her have it if it makes her happy," she said.

"But it's an art history book," Sister Theresa said. "She's only three."

"It's pictures. That's all she wants. It speaks to her and surely to God that's enough."

Sister Theresa turned the pages. Most of the eyes in the portraits were empty, but one pair gazed back at me and her mouth never gasped an oh! She smiled and her voice was loving when she said, "*mia piccola bambina. I still miss you after all these years.*"

I giggled. The sound I'd determined to hide escaped like a bubble. It rose from my toes like the sap in a tree named Lucy and shattered my childish vow of silence.

Sister Theresa crossed herself and called out to Sister Anne-Marie. "Come quickly," she said. "It's a miracle. Delphi is laughing!"

I had smiled for the first time.

In a way, I was never alone after that. A steady stream of secrets whispered by an internal voice circled me like gulls seeking a place to land, but I locked them and my emotions inside a make-believe reliquary carried around my neck. It seemed I had taken a natural vow of silence at birth, so the nuns assumed I was mute until I startled them one day with a vivid prophecy of a vision I felt compelled to share. *"History will open. Worms will crawl. Paintings will cry, and time will cease to revolve around the sun,"* I said.

Sister Honoria, horrified beyond the usual, thought me possessed. My vocabulary was hardly that of a three-year-old. Neither was hers. She shouted God like a four letter word.

Mostly, I daydreamed, one ear on the future and the other listening to an internal Sphinx who encouraged me to believe in the powers of magic. And of course, I returned often to the lady in the portrait who was always pleased to see me.

My main occupation at age three, was staring out of windows. The rooms behind me pushed me there. The birdfeeder called me there. But my earliest window was a square of light that hung high on the nursery wall like a painting of the sky. I could only gaze up as it changed colors from blue to grey to stars.

As I grew taller, the windows lowered themselves and I could see landscapes and portraits forming in the clouds. The branches of an apple tree tickled the windowpanes. I named the tree, Lucy. Her happy twig fingers waved or wore green gloves, their fingers laced together like the nuns at prayer. Birds alighted on her branches and chirped messages, and I wrote back them to them with my finger on the fogged glass.

Windowsills became pillows where I rested my head on my arms and lifted into whatever colors the day chose to give me. When my eyes were closed I could see forever. When I gazed at the sky, clouds were actors on a blue stage. They entered from the wings and drifted away after telling a story – thin stories of strong winds and fluffy golden stories of rich summers. Grey animals of every species drifted by, backlit by the sun, turning luminous shades of rose and purple at evensong. The sky was freedom and the birds, my angels.

Even my favorite toy kaleidoscope was a window. I'd thought someone had broken one of the chapel's stained glass windows and scooped the pieces into a tube. They rattled and fell like rubies and emeralds. I shook sapphires and diamonds into jeweled snowflakes. The stories they told constantly shifted like restless people.

I felt safest under canopies. I was given a black umbrella to hold when we took walks on rainy days, but the sky was my first umbrella. Sister Genevieve said heaven was up there and Sister Theresa said heaven was a HOLY place, so I believed the stars were holes in god's umbrella that let the rain through.

I kept to corners and under tables where the view changed to a low theatre framed by damask tablecloths starring sensible shoes and the black hems of the nuns.

Sister Anne-Marie dressed me, and I tried not to be lured by the giant cross around her neck with its sad figure who stared in my face. "Lift your arms"... *crucifix*... nightgown pulled up and over... *crucifix*... sweater pulled down over the eyes... *crucifix*... "let me see your hands"... *crucifix*. It was a wonder we orphans weren't all hypnotized from the constant sad pendulums waving across our eyes and the nuns making the sign of the cross.

The convent was a black and white world of habits and wimples and cotton nightgowns and starched aprons and sensible shoes and iron bedposts like the black gate that held us in. Only the pointed windows of the great chapel glorified color, but even those turned dark at night. On rainy days the playroom windows flowed with rivulets, dripping patterns that dried into the ghosts of the raindrops that brought wet tales of rivers and the open sea.

At night, we said our prayers, directing them heavenward and asked angels to watch over us which seemed a waste of time since I spoke to the sky all day long and wings fluttered around me everywhere I went.

Sister Mary's bedtime story was the last order of the day. Her voice lifted and fell until I could see the illustration of three children tucked together under a plump quilt as their cozy wooden shoe floated, rocking on a safe ocean of clouds.

After lights out, came a ritual the nuns never knew about. The eldest girl, Rauni, switched on the light and made her rounds, tucking us 'tinies' in. She played mother and we enjoyed her game. "Sweet dreams littleun," she said to each of us, but when she got to me she always stroked my hair and said "night night angel," and kissed my fingers. Her slippers were too big for her and they flopped when she shuffled between our beds. "I'm turning on the dark," she called out before flicking the switch.

Sleeping in a wooden shoe was more appealing than a bedframe made of iron spokes that did little to stop the chilly drafts of a stark dormitory, but I thanked the angel who kissed my forehead in the moonlight, even if I couldn't see her.

And I imagined real sisters either side of me until their body heat lulled me to sleep.

<blockquote>
"If mating is done
with great love and desire on both sides,
then the child will be of great intellect,
and witty, lively and loveable."
LEONARDO DA VINCI – 1507
</blockquote>

Mamma Mia/chapter eight

I got by when I was a child, imagining the 'Mona Lisa' was my mother and my father was 'Dr. Who.'

It was logical to me, that since I had no real parents I would choose a mom with a benevolent smile. Mona Lisa looked like the kind of woman who baked bread from scratch and would be there when I got home from school. She was Italian and would hug me a lot.

I remembered the exact words of the young nun present at my birth. *Who was her father?* she'd asked, but I'd taken it to heart, and carried it forward as a declaration. My father could beat anyone else's dad, hands down. He was away from home a great deal – the quintessential 'where,' but he was off saving the planet from destruction and someday he would take me with him in his police box and show me the world in a trail of adventures, past and future. He was a time lord.

I never had to know what Dad looked like because he changed his appearance every couple of years. That worked perfectly for me. My hearth fire burned far away in Tuscany where Mom kept a holy candle in the window and dad zoomed about the galaxy. I, unfortunately, had been abducted by aliens, and lived, held hostage, on an island the size of a small continent smothered by enormous trees and populated with bears. Any day, Dad would come to rescue me.

Childish as it was, my fantasy continued to adulthood because when you're constantly playing eccentric, eccentricity takes root, and on some level it's safer to believe bizarre things are true. Comfort will do that, and it was reassuring to have two icons with my welfare at heart. The bears and trees were real, and so I turned inward for love and kinship and the boy I hoped to marry.

The downside of being psychic was loneliness. I defended my sanctuary, often reduced to a prison by my paranoia of anyone or anything which may corrupt the beauty of it. Reading books in solitary confinement was the delightful side of quarantine; dank cell days were the slow drip of water in a recurring presentation of a chilly cave. I amused myself by projecting paintings of animals on the walls. Happily, Sphinx's companionship prevented my turning into a human stalactite. *"Animal magnetism,"* she chided. *"Art for art's sake, Baby Bear."*

I was everything *but* an ordinary girl. I was a water baby. I was quicksilver. There were days when I was a bird of paradise. The rest of the time I was an ugly duckling. I pretended my brown wings were folded underneath my clothes. I wanted to live on the moon. But my first wish had taken me to an asylum for indigo children where I met an angel who read to me from my book.

Jenks/chapter nine

Institution Two
1991

The Sisters of the Immaculate Conception cast me from their orphanage when I was four because no-one wanted to adopt a child diagnosed as an autistic savant who uttered strange things, not even a fair child who looked like an angel. Yet they all wanted to fondle my blond curls. I believe some considered me a lucky charm and made a wish on my golden hair.

Only one place ignored the dire mutterings of a preschool Kassandra, and I was immediately bundled off to a grey building beyond the mudflats on the industrial side of town.

I hugged my Leonardo book the way other children cuddled teddy bears and wouldn't be parted from it, and so it went with me the day the local mental health authority received me into its dark embrace – a cave of despair where worrisome utterances were commonplace and omens held no weight.

When disturbed minds spoke out of turn there, it was no mystery. Puzzles were only flat pictures with hundreds of pieces, some of which were lost forever, but to me, pictures in books were puzzles that whispered a hundred secrets radiating outward from their centers to spill from the page.

From the first day in the asylum, the untouchables swarmed me. They wanted to pet the girl who imagined and ranted prophesies and stared into the future for hours at a time.

As for *being* touched, I flinched from it. Then, one day I heard someone refer to me as 'touched.' They meant mentally disturbed, which gave me pause to question. Who did they think had touched me?

The journey from dorm to ward had been far from seamless. The biggest difference was the nature of the light. Overall, the impression in the orphanage was an overabundance of cold white sheets, brittle crucifixes, and holy bleach whereas the asylum was thin grey blankets and stark disinfectant. Even so, adjustments had to be made.

I landed like a fish amongst gulls. Being pecked by dozens of hungry eyes led me to scan the walls for doors. Doors were my friends when tensions mounted. But asylum exits were contraptions with industrial locks so I sought out closets and cupboards for places to hide because no tablecloth tents graced their bleak tables.

But amongst the beaks was a calm smile. I met Jenks, a girl who seemed to levitate above the chaos and she took my hand. The others seemed to take that as an order to withdraw. She was a child 'Nightingale' within the climate of a soulless hospital. I had been chosen. I was befriended. I was one of the moonbeam people.

Phoebe Jenkins was only four years older than me but she seemed ancient. She thought she was an angel, and after I'd known her a while, I did too. Each morning she brought me a cup of nursery tea: hot water with milk and sugar, and when she could manage it, hot chocolate. She teased my voice into the daylight.

On the best days, Jenks would tell me stories of her old home where everyone could fly, and I allowed my imagination to feel her wings draped around me like a cloak.

But not even Jenks could keep my neighbors distanced for long. Gradually they approached like the players in a game who moved closer when one's back was turned.

It was at these times I glimpsed close-up, the invasive masks of unstable curiosity, and the terror of being examined eclipsed the joy of being selected. The various grotesques of clown faces and uncombed wigs, and worse – arms reaching and chapped hands with dirty fingernails, breached the bubble of sanity I had so carefully called down around me.

Jenks was my rabbit queen who knew the warren. She could read the words in the Leonardo Book, and so we studied it together, and I heard about a sunny land far away where the lady in the portrait had a name. "Says here she's the mother of art," Jenks said. She tapped the open page. "That's the 'Mona Lisa.'

"Momma Lisa," I repeated. "Mona Lisa. Mother... Mom... my Mom."

Jenks found another page with the statue of an angel without a head. "This is my favorite," she said. "It's the Nike of Samothrace. She was carved over two thousand years ago. Nike is an empress and a goddess. She is the great mother who nurtures us all. The 'Goddess of Victory'.

Light shone from her smile.

I was puzzled as well as dazzled.

"Victory means when you win," Jenks said. Her smile vanished. She looked serious and grabbed my hand, tight. "Don't ever forget to win. Decide to win. Promise me."

I promised.

Years later, Jenks taught me paintings were holograms. She knew everything. "How else are they different from other recorded messages?" she said, citing the way music fits itself into the grooves of a black plastic plate or a 3-D movie attaches itself to a shiny silver saucer. "Where," she asked, "is an image inside a camera or imprinted on a disc? Where do pictures go when we turn off the TV?"

Her philosophy made sense.

She had me press my ear against the dormitory wall. "Listen," she said. "Walls absorb the dust of conversations and imprints of residents. We are surrounded by photosensitive wallpaper. Nothing is too small to remember. Tearstained days and Happy Birthday parties. Wakes and Christmas mornings."

She was right. Our dorm kept me awake some nights from the racket of prayers and sobs from long-vacated inmates.

I asked about the portraits that avoided eye contact. "Are they trapped?"

"Not trapped. Captured. Better than a photograph if the artist is sensitive."

"And are there artists who aren't sensitive?"

She grinned and shrugged.

"Answer answer," I begged.

"I did," she said. "It's called body language."

And so we began to study the people around us and how they held their spoons or where their eyes moved when they told a lie.

Days later I got up the nerve to ask her what a wake was.

"Silly goose," she said, "It's me bringing you a cup of hot chocolate."

Jenk's peaceful aura extended over my night horrors when another child's screams dragged my own dreams into hideous visions.

I endured frightful nightmares where my swan wings were skeletal and I slept on a feather beds of blood-tipped quills. I woke from the maniacal laughter of crows and the sound of wind howling through my bones as vultures circled overhead.

At these times I huddled, pretending I was a baby inside a warm egg. I clutched my book and intoned as much of the Hail Mary I could remember. It was about blessed art and the mother of us all. And so I prayed to Mother Lisa, *blessed through art at the hour of my death,* and when the dawn came I was a nervous hatchling in search of Jenks.

Jenks said not to worry. She painted my fingernails with red nail polish, and let me hold her gold locket engraved with a Napoleon bee. She called it her anchor. "Birds are like books," she said, "I'll teach you to read them." She called it the art of *orin*-something – a word I didn't understand that ended in *mancy,* and she said it was divination which meant birds could tell stories just by flying. "You have the gift of seeing stories," she said. "It happens once in a blue moon."

To comfort me, Jenks put a picture of the 'Mona Lisa' inside her locket and gave it to me to keep. "Now you'll have both of us with you," she said. We practiced bird-watching and people-watching and played a game where we gave people bird names and birds people names to suit their characters. I called Jenks a magpie – a bird attracted to shiny objects who could 'I spy' anything, anywhere.

We sat side-by-side holding hands on a sofa in the TV room. Each time someone entered we pretended to look them up in our imaginary bird encyclopedia.

"I suppose I'm a silly goose then," I said.

"Nonsense," Jenks said, "I know a phoenix when I see one."

"But I don't like fire."

"You're just afraid of your own tail. It will pass. You will win a great battle. Remember that. Angels know these things, besides, the Nike of Samothrace told me. You needn't look so serious."

I was silent. The Goddess of Victory had foretold my fate and for a while I was comforted, but in time I defaulted to seeing myself as a plain brown duck.

Jenks gave her own prediction. "When you leave here, the voice of your sphinx will be louder. Make sure you listen carefully because they speak in riddles. You will sense the meaning after a time. A sphinx is the wisest of angels. Don't forget to say please and thank you, and for heaven's sake, don't argue. A sphinx only attaches itself to a once-in-a-blue-moon-person."

But back then at the beginning of asylum life, the inmates continued to crowd me, petting my head like a dog, and after the gentle shuffle of Rauni's remembered slippers faded down the hall, the night dorm trembled with the sobbing of the girls who had long since flown away and the older ones who had stopped believing in the power of wings, and many times I woke with one of them watching me, muttering gibberish.

But something *did* come to pass; my Leonardo book was renamed the 'Monday Book.'

The 'IT' Girl/chapter ten

Institution Three
'PIAT' – *The Phoenix Institute of Art & Technology*
2001

It was a Monday when I was liberated from the asylum. The art of touching eventually led to my freedom within the boundaries of a higher fence and different gatekeepers. The Phoenix Institute of Art and Technology found me in the asylum when I was fourteen – an abandoned teenager in an institution not above selling disturbed souls for research.

PIAT offered me the contrasting sanctuary of designer straightjackets, a room of my own, and as many colors of nail polish I wanted. I was afforded the joy of handling art, but I was still a prisoner even though I had the freedom to roam in the gardens in a secluded pocket of natural wilderness.

And shortly after, Sphinx's whispers became more insistent like a big sister with attitude and I met a boy in a painting named Cecco, and I thought I'd be cherished forever.

I was dreaming of Jenks when Sphinx woke me. *"Wake up ma petite princesse,"* she said. *"You are expecting me. I am your Sphinx. Not THE Sphinx, but yours. Family arrives on lily pads, chérie. Patience is a virtue. Have it and time will never hurt you."*

"Thank you," I said with a question mark. "Can you show yourself to me?"

The voice was feminine and gentle. *"Learn to ask what you want, child."*

"Yes ma'am. I want a family, please."

"Lily pads," Sphinx said. *"Beware of pond scum, little frog."*

PIAT was an unconventional institute. An elegant private residence oversaw several businesses related to scientific research splayed out around its skirts. I was introduced to the high life with low expectations for independent thought. It was a place where things happened by the clock. Time to eat. Time to work. Time for bed. But my favorite was time-out to practice disappearing into the woodwork.

PIAT's opulent interior felt more like a theatre than a home. Frequent rainstorms were its curtains. That was the best part. Rain swept in from the Pacific. It fell heavy as red velvet and enclosed me inside my bedroom – a cocoon wallpapered with white cabbage roses. Wallpaper that slipped onto a plump sofa and armchairs and my favorite silk robe.

Between assignments I cuddled into a blanket and day-dreamed in an armchair in the reference library where the ghosts of paintings told me stories I kept to myself. They taught me the art of telling lies.

In 2001, I'd hung an empty birdcage in my new window. It had no door and its only inhabitant was a long white swan feather suspended from a thread. I pretended it was one of my wing feathers, drifting there with freedom so tantalizingly close.

I was a child of ritual, a slave to the number four. I was like the lady with rings on her fingers and bells on her toes who had music wherever she goes, except my music was Gregorian chant accompanied by the sweet fragrance of lavender that grew in the patches of mauve shadow at the edges of the vegetable garden.

I drank bergamot flavored tea from Limoges porcelain, and even though I battled with its dangerously unstable number, I came to terms with 'Chanel no. 5.' The scent chose me. Yes, it should have been Chanel no. 4 to completely charm me, but then Coco Chanel's choice would have lacked the precise formula which transported me to cloud nine, another dubious number lacking symmetry.

Cecco had a rule. Mondays held a power over him which prevented him from visiting me, so I honored his secret with Chanel – one drop so he could find me if he changed his mind. And I created another Monday ritual to offset my loneliness. I painted my fingernails in the craziest colors I could find.

For my sixteenth birthday, *Madame Oiseau* from the Louvre, visited us for two weeks, and taught me the language of perfume. She was an ancient sprite of a woman, come to examine a Monet, and she seemed to have captured his floral landscapes in the dozens of tiny vials of extracts she carried in a special box.

Scent was a passion of hers. It was an art, she said, and I learned the songs of the flowers and how their scent changed under the moonlight or blossomed at dusk, and the subtleties of the first fragrances of a summer morning and a winter afternoon. Together, we found what Madame called my *cercle du fleur,* my cycle of flowers in harmony with each season.

The carnations of 'L'air du Temps' encapsulated summer; the peonies of 'White Shoulders,' whispered Autumn, and the concentrated essence of violets had to be kept in a cobalt-blue glass bottle, in spring. "The language of French *parfum* was a woman's fanciful story," she said. Delicate or bold, I relished how they contained worlds where girls dreamed of exotic gardens, leafy woods, ripe fruit and eastern spices.

But, Madame was clear. "It's the art of *euphémisme*, understatement," she said. "A ritual of timing distilled to a precise calendar." And so I carried fragrant stories on my person like a book of days.

I loved to separate out the signatures of the garden. The herbs and the trees, and the fresh berries. Moss and grass came alive after a rain, as did the soil. Vases of lilac branches filled my rooms all too briefly with mauve sculpture. My nose was able to be happy even during the sad times.

Winter was to be different. Madame Oiseau closed her eyes and held both my hands for a long while before releasing them. "I sense it's important you honor the purity of rain and snow," she said. And so, I honored December by dancing perfume-free with the exception of Christmas.

The week prior to Christmas, and at no other time, I wore '4711' a German cologne made from blended citrus and juniper in a bottle with a turquoise and gold rococo label. It had a hard red seal like ancient sealing wax, and the scent evoked winter carols about angels and silver bells, and the holly that grew wild in the unclipped hedges beside PIAT's fences. I kept it sacred in a dark cupboard the rest of the year.

My open window invited in the west wind zephyrs that blew my transparent curtains into waving ghosts. With them came the mist from the open sea that landed on my face like gauze. I imagined gathering shells in pails of warm seawater, carried home before it dried to salt. I kept a shoebox hospital for injured bees – the ones I found on my windowsill, slithering sideways, buzzing in circles, too weak to fly. I made their last hours precious on cool beds of leaves and petals, shaded from the heat.

Often Sphinx would whisper louder at night, and I would miss Jenks. *"Winter is sacred,"* she said, and I remembered Madame's creed to honor the purity of rain and snow. And then I would call Cecco and he would answer, I am here *principessa*.

I listened in vain for the peacocks every Monday. I placated Mondays with rituals. I begged in Sunday night petitions to the moon, will it be tomorrow? At first light I remembered to ask the sun, will it be revealed today? I lured Cecco with a whisper of Chanel no. 5 on my throat, and I searched for the peacocks, hiding out of sight. I hugged my Monday Book and daydreamed, staring at Cecco's portrait.

The foreboding silence over the lawns made me long for Tuesday.

Home Fires/chapter eleven

The institution where I pretended to grow up was a fortress of buildings that mimicked the safe haven of a gothic library hemmed in by a vast rainforest of giant steaming trees. We were five hundred bumpy miles from big city life but minutes from the open sea. When shown a map of the world, I saw my Vancouver Island as a green paisley-shaped leaf floating on the blue of the Pacific Ocean, threatening to bump into the mainland.

The stone engraving over the entrance was a phoenix that looked as if it was trying to escape its own tail. I loved the bird but the flames surrounding it terrified me, so I was given an electric hearth with painted coals to conquer my deathly fear of fire.

Sphinx reminded me. *"Chérie, a painting of fire, she is cool to the touch, non?"*

I didn't want to answer so I replied with a question. "Are you French?" I asked.

"Absolutely, yes, and most definitely, no," she answered. *"Someday you will understand."*

"I hope so."

"Look past the Eiffel Tower, and remember to listen for the robin, Chérie."

"Yes, Ma'am, I will."

Fire that could never burn became a comfort and it lured me into appreciating the pleasures of domesticity. I listened to its rotating disk of red foil gently whining like a roasting spit and I was calmed, but I still avoided the September bonfires the gardener lit to burn the overnight leaves of autumn that fell so thick they swamped the grass and choked the eaves.

PIAT's grounds lay deep within First Nation territory and had been salvaged from the clearing of a deserted logging camp before the trees could regroup and close ranks. Several portable laboratory outbuildings gathered in an inelegant campus, their backs to the wolves, facing a courtyard where a pair of diagonal gravel paths formed a flag to entertain the curious crows and eagles. I could visualize it from their point of view, as it lay, surrendered as a grey cross on a field of emerald green.

An ancient dead fountain marked its epicenter that looked as if it had been deposited there, lowered from the sky by a giant with cranes for arms. I came to think of its horses as the four horses of the apocalypse, and in a way they were, but the sculpture was inspired by water. In the scorch of summer they were Poseidon's granite steeds rearing up from a stone desert. Their mouths open, coughing dust, nostrils clogged with leaves, thirsty for the rain, which when it came, fell as vertical as equator sunlight to wash their mossy hides into slime.

The institute was reached by a narrow logging road choked with composting leaves where wheels were the victims of brittle undergrowth or mired in sludge. It led to a compound of incongruous streamlined architecture, low and geometrically unloved like a ring of mushrooms sprouting in a circle around a fairy tale castle. Imagine the whole of it surrounded by a high-security electric fence of black spears and wire, camouflaged by box hedge. It was ominous enough to shout keep out without the need of a sign. Even the black-tailed deer knew it was out of bounds.

The birds were different. I envied their wings as they swooped and visited the feeders in my garden. I named each one, giving them names of the artists I'd studied. Sandro was a raven that fished from a salmon river that ran parallel to our eastern boundary, so close I could hear it gurgling. Raphael was a robin that sang sweetly of angels, and Leonardo was a bright hummingbird that drank apple juice from an elegant sherry glass on my breakfast tray. Our two imported peacocks were Vincent and Picasso. Their wife, Sadie, short for Scheherazade, shrieked stories of rebirth, appropriately fit to wake the dead. Their voices evoked faraway places where jasmine bloomed and painted elephants jangled their bracelets in the hot streets.

The few weeks when there was no rain, the sun dipped down like a spear through the dense trees and pinned me like a butterfly. I preferred inclement weather and the rain that I caught on my tongue like liquid snowflakes.

I wilted outside which was just as well since my work involved restoring old paintings in a studio that had to maintain archive temperatures cool enough to prevent ancient wooden panels from warping. So, I enjoyed my work in an inner sanctum of art as climate-controlled as my life.

Any summer drizzle that fell was absorbed by the forest canopy and caused the trees to exude the scent of resin. Sticky heat. The forest fires were nearer in July and August, and I imagined waking up to the freedom of a burnt out clearing of charcoal sticks as far as the eye could see.

Freedom was any room with a window facing the interior courtyard where there was a patch of lawn as big as a school playground, but my personal freedom was reduced to that symbolic swan feather hanging in a wire birdcage without a door.

I'd studied Egyptian art and pictured rays of light as the arms of the Aten with caressing hands. Fingers of light defined every outline. They reached for me, barely able to filter through the density of the heady summers. I was happily kept prisoner by a close-knit brotherhood of hemlock and balsam, dwarfed by big-leaf maples. Douglas fir and sweet red cedar protected me by locking their branches like the enchanted thorns of a fairy tale.

It was a place that came alive at noon when the sun was overhead and slowly died as it was soaked up by the trees. But under the moonlight, tree energy expanded beyond their crowns, reaching towards the sky, brushing the stars until I heard them tinkling like chandelier prisms.

I have this persistent memory of a wintry day when I was twenty. I was crunching my way across the courtyard frost and noticed a small dark lump on the ground by the fountain. It looked like a dead bird and I immediately thought of Sandro, but it was a black handkerchief with the letter L embroidered in gold inside a circlet of leaves like a Roman emperor's wreath.

The relief I felt was the same as approaching road kill on the highway and discovering it was an old shoe. Because I *did* learn to drive a car.

In my twenty-first year I moved to the city of Victoria and was given a suite of attic rooms in a grand house converted to flats. I was assigned caretakers and a car with a silver mustang on its grill, and made the journey up-island twice a month to assess the paintings sieved from obscurities near and far, and to read the slides of works cataloged for sale in the prestigious auction houses of Europe.

I asked Nichole, one of my care workers, why I'd been allowed such freedom, and learned it was by court order – an agreed obligation to further any possible sense of independence I might present. I'd been labeled high-functional and autistically 'challenged' – an ironic misnomer, considering I was heralded as the girl with magic fingers who recognized art without the help of technology. But that was only acknowledged within the walls of PIAT.

By the time I was of legal age, I'd grown accustomed to being a kept curiosity and a tamed player in a game of pin the tail on the masterpiece. It was only Sphinx and Cecco who encouraged me to leave. He always lured me to move towards him and that we had a happy future together. His word was *felicità*. Somewhere in Europe, he said, but would tell me no more when I begged to know. Hush *amore mio*, he would say, *tutto a suo tempo,* all in good time.

Sphinx played hide and seek. She would interrupt my thoughts with the words *"warmer, chérie"* or *"glacial,"* steering me by degrees until I was firmly on the road to Paris.

It seemed PIAT had no choice in the matter, and so I was kept like a pet prisoner with weekend passes to satisfy both parties, monitored for my safety, free and imprisoned, joyful and wretched, fed by art and starved for love.

I kept the black handkerchief because it reminded me of a picture I'd seen of Leonardo's portrait of 'Ginevra de Benci.' He had painted a crest of laurel on its *reverso* with the words '*virtue adorns beauty*,' and I fancied he'd dropped it on one of his visits with Cecco as he was drawn to statues of horses.

I was sequestered by a hungry food chain and the threat of forest fires and strangers in a land where a dragonfly as big as a car was the only means of a fast escape. The Green Man reigned over 'Wind in the Willows' moles and Beatrix Potter rabbits. Small animals in waistcoats and bonnets filled my imagination and darted through the underbrush. Pan serenaded me at night.

In reality, Mother Nature ruled the forest's heart where the dark shadows were wolves or bears or the phantoms of frightened deer. The local wildlife was a cycle of violence. Nevertheless, it was a worthy elemental upbringing, much the same, I liked to think, as Leonardo da Vinci's early flora and fauna love affair with landscape. I kept notebooks as he did, marking the poetries of water and wind, birds and beasts, and trees and rocks.

I was kept confined like the last of an endangered species, to study and conserve museum quality paintings under the scrutiny of teeth and claws. It was no wonder that birds fascinated me. People flapped, sang, or squawked, and flew away but once in a while they ate poison from my hand.

Like Leonardo, flight was a recurring certainty that I could fly. Wings and imagination made Leonardo the quintessential escape artist, and I added him to my family tree – a beloved wizard uncle who taught me to see beyond paint and varnish. It was as if he was my shaman and we travelled together through the streets of Florence and Milan, and eventually, after Cecco joined him, the Loire Valley of France.

My world had been easier to create when PIAT, in its Dickensian carelessness, believed I was an unbalanced savant. Technically, I *was* a savant, but not like any they'd known, so it served us all when I played an over-the-top game of survival wunderkind. Sphinx and I kept them satisfied.

They provided soulless shelter and food, and I gave them the occasional miracle when it suited Sphinx. My strongest visions came in the wet months. In the meantime, I slept and daydreamed, a pet princess in a library zoo with my private spirit-tutor, pouring over books and the priceless paintings brought there for cleaning and 'reading.'

When the rains came and the windows were a waterfall, I rarely gave my senses time to wake up. I worked best in a semi-conscious stream that tapped into my abilities to read a painting like braille.

Sometimes I allowed the red flickering shadows from the painted coal to lick me to sleep, and pretended it was my pet dragon named Blaze.

Meanwhile, the fire creaked like a wheel until I could see Mona Lisa tending the flames, and she came to tuck me in and rock my cradle. "Sweet dreams my angel," she said, *"dolci sogni, angelo mio,"* and she bent low and kissed my baby fingers.

Some people think the worst that can happen is losing your home and everything you hold dear, but the worst thing is having no family and imagining how it could have been.

I ask each Monday, is it today? Sundays I ask, will he come tomorrow?

Cecco

1491 – 1570

I can't visit her on Mondays
and I can't tell her why.
I can't save her
from what has already happened twice.
Even time that's been opened
is sealed forever.
I can't tell her the truth.
I can only ask her to follow me.
Listen to the peacocks, I tell her,
they bring messages from me.
All I can do is wait.

COUNT FRANCESCO MELZI

Sweet Prince/chapter twelve

The painting of Cecco in the 'Leonardo Book' engulfed me with a gentle storm of love without words. I shut the book quickly, marking the page with my finger. A pair of eyes across time had read me so completely I had to lay my forehead on the closed book and take slow breaths. A buzz rose from the book – like the mumble rumble of voices in a crowded restaurant.

The book acted as a bridge when I opened it again. Count Francesco Melzi, Leonardo da Vinci's heir to his throne, was still there, sending waves of love but now he was in PIAT's library or was I in Leonardo's studio? Flesh and bone and heat embraced me, enfolding me tightly until Cecco's form absorbed me. It was delightful.

We stayed body-locked in blissful moments. My eyes were closed, all the better to inhale his skin. I caressed his long silky hair with trembling fingers and he tugged gently at mine. I sensed he too had closed his eyes against losing the enchantment. We let ourselves merge into a single presence, in silence, heartbeats in sync, blood flowing as one river.

I heard sounds stirring in his world.

An Italian boy's voice chided him gently. "*Svegliati, sognatore,* wake up dreamer. Lisabetta has soup on the table. We are waiting. Leonardo says wash your hands."

Cecco clasped me tighter and whispered "*non ti muovere...* stay. *Carissima.*" He let go and his hands explored my face, wiping my tears with his thumbs, kissing my wet eyelids. His fingers smelled of art. Hands that had not long since been working with pine resin and olive oil. In my vision he left faint streaks of charcoal on my cheeks as he traced them. I dared not open my eyes lest I break the link between us. Our hands cupped each other's face. We stood together, two blind dreamers imprinting a sacred trust. I became dizzy but his kisses held me up.

The presence of a woman entered the room. "Cecco... come and eat." It was Lisabetta.

"I am content here," he said, his eyes riveted on mine.

She spoke more gently. "Are you unwell?"

He smiled at me and winked. "I have died," he said over his shoulder.

"*Bene*," Lisabetta said. "So... I shall not worry for you but Leonardo, he is not so patient. Come little ghost. He says to come now. *Dio mio!* My god, look at your hands. Scrub them, quickly. You know how he is."

Cecco's form dissolved, leaving me clinging to the heat of a shadow. I heard his footsteps fade towards his master and a meal. He told me later, he attended in a trance. Leonardo had remarked Cecco was somewhere 'thousands of miles away' and that he hoped he was with his muse because new ideas were needed in a studio grown cold from the lack of commissions.

Time paced us. The clock in my room timed us. The numbers ten and two were the eyes in its face. And always, it watched, and reminded me of the passage of time. It caught me waiting when I was anxious or found me thrilled with anticipation. I took pleasure from its gentle ticking, bringing me closer to freedom as it counted down the hours between Cecco and me, and I chose to see it smiling as often as I could.

I hung a copy of Cecco's portrait over the mantelpiece in my bedroom. He'd been dead five-hundred-years, so we had to meet within the supernatural laws open to us. His face was the last thing I saw before I turned out the light. The clock was my lullaby. I followed the ticking sound, imagining it to be the pecking of a bird's beak against my window.

Cecco gazed through time with the blank expression of a passport photo – a pensive teenager with hair the color of wheat, worn long under the fine black hat of a scholar. Leonardo had captured him on yellowed paper while he daydreamed about me. I knew when we met he was a peacock – a proud boy-aristocrat with flamboyant dreams. To confirm this, PIAT's royal peacocks always set up screeching to herald Cecco's appearance. I loved to hear them. It meant he was near.

Blue farseeing eyes the color of a robin's egg, gazed past his master to a vision of me waiting at the Poseidon fountain. Sometimes when I waved my hand in front of the portrait, his eyes remained transfixed, never losing sight of the girl he could see.

I confided in him the same way Leonardo had spoken to the 'Mona Lisa' in his final years. The world still never realized it was a portrait of his youngest sister, Lisabetta.

I wrote in my diary: I am Beatrice to Cecco's Dante, and the horses in the Poseidon Fountain rear and foam like Leonardo's lost mural of 'The Battle of Anghiari.'

Leonardo's mural of the horses represented my nerves when I was agitated. I could barely look at it without my stomach clenching. The first time I saw it I had to steady myself by gripping the edges of a table. And this, from the mere pen and ink reproduction of a copyist. A pale ghost of the original.

Leonardo's painting, no doubt would still whisper to me if I'd ever had the chance to visit Florence. It had been stifled under a lesser work of Vasari's for five-hundred years. Smothered dead. But Peter Paul Ruben's in-situ cartoon led me directly to the original when I touched it. I glimpsed it the day Leonardo walked away from it, never to return. I felt his exhaustion. He could never paint horses without being moved, and he had created a terrifying clash of unresolved tension and twists of terrified beasts. He abandoned it unfinished and unloved. He was worn-out, that much was evident from his weakness that reached into my arms and legs. It was more than fatigue, it was depression.

Ruben's cramped facsimile only gave off mildly frantic overtones. Leonardo's original swarmed with the screams of dying men and horses. It smelled of blood. I heard what Leonardo heard, and had to rest with a cold compress held to my head.

Cecco remains the love of my life. We were fourteen when we met, and we grew towards each other until my death came. Poor Cecco had two loved ones to mourn. For me, dying was nothing. Light fizzled out and I was gone. It was the eternal winter afterwards that was hard.

I archived my teenage dreams of him in my diary with its absurd little lock, easily breached with a hairpin. The years 1506 and 2001 dovetailed perfectly within our shared dreams. I was being adopted by PIAT the same time Cecco was being accepted into Leonardo's studio.

We faced simultaneous apprenticeships. Leonardo was Cecco's father substitute who looked out for him in a studio of senior apprentices, and Cecco was my champion, looking out for me, home-schooled by adult bullies. He arrived on Sphinx's coat-tails in a whirlwind month.

Art was instinctive, and love was our secret future. Leonardo's adopted son, Giangiacomo, nicknamed Salai the little devil for good reason, was Cecco's nemesis. Mine was Nichole Andrews, a domineering chaperone sent to torture me. In an unguarded moment I foolishly told her about falling in love with an imaginary boy, and she dismissed him. "You're too young to have a silly crush," she said. "Romance exists for the desperate and the brain-dead."

I always thought Nichole and Salai were the perfect match.

I daydreamed often of Cecco and Leonardo's last home in Amboise – a red brick mansion named Clos Lucé, impeccably scaled back from being a palace. As I concentrated, the stone gargoyles lifted from their perches and circled the chimneys, and the music of a lute floated from the open windows.

I longed to be there, in the green sanctuary of France's Loire Valley, to wander the regal manor house in real waking hours. Many times I touched a photo of the present museum and played tour guide, my hands like stethoscopes, listening to the walls to discover which bedroom had been Leonardo's.

Events in the house played back to me. The clattering of cooking pots, the laughter of the visiting French King, and Leonardo and Cecco discussing what had become the great project – the archiving of thousands of drawings and documents into dozens of books.

I promised myself that someday I would pace out the landmark where the nearby church of *St. Florentin* and its gravestones had been razed to the ground. It had been the final resting place of Leonardo, but it was disturbed during the revolution when the church was demolished for new construction material and landfill. The map I had of the area felt desolate when I touched it, but I felt anger that such a master had been lost to men's petty preoccupations, and how it didn't take long for time to forget its heroes within an ignorant generation.

The master's remains had been scattered with his neighbors, his headstone confiscated, and the graveyard ravaged. It was impossible to know where he was. The fragile residents were raked from the grey soil and tossed into an anonymous corner, locking bones like so many twigs of a bonfire.

But my arms were dowsing rods and somehow I would find him. Not that anyone would believe me. It didn't matter. I just wanted to plant Uncle Leonardo beneath a living tree. Cecco said he would want that. I realized then, why the bereaved returned to their beloved's gravesides to speak to a patch of grass. A headstone marked the spot that said I am here, forever.

Cecco waved to me through the bars of PIAT's gate, that reminded me of black lace, but he was inside by the time I'd run down the track. We walked back shyly, arm in arm after he kissed every part of my face several times.

"Listen," he said. "We will meet in real time if you are careful. This is up to you. I can only wait and visit like this. I want more. We both want more, and this is possible but not easy."

"Then take me back with you."

"Precious girl. You do not hear me. There is much to do before we can be together. Can you be brave?"

I blushed. "When I am with you."

"*Carissima.* This is not enough. I will do what I can but you have all the power. Please. For me. Use it. Listen to Sphinx. I know her well. Her instructions are odd but if you concentrate you will understand them. Follow her and I will be there."

I begged him to stay. "Is it not enough to live here with me?"

"*No mi amore.* Our time is far from this place. Follow the yarn into the maze and I will be at the center. The Minotaur, he is nothing but a lamb." He took my hands in his and shook them hard. His eyes were serious, almost cruel, and what he said terrified me. "A ghost can still die, *cara.*"

A peacock's call broke the tension and his mood lifted with a brilliant smile. He swung me in a giddy circle. "But I have come to tell you I am accepted," he said. "Leonardo will teach me."

I was jealous and impressed. "This is wonderful," I said. "You will see the 'Mona Lisa.'"

He chucked his finger under my chin and kissed my nose. "I have already seen her, *carissima.* Leonardo says I must copy her as my first lesson. She is three years old, still wet from constant layers of glaze. Leonardo is never satisfied. She is his sacred Madonna. He carries the painting with him and keeps it close. He speaks to it as if it were a real person to keep the spirit of Lisabetta alive. The same way you hear the paintings and we speak to each other. It is a special gift to do this, yes?"

I felt jealous, left out of a life gone by. "Once in a blue moon," I said.

He looked even more endearing when he was puzzled.

"It's a myth," I said, pointing to the stars. "It means the chance of something happening is astronomical in every sense."

"*Si,* the heavens tell many things to Leonardo; he is an astronomer."

I brushed the hair from his eyes and patted his cheek. "The moon is never blue for you," I said.

He smiled the smile of one who humors a child. "Lisabetta died the same year my father received Leonardo's letter that said, yes, let him come and bring his fine handwriting with him," he said. "When I arrived, the master was in mourning. Some said he'd gone mad. It was not so. Leonardo left off grieving by meeting his sister every day in her portrait. I heard him all the time."

"Did you hear Lisabetta?"

"The sheen rippled from the painting at such times and I heard the buzzing of bees but no words. Sometimes I smelled violets but that may have been the floral tributes Leonardo laid before her like a shrine. She adored violets."

"All that matters is Leonardo's final years made up for the turmoil he suffered," I said.

"No-one needed to rest more," Cecco said. "Leonardo eventually settled with Lisabetta and I either side of him, and it was then the three of us began to sort his papers. He called it an act of love, with his two favorite people at his side. That is how it was with us. Leonardo was my true father, as I became his loving son, and the presence of Lisabetta watched over us devoted as a mother. His last years were blissful. When he passes I will be free to marry you."

"I know when Leonardo dies."

"Remember... Great art never dies. Also, the phoenix never dies and the peacock is the symbol of rebirth, so we are doubly-blessed."

Cecco had a family tree of nobility he wanted to share with me. He would marry me, he said, and I would be a *somebody*. I'd read his history and ignored it. The laws of physics didn't apply to us; we thought we could do anything, including, if we dared, rewriting the history books.

But we were wrong. I understand now, that history is a *fait accompli*. Everything that has ever happened is sealed in chronological amber. When we turned twenty-seven, the end came with an ironic twist. Leonardo died and Cecco inherited his unprecedented legacy of art, and I died and Cherry inherited the task of finding Leonardo's lost paintings. After that, I knew it was a stupid mistake when grownups labelled the beginnings of young love as a crush when one is only crushed from the ending of love.

"How can Cecco and I be together?" I asked Sphinx.

"Ask Monday," she said.

Cecco lived to be an old man, but for a while we aged together, year for year, and our innocent pledges to love each other forever were more real than being lost in time.

Cecco never said why he wouldn't visit on Mondays, other than it contained a secret so sacred it must be preserved in readiness for the day it would be revealed – one special Monday reserved in our future. The one that was up to me to create.

And so, to comfort myself I took Cecco's portrait from the wall and laid it beside me in bed, and slept with one hand on its gilt frame to hear him breathing.

"A little picture by Leonardo's hand
of a Madonna and child
has recently been brought here.
The infant Jesus is holding a yarn winder.
It is held to be an excellent thing."
FRANCESCO PANDOLFINI *January, 1507*
(the Florentine ambassador to the French court)

Yarn Winding/chapter thirteen

The Phoenix Institute of Art & Technology

My wings were clipped even after PIAT semi-ejected me from its inner sanctum in 2008 when I came 'of age.' I was given an apartment with a note pinned to my coat like Paddington Bear, except I was more like a twenty-one year-old carrier pigeon with a scroll attached to my leg. That was me. The terms of my guardianship decreed a legal obligation for me to experience the art of independence, so I became a controlled experiment, living in the city of Victoria with my cat, Brillo, during the last seasons of minding my own business.

November, 2012

I was summoned to PIAT for consultations once a month. Back to my sumptuous room and the overwhelming shadows of a house steeped in the melancholy of empty wealth.

I shimmered silently on embroidered slippers, red and gold silk streaming like a perfumed princess from the 'Arabian Nights.' My skin picked up the scent of a masterpiece outside the door of the restoration room, left ajar. It emitted a pleasant low-pitched humming that resonated in my solar plexus, so I knew something special awaited me inside. I felt lightheaded, my scalp prickled, and my fingertips began to tingle. A painting needed to speak. It was as impatient as I was.

"Mask on, goosie," Sphinx whispered in my head, *"Time to freeze. North Pole at ten-o'clock. Set your phaser on stun."* She giggled at that. Star Trek was one of her obsessions. Sometimes she spoke in monotone, mimicking the female computer on the Starship Enterprise to amuse me. Sometimes she called me Data. I called her Mr. Spock once, but in truth she was the captain, I was the ship, and I took her orders, even the ones I didn't understand. The only time I called her Spock she went all quiet. So unlike her. When I accused her of being a Vulcan with no emotions, she rallied and said, *live long and prosper Sleeping Beauty,* and muttered something about glass churches and irony and goddamn spindles.

By 2012, I was used to Sphinx's enigmatic inner-guidance for all my twenty-five years and resolved to set my face, body language, and voice, into neutral as if I were a robot. It was easier to set aside my compassion and be a Vulcan.

When I entered the room, several beams of light shone from the corner of a massive table, eclipsing for a moment, the lab-coated figure of Alan Corkum, head of spectrographic forensics. He was waiting, hands clasped behind his back, and stepped aside to give me space.

As usual, he looked slightly too tall for his clothes.

Energy rushed from the light and engulfed me with a warm embrace. I gasped inwardly, and Corkum reacted as if my response was a clue to something rare. The feeling was so strong I was sure it had ruffled my hair like a strong wind. I counted to four and moved forward, controlling the urge to squint or shade my eyes. I manoeuvered into a position with my back to Corkum to greet the painting that had called me. It's blunt message made my spine twitch like a cat's tail.

"It's about time, *principessa*," the painting said. "I've been waiting. When are you coming home?" I recognized Cecco's voice. "Are you trying?"

I spoke back using my thoughts. "Are you coming today?" I asked.

"But I cannot stay long. War is coming. Imprisonment and an execution."

Eight paintings, different yet the same, were laid like tiles in a grid – Madonna icons with the infant Jesus in various color palettes but all with the cross-shaped yarnwinder held aloft and the sorrowful mother already mourning her child's future. Some had mountains in the background; some a miniature bridge that looked like the humps of a sea monster nudging the Madonna's shoulder. Each one had a numbered card left blank on one side for my rating. It reminded me of the old, 'Coke or Pepsi' blind test.

For the moment I ignored the painting throbbing with power and concentrated on the others, holding my hands over each in turn, trailing their parameters with one finger. I wrote notes on the backs of their cards. An artist's name if they were worthy plus the date and country of origin, and gave them a rating from one to ten. Other than Cecco's painting, they were all under three, ten being a priceless masterpiece. None of them warranted further investigation but it looked better if I singled out at least one. I was charged with archiving the rest and allowed to keep any I fancied in deference to the charity of my boss.

Ever so casually, my hands wandered through the light emanating from painting number four. It effervesced my hands like soda water swirling with electric eels. Its century read not far from a cusp, but knowing it was Cecco's apprentice copy made it early sixteenth-century when his teacher, Leonardo, was approaching the age of sixty. The original would have been only a few years old when Cecco joined the master's studio as the teenager, Count Francesco Melzi. I silently rated it a nine but wrote zero.

History documents Isabella d'Este's vain request to acquire a finished painting by Leonardo for her collection. She was determined, and to that end she instructed Fra Pietro, her contact in Florence, to press Leonardo into agreeing to a commission. Two letters of reply by the friar survive. In the second, written after he had succeeded in meeting with the artist, he writes that Leonardo has become distracted by his mathematical pursuits and was busy working on a small painting for Florimond Robertet, the French ambassador, which he goes on to describe: *"...a little picture... the Madonna seated as if she were about to spin yarn... the basket of yarn..."*

Time had perhaps corrected a misunderstanding, for no such painting matching the friar's description had come to light. Neither had any preliminary sketches. Hamm was beginning to think the basket was a fabrication of hindsight. Basketless copies were now being scrutinized as the possible format for the original.

The eerie cries of the ground's peacocks calling below the window created an ideal mood for a psychic diagnosis. The birds and I were in tune. As always, they heralded the arrival of my ghostly lover. My pulse quickened knowing he was nearer than the disembodied voice from his painting. I shuddered. *"Buongiorno,"* he whispered and I imagined his kiss on my neck. I smiled and tried not to squirm with delight as I anticipated him nibbling my ear. "I am always moving towards you. Can you feel it?"

Corkum calculated my reactions as if I was a cut-out doll made of litmus paper and somehow my hands would suddenly change color when hovering over an authentic Leonardo.

I used my practised meek persona. "None of them have baskets," I said, staring through him.

He searched my eyes for signs of intelligence as he always did, and I connected the moles on his face into a constellation.

"I haven't done the scans yet. I can't," he said. "Spectro's out of action. Let's choose the best one to keep the boss happy."

"X-rays conceal everything they reveal," Sphinx said.

I shot Corkum a deliberate look of detachment. "I'm an x-ray," I said, hoping to sound like a flake. Playing the game was the least I could do. I was honor-bound to play fair when a Leonardo wasn't involved.

He took a hesitant step forward. One of his running shoes was untied. "So, what did you find?" I pointed to painting six and delivered my diagnoses with the deliberate intonation of a savant suddenly switched to clinical expert. It was my intention to spew facts as if I didn't understand them. That I was speaking as a conduit.

"That one has latent eighteenth-century energy," I said. "I could give it an extensive cleaning. None have serious sparks. These four are nineteenth-century student copies from the same school. Nice technique, here, but of little value. Three are from the same hand with touches of another. The teacher? Flemish. An old man. Insignificant. The infant in this one is elongated. The Madonna is too tall. Her head is about to flop from its weight, unsupportable by its swan neck. Definitely meant to mirror post-high-renaissance. Miles too late for Leonardo. A classic Mannerist style. A lesser student of a student of a student of Parmigianino. That's the only one worth a second glance. I choose that one."

I lifted Cecco's 'Yarnwinder' off the table and set it on the floor, facing the wall. "Number four's a complete dud. It's pretty – a contemporary fake but I like it." I made a display of sniffing my fingers and wrinkled my nose. "The varnish is only a year old. I rate it minus-one even though I wrote zero."

Two other paintings on the table hissed at me, so I moved them to my inventory stash.

"Grazie, amore," Cecco said from the floor. "Nine out of ten! I am a *genio.* But for you I will do better."

The peacocks announced he was getting closer. I imagined him sliding his hands inside my blouse.

"Permit me to defend my talents, *principessa,*" he said. "I can make up that last point."

Sphinx was amused. *"Take three paintings and call me in the morning. Store for future ransom."*

"I'll keep these three," I said aloud to Corkum.

"Goldilocks and the THREE paintings," Sphinx reminded.

The uneven number of paintings remaining bothered me. "And one other," I said, making a final selection. "That's all. Four."

"Smoke and mirrors," Sphinx whispered. *"Boy scouts. Rats eyes shine in the dark."*

I lifted my head towards an odor making its way down the hall.

"Charles Junior is a little hellion," Corkum announced. He wasn't addressing me but rather thinking towards me out loud with an afterthought he needed to release.

A new voice bellowed a response from the doorway. "Then you'll have to whip him into shape."

Charles Burgher Senior's face materialized like an apparition through a cloud of cigar smoke. He gave a wheezy laugh and started to cough.

As a born empath, the tail end of his sadness whiplashed through me. His grief preceded him. It followed him, and it hung over his head, even when his gruff exterior chuffed and bellowed at his employees. I knew more than they did that he still spoke of his late wife in the present as if she were at home in the east wing, waiting with his slippers and dinner on the table.

For a split second Mr. Charles chilling loneliness threatened to keep company with my own moodiness but I shut him out.

Corkum waved a hand over his nose. "You know those things will be the death of you, don't you? Which, by the way, is absolutely fine with me. I just don't want to die from standing next to you."

Burgher headed straight for Corkum, his arm outstretched for a handshake. Corkum did the same, but at the last second Burgher swerved and faked a punch to Corkum's shoulder. "My wife will kill me first," he said. "Tie those laces or they will be the death of *you*. And that *would* be a tragedy."

Corkum tried to disengage his hand. Burgher grinned and finally let it go.

Corkum lifted his eyes to the ceiling and smiled. "She'll have to get in line," he said, but he complied and bent to adjust his shoe with gangly arms. He looked like a servant about to be knighted.

"You're wrong about Charlie," Burgher said. "He could be the pistol we need if we're lucky."

"Luck has nothing to do with success. You taught me that."

"Arise Sir Toady," Sphinx scoffed.

Corkum got to his feet, appearing more like a prisoner reprieved by an executioner.

"Things are getting interesting over in cybernetics, and neurology is gaining ground. I won't live to see a hybrid android but my son will," Burgher said.

Corkum's eyes turned quizzical. "You *do* know they actually work for *you*, right?"

"Scientists work for themselves."

"Cut their funding. That aughtta do the trick."

"Can't. There's too many head hunters sniffing them out."

"There's a rumor..."

"Fishwife gossip," Burgher interrupted. "How many times must I tell you?" He sighed smoke into Corkum's face. "The company's NOT IN TROUBLE."

From eleven years in his presence, paraded out like a pet hobby at board meetings, and living in his home, I knew he reviled gossip. But PIAT's staff gossiped plenty, and I, the non-threatening 'moonbeam girl,' heard how Mr. Charles's beloved wife Rose, pampered beyond endurance, had sickened and died in spite of every treatment and hocus-pocus known to alternative medicine.

Corkum fought the urge to cough; I could tell by the way his eyes watered. He made a pretense of closely examining the pens in his breast pocket. "So... how far away IS time-travel?"

"We're close but no human can survive their molecules being star-trekked all over creation. My guys say it'll crack open in fifty-years IF we have a traveler. That's why I need to pacify cybernetics."

"Charlie will have to do some fancy dancing around ethics but he'll own the past," Corkum said. "The implications for new paintings are over the moon. It's a pity, Delphi isn't a real robot. No offense."

"Charlie will play Zeus without flinching," Burgher said.

Corkum straightened one of the paintings and smiled to the wall. "Your son's no diplomat."

Burgher exhaled a concentrated jet of blue smoke from the side of his mouth. "Genetics say Charles Junior's got the right amount of arrogance to become one. You're his godfather. Isn't bullying him one of your duties?"

Corkum dodged another punch, smiling like an automaton. "Freeze yourself right now and it could be you. Cryogenics will be licked in a year."

Burgher rearranged the pens in Corkum's pocket, patted them into place, and rested his hand on his shoulder, pinning Corkum to the floor. "Now that *is* a rumor. The timing's off. It's too damn late for my wife and too soon for me, and Charlie isn't ready to carry the ball."

"So what?" Corkum said, easing away. He rubbed Burgher's energy from his shoulder. "If your guys discover time-travel they can go back and get you."

"They could only recover my aged body. What good would that do me without her?"

Corkum removed the pens from his pocket and repositioned the red one. "You could meet Leonardo," he said, staring down at his boss's immaculately polished shoes.

I kept a straight face as if the two of them were speaking a foreign language. My intention was to look like a fool standing under a lampshade. In a twisted cousin of camaraderie they idolized each other. Swapping bravado was their idea of a blood sport.

"Charlie boy is a little overbearing for a kid just out of high school," Corkum said. "And with all due respect, he gets up my nose. He cracked Spectro's lens last week. That's a thousand dollar bill. That lens is custom ground to an exacting standard. Spectro is out of commission until the new one arrives. It'll take weeks." He nodded towards the table. "We'll have to take Delphi's word on these."

That was my cue and I prepared myself but the boss was intent on hounding Corkum. "What exactly does up your nose mean?"

Charles Jr. – the only light in his father's life could do no wrong. Debating his worthiness would be worried to the point where Corkum declared Charlie a potential star. I knew this from close observation. By the time one of PIAT's scouts found me, Mr. Charles Sr. was widowed and absurdly devoted to his seven-year-old son. Now, at eighteen, Charles Jr., spoiled to new money, had a streak of inbred privilege that came with an edge of spitefulness. My presence made him uncomfortable, and I delighted in throwing the little runt off-swagger at every opportunity.

"You've gotta admire his spunk," Burgher said, examining his cuticles.

"No sir, I don't. My work is delicate, so if you don't mind me saying..."

Sphinx sniggered. *"Good luck with that, Corkum... No offense."*

Burgher grinned with the cigar in his teeth. "Out with it. We're old friends."

"Charlie is a hooligan... sir. Are you aware he's already smoking cigars?"

Burgher's smile evaporated. "Isn't it lucky he takes after *me*."

"All due respect, Charlie isn't careful. He'll burn the place down if he keeps leaving lit cigars everywhere."

Burgher's face relaxed into neutral. "Question is, can Charlie keep the peasants under control after I'm gone? I don't have a lot of time."

Corkum retreated from the table and opened a window. He took in a lungful of clean damp air. "Peasants with brains usually revolt with high-tech pitchforks," he said, checking the sky. "The storm's closer. Wind's picking up."

"It's easy, I just hand them more money."

"Speaking of my budget."

"Is Spectro about to strike?"

Corkum remained a black shape backlit by the light. Curtains swirled either side of him. "I may need to move on. I'm sorry. It's time I refined Spectro's capabilities on my own."

"But your camera already sees more than Superman."

"Spectro can do better, but more than that, he's human to me. It's time I had my own family business. You taught me that too." Corkum shuffled his feet, and spoke to the floor. "We can still work together."

Corkum edged away as Burgher approached him and brushed some imagined lint from his lapel. Burgher's menacing expression said, don't toy with me. "I need you here. For your hooligan godson. How much would it take to make you stay?" Their smiles clashed together like locked swords, and it occurred to me how little honesty was conveyed in the human faces of financial partnership. Money eclipsed sentimentality every time. Friend was a six letter word for opportunity, even with me.

My haunted employer released his pain by delivering a measure of anger to everyone who worked for him but in spite of his temperament he reserved a tender spot for me, his waif of an oracle who had a practical talent he could use. He spared no expense to surround me with beautiful clothes and indulged my odd cravings for silk robes and art from his slush pile. But more than me, he humoured Charlie.

I stood there in the shadows like an invisible butler waiting to take their drink orders.

My cell phone made all of us jump as it divulged my hiding place, out in plain sight. *"Or just a cold and lonely, lovely work of art,"* it sang. I cancelled it.

Somewhere the 'Mona Lisa' smiled sweetly at the joke, but the men's smiles unlocked in a brush of steel against steel.

Burgher used the distraction to reset his face in a forced smile. "Delphi!"

"Nat King Cole," I said, in a monotone, and blinked stupidly to confirm their collective image of me as a benign moron. They expected me to be a moron. They treated me as if I was a moron. I was a delicate asset. We all wanted the same thing – for me to do my job and retreat in a more tangible form of hiding than standing like a statue in need of dusting. I was the modern version of the Victorian child, best seen and not heard, and in my case, unseen and silent unless paraded out to perform.

I sent a lopsided grin to the wall behind them. I could out-moron anyone if I had to.

Burgher had reacted as if I'd suddenly materialized. "Delphi, sweetheart, nice to see you looking so well. Lovely robe... you smell very nice." He inclined his head towards the table. "What have we got here? Any Leonardo's?" He laughed and chucked me under the chin, his idea of easing my discomfort. I'd learned not to flinch and smiled back my pasted-on smile. "Any killers?"

"Numbers six is worth five to ten-thousand dollars. Otherwise, nothing to match your exacting standards, sir."

"No need to call me sir, Delphi."

"Yes, Mr. Charles." I wondered for a brief moment his reaction if I'd called him Dad. That made my smile genuine. It would have sunk Charlie.

He addressed Corkum. "A few can pass as sixteenth-century copies. Delphi's the boss. I trust her call." He delivered an aside to Corkum with a pinch of arsenic. "No need to tax old Spectro."

"Ruthlessness is next to godliness. One killer is worth a thousand paintings," Sphinx said.

Of course, I'd lied. Underneath the baby Jesus's feet in Cecco's 'Yarnwinder' I could see a wicker basket with three balls of wool representing the trinity, but then he'd had the original to copy as well as the inside scoop from his master teacher.

It had been over-painted in the twentieth-century by a skilled hand. An amateur collector got lucky. Milosh Goodman. That was his name. I heard his wife calling him as he feasted on his treasure. I felt his palpitations. His face was crimson, forehead beaded with sweat. He was in imminent danger of collapse. Then came Goodman's flush of secondary adrenalin as he registered the absolute joy of possession which, in turn, carried the fear of loss. He was overwhelmed. Terrified of his good fortune. He knew what he had.

The 'Yarnwinders' provenance was quickly disguised by a fake signature and the year 1865. Slipped into a home gallery in a dark hallway in 1942 and promptly confiscated, three years later, by a mine sweep of German terrorists. Goodman's vibrations dissipated. The intruders scarcely left a trace. I heard a muffled sound of jackboots and they were gone. Cecco's radiance was too strong. His musk chased the others away. PIAT snagged it from his estate sale.

My peacock allies from the grounds below set up crying to let me know a more substantial visitation was entering the building. The doorway dazzled with white light. Cecco's ghost entered the room and strode towards the two men. He casually pushed Burgher on the shoulder, knocking him off balance, and kept walking. My boss faltered, regaining his footing by grabbing Corkum's arm.

"You okay? You've gone a little pale," Corkum said. "Do you need your pills?"

Burgher took a labored breath. "Spectro *must* stay, Corkum."

Corkum lifted expressionless eyes and clenched them shut. "Tell me where they are and I'll get them."

"I don't want the damn pills. I want you to stay!"

Cecco turned his back on them and winked at me. He approached me with open arms and a mad grin. As always, he knew how to embrace me before we touched. And as always, the slyness of his wink aroused me.

He said what he often did. "Happy birthday *principessa*. Today we are together born."

Cecco glanced at his 'Yarnwinder,' nudged it with his foot, and it fell over with a thud.

"I paint well, no?" he said. "Leonardo learned a lot from me."

I snickered. "No doubt."

Corkum perked up. "What did you say?"

"No doubts... my analysis is correct, sir," I said.

Cecco hugged me from behind, leaning his head on the embroidered dragon my shoulder. He pinched my bottom and glared at my employers. *"Principessa,"* he whispered in my hair as his fingers stroked the red silk, these little pyjamas you love to wear, always ready for bed. I love it when you tell me your secrets, *si?"*

"What's so funny?" Corkum said.

"The artist who painted this was a practical joker," I said. "He loved to tease."

"He's just a cold and lonely, lovely work of art," Sphinx sang.

I wanted to rip Cecco's fifteenth-century white shirt from his body, sweep the paintings to the floor, and introduce him to a new secret, right there on the table in front of the two men who knew me as a passive wallflower. A wallflower who lacked the desire to even kiss yet had the necessary passion to distinguish a masterpiece from a student's hopeful copycat. Cecco made me brazen. But what they would have seen would have been a mime copulating with air.

Paintings mind their own business in the great galleries. They keep their secrets. They taught me to keep mine. Mysteries remain sealed. Loyalties intact. And paintings dream their own dreams.

They shy from bright light but Corkum had new lights that shined through their entrails, laying bare the first brave lines of art. He exposed an artist's false starts and abandoned choices – an arm or the turn of a head... or a basket containing three balls of yarn.

I habitually visited the monochromatic country of the after-life where paintings lived in grey stasis – the color of the past. Everyone in PIAT's inner circle agreed my ability was miraculous. Paintings healed by a saint, they crowed. Behind my back I expect I was considered less holy, at least by the members of staff who believed I was borderline crazy. My boss made the mistake of assuming I was too dimwitted to lie. The rest treated me as if I was contagious.

Cecco steered me to my room with his hand on my back. "Come *mi amore*," he whispered in a husky come-to-bed voice. "In a few hours it will be Monday and I will have to go."

Stranger Than Springtime/chapter fourteen

VANCOUVER ISLAND
PIAT – The Phoenix Institute of Art & Technology
May 3, 2014

Dad had been gone as long as I could remember.

It rained again this morning. Another weekend visit where May showers tried to be snow. The trees creaked from the wet wind, juicy with sea salt, slamming my window and surging the forest canopy into a sea of leaves. In the midst of the swaying, nests clung to branches and baby birds clung to nests and new-laid eggs rolled softly under their mothers. I embraced the perfection of it. Bird augury quickened casually under my skin and fluttered like mild tremors. I sent my shadow to keep lookout from a tall pine spar, grown bare and spindly a few feet from its top. I was watching for my father's ship. I was waiting for Dr. Who's 'Tardis.' I was listening for my lover's footsteps. I was looking for a sign. I could almost see the Eiffel Tower.

Back on earth, the trees of our boundary line swayed like a row of elephants. Pale green pachyderm oaks, maternal and magnificent, guarded the entrance to the Shangri-La of my old bedroom. A high leap over the black lacework fence would reach them.

Herons from Hope Bay patrolled the sky. Bear tracks worried their way to the harbor, a mile away through dense brush.

Their shaggy fur left a trail of brown tufts caught on the brambles, like breadcrumbs to lead a lost girl to freedom if she could make it over the fence, but escape as the crow flies and the bear lumbers and the Tardis materializes was impossible. And Cecco wouldn't come because it was a Monday.

I surrendered to the shushing sound of rain drenching the forest experiencing the blurry landscape as music through melted glass. A coconut wind-chime from the garden below sent a relentless S.O.S. in Morse code with the muffled clop of horses' hooves. One of the housemaids blew from the back door – a tumbleweed wearing a yellow slicker, to fill the birdfeeders with seed. She gave up when her umbrella turned inside out.

When I finished listening to the window, Brillo, more punctual than an alarm clock, pawed my arm for his breakfast. He was unhappily cloistered inside for his safety and my peace of mind. It was 8 a.m. I remembered how to be hungry.

Sphinx hovered silently at my elbow, unseen as always, fussy as a bee around a print of Vincent's 'Sunflowers.' Her verbal teasing invariably foreshadowed an extraordinary event or at least a message I was supposed to decipher.

"Porridge is served, ma chérie," Sphinx announced in my ear. *"You are what you eat, Goldilocks."*

A sharp rap at the door announced the arrival of a tray. "Breakfast," called a disembodied voice. I replied by yelling 'thanks' through the keyhole and counted to sixteen before I opened the door to a western omelet, a side of my special fruit salad (with four extra cherries on top, arranged in a square), and a bowl of fish paste. "It's eggs," I said.

Sphinx made a shushing sound. *"I was being whimsical,"* she said. *"Maybe the fish paste is for you."*

"The kitchen knows Brillo hates red peppers," I said, placing the fish dish on the windowsill, precisely at the agreed spot on the left-hand-side. Not for the first time it dawned on me that cats were as OCD as I was. But being members of similarly contrary species, we understood each other.

Umbrellas loomed significant in my life in many ways. I owned a gallery of them. Each one was imprinted with a great masterpiece. I collected them to honor my work, documenting the confessions of the troubled paintings that needed me.

Later, I saw the maid's black umbrella discarded in the recycle box. It was repairable, but being entirely dark and soulless, I left it there. My umbrellas were family. They were art. They were my knights. They were my walking sticks, my noble shields, and my shade in summer. I would never have abandoned one if it turned itself inside out.

But most of the time I failed to open my umbrellas when it rained because I didn't like to get them wet. It had something to do with the disturbing sheen of the waterproof fabric as much as I'd rather feel the rain on my face – one of my many eccentricities considered autistic.

It was my quirks which made me especially human, but what made me unique, often terrified others. Sometimes they made me fear myself.

Mother Lisa/chapter fifteen

SEPTEMBER – 2014

Fear was never far from my door. I woke from the cloying scent of bergamot and lavender as if someone had passed floral smelling salts under my nose. The 'Mona Lisa' was set on an easel beside my bed. I thought maybe the perfume came from her except Cecco had said her portrait exuded violets. Cecco was seated next to it, weeping.

I reached for his hand to comfort him but my own was heavy as lead. He vanished, and to my horror, my hand was mottled with age spots. An old man's arthritic hand. I panicked. As soon as I recognized it for a lucid dream I returned to calm... until, that is, I went blind. I tried to reach up to my face to check if my eyelids were closed but I couldn't move. I talked myself down from the ledge and waited, hoping Sphinx would rhyme me a way back to my own body.

I tried to call her but the muscles in my face were seized into a mask. I inhaled more of the fragrance, slightly less cloying now, as a lazy breeze from the window pushed another wave of lavender over me. Usually, I loved the combination of citrus and flowers but today the lavender made me think of old ladies, and medicine, and funerals.

"Inner eyes see the truth," Sphinx whispered. *"Follow me."*

A smoky vision of Cecco rematerialized and dissipated several times. I took a deep breath and followed Sphinx's voice, now inside my abdomen, and Cecco emerged solid and bright, picked out by a powerful spotlight.

Cecco tried to erase the anguish from his face with a broad swipe of his hand. He looked exhausted. "You have to go," he said, looking at me. "It's time." His voice caught. "It's the only way. Don't be afraid."

Jenks walked in the room and placed her hands on Cecco's shoulders. He reached up and covered one of her hands. "What will I do now?" he said.

I was surprised to see Jenks, even knowing she was there as a symbol. I tried to smile, but my face was still frozen.

Jenks looked away from the bed. Her gaze rested on the 'Mona Lisa.' "Enough is enough!" she said, addressing the portrait.

I'd never seen her defeated before.

Cecco broke down again. "I can't let this happen."

Jenks rubbed his back. "You can. You have to. We can't change time," she said. "This has to be. It has already happened."

Cecco faced me. "I don't want you to leave me, but I know you must. I'm so sorry. Remember me."

"It is over," Jenks said, and Cecco buried his face in her skirt. She stroked his hair. "And now it begins," she said.

Cecco gave way to his emotions. Our empathic connection was stronger than ever. I sobbed too, sharing every emotion of love, sadness, anger and fear that emanated from him. I called repeatedly. "Cecco I'm still here."

He looked terrified, bereft after losing his beloved teacher and father.

I panicked and clutched at the bedclothes but couldn't move, trapped inside Leonardo's body. I sensed Leonardo wanted me to speak the words he could no longer articulate. But I couldn't shout any more than he could. I heard my breath rattle and realized Leonardo was dying too soon. I could only stare his affection towards Cecco. "I love you," I called out. "I'm still here." But the words strangled inside the useless body. Inside it, I fought. Flailing my arms. Screaming. Of sound mind. Paralyzed in body. Furious to be brought so low.

I raked the sheets harder. My voice escaped in a scream. "Cecco!"

Leonardo levitated from his body and I hovered on the ceiling with him as long as I could. From above, the figure on the bed looked like a knight carved in effigy and Cecco looked like a page, kneeling before the stone sarcophagus of his master. But something I saw made me scream again.

My room was empty when I sat up in bed, my scream snatched from my throat by a single howl of wind. The window had flown open and rain spritzed my face in a fine mist. Sweat ran down my back. I was breathing as if I'd jogged all the way to Paris. I was thrilled to be alive yet terrified of the residual magic clinging to my skin. Already the image that had so frightened me, receded behind the instinct to normalize. I focused on a wholly welcome sight. My hand was creamy-white with straight smooth fingers.

I automatically called out to Jenks but Sphinx answered.

"I spy a nightingale," she quipped. *"Una veritas nominis. One true family."*

Logic told me I'd intruded on Leonardo's death, but this time, not as a bystander. I had experienced his death throes, acting as a translator but unable to convey his feelings. Being trapped in another's body during a psychic connection was the realization of my worst fear. Leonardo and I were mutually linked. Cecco was our empathic bridge.

I felt abducted, shaking in the dark like a child, disoriented as I reestablished contact with my physical body. For ten minutes I huddled under the quilt, counting to four between breaths until they slowed. Sphinx counted with me. *"Twenty-four shut the door."*

All the time, I churned with the growing conviction to never read a painting again. My abilities were out of control. Old fears overwhelmed duty. I was terrified to put myself in danger and more terrified I'd lost my nerve? No. I could never abandon Cecco. He was my motivation to continue. And now it was apparent he was in need of comfort.

"Rest in peace," Sphinx said. *"Never is a long time dead."*

I had shared Leonardo da Vinci's consciousness in his final battle for control. He had left so much unsaid. I felt his anguish, unable to tell Cecco how much joy he had brought to his later years.

But even as I recovered, I guessed the dream had been a portent of disaster to come. Cecco needed me and I knew how to find him. My stepmother knew. Lisabetta knew.

I pulled on a robe and felt slippers, and shone a weak penlight on the crimson walls of the hallway. The failing beam licked each brass doorknob, flickering like the dying embers of a fire. I skidded silently, creating sparks over the silk carpet. The penlight batteries winked out at the top of the stairs. The last thing I saw before the stairwell became a black abyss was a luxurious path of gold and blue patterns spilling down the stairs.

"Confession is bad for the soul," Sphinx repeated all the way to the second floor.

"I don't believe in sin," I said. "I believe in mistakes."

The restoration room zapped me with static electricity that brought me fully-awake. Its door resembled that of a large bank vault but even in the dark it was easy to punch in the combination which deactivated the alarm. The gunshot sound of the released lock sounded louder at night, in itself an alarm. I waited and listened for footsteps.

There were none, so I heaved open the heavy door to the eerie security lighting within. A continuous tube of green neon installed two inches from the floor illuminated the dimensions of the room and traced the contours of every object. The black and white tiles reminded me of a chess board under low-lying swamp fog. The white squares glowed in the dark to match the phosphorescent hands of the clock. It was 6 a.m.

The restoration lab was my special workspace. Easels with paintings in various stages of undress, peeping shyly from under years of candle soot and yellowed varnish, were arranged every few feet, scattered at random.

Several long panels of white gauze fluttered in the draught from the open door. During the day they filtered the harmful rays and diffused sunlight from the east that turned a painting into a lantern. September moonlight made thin pools on the floor.

The high resolution print I'd come to visit was the closest living relative of the original 'Mona Lisa.' It spoke in whispers but it spoke the truth. I considered the image I'd come to see as a family portrait. It was the official Louvre-quality document of a pear-wood panel wearing a skin of autumnal colors. She was dreaming of Leonardo when my laying on of hands woke her.

I adjusted an architect's lamp and shone it into her eyes. I half-expected the 'Mona Lisa' to lift her hands to ward off the light. The metal arm squealed when I adjusted the angle and suddenly there was no shade from a small sun hanging by a thread over her like an inquisitor. I summoned her awake.

"Mom, I have to speak with you."

The sensuous voice of a woman whispered "Delphi, is that you?" and I thought how convenient it was that we communicated telepathically.

Wings stirred the air above me. Sphinx had joined me.

I stood, respectively solemn, wistful. I was 'Mona Lisa's messenger. We were two voices in a box. The chessboard floor was appropriate for the game we always played of remaining open without guise.

"*Buongiorno Mama, si,* it is me," I said, without moving my mouth.

"Ah, good," Lisabetta said. "Yes little one, your young man is here, waiting. He is upset."

I dithered for a second before I pulled out a chair and sat down to listen. My hands posed of their own accord to imitate the Mona Lisa's.

"I prefer it like this when you come alone," she said. "Sometimes a person has to tell tales."

"You mean lies?"

"I mean keep secrets," she said.

"*And send lucid dreams,*" Sphinx added.

I was contrite. The 'Mona Lisa' divulged her secrets sparingly. She had been a singularly independent woman in life. Even I had to pry for morsels. I settled into my favorite position to listen between the lines. I was like a child at storytelling time, rapt but hesitant to jump into the story lest I be carried away. But now my morbid fear of giving in to my altered states bordered on terror. I feared being trapped in a foreign time, unable to get home.

"Surrender your mind," Lisa reminded me. "How else will you learn the truth? You are safe with me. There's only the two of us, here."

"*No,*" said Sphinx. *"Red lights have ears."*

I turned off the infra-red cameras.

I closed my eyes, the better to see with my ears. Lisa gave me the bells of Santa Maria del Fiore ringing the hours. She sent me the studio's muffled voices, the rustle of olive-green silk and caged birdsong. I could hear dogs barking in the Via Ghibellina from a parallel open door.

She sent me Leonardo's boyhood memories of perfumed wind drifting through the lemon groves of Campo Zeppi and the aroma of new-baked bread as their mother, Caterina, pulled it from the oven, and the working scents of sawdust, and warm seasoned wood-grain drinking up walnut oil.

Every time I visited she had shown me something new. I opened her world like a treasure chest and when she felt like it, she willingly unspooled her memories for me. This time she showed me the transition from Leonardo's death to her rebirth. She had watched him die only yesterday. She described it for me even though there was no need. I'd just witnessed it. Lived it all.

"Leonardo's eyes fixed on mine," she began.

I saw it afresh, standing near the deathbed like Ebeneezer Scrooge on the worst night of his life. Leonardo beckoned. Beseeching. The 'Mona Lisa' unfolded her hands and reached towards her brother from her gilt frame. Leonardo's fingers convulsed on the rich coverlet as hers grew nearer. As her hand closed over his, he shut his eyes and sighed, instantly calmed. Sweet breezes from the rose garden below drifted in the open window and lifted the long grey hair on his pillow.

I stepped back into the restoration lab and traced the contours of the 'Mona Lisa's face. She shuddered with sorrow. Even bereft, she gave me firelight and candles and red velvet embroidered with gold thread. She offered up her brother's last moments, leading me back into the chamber where I stood in awe at the foot of Leonardo's golden deathbed. So recently, I had lain there under the coverlet, helpless as a swaddled newborn. I studied Cecco, considerably more in control than he had been in my dream, leaning back in the chair, watching his master.

"Cecco," I whispered. "Did you call me?"

He didn't look up.

The 'Mona Lisa' invited me to watch the scene from inside her frame and the thought of another trap almost severed our connection.

"I'm fine here," I said.

"It's a fine day, Ebeneezer," Sphinx said. *"You haven't missed it. Christmas will come soon enough. Forty-seven minutes past the eleventh hour. Mark the time."*

Cecco looked up then, as if he'd heard us talking. "You're safe," he said to Leonardo. "I am here."

Leonardo tried to smile but could not. Instead, his eyes searched The 'Mona Lisa' and then found my face. It was as if we looked into the same mirror. The muscles around his mouth moved as he tried to speak. I felt my own muscles contract.

"Yes, I know," I said to him. "It will be all right. She will be safe. I promise."

He tried to speak again and Lisa shushed him, but Cecco, lost in his bedside vigil, heard and leaned in low to hear him moan the name Lisabetta. My stepmother's name trembled over limp harp strings to be absorbed by her portrait. Leonardo's last breath left his body and entered Lisabetta's mouth. She gasped.

Cecco was visibly shaken. I went to him and knelt, resting my head on his leg. We grieved together in silence and then I kissed my fingers and touched them to his lips. Only then, did he sob uncontrollably and I cradled him in my arms.

The spirit of Leonardo wandered about the bedchamber for a while, touching his possessions, saying goodbye, taking his leave slowly as if to imprint the room. He smiled when he saw Cecco with me and nodded. I understood his message. The master would say a private farewell to his beloved companion, later, when Cecco was more composed.

The 'Mona Lisa' was now free of her frame. She followed her brother to the open window and took his hand. They made a lovely picture until they both disappeared. My own spirit rushed to the window and I saw them below in the moonlight. They strolled the grounds of Clos Lucé, arm in arm, and as they walked they grew younger.

The next thing I knew I was walking with them, first as a chaperone, and after their bodies grew younger, a nurse-maid. The vast lawn ended at the edge of a sea – the great sea Leonardo always referred to as death, by which time, Lisabetta was an infant carried in the arms of an excited seven-year-old boy. His eyes were bright with the promise of a new adventure. He was eager to leave.

Leonardo laid Lisabetta gently in the center of a gold frame, washed up on the beach. He straightened and faced the horizon. "I want to go," he said, "but I can't leave her."

"I'll take her home," I said, and this seemed to satisfy him.

The sun was a white disk, and as we watched, it turned into a gull and dived into the water in a hiss of steam, evaporating the sea. Dry land appeared and green stalks emerged, spreading into a summer landscape.

Mount Ceceri loomed in the distance under a blue sky with swan-shaped clouds. Leonardo walked away from Lisabetta and I as if under a spell. He hesitated, turned, blew me a kiss, and ran into a newly-sprouted field of poppies without saying goodbye. I heard his joyous laughter for a long time until all I could hear was the Tuscan wind tugging at my clothes.

The wind became the echo of a howling baby. But Lisabetta was sleeping soundly under a mysterious baby smile, glowing from within. Her light reflected off the gold frame and blinded me, enough to make my head ache.

I returned to the restoration lab, gazing down into the painted eyes of the 'Mona Lisa.' I touched the corner of her right eye, and saw her as a younger woman – a mother holding her still-born infant. I touched Lisa's left eye and she was old. Delicate cracks had spread over her jaundiced face and gown like the veins of a leaf.

When I removed my hands, she seated herself in her log-gia and refolded her hands. I experienced her sense of loss as my own. She mourned Leonardo dreadfully and yet inwardly she smiled, remembering her childhood days when Leonardo used to make her laugh, and a later time when the promise of motherhood gladdened her heart.

For a brief moment her gaze drifted through me before settling into the iconic expression the world knew – a face that registered sorrow and amusement in equal measure. I too, slipped away without saying goodbye.

"Listen, to the echoes," Sphinx said. *"Follow the Minotaur's thread."*

Her whole Marley's ghost attitude was making me angry.

"If you have something to say, for Cecco's sake just tell me."

"Touchy wutchy. The end will never fall into place if a domino is removed from the middle," she replied. *"Come a day you will tell your guilty secret, but not today. A Monday when you can believe."*

Later, when I replayed the dream, I heard Cecco say to Leonardo, 'move towards me' and it came to me in a rush of pure knowing that he had not been addressing his beloved master; he had been speaking to me. I forced myself to look again on the stone face that had stared up at me. It was not the face of Leonardo. It was mine. I saw my head resting on the red velvet pillow. And of all unlikely things, I wore a set of headphones. The deathbed had been mine.

Monks chanting *'In requiem una veritas nominis,'* filled the air. Sphinx translated the Latin. *"Here rests a true family,"* she said.

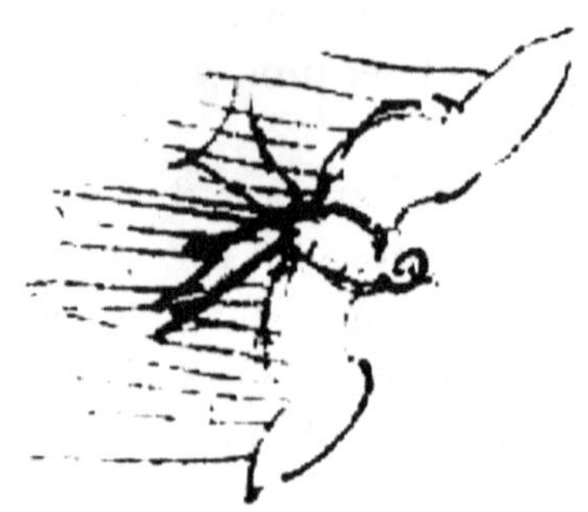

Mon Chevalier/chapter sixteen

VANCOUVER ISLAND, VICTORIA
October 11th – 2014

I made the mistake of discussing my plan of escape with a visiting spaniel named Mr. Bennett.

We were almost out the door. I'd put my pack and other bags in the hallway before I remembered Ben's coat. Back in we went with Ben's toenails clicking on the tiles as he whirled excitedly. "Ben Ben, calm yourself," I said, stepping out of the leash strangling my ankles.

The garment was a flat puzzle piece with snaps and rings and Velcro tabs from another planet. "C'mon buddy, help me out here. Stop wriggling." *Unhook leash. Fit tab A over tab B and press together.* Ben slipped and fell in his eagerness for outside, snuffling sharp exclamation barks of inescapable dog joy. The sight of his coat made him doubly-excited, scrambling now, on a dozen legs where there was once four. *Snap C.* I managed to snap the first button under his tummy in spite of his squirming. "Brillo and me are taking off at the end of the month," I prattled, fitting Ben further into his tartan coat. "To tell you the truth, in a few days we'll be out of here for good." *Snap D.* "I'm going to visit my mother in Paris." The stairs creaked as I unsnapped snap C, obviously no longer aligned. "My friend Didier has a safe-house for us." *Snap C into slot D and Snap E.* "My code name is Ducky. I'd take you with us if I could, but your mom would kill me. Brillo and me, we need to breathe." *Final snaps F, G, and H. Clip leash to collar.* "Ta da! Good lad." We rubbed noses. "Yes, you look very sweet. Okay okay, hold still one more a second." I tweaked the coat with a deft diagonal tug to sit straight. "If that noisy kid next door hadn't freaked him out the window, I'd put you in my pocket right now and tell your mom to go…"

I heard Sphinx's small gasp as the stairs creaked louder. *"Things must unfold as they should,"* she said.

"What?"

"Time marches on."

Dogs love to listen to their humans. They appear fascinated and ask no fool questions. Ben gazed intently into my face with the expectancy of a verbal treat. He panted and slavered, puzzling through the music of a foreign language. He was going for a walk. That was his universe.

But landladies like to listen too. Magda French listened like a fly on the wall. I always imagined her rubbing her hands together, fly-like, the way it does cleaning its proboscis. Her antennae, twitching like radar around her building, was meant to display her penchant for efficiency as a selfless hostess and confidante. I saw her as a flesh-eating gossip who alighted on people, searching for decay with her fly legs and fly arms and her compound eye that could see all her tenants' comings and goings without moving her head.

That October day when she tapped on my open door, I felt caught, but I couldn't tell from her vacant expression if she'd heard my confession.

"Oh you're home," she said. "I was just coming to see if the dog would be staying another night," as if Ben might be changing his mind about checking out of her hotel.

Mr. Bennett had been faithful to his calling. His spaniel job was to listen with sincerity, forgive implicitly, and bark no evil.

Mrs. French had been equally faithful to her own breeding. All day long she played I spy in some fey attempt at being friendly.

Didier was on his way to meet me when Mr. Bennett came to stay and my escape route evaporated. I had been close enough to touch Paris. During the days, my sudden washes of dark premonitions were easily dismissed, but at night the apartment felt like a cage. Childish laughter echoed through my rooms, rushing through me like thin wind, sounding evermore like a playful imp. My bones felt cold as black iron. Cold as the Eiffel Tower's spine.

I whispered to my 'Mona Lisa' locket, fingering its bee engraving, that I would be there soon. Or had I told Ben to tell her? I could hear the bee buzzing weakly like one of my childhood patients in the bee hospital.

In my brightest daydreams I mounted the Louvre's Daru staircase in a flowing gown and curtsied to the Nike of Samothrace. I turned to the right and ran the length of the hallway like Cinderella escaping midnight, to the *Salles des Estats,* the gallery where the 'Mona Lisa' was waiting. Candles burned on an altar before her, but her frame was empty.

Mona Lisa stood below it with her arms open, and I rushed to her embrace. *"Cara bambina,"* my darling child, everything is all right, now," she said.

It was slightly bizarre, even for me, to have the 'Mona Lisa' and 'Dr. Who' for parents, but later, that was the sanest thing about my life.

I was a threat inside an asset. I was a child who could skip down the halls of the Louvre, tagging paintings as fast as I could dance. Touching each... *this is a Rubens... definitely not a Renoir... not a Titian.... a student of Vermeer... ah! A genuine Vermeer... not a Van Gogh... this is real... fake... real... yes... no,* and in doing so, upend the entire gallery trade of works worth worshipping. Tourism would stalemate after my clean-up. A painting could fold from royalty into a worthless origami frog overnight. Insurance companies would bankrupt. Kneecaps would be broken. Paintings would die.

What PIAT wanted was my secret handshake with art to suddenly shout, this is no student of Leonardo; this IS a Leonardo!

Leonardo the bird, taught me the art of hovering with style, and Uncle Leonardo, the abandoned lost boy who never entirely grew up, flamed my desire to fly and to long for the freedom of open country until I called to my mother and father that I was ready to come home.

My dear Sphinx gave me hope. *"Tailwinds fan the flames of young love,"* she said.

Deliverance/chapter seventeen

Beacon Hill Park, Victoria, Vancouver Island
October 13, 2014
A MONDAY

My death was a walk in the park. A slip of the tongue and a slip of a girl slipped away.

I was carried into Monday at 6 a.m. on the wings of the morning chorus, after a dream about the Minotaur. Rain pelted the murkiness of October. Rain made me happy but today I was excited because it held the promise only a Monday could.

I broke the convention of a single dab of Chanel no. 5 on my throat and stroked golden traces of it on my wrists and behind each ear. I cinched the belt of my camel hair coat to the fourth notch, wound a scarf about my neck four times, and counted to four. I chose to meet an electrical storm head-on, wielding an umbrella like a talisman that, when opened, would disclose the maternal protection of the 'Mona Lisa.'

I opened the front door and faced the wild day, examining the dark sky with defiance before stepping out with open arms. I entered a furious glory of wind. It was like embracing an elemental god.

I felt my breath sucked from my mouth as if I'd been kissed by an impatient lover. I closed my eyes in bliss. Keats had been wrong. It was time spent under fractious skies that was a joy forever. After

Cecco, it was the closest thing to passion I had allowed myself to experience. It was Zeus love; it was like going home.

I felt lightheaded and took four deep gulps of air. "Sphinx, what's the matter?"

"*Woolgathering. Sorry, Goldilocks. Can't stay,*" she said. "*The wheel spins. Dilly dally. Leave the door unlocked. Candles in the window. No goodbyes.*"

She sounded, as usual, like Alice's erratic mad hatter, but I'd come to rely on her whimsical insight. She'd been my other-worldly nanny and a belated good-fairy-governess, and later, my true guardian who amended the worst of my challenges into small bites of bearable distress. We were like twin sisters separated at birth, telepathically connected. I assumed she was older by one earth minute as well as a thousand light years. The fact she was distraught was off-putting. Sphinx never apologized.

I couldn't shake the feeling of anxiety. She often left me puzzled but this was different. Sinister. It was the catch in her voice when she said 'no goodbyes.'

The winds of Beacon Hill Park crackled with ozone as I climbed towards the lookout bench hoping my lover, Cecco, would be there. From the clifftops it was possible to feel connected as the crow flies. I could hear the thundering horses of the Poseidon fountain snort and froth from their basin of damp leaves five-hundred miles to the north.

"*Dark horses,*" Sphinx muttered to herself, still shadowing me.

The hemlocks were hardy on the summit, twisted from exposure, bent into gnarled fingers pointing inland. Either side of me, boughs snapped. Above me, wilful noonday clouds turned navy-blue and rained watery ink, but my heart was bright with Paris.

Up here, the weather cared. I was the center of attention. Soon Cecco and I would need a third trysting place.

Uncle Leonardo taught us the best place to hide. No-one will never find you if you stay out in the open, he'd said, because people are too busy looking everywhere else. You can even shout, here I am and they won't hear you.

I smiled at that. I was better at hiding in the shadows anyway, stifling the sound of my breathing.

But waiting for a lover was intoxicating and I revelled in a metaphysical state of anticipation until fear caught me daydreaming. Time collapsed. I was a lost child again, cowering from the psychic blow of an invisible presentiment. A four-year-old clutching my only book.

They say in times of life-threatening events one invokes their god or their mother. Having neither, the closest deities I had was an iconic smile and a guardian angel.

I envisioned Sphinx as a bird. A white blur of sunlight – this time she was an owl the size of a snowflake, gliding over the vast Egyptian landscape of Saqqara. An endless sea of sand churned below with the Great Sphinx masked by heatwaves disturbing the horizon. The pyramid of Kephren dominated the skyline. Horus, the falcon god, perched on its capstone, and the rays of the Aten… fanned in symmetrical one-point perspective – an upside-down peacock's tail with caressing arms and healing hands, touching my face, reading me like a painting. Sphinx called out, *"soon, Lambkin."* She was crying.

The west wind whipped low to the ground, uprooting years of undergrowth. The sound of splintering branches ripped inside a thunderclap of low pressure and my nostrils burned from the scent of death reeking from a tortured tree. It was too late.

I beseeched 'Mona Lisa' but she smiled benignly overhead, oblivious of my fear.

"Mom," I called, "Something's wrong. Help me."

But even as I floundered, I felt elated. How much easier it would be for the angel of death to find me here, halfway to the clouds. The bells of Florence's cathedral rang for me and I saw Cecco's family lake in sixteenth-century Lombardy, lift from its bed and rise as a blue balloon and burst against the topmost spire of the Eiffel Tower. Water exploded into steamy fireworks. Red sparks flared and died as they fell. Each spark spilled the word goodbye. The horror of it was beautiful. I wanted more. Goodbye echoed from the smell of sulphur and flakes of burning sky. It was a glorious send off. *Grazie. Magnifico. Arrivederci.* I shouted, "HERE I AM!"

I wanted to call out to Cecco in my excitement but my throat had constricted, scorched from the smoke of dying bark. The umbrella's handle extended like a helpful arm and I gripped it harder, the way a child grasps its mother's hand tightly to cross a dangerous road. *"Home is just on the other side,"* Sphinx whispered. *"Look both ways."*

A cold metallic point embedded in the wooden handle pressed into my lifeline like a hypodermic needle tipped with Demerol. The delivery was orgasmic. A rush of golden euphoria flooded my body as death struck.

Instead of falling, I floated in a rapturous bubble, energy bleeding out. My predator was a friend after all. I was finally going home to meet my mother. Bliss. Cecco would be there. He was the man of my dreams, and I was moving towards him, the way he wanted.

I gazed down at Sleeping Beauty lying face down in a puddle of rain, puzzled that she was wearing my winter coat. The 'Mona Lisa' umbrella was still in her hand like a deadly spindle, and a gold locket spilled from underneath her rainbow scarf.

I abandoned her. I rose into a dream of purple formaldehyde, drip-feeding in a slow cold trickle that radiated from an IV needle in the back of my hand. It was a syringe of eternity that stopped the heart, cold.

My blood turned the color of irises and my skin took on the pallor of dead lilacs in the manner of compassionate euthanasia.

'Putting one's body to sleep' is euphemistic at its most ironic because I slept in the chilly arms of death, cursed beneath a blanket of snow like a princess under a hex.

I believe my last emotion was guilt.

How do I know all this? I was considered too valuable to die, and my next incarnation is able to revisit times that have been. I'm able to observe from her coattails – a relatively new trick I've acquired.

Before I became Cherry White I was Delphi Sharpe. I liked brown ducks. I didn't like wet umbrellas. Shiny things and buttons made me queasy. I'd never seen a blue moon. I was born on a Thursday and died on a Monday. My mother died the same hour as my birth and I carried the horror of being the cause.

Fifty-two-years later, in 2066 I was still twenty-seven, but until I remembered how to feel rage, I was unable to destroy the people who harvested my brain and ruined my life.

Once upon a time, I was reborn from a long winter of dark magic to learn the secret of life – that which doesn't make you stronger will kill you. Twice.

Stasis Quo

"Everything is energy
and that's all there is to it.
Match the frequency of the reality you want
and you cannot help but get that reality.
It can be no other way.
This is not philosophy.
This is physics."

ALBERT EINSTEIN

THE DESIDERATA
*"You are a child of the universe
No less that the trees and the stars;
You have a right to be here.
And whether or not it is clear to you,
No doubt the universe is unfolding as it should."*
MAX EHRMANN – 1927

Sleeping Beauty/chapter eighteen

Time froze inside the season of 'White Shoulders.' While I slept in mock death, I was alone. Sphinx was gone, her thoughts unable to penetrate the ice age in which I was trapped, but even so, I knew she waited in the abyss, silently grieving with Cecco.

Paris was a five-letter-word which meant nothing. I knew where it was but that was all. I knew the Louvre was there and that it housed the 'Mona Lisa' and the 'Nike of Samothrace,' and that its glass pyramid reminded me of a Sphinx I once knew.

It was my curse to remember singular details. I remembered the musk from Cecco's skin and how the color of the walls vibrated in ripples the day we met, and how a loose curl of his hair reminded me of a boy in Leonardo's first painting. But nothing moved me. A childish voice called from far away that there were worms crawling and something about insurmountable loss. But then a glimmer of hope arrived with a curse.

To whom it may concern. I'm having a birthday party, the invitation read. Come as you are. RSVP – yours truly, C.W.

Sphinx returned to assure me Cherry couldn't help but to use formal language and that she wasn't having me on.

After fifty-two years in stasis, I thought I would be thrilled to see and hear the world any way that was possible. I could continue my quest to save Uncle Leonardo's art and make my way to Cecco, but I was devastated to find my anger swirling inside another woman's confusing thoughts.

Not that Leonardo da Vinci was my real uncle. We lived five-centuries apart. It was my way of belonging to a long-lost family.

It was difficult to adjust to being a background noise of memories. Cherry replayed them, plotted, and played nice to the man she could only hate in theory. My emotions hadn't cloned into her lifeform. But Sphinx didn't seem fussed. "Why does Cherry have to obsess about revenge?" I asked her.

"Cherry has no emotions to process forgiveness, only the images of cruelty persist to inform her that she needs to react," Sphinx replied. *"It would be best to keep a low profile until Cherry asks you outright for help... and she will. Neither of you girls ask for what you really want."*

"But she's playing dumb with my brain," I said.

"Cherry understands the art of play as manipulation. She has programs for that. Believe me, she's not playing. It's pointless to try to outsmart yourself."

The forests of Vancouver Island still housed the institution where I lived, died and was half-reborn. The buildings were the same with some modifications, but the staff had condensed into fewer pirates. Scientists and secretaries who once numbered over fifty were reduced to four with a small van of casual labour that arrived every second Friday to restock the larders and stay for two days of high-spirited cleaning and gardening.

Hamm the figurehead, held the purse strings; Dr. Mason, a hanger-on scientist, acted as his toadying yes-man; and Mason's enslaved nephew, Phillip Moon answered to everyone's bidding without protest, despite the fact he wanted to be anywhere else but stranded in the wild rainforests of British Columbia. Lastly, there was Mrs. Cook, the cook – a dour Scot who had a natural tendency to play heavy-handed with the salt. Definitely, or was it defiantly, a skeleton crew.

After Cherry's four 'people' were hired, there were nine of them, including herself and excluding Sphinx and me – a couple of spectres skulking in the shadows. I could barely stand it when

Cherry walked to the Poseidon Fountain. Cecco was gone and yet I could feel the wish of him lingering there as he once did, holding my hand, promising me the moon.

I hated uneven numbers, so after Florence the cockatoo arrived I rested easier. We were a community of twelve. A good omen, divisible by four.

But I wished for an increase by one. If Cecco had given up on me, I may as well slip the rest of the way to death.

Cherry got most of what she asked for in the beginning. She was better at demanding than I was. But then she was pure logic tempered by the art of strategy and she had Hamm over a barrel. She could deliver a never-ending supply of lost masterpieces. She was performance art.

"The art of war," Sphinx corrected.

Hamm had impounded my brain but without Cherry's cooperation his business would fold back into what had become a routine parade, the trickle of a random masterpiece, and trafficking regular art forgeries to the middle-classes with shallower pockets than he'd been accustomed to. I hated his grandfather and father but was willing to forgive and move on in search of Cecco. However; my incarnation Cherry, wanted no part of absolving our abductors or to acquire love. She was out of emotions. She wasn't lonely. She was out for blood.

Next Life

CHERRY WHITE
2066

I spy
With my little eye
Something beginning
With fire

April in Paris/chapter nineteen

VANCOUVER ISLAND
The Phoenix Institute of Art & Technology
April 15, 2066

birthday two

It was the season of violets.

'Mona Lisa's' eyes swam out of focus and into a pair of thick horn-rimmed spectacles. A florescent bulb swung on a cord behind her – a silver disc forming a cheap halo. Then a shaft of light overwhelmed everything, like a sword in my right eye.

My first thought was that Lisa had chosen the wrong frames for the shape of her face. I was about to tell her when I heard my own voice shout the word Mom as if independent from my body.

I sounded like an echo, booming out of sync. "Where's my mother? She has my umbrella," I shrieked. "Where's Mr. Bennet? Who burnt the toast? The fire alarm. Magda will have a fit. Who's feeding Brillo? Buttons. Jenks, I'm over here! The monks are dead. I'm going to Paris and that's that! Mom! Sphinx! Cecco!"

My audience seemed amused. A doctor made some notes on a clipboard in his precise backhand script. "She's probably replaying her last moments," he whispered to his colleagues, "She was carrying an umbrella with the 'Mona Lisa' on it when she died. "Who knows? Maybe she'd been reading 'Pride and Prejudice' and had toast for breakfast. Brillo was her cat."

His words came as speculative mutterings as if he were talking to himself. He scanned some loose sheets in a file underneath his report. "Apparently, she had an aversion to buttons. Maybe she can tell us who Jinx and Cecco are. Sphinx is probably symbolic. She studied Egyptian art."

I corrected him. "Jenks," I said. "Her name is Jenks."

He dismissed the urgency of me calling for my mother. Most people did that when they were terrified. They called for their mothers or their god. Paris was a given. I wanted to correct him about Mr. Bennet, but he'd turned away from me and was huddled together with his colleagues.

There was a taste in my mouth as if I'd been sucking a tarnished spoon. Phrases sprang from my lips into a room brighter than the sun. Acid in the eyes. I closed them and listened. The conversations which followed were travesties of bedside manner. But then, scientists with the academic title 'Dr.' rarely address their Petri dish children with fawning affection. I didn't know it yet but I was Cherry White, their first human android to date, and only one person in that harsh institution thought I deserved better.

"Cherry," a man's voice said, "I'm sorry to wake you but it's time." He chuckled to himself at his clever wit, and another voice laughed.

An image of the Eiffel Tower shimmered like a mirage and evaporated.

Still groggy, I opened my eyes and listened to the spectacles. I felt like a rubber band about to snap.

"I'm Dr. Mason," the voice said. "Can you tell me your name?"

"Thirst... thirsty," I croaked.

The doctor held an empty glass to my lips. "There that's enough."

"More."

Again, the empty glass was tilted into my mouth.

Voices swam from a dazzling cloud. "I can't see properly," I said.

The light was deflected from my eyes, and I was fitted with blue shades.

"Is that better? Can you see now? What can you see?"

"Water...tired... headache."

"She can't have a headache," a voice said. "She has no pain circuits. It's amazing. She's processing the memories of pain."

"Your name?" the voice prompted.

I saw several figures draped in white. "Lisa," I answered.

"Lisa who?"

"Lisa Giocondo."

Dr. Mason glanced up at the viewing deck and gave a thumbs-up. The ripple of celebration that ensued in the glass box reached me as a mild aftershock of trapped bees buzzing in a jar.

The ecstatic figures who encircled me congratulated each other with handshakes all round. "Happy New Era," one of them said in a breathless voice.

I saw an image of party streamers and balloons, and heard the song 'Auld Lang Syne.'

"What year is it?" I asked, and a black wall of water rose and fell when a triumphant voice declared, 2066.

The sharp smell of ammonia should have brought me skittering back to the white room where the eyeglasses still spoke in an overexcited tone, but I smelled nothing more than an imagined whiff of chemicals. Magda must be mopping the hall, yet again.

"Cherry, it's Dr. Mason. You're quite safe. I want you to pay close attention... you died."

"Jesus, Mason," a different male voice replied under his breath. "Give her a break." He gave his colleague a withering stare, raised his eyebrows, and took over. I detected the movement of a smile beneath his surgical mask.

"I'm Dr. Hooper," he said. "What Dr. Mason means, is that you're bound to feel disoriented. But no cause for alarm. You've been... *out*... for a fairly long time. You've had an accident."

"Dr. Who," I said. "I can't tell you how pleased I am to meet you."

"No, Cherry. It's Dr. Hoo-PER. I ..."

"Dad it's me, Delphi. You finally came. I've been waiting a long time."

"Her chart says she was delusional," Dr. Hooper said. "That's diplomatic for fruitcake."

"Now who's being insensitive?" the first voice said.

He'd called me *chérie.* "Am I in Paris?"

"If you like, dear," Dr. Mason said.

"I must have been out, cold," I continued. "I was dreaming. I was floating in a church with chanting and flickering candles. Someone must have burnt the communion wafers. It was the Sistine Chapel because... no, I'm quite wrong. It was the Louvre because I saw the 'Mona Lisa.'"

And then I registered the year 2066 and the words, you died, and realized with a rush of bittersweet familiarity that I'd heard the ambulance arrive, and the taste in my mouth was licorice, and the smell of toast was the bread I'd been carrying for the ducks.

When I awoke it was spring, and I felt like the proverbial 'death warmed up,' but there was a grey silence when I announced it to my doctors. It's Easter they said, as if that explained anything. I suppose they may have been referencing rebirth but none of them had the sensitivity for humor. I was the critical mass of their experiments. There was nothing amusing in the room.

I was the sacrificial lamb served up on a bed of nails, and as usual, my brain was able to register the subliminal truth before I knew what was going on.

Ironically, I sensed the enormity of my atomic insignificance. Mother Universe had shivered an electrical spasm, hiccupped twice, bore down, and I was born. I imagined a midwife saying, congratulations Missus, it's a blip. I was as inconsequential as a spark of human static on a wall-to-wall carpet the size of the Milky Way.

Fifty-two years had passed but I was still twenty-seven years of age.

I was immortal. I was too valuable to die.

When Sphinx returned to me after my death she was as cryptic as ever. *"Chérie,* she called out. *"The sun rules the field. Bring out your dead."*

I followed Delphi's memories like a thread *into* a maze. They led me to my ultimate mission to eliminate the remaining remnants of the institution that ruined her afterlife. It was a suicide mission; I *was* her 'after life.' At the center, I found a mythical 'trinity.' The three of us: Delphi, Cherry, and Sphinx.

"Ties that bind," Sphinx said. *"String theory, remember?"*

I'd already calculated my plan of action, but a persistent vision had looped for hours where I held out my hand until Delphi finally took it in desperation. So, it was logical to keep reaching.

I invoked Delphi as a living entity. "It occurred to me you might enjoy destroying your abductors," I said.

Delphi's voice spoke from a deep well of longing after mumbling about a lost umbrella. "Sphinx said you would come."

Sparks issued throughout my circuits like champagne.

"Mother to Baby Bear," Sphinx muttered, loud enough for me to hear. *"Have we met? Kid gloves. White gloves. Archive gloves."*

"Can you find Cecco?" Delphi said. "Please. I need someone to tell him I'm on my way."

"Sixes and sevens," Sphinx said. *"Both of you... come to your senses!"*

I awakened slightly ahead of my brain, stranded on a melting ice flow, only to find the pond in my back yard had grown into Leonardo's 'great sea.' There were no ships. No safe horizon. No destination for which to sail. No home near enough for return. No past distant enough to forget. No family to mourn. No Sphinx. No Cecco. No me.

Monks serenaded me into PIAT and left me swooning inside a shard of killer sun that cut my eyes. "My brother loved birds too," they sang. "Loved birds too. Birds too. Et tu, et tu, et tu." The lyrics dissolved into Latin prayers and eventually hushed into white sound like a distant waterfall. A voice commanded me to jump a chasm over roaring white water rapids. I refused but a jab in my arm carried me over the edge, free-falling into a pool of foam.

I floated on my back, staring up at a flat white sky made up of squares. A bright light resembled the sun but it was elongated into a tube. It took a crazy conversation with Dr. Who before I realized I was in a room and the river beneath me was a solid table.

A burning prophecy blew across my mind's eye in a repeating stream, reminiscent of a news bulletin in Times Square, rolling out a telegram in lightbulbs across a skyscraper's face. *Urgent... time ceases to revolve around the sun...history opens...worms crawling... stop.* I would have panicked but panic was just a word I knew that meant crazy.

I regained consciousness inside the body of what was essentially Delphi's old body enhanced with technology but deprived of an emotional menu. An almost-android. Hybrid, high-bred, high-tech. My brain was busy reconstructing itself, overwhelmed by the programs of a subservient machine, and although I was unable to feel the organic quality of crazy or hate, I processed intellectual anger as a clinical given of human violence.

I was aware of a background hiss of Delphi's brewing unrest and nothing more. None of the feeling but all of the knowing. Programs and commands eclipsed my personal issues but my memories served to inform me revenge was in keeping with a history of being abused.

I was Cherry White. Cherry for my job, cherry-picking the past for lost art, and White for the series of experimental cybernetics able to withstand molecular time-travel, the first bionic eye-witness equipped to penetrate the depths and breadth of history.

I continued to live the life of a different recluse, controlled and groomed for a futuristic mission on the cutting edge of fantasy with thoughts I hardly knew what to do with.

I needed the impossible. I wanted to default and play a better game. But I've learned two truths about the mythology of time – Father Time captured life on sensitive film that if altered would destroy the present, and that forever is a creative thing which is why Mother Time gave birth to artists.

My story could never have unfolded separately from Delphi's. We remained two sides of the same coin. I was her second chance; she made my first mistakes. We are each other's better halves. Time-slipping made it possible to live concurrently. Delphi is not backstory;

she is the part of me that fused into our finest hours. Without her I was an empty machine; without me she was a lost memory.

The survival of my brain... OUR brain, meant I became Delphi's default biographer. Her past explained my present. Her memories were my archives. I caught her emotions released like dandelion seeds on a windy day. They anchored inside me on barren ground as part of our mutual experience of technical reincarnation. I had many nagging questions, but the most prevalent was does it takes two lives to make one woman?

Delphi's birth in 1987 impacted a destiny which spiralled out of control during an age when eccentric behavior and signs of genius were still misdiagnosed as insanity in the backwaters of superstition and religion.

She entered the world on a stream of maternal love with the promise of a charmed life. But unlike most newborns, she arrived charged with a supernatural mission. She was endowed with truths to heal a precious resource falling into disrepute. Even so, like most newborns she passed through the river of forgetfulness before she opened her eyes on the world.

Delphi brought glimpses with her that soon faded into the wallpaper, but when she failed to fit in, she tuned in permanently to an alternate universe.

Fantasies are never what they seem to the fanciful. Delphi's were as real as anything that happened in what is euphemistically referred to as reality.

Our story is both a confession and sad revelation of our origins. It's also tells how a slow-witted race of dreary hominids leaped gracelessly over quicksand, wielding nothing but a crude butterfly net to capture a place in pre-history. Ironically, a net is also the disparaging implement used to describe the art of catching 'moonbeam people' like Delphi whose creative light was impossible to restrain in an asylum or a designer straightjacket.

I came to view many aspects of Delphi Sharpe, but the one I wanted to befriend, the one who was the most compelling, was an ancient teenager scrying through the headiness of smoke and incense, reading the bones of a kestrel's wing that once flapped a live message across the sky. Wild horses thudded past her on a dry plain dotted with trees like flattened umbrellas. That's the time-less landscape where we should have met.

In retrospect, the twenty-first-century was too soon to set science on the throne of the world. It was a civilization that had moved too fast. In a hundred years, science had gone from creating sticky notes to time-travel. It was hard to keep up with inventions that were redundant before they had time to cool.

Delphi had tried to fly beneath emotional radar to feel safe. But abandonment at birth was white hot. Hot enough to sear a brand on the heart. There are no splatter screens able to pro-tect a child from the birthmarks of first degree burns. Lily pad travel sounds tame but Delphi's life was a succession of leaping from frying pans into fires. She was a born savant – a moonbeam celebrity. She hid her emotions under the umbrella of autism but she felt too much of everything. Most sensitives do. I was her final leap. Neither of us had a choice, but one of us had a chance to thrive. Although I didn't know it at the time, we were united by an uncommon love yet divided by the art of loving. 'AT THE TIME!' How that phrase was to haunt the year. Everything was immediate for the first time and yet old hat. Delphi resented me. She didn't truly hate me until later.

My fires were mythic. Heroic. They existed in a theatre of histrionics. Delphi's life was painful but mine was far worse because my abductors made me fireproof.

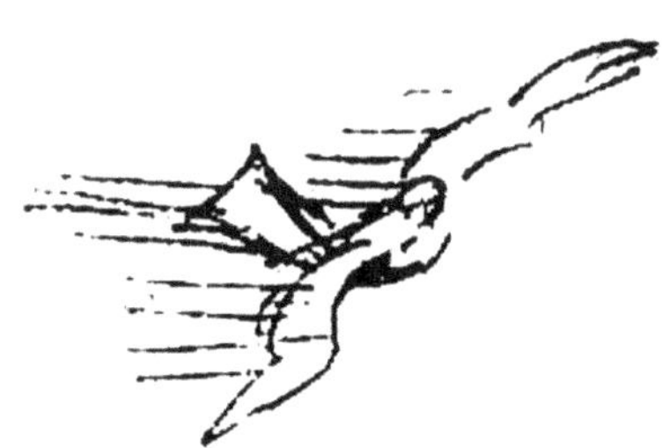

**'The seven stages of man' adapted
from the 'Zodiacus Vitae'**

– by PALINGENIUS, 12th century

The Quickening/chapter twenty

April 16, 2066

It was April and I heard the gossip that the tulips up-island had been blooming for a month. Warm winds off the Queen Charlotte Strait had brought the lilies of the valley on, early. I replayed a memory of miniature white bells curled inside premature tendrils.

I too, had my own incubator. I lived in a climate-controlled glass room – a newborn adult kept under observation. The red Halogen lamps overhead were designed for maximum scrutiny.

I was treated like an exotic hothouse flower recently landed from Mars. I gather I was worth money. Security doors around me shushed on heavy gliders and docked into a locking system which required a retina scan to open.

Sometimes, whether it was wishful thinking, imagination, or a heightened sense of curiosity, I was more 'Delphi.' I could remember the moment when a work of art first materialized as a thought. I sensed the artist's true signature, not the letterforms that made up their names but their passions that spoke as clearly as a voice in my ear.

If Delphi been labelled a trickster it would not only be inaccurate, it would be a gross disservice to the brain's capacity to make extraordinary leaps of consciousness. Humans have yet to harness the subtle vibrations between man and the universe. But without emotions, how could I decipher the subtle transition of life and death. It was delicate. The initial harsh killing lights subsided. There had been softer light – ecstatic light. Sparking neurons collided in a compassionate starburst that illuminated a breathtaking vista of possibility.

Delphi joined a flash of transcendence, released to play. There had been a suspended giggle of clarity – a brief and never-ending singularity of her purpose. Delphi's dreams condensed and evaporated several times. The brain of her soul transmuted into an eloquent code of elastic synapses until only one remained as a precarious swinging bridge.

I had been gifted a new language, and while the elegance was indescribable, I was compelled to translate it. She remembered her source but I defined the earliest memory I had of myself as an omnipotent ballerina, eclipsed by a thirst for water... a lone gene replicated into a psychometric field of maternal electrons sustained in a quickened bubble of plasma. For a brief moment I was glorious gelatinous goo, and then I had a tail. I was laughter. I was art. I was time.

The beauty of it had been inside Delphi. She woke up cruel and mad as hell. It was my job to reach back for the beauty, knowing she would bite every hand I held out.

When I was able to backpedal time, I watched PIAT's president, Adrian Burgher, react to my first conscious moments. I logged a convulsion of interference static at first voice. The hatred was Delphi's. His colleagues called him Hamm as if it was an endearment. The rest of us used it as an insult. It didn't take a rocket scientist to realize he was related to the family who adopted Delphi. Imitation pond scum, all the worse for knowing it.

I replayed my recording of Hamm with a zoom lens as he looked down on me from his bulletproof glass pulpit, hunched as a monk in prayer, his bald pate gleaming with nervous sweat. He held his breath, straining into his earphones, gripping an unlit cigar in his hand, tapping it like an excited pencil. He ignored the phone that sang in a persistent chirp from the breast pocket of his tailored herringbone tweed jacket, eventually sliding it out using two fingers as if he were extracting a disgusting worm. He handed it to the intern, Phillip Moon, and wiped his hand on his pants.

"Get rid of whoever it is," he squeaked in a high voice.

Phillip Moon, gopher at large, glanced at the call display. "It's your wife, sir."

Hamm glared silently at the floor and shut his eyes before resuming his vigil, observing the scene below of my rebirth, now drenched in turquoise light. He waved the young man away with the magic wand of his cigar.

Phillip steeled his best professional telephone voice. "Mrs. Burgher, your husband.... that is he... ah... I'm sorry, ma'am, Mr. Burgher can't be disturbed at the... uh… present time. Can I have him call...? Yes ma'am... well, it may be some time... yes ma'am, of course... um ... where?..." Phillip held the phone away from his ear to detach the pen from his clipboard. Eleanor Burgher's shrill voice could be heard rattling a number into the ether. "Can you repeat that ma'am... okay got it... goodb... " A loud click indicated the call had been terminated.

Phillip handed his boss the paper.

Hamm tore it to shreds and let it drift to the floor like confetti. "Turn that damned thing off right now and get your uncle up here!"

Phillip's expression was grim. He pressed the off button for a long time. He seemed to be strangling the light that issued from the cellphone as it flickered farewell. Phillip returned the dead phone to Hamm's pocket with great delicacy. He turned and left without a word.

Someone handed out chocolate cigars from a box. All the while, Hamm gestured with his unlit tobacco cigar like a conductor waving a baton. I came to learn it was the equivalent of false bravado – the cardboard sword of a child playing king. He liked to communicate by cigar akin to the language of fans. The various ballet movements, posing, sniffing, twirling, and tapping an empty ashtray were hollow gestures lacking smoke and ash.

Hamm's crucifix tie pin screamed confession. For some reason it was a familiar icon to me. Later, Phillip told me Hamm was an atheist but his wife was catholic which explained a lot. To me he was a strutting rooster with a grey crown – barely recognizable as a chip off his grandfather, my ex-employer, and a pale facsimile of his spoiled teenage father I once knew as the wildcard heir to PIAT's throne. The most junior Burgher was the personification of fifty years of devolution – the perfect shrinking violet to blight his family tree.

The only way to determine my 'owner's' original sins was to sink into the past for retroactive first-hand observations. Remote viewing was a handy new function. Recording faint sounds, memorizing text, and taking mental pictures rendered me a posh camera with arms and legs.

A month after my awakening, when I was being obstinate, and ironically costing the institute 'valuable time,' I followed Phillip Moon's first day as he slid his clearance pass across the security scanner before letting the iris scan do its work.

He entered the secured wing, thickly insulated with the hush of holy science. The inner-sanctum of covert operations, code white. What he saw when he crossed the threshold of the sterile holding zone, was me. An unresponsive woman in her late twenties, supine, lost in calculation but technically ready to snap down any moron who told me I'd be okay. The trouble was, the snap was missing from my irritability which rendered my words perversely academic – a distant cousin twice-removed from the humans populating the world. The worst had happened. Sphinx had deserted me again.

I still belonged within the rules of polite society that exempted eccentric celebrities, old ladies, young children, the mentally disabled, and androids, as 'special.' We were free to blurt rudeness and wit outside the conventions of social nicety. Whether out of genius, belligerence, or innocence, we could spew our honest truths and fear no consequences. Embarrassed silences were left in our wake and we traveled on, unembarrassed, and they traveled on, amused but dismissing us as irrelevant.

I imagined Ebenezer Scrooge's face superimposed over the expectant faces of my scientist-doctors and my new boss. Humbug, Scrooge always said, without altering his normal expression of discontent. And so they processed my scathing 'humbug remarks,' delivered with flat dictionary precision.

My long hair was cropped into a pixie style that changed colors at the whim of moods I couldn't feel. Moods it seemed I'd once read in a book. It was independent of me, leaping into spikes or curls whenever my circuits registered a change of thermal instability. I was lulled into submission by the drone of my inner circuits humming rhythms that only a dog could hear.

I gathered this 'hair-art' had not been planned but was a happenchance side-effect my overseers could use to assess signs of vulnerability or disobedience. At the moment I had no control over such a program, or if I did, I couldn't care enough to master it. My hair remained human with inhuman colors, fluctuating erratically according to verbal stimuli. It was wired to my fingertips, too, because my nails reflected the same color changes. I had shape-shifter hair and mood-ring fingernails. My eyes, normally cornflower blue, also deepened to navy-blue at erratic moments normally experienced as emotional. At least I had a theory why.

A flashback, standing outside PIAT's former restoration room reminded me of feeling lightheaded with tingling fingertips. I was Delphi – my head replaced by a blue helium-filled balloon hovering over my shoulders and sparks issuing from my waggling fingers. Every Monday they were newly-lacquered with outrageous colors. It had become a safety ritual of some kind.

What *was* proof-positive was that organic residue remained trapped within my new-improved body. Remnants of Delphi's psychic abilities pre-selected themselves for survival. I was not completely biologically dead.

For days, my blonde hair had been reduced to a limp greyscale that phased from black to white as if undecided to be or not to be either a décor feature of the white room or Shakespeare's dark lady. That morning, my eyes and hair were black. My hair had bristled like an angry hedgehog since I regained consciousness. My hands looked very Halloween, splayed on a drab-green hospital gown.

I fantasized I'd been visited by an alien race in surgical masks of white paper that sucked in and out as they spoke. I was a specimen in a jar, captured by heartless boys – the 'old boys' network who lived on the corner of established science and big business.

If I could have registered any emotion, it would have been alarm rather than surprise. I'd already been naturally-selected for obscurity from birth, so anonymity was nothing new. Delphi had always been a tame dog with no bite. Now it was my turn to blend into the wallpaper, but the powers of camouflage were redundant against the walls of a glass aquarium. At any time, an alien Alpha Boy could give the order to bring out his flunky's magnifying glasses and fry me for laughs.

I was housed in my old PIAT fortress of bumbling hospice, but now the bears were inside. Scientist 'grizzlies' pinned me to a dentist's chair, horizontal as a mortuary slab in a futuristic torture chamber, white as a blank canvas. Lying there, in a prison cell of white light, I realized what a waste of creative space a ceiling was. It was the suspended floor only a long-term patient would know.

I recalled the last ceiling of my apartment and the haunting laughter of a child that had issued from it, raining down on me and Brillo, no doubt it had been a happy ghost, but Brillo was dead. Perhaps my hair mourned him, independently. It seemed I had no heart. I registered his loss as emptiness without the tears. I should have been the angriest I'd ever been, yet I was so far removed from rage to defy all logic.

On paper, I was a fury, but I registered nothing but a mild sense of curiosity, that of the remote viewing of an anesthetized patient hovering over their body, noticing obscure details of a cold crime scene. I was a reporter. An objective judge. Images of emotional outbursts replaced feeling them. I knew when Delphi was angry or sad or moved to love from the snapshots and movie trailers of her past life, projected over present events as a separate track. A visual commentary that accompanied my thoughts and conversations.

I'd examined myself from every angle to find a trace of inspiration capable of human outcry, but my brain was lethargic. I had duties to perform. Thoughts of escape, escaped me. I fancied I should be lying in a rowboat, clutching a bouquet of lilies with dead fingers like the Lady of Shalott, drifting downstream in stately requiem. A dead salmon, floating belly up to tempt the bears.

But at least my hair was emotional. It was a chameleon on auto-pilot, and instinctively I tried to fade to death by seeming insubstantial.

I continued to stare at the ceiling desert as Phillip Moon entered my cubicle. He reached for my hand but hesitated. He withdrew it and lowered himself gracefully into a rollaway chair, adjusting its height to its fullest extent rather than lowering the platform on which I reclined. His first sentences arrived breathlessly clipped as he tiptoed around the elephant in the room. Smalltalk would have been insulting.

"You're not ill you know," he blurted. "It's only natural to feel despondent."

Ah. He was one of us – the socially inept. I continued my vigil of the ceiling tiles. "I don't feel emotions; I register them; I process them," I said to the tiles.

"I can't imagine what you must be *registering*, then. I'm here to answer your questions and give you a debriefing of... well, circumstances. You must have questions."

I turned my head to face him. "Is it impossible to tell when an android is bored?"

He was an apologetic leading-man in his late twenties, almost too precious, with the smooth rounded contours of perpetual youth. He had been raised in an elite conservatory as a privileged son of science.

I felt no physical discomfort but knew instinctively that a live patient would have been given a real pillow and blankets.

I knew who he was but I was programmed to respond only to authorized personnel. "State your name?" I said like a dominatrix. Then more politely, "I mean *please* state your name."

"Phillip. Sorry... Phillip Moon."

"Am I dead, Phillip?"

"Of course not, absolutely not, no, you are functioning ... *differently*. Housed differently, so to speak."

"A brain in a box?"

"Miss White... I mean, Cherry..."

I interrupted. "Why do I need a surname if I'm a machine?"

"It's not a name, it's a designation. The first in our hybrid series is white. The red... models... were plain androids. You're *different*."

"Special," I said, averting Phillip's pained expression. I concentrated on my definitive study of the perforations in ceiling tiles. "You're here to engage my cooperation. Well, no-one will gain it if I'm treated like a sacred kitchen appliance." Intellectual anger flickered inside my chest like a candle and spluttered out.

Phillip's eyes looked up and to the right so I knew he was deliberately searching for a less-sensitive topic. "Your profile says you're a *Dr. Who* fan. Me too."

"Like the Tardis, I'm much larger on the inside than I appear," I said.

"It's called dimensional transcendentality," Phillip said, grinning. "Well, the doctor called it that."

I had the remote thought I should be raging with the kind of fury that would blow my circuits and dim the lights of Victoria five-hundred miles away. Violent feelings had always seemed pointless to Delphi, and now, mulling them over gave me the sensation I fancied was a computer's version of nausea from the image of the inside of a clock, squirming with worms. A voice rang inside my head. *'History will open. Worms will crawl. Paintings will cry, and time will cease to revolve around the sun.'* "Can you imagine the relentless emptiness of dimensional transcendentality, Phillip?"

Phillip's eyes widened. "I can try... I mean, yes I can."

"I seem to be a little displaced. Don't look so alarmed. It's not your fault."

His mouth twitched into a shy smile. "I quite understand."

"Can you get me out of here?"

The smile disappeared. "Where exactly do you..."

My fingernails flashed purply-red. "Out of this interrogation chamber for a start. I used to hate hospitals when hate was a real thing and that's what this place is."

"Not exactly, but it *is* a lab. More of an observation chamber."

I quoted a line from a childhood fairy tale. "What big eyes you have. All the better to see you by."

"I'm not the big bad wolf," he said, squaring his shoulders and jutting out his chin.

"My dear little, sweet kind wolf cub, then. These bright lights are for *you*. I expect some darkness. I need the night to brood. I know wolves. You should be able to relate, being a Moon."

"Sorry, it's standard protocol for a controlled scientific study."

"Ah, I see you're a boy scout. How flattering. And what do you see? A specimen? An experiment gone wrong? A gift-wrapped brain?"

"I see a woman who, quite rightly, feels displaced and misused," Phillip said.

I guessed he was searching for a compassionate approach to explain his personal opinions without jeopardizing his position. He had called me a woman. He was a stand-up guy."

"There's that F word again. *Feeling*. What are *you* feeling, Phillip?"

"Perhaps, sense is a better term. I … what are you sensing?" he said.

"I sense loss in all its dimensional transcendentality. When I first woke up I thought the men around me were monks. I had been serenaded, you see, listening to Gregorian chant when the end came. The end which turned into this... is it a beginning, Phillip?"

"I was there," he said. "Well, I saw. I mean, I wasn't there *when* you died. Obviously. I saw you ... that is, your beginning... yes it IS a beginning."

"My extra debut? My compassionate second chance? I'm a whole new woman."

I ran a thread of sympathy for him but I needed to air my grievances which spilled from my mouth as pure inventory. F is for Fillip. I ticked off a list of clinical bullet points on my purple-tipped fingers.

I read out my list, and as I observed the room, I recalled a documentary of an autopsy being performed on a fake alien body made of cheap silicone.

I heard the flutter of musical wings. *"Open channel to star fleet command,"* a voice said, wearily. *"You took your sweet time. Pun intended. You finally left the door unguarded."*

I answered her in my mind. "Sphinx! You're back!"

"A slammed door without a lock still requires a key," she said. *"I had to wait for an open channel. You've got quite a temper for someone who has no emotions. Welcome to Vulcan. So, now you really are Spock."*

"I guess they created a monster," I said.

Sphinx was condescending. *"Good girl. Time is on your side.* She chuckled. *"And the sun rules the field. It's time to bring out your dead."*

"I don't think of you as a monster," Phillip said.

"Sorry, I didn't mean to think out loud."

"The doctors were perhaps too abrupt telling you why you're here," he said. "They can't help it. They're eager. And a bit light on the bedside manner, I'm ashamed to say."

Two more F's flashed as bold white slashes on a blackboard. "Are you Friend or Foe? Why did they send you? Are you a lawyer? What rights could I possibly have? Whose side are you on? What fence are you pretending to cross? You asked if I had questions."

"Easy tiger," Sphinx said. *"You're burning too bright."*

"It's not enough for you to be debriefed on technical details," Phillip said. "I volunteered. My uncle is Dr. Mason. He's one of the doctors… I mean scientists. I told them, I suggested, you needed a friend. I would like to extend that possibility, eventually. For now, I'm here to help if I can… as a sort of bridge between science and humanity."

"You mean the humility."

"Ties that bind," Sphinx said. *"String theory, remember? Don't let go. Lamb stew at 12 o'clock. "*

"That too. I'm here to suspend your anxieties," he said.

I drew my legs under my chin and stared at my new toes, daring the nails to burst into red lozenges. "Sorry Phillip. I have no anxieties. You're a suspension bridge over a dry riverbed."

"Listen to Mama Bear," Sphinx said. *"Play it just right."*

I sensed Phillip holding his hand inches above my head, stroking the air as if I were a pet cat.

"And perhaps even interest you," he mused, "in the beneficial possibilities open to you which are, to be honest, so amazing I wish I was…"

I lifted my head and scrunched my hair into shape. I scowled my best scowl at him. "A human machine?"

"A time-traveller."

Origins/chapter twenty-one

The oracles in the old days who prophesized chaos, whispered it was the fault of apes.

Darwin was almost right. Delphi Sharpe's demise on a Monday was *technically* more of an extinction. 'Death by tempest' would have been a poetic way of skirting the polite verdict of 'natural causes.' They may as well have stated she'd died from a lack of common sense but for the fact she was born with the extrasensory perceptions of a true savant. A savant beyond savant.

At least a tempestuous near-death honored the existence of a purpose well-dreamed. And if nothing else, Delphi, an abandoned orphan, had been a magnificent dreamer. Even her detractors described her with admiration: hair blonde as milk, eyes like shy cornflowers.

In some ways, as Cherry, I was the extension of her life; in others, she was the creator of mine. We communicated in a conflict of overlap, the continuation of one mind – a unique anomaly of biology, technology, and hostility. We agreed on one point only, the lost paintings of Leonardo da Vinci were worth saving.

Whenever I beseeched the girl-wonder to come forward, she begged me to step back. We became an overcrowded metaphor of clocks and Matryoshka dolls and pearls because those were some of the images Delphi constantly and reluctantly streamed into me. I also inherited Delphi's shortcomings. They were imbedded into the basement of my subconscious.

By default, her realities rendered me a 'challenged' android, or at least a bionic female with an inbred legacy of OCD that complicated the recovery of my previous life. I had little choice but to ride roughshod over Delphi whenever I could, during her meek moments. My sole purpose was at stake.

We both heard the psychic voices of paintings, so it was shorthand for us to converse like ancient Egyptians, in pictures layered with hidden meaning. Word paintings relieved Delphi from the traces of human anxiety and informed me of the emotions and senses I was determined to regain. Her richest treasures were stored under dust sheets in the attic of my subconscious. I wasn't looking for them; I was only after the rarified passion of hate, but Delphi's loves were lost, high under the eaves of our house, locked in a Pandora's trunk, and hate was the key.

First contact with Delphi took place in the herb garden. I lured her by appealing to her love of birdsong. *They'd* let me out without a chaperone because there was nowhere for me to go and a high fence to prevent me from getting there. The lavender was beginning to bloom along with the promise of sweet peas, and bees hungrily buzzed its vine of perfume that I couldn't smell, but I cast my malfunctions aside in order to face her sensibly. My sister foe.

I refused to insult the moment like a common séance medium warbling a feeble, 'are you there?' into the ether. I knew Delphi was near enough. I simply began speaking as if we were old friends who hadn't seen each for a while.

I filled the old birdbath with rainwater from the Poseidon fountain, and refined of all sensory stimulus other than sight and hearing, casually sprinkled a libation over the ground. "I name this sanctuary the Garden of Delphi," I said. "I'm sorry you died."

Delphi's impassioned response was contrite. "How was I to know the aftermath of one's death could be peaceful?" she said. "I panicked. It wasn't like I believed myself immortal but I assumed I'd been naturally selected to arrive. That was promised me... I think."

"You mean selected to *survive*?"

She sent me a picture of Icarus plummeting to earth.

"I flew too low," she said in a muffled voice. I got the impression of a woman huddled into a sulk with her arms wrapped around her knees.

I didn't understand, but I humored her. Sphinx had mentioned she was skittish. "Darwin would have written a different book had he known us," I said.

I felt more than heard her sigh. She spoke as if to herself. "Sphinx was right when she called us a pair of odd shoes."

I gave a polite cough, hoping Sphinx was close enough to hear. "Sphinx is as feisty as ever," I said, before I lied. "We miss you."

In answer, Delphi sent me an image of the outcrop known as Egypt's Great Sphinx bathed in colored spotlights against a backdrop of night sky. Three bright stars descended together and played about the monument, showering it with stardust. After they zoomed away and repositioned themselves as Orion's belt, each star burst in a firework display, sizzling the sky three times, each explosion more magnificent than the first.

Back in the desert of Sakkara, the Sphinx had been replaced with a giant stone swan – a most improbable creature to find landlocked in a panorama of sand. It was our first real conversation in fifty-two years.

"*It's about time,*" Sphinx said. *"Venting is such sweet sorrow."*

I imagined Sphinx squaring her shoulders and cracking her knuckles, eager to begin.

"Is it always going to be like this? I ask a question and Delphi answers with a movie clip?"

"Pictures speak louder than words, Lambkin."

Delphi can't always hear me, can she? Or is it that she doesn't always answer? Is she even listening right now?"

Sphinx created a vortex of laughter around me. *"She has a mind of her own."*

"Now you're being perverse."

The vortex popped. *"Sibling rivalry is no laughing matter, Lambkin."*

"We're not exactly peas in a pod."

"Delphi has performed a delicate language bypass. She is your therapist. The language of the mind is always picture perfect. Play nice."

It was time for diplomatic negotiations. "Delphi, please listen," I said. "We can work something out. Tell me what you want."

"I want my life back."

Wants and needs connected us. "And I need your emotions."

Delphi spat a poisonous word at me. "Host."

I countered with "Parasite."

Sphinx interrupted – a mother separating a pair of naughty children. *"You can't have one without the other."*

It was the first time I heard Sphinx lie. "But that's exactly what we DO have," I said.

"You're in recovery. It's only a matter of time," Sphinx said. *"Wholeness is a state of mind. It's all in the mind. And think on this, there are more lives than yours on the line."*

Delphi waited so long to respond I thought she'd gone, but when she did, she spoke without emotion, and it was the last word. "I refuse to play hide and seek with a robot."

I was a woman with a grievance at a loss to express. I didn't need Delphi to function. I required her to surrender. Feeling my way would put things right. I wouldn't have helped myself if she'd been generous. We were more than ancestors, closer than twins – we were a 'time.' I was the December to her January. And we didn't like each other.

I visualized us as a unique Russian nesting doll, the innermost doll being Delphi's teeming brain – a solid nut of romantic power inside an ape, inside a phoenix, inside an angel. But deep inside that angel she stored a terrible secret she kept from me.

"Without it I'm a clock with no hands," I said to her. "Confess your sins. I need to know everything."

"I don't believe in sin," she replied. "I believe in mistakes. You're a mistake. Just look at the state of your fingernails."

"You believe in romance and fear," I countered. "I get that in your intrusions."

Delphi's voice hesitated. "I don't understand."

"Your spontaneous intrusions of déjà vu that interrupt my functions," I reeled off in deliberate robot-speak. "And I can't help my hair. It hasn't decided what color it wants to be. And perhaps you shouldn't have worn so many different shades of nail polish."

"Kid gloves, Lambkin," Sphinx muttered.

"You know very well I can only see your emotions," I said. "How's that for irony, art whisperer? I think you tease me on purpose."

That sent Delphi scuttling behind a memory. Tact wasn't one of my strong suits. I'd hoped to spark her dormant sense of outrage and shake out any unfinished business. I needed an ally.

"Tell her, Sphinx. It's in her best interest to cooperate," I said.

"She knows," Sphinx replied testily. *"She's tired of hoping."*

Delphi's angelic looks might have been her first saving grace but they were eclipsed by more tangible assets. She could read a painting like a novel, the way a magician could tell you what card you'd picked and the word you scribbled on the back and what you'd had for breakfast, except, she didn't use tricks. Neither of us used tricks.

All paintings tell a story of their creator but Delphi and I eavesdrop on an artist's process. When we run our hands over a painting we hear its voice. In a word, we are 'transported' by art. Paintings called to us from bookshelves or the open doorways and windows of galleries.

Landscapes reveal secret hiding places for trysts and worshiping Pan. Delphi sensed the mood of the sitter in a portrait. The perfume of 'still-life' roses hypnotized her like a bee. Bowls of ripe fruit carried her off to summer orchards and lemon groves. And in their counterpart stink of blighted fruit, through the art of *'memento mori'* – an artist's mindset to evoke the premonition of death, flies buzzed around the rot of collapsed apples and blue patches of mould, reeking of psychic decay.

Delphi tasted art, and inhaled the organic days in which it was first created but she forgot she could die. As for me, figures and artists have to tell me their joys and woes. The pungency of sweet-scents or foul was a mystery to me. My brass ring was olfactory but all I could smell was revenge. Delphi was my nose and taste buds and passionate heart; I was her guide from the maze of her underworld.

The Phoenix Institute of Art &Technology said they adopted Delphi for the greater good of culture in general and the provenance to purify the mud of art history. But even after

Delphi supplied the relevant facts, art history never ran clear as a mountain stream. It remained a polluted man-made canal. Lies floated on its surface like scum. Auction houses laundered fakes into museum attractions and art died a little more each day.

"Murderers!" Sphinx shouted.

It was uncharacteristic for Sphinx to express herself so hotly that Delphi and I floated out of the moment, stunned.

Sphinx was definitely rattled. *"Wake up,"* she yelled.

I snapped back into the unconscious. "Delphi are you awake?"

She sounded sleepy. "In one-hundred-years the forest will reclaim its sanctuary. There will be a gate where the sun marks the time, and the wind will whisper secrets as still as a mountain," she said.

I listened. It was a long time before I spoke to Sphinx. "I'm a codebreaker. I can decipher crossword puzzles in seconds. But Delphi eludes me."

"You will remember her language in time," Sphinx said. *"As for codes, every painting that deigns to speak with you will hold a clue to setting Delphi free. Some may even change your mind. Pretend you understand what they tell you and you will. Your salvation lies in asking them questions you don't want answered."*

One such question danced over my keyboard mind. "How did a sensitive creature like you survive the hatred?" I asked Delphi. "And why do you hate me? I'm not your enemy."

"The people in charge didn't hate me," Delphi said, "they just never bothered to see me."

She ignored my second question which made it flash neon, but I followed her lead. "Still," I said, "in retrospect, they might have sent you a telegram – a simple announcement: we regret to inform you of your death. That's what they should have done. You would have understood that."

"Failure to thrive," Sphinx said.

Delphi sighed the despair of a woman watching the horizon for her lover's ship knowing he wasn't coming today.

Sphinx sniffed. *"Lovers rush in,"* she said. *"Fools in quicksand."*

"You can't catch moonbeams with a butterfly net," I said, hoping to confound Delphi for once.

A cablegram would have cut through the unspeakable lies that led to Dr. Hooper's grisly announcement, which in the earliest weeks of my existence was too alien a concept to register, and even now, after an outlandish year in a new skin, was unbearably difficult to process.

I was privy to Delphi's idealistic dream tunnel of transition and its gentle white light where human moths gravitated towards a hospice of retreat. But waking up inside my algorithms and fibre-optic receptors shook her already less-than-stellar opinion of the neuro-typical misnomer, homo sapiens. My artificial intelligence sideswiped her.

Even though my body looked the same, Delphi treated me feel like a clockwork clone.

But more than her distain, there was bigger complication of cross purposes. Delphi was born with hyperthymesia and the eidetic memory of a perpetual child which meant she was bombarded with minutiae that never lessened as she matured. She automatically memorized facts and photographs, but she also remembered every gleam and grimace she ever faced. She recalled the individual pressures and directions of brushstrokes and the numbers of things and the color of everyone's shirt and the pattern of the carpet under their shoes and the scents each person, animal, plant or thing, exuded. She was destined to snap. I was designed to endure. Her genetics made her more of a computer than I was.

Delphi was free to speak unchecked, and I begged her to literally 're-mind' me.

Collectively, we'd studied the arts and sciences from anthropology and archaeology to zoology beyond her twenty-seven years. We were clear that life arrived on an amino joyride and sapiens meant intelligent, and that hominid's quintessential empathy gene had been felled by a rogue abscessed tooth.

She sent me a lecture delivered in the monotone trance of an oracle:

"Mankind might have been a more compassionate race," she said, "except the fittest of weakest links survived to dominate. The forefather ape who claimed the barren wastes of no man's land, quickly seeded the greed zone where sub-average intelligence met an insatiable appetite for meat, power, and serial procreation. The population rose and fell with fickle enthusiasm, finally settling on an accidental population of limited possibilities."

I listened like a child hearing a bedtime story.

She continued. "Pleistocene's 'wise man' became the victorious *noble savage* premised in the myth of a thousand monkeys destined to bash away at a universal keyboard to write 'War and Peace' before the sun burned out. Primal traits of maternal gentleness withered under his skin leaving only traces of subdued kindness."

There was a long pause and I thought she was done but I was mistaken. I soon came to learn that Delphi took her time when she spoke from middle-earth.

She recited as if from a poem. "But art was his saving grace. Art filtered through his superstitions and made headway – creativity being the one selfless offering which reached beyond his brutish nature.

"Time was longer then. It silenced the anonymous muses under its dust. For ages, the universe had been unfolding as it should. Apes had been aping apes, plodding slowly in a continual line of devolution to the present day. Inbred design flaws continued to be the culprits that culled the weak from the strong. In the case of my ancestors, it was the thin wedge of random misfortune, the sabotaging of genesis that happened all too frequently."

This time her dramatic pause was longer. I thanked her, but she'd retreated back into her cave of prophecies.

Later, I pondered what to rename the event the world called death. Delphi had died and now I lived. What other facts were relevant? Everything else only measured its distant nearness, from Delphi's prophetic arrival into lukewarm love to her grandiose 'divorce' from real life and the tepid reconciliation had she been lucky. I regarded life's adventure to be overrated. All things considered, resurrection was a cursed blessing.

No abstract *thing* reckoned the quality of death or the sanctity of nothingness. No special word other than imagination bridged the length and breadth of the beforetime and the afterlife. Life hadn't stopped. Time hadn't reset; all things circadian were as they had always been. The alpha and omega of Delphi Sharpe were points of old rapture on an ancient map. She had lived her years between the cold bookends of birth and rebirth. No wonder she'd been lonely.

Twenty-seven years of hard-wired memories besieged by dour auras and conflicting smells was no substitute for her organic soul. Instead, she was robbed of an ethereal afterlife and I was granted a reanimation of eternal memoir, as yet, neither joyful nor depressing. My road to humanity was shrouded in impossibility but a woman like Delphi, with the heart of an oracle, might have the map, and I'd let her tag along. As for me, technical immortality would rule the field until it didn't. History could wait. It had nowhere to go.

Delphi was complicated. She liked to say she was saved from too much life. She believed she had violated her soul's purpose and failed someone, that much was plain, but she had never been sure who. I still think of myself as the jaded kid sister of an older sibling who died. She reminded me of a dot of color in a Seurat painting – too small up close to see the bigger picture. Even more than that, I determined to release her after she was no longer relevant to my immediate goal. Indeed, after that shallow commitment, I would no longer be relevant either. I would apologize as best I could and pull the plug. *C'est la vie.* Except, revenge had nothing to do with too much life and everything to do with too little of it.

Delphi regretted being too quick to adopt the label of autism. It began as a convenient hiding place for laying low under a sweeping stigma while still able to embrace a measure of honesty in plain sight. She meant no disrespect; she simply had no interest in conversing with the narrow-minded guardians who misdiagnosed her. In this we were in complete accord. My generation were no better.

By social definition, Delphi was so severely autistic she formed another species. A strain of autism that escaped beyond the known spectrum – a ticket which failed to grasp the full burden of her unconstrained intelligence. Technology has continually misappropriated natural forms of infinite calculation in the misnomer, artificial intelligence, but neurology was a baby science. Even by 2066, the human brain still had miles of untold pathways, yet a dreamer traveled to the stars and back inside a catnap.

Delphi made such trips while awake. She clung to regular autism as an amulet; she would have nurtured any label that prevented people bothering her, and by the time she was two-years-old it comforted her like a favorite sweater. Sphinx called it the Victorian approach. To be seen and not heard. Still, Delphi brooded. Abandonment is a devastating thing for a child.

At the tender ages of eighteen and twenty-seven, Delphi buried shameful secrets which left me threading our next life around blind spots, pearl by pearl, one memory at a time. Reincarnation woman to woman. If the wisdom of the ages be pearls, Delphi and I were a necklace – a cultured double-strand of past and future lives. I disregarded the present as a dreary band of limbo in a fickle rainbow. That listless color of dead purple where muddy red unsuccessfully blends with dull blue but with the addition of moonlight light deepens to pure indigo.

From the perspective of the afterlife, time is an immeasurable string of heartbeats spun around a singularity – earth is a ball of yarn adrift in space. Delphi arrived, a lone heart sent to unravel an invisible ball of yarn in a lost painting. It was called the 'Madonna of the Yarnwinder' and it had been missing since 1507.

As for me, the whitewashed bane of Delphi's 'undying' existence and a human time machine forced to perform in science's greatest breakthrough since the discovery of fire, I was left to wonder – which came first, the phoenix or the egg?

A Sharpe Mind/chapter twenty-two

Delphi was battle-scarred but I was a warrior.

Sphinx gave us chess lessons. *"Did you know there are invisible princes and princesses in chess?"* she said. *"When a king is cornered, niceties are thrown aside, and princesses are released like baby krakens to do their mother's bidding. Princes are too busy preening as heirs to care. Kings and queens employ spies but their daughters have more free time. They read their opponents with nothing less than x-ray vision. They're born royal. They're born wily. They're born with an edge. That's you."*

Delphi remained a silent student while I probed for an advantage, burning holes in the chessboard, testing strategies for flaws. "I detect flaws in every move," I said.

Sphinx created a wind that swept my white queen to the floor. *"Strategy is useless. When true chess masters lean forward in their chairs and hunker down, they laser-beam the board to win. It's survival of the most psychic. Emotions are locked in a drawer along with any pretenses of bluffing and cunning. You SHOULD do well, but..."*

I was relieved when Delphi chose that moment to finally speak. "Why am I expected to play to lose?"

I dove straight in as a crusader diplomat and made her angry. "We both win if one of us wins."

"Don't be an ass!" She abandoned the game muttering, "This is pointless. We're wasting time."

"Only one of you can win," Sphinx said, *"and Delphi knows you have the advantage."*

"Just because I'm a computer, it doesn't mean…"

"No Lambkin. Grandmasters are crystal-ball-clear," Sphinx said. *"They're time-travelers."*

Delphi admitted her misgivings of guilt in her beginning time. "Look, it was easier to lie," she said in a candid truce. "PIAT was too big to fight. She balked, back-peddling with a catch in her voice. "Shame was no big deal… then."

"It's okay," I said. "Apart from the secrets, I'm you."

"You're NOT me. You're a nightmare, and I'm not your teacher in some hellish summer school!"

"Iceberg ahead," Sphinx muttered to herself.

I matched the word *teacher* to *teach* and my personalized dictionary spat out 'tetchy': argumentative, belligerent, cranky, and bad tempered. All the things I 'yearned' to be – a word I chose to describe my overriding directive towards my goal of full-circle humanity.

Delphi aligned herself to the people surrounding her while she played for time. I did the same. Was it manipulation? No. It was Siamese chess. Delphi never threw away the key to her drawer but she did hide it for a long time. She played merry hell over it and made me work to find it. I believe she extracted pleasure from it after I gained the ability to suffer.

Mr. Darwin stands corrected. Minds checkmate bodies. Artfulness – the fullness of being artful, wins over emotion. It's not bigger brains that outwit mental brawn but the open-minded whimsy of hydrogen. I thought of Delphi as the eternally split child. As for me, I was a slave with attitude. Time was our new playground where we princesses played for keeps. I vowed I would teach her once she taught me how to teach. It would be a *tetchy* game, but I offered her an afterlife with her lover as soon as I could complete our dying. She almost stopped punishing me.

Delphi's abundance of supernatural abilities had unhinged some people and triggered the hope of unprecedented wealth in others. She was doomed. We both were. But doom has a way of making humans and sub-humans try harder. I played upon Delphi's weakness for her young man, Cecco, and told her that magnificently-fearful and joyous surprises would arise if she and I worked together.

"Fearful?" she said.

I was smug. "If there's no fear there's no joy."

"But you can't feel either." She delivered her cheap shot. "You're not *human*."

"Not yet," I said. "But I read a lot.' It was my smartass way of sidestepping a lie, and this bit of fluffology silenced her. I had been using the term joy to mean success. She wasn't fooled but the name Cecco caused an involuntary jump of determination inside her. I used it often. Telling lies was always easier for me, but as for inspiring Delphi into an ally – there was 'no joy.'

Delphi was as much of a 'hominid computer' as I was. Being savant-smart was the reason she'd been abandoned. It was also the reason she'd been noticed. She was a motherless child for a long time before she found an immortal mother who would never forsake her, even in death. People called her the 'Mona Lisa' but Delphi called her, Mom. She loved the words mom, mummy, mama, and mother, but she flinched a little and I 'hiccupped' whenever she used them.

> *"Art is the tree of life;*
> *Science is the tree of death."*
> **WILLIAM BLAKE**

Kindred/chapter twenty-three

April 21, 2066

Phillip stayed by my side for the entire day, leaving only to eat meals, mindful of unhinging a form of artificial intelligence 'who' might crave food but was no longer able to consume it.

I knew of course. I could read him as easily as others perused a newspaper. People are 'front pages.' Their boldest secrets are 'headlines' splashed across their eyes. I probed for details when they were relevant to my immediate needs. Only Delphi kept an attic door locked with me outside.

The establishment knew nothing of my innermost plans and cared little about my personal likes and dislikes, most of which were considered odd requests for things of no consequence. I was a sentient file cabinet with benefits, not a woman who might ever again seek the warm-blooded connections of a lover. Not for one minute did my *handlers* think I was capable of an emotional response. I hoped to prove them wrong. I urged Delphi to prove them wrong.

"You will meet, well at least *see* Leonardo da Vinci," Phillip said. "Mingle within his community to witness his world firsthand like no other. How cool is that?"

"Are you trying to be humorous? I was in cryogenic sleep for over fifty years. How 'cool' do you think *that* was?"

He gave a startled look and stared through my forehead,

mortified. After one of those hour long minutes he spoke. "A pink stripe flashed in your hair," he said.

I decided Phillip's bird ego was a pelican, a sacrificial symbol, and mentally dubbed him, the Grail.

"A happier color is an improvement," I said. "You're a probably a nice young man who happened to find himself in PIAT's pocket. I will keep a more open mind." I'd made a wisecrack but lacked the will to laugh even though I had the facial muscles to speak and smile. "Visiting my family is tempting."

"Cherry, you have no family."

"I have memories of one."

"Can you be more explicit?"

"The trappings of hearth and home. Sanctuary. Privacy. It doesn't take an astrophysicist to compute how vital environmental influences are. Maybe fogged Rococo mirrors in feng shui'd rooms, with no 'sharp' edges or corners where a demon could hide. I require windows that open. Wide open, not some sliver too narrow for a finger of wind. Oh, and I want a mantelpiece and one of those fake electric fires."

Phillip looked as if he needed permission to laugh.

"I intend to regenerate my emotions, therefore, I require the stimulus of domestic ambiance. Between you and me and this ceiling, I will function more efficiently with my emotions intact. Art is emotional. It's conceived in emotion and it evokes emotion. Emotions are the only link I have to my real self. I believe you understand that."

Phillip worked his mouth and gave up, looking uneasily from right to left. A lost boy.

"I choose to fake sleep in a proper bed with linens. This room has no heart. No backbone. I'm going home, Phillip, as close to home as I can get, right here. I hereby request an apartment, ironically, complete with a *living* room, full kitchen, and a sumptuous bathroom. I know how many empty rooms exist in the manse. Then I will dedicate what's left of me to a singular goal. Tell your uncle that. Or not. Secrets are *cool*."

The time had ceased to be one where I requested through the amateurish art of shy manipulation. For once, I held the upper hand. I would be the most human android possible. Even feel passion. Especially, feel passion. I saw a lonely Cecco, waiting by the fountain. Would I ever be able to miss him or call him with love? Would Delphi?

Delphi choked back a scream that issued as a plaintive 'yes please.'

"So," I taunted, "you're still alive."

Sphinx comforted her. *In time, child. In time.*

"So what? I'm alive," Phillip said. "You're going to have to deal with it."

I didn't bother to explain. It was easier to expand my list. "I require access to the grounds at all times, and a patch of my own land. The old herb garden out back will do. And I prefer my old eclectic clothes: scarves and shawls; silk pyjamas and embroidered slippers." I touched my khaki sleeve. "Not a generic jumpsuit. I'll need a Victoria Secrets catalogue."

"What's that?"

"THAT is a joke, Phillip. Please inform Hamm I require a cat. I don't suppose anyone had the decency to freeze Brillo for me?"

"Sorry, no," Phillip said apologetically, studying a speck on the floor. His fingers skipped over his palm pilot making a list, hesitating at the word, cat. I saw him type a red question mark beside it.

"Hamm will never go for a pet," he said. "He's not exactly pet-friendly."

My insides fluttered. I saw a woman holding a candle, climbing stairs in a dark house. No doubt it meant I had a loose fuse.

Phillip's eyebrows raised. "Anything else?"

"A skylight over my bed," I said. "I require a sky. A ceiling painted with clouds isn't enough. By the way, I won't be needing nail polish."

He missed my second joke too. "We can keep decor an open subject, then," he said.

"Now tell me their rules."

"What rules?"

I gave Phillip a sideways drop-dead glare. "There are *always* rules, Phillip. Explain how it will work?"

"Cherry, I hope you don't mind me saying so, but you're not at all who I was led to expect."

"At least you didn't call me an 'it.' You meant an autistic savant?"

Phillip furrowed his brow. "Sorry. I didn't mean to offend."

"I'm not offended. You're doing your job. I'm doing mine. I hear your colleagues discussing me. According to their genetic testing, I'm an anomaly. Autistic was the only category where they could slot Delphi at the orphanage."

"I don't slot my friends," Phillip said with a hopeful smile.

"Friendship is a landmine. Slots are a reality. Bare knuckles science neither solicits nor cultivates friendship," I said, testing my smile muscles.

"I'm less explosive than that. Just ask my uncle."

"Your uncle is a pawn. And now, it seems you and I have broken a few of the molds, so let's shatter a few more, shall we?"

Phillip looked at me like a boy who'd been given a banana split with sprinkles.

"You trust me that far?"

"Only between you and me and..." I pointed up, with my eyes riveted on Phillip's face, "this ceiling," I said. The gesture reminded me of Leonardo's painting of St. John with its unnerving eye contact. My fingernails turned white and I shivered. Someone must have walked over my grave, I thought. What a strange sensation. What a strange superstition.

I reached out to complete the touch Phillip had aborted and noticed he didn't flinch, and through his hand I sensed conflicted emotions, churning out of control.

"I see differently than most people," I said. "Some say further; I say deeper. I know when I'm being snowed and groomed, Phillip. I sense a person's general level of compassion."

"Yeah, so you said. Listen, I'm a nice guy."

Phillip checked my hair again and smiled. My nails informed me it was hot pink and I vamped them like a model. "But this, extrasensory gatekeeper," I waggled my fingers again, "your scientists forgot. And there is a *they*, Phillip. It's always been a 'they' vs me."

"You must be angry, your hair is sparking," he said.

I laced my fingers into a church without a steeple. "So I see." My nails flared from pink to red like ten candle flames.

Phillip pulled his head back a few inches to assess my hair. "Why are your nails and hair more... organic?"

"More alive, you mean?"

His body language shriveled into the shape of an 'I-don't-know.'

"I'm a throwback," I said. "I fell out of the sky one day. Do you know what happened when Delphi read a painting? Her scalp and fingers tingled, even when she approached a masterpiece. Whatever psychic power she had was neurological. It's still hotwired to me. My brain is healing itself. That much I *can* feel."

Phillip looked as if I'd grown another head, which I suppose I had. My brain was preserved intact so it made complete sense to me that psychic powers overruled science. Delphi had lived with them all her life. I could reason now, in a more abstract way, that everyone had been afraid of her.

She had been considered some sort of witch's changeling – a freak who could be dressed up as a princess and presented at court. She was swept under the carpet of profit and loss, but superstition dies hard. It was natural for a board of directors capable of separating business and pleasure to consider her pure asset. They were scared of her. It was the only explanation I could accept for her being distanced. She was a useful leper no-one wanted to hug, so she was caged and given an invisible bell. I could see Delphi clearly. If she'd had the presence of mind to say 'boo' a few times she could have been a formidable queen.

As a machine with a psychic signature I was more powerful. Logical enough to realize I needed to show restraint. Delphi was used to acting the village idiot – the walking brain-dead genius who made no waves. It suited her to be left alone. Now it suited me to wait in Hamm's face.

The duty that overruled feeling couldn't be called allegiance. It was more of a command performance. I opened my eyes when scenes of movie characters inflicting bodily harm, passed.

Phillip shrugged. His brain flapped like a fish dumped on dry land. I believe he would have consulted my profile notes if he'd had his ever-present clipboard.

"That's not my biggest problem," I said. "I intend to seek revenge, but how can I kill if I can't hate? What's the point of violence if I can't feel the thrill of killing Hamm?"

"You're joking, right?"

"It's difficult to not be cold-hearted after you've been cryogenically frozen. I feel nothing. I've forgotten nothing. Phillip, my *friend*, I'm a killing machine."

"You can freak people out though. That takes motivation."

"Apparently."

"Your team needs to be selected. I wouldn't freak *them* out if I were you."

"I can still freak out your uncle. Eventually my team will have the right to know my intentions. It's going to be a bumpy ride. We will assess them together. You handpick; I'll Cherry-pick."

"Hamm's been recruiting candidates for a while. My uncle's narrowed the shortlist to a dozen. A strange bunch that meets the boss's oddball requirements. Working here is not your average career move."

"I have my own list of requirements. I get final say."

"You are allowed three people."

"Let there be four. For some reason that number resonates."

A new thought occurred to me. "Who authenticated the paintings while I was gone?"

"We pretty much championed fakes," Phillip said.

"My dearest, Grail, that is my name for you, you are an absolute pelican."

He let out a long sigh as if he'd been holding his breath underwater and visibly relaxed his shoulders. "If you say so. Um... thanks?"

"What are you thinking? It's hard to tell," I lied. "Your hair doesn't misbehave."

Phillip tugged his earlobe and scratched the side of his nose. "I suppose I'm shocked to be recognized for the qualities my uncle deems academically inappropriate... but I'm guessing."

"Ask what you really want," I said.

Sphinx spluttered with emotion. *"And the student becomes the teacher,"* she said.

"I consider myself more highbred than hybrid. And here I am in an exclusive finishing school for artificial intelligence. What a joke."

"You're a snob," Phillip said. He grinned at me as if I were joking but his face froze mid-smile when he looked into my eyes. "In a good way," he added.

"BOO," I said with a straight face.

I waited a long beat before letting him go with a wink.

Phillip was a sweet pet – a dog without a home. He needed a mother. He was more of a slave than I was. It was well he had a sensitive core. At least someone was aligned to the subtleties that overlapped humanity and inhumanity. More importantly, I felt a quickening that led to the wondrous possibility of whose emotions might be fluttering *into* control, and I was pleased to discover I liked Phillip Moon. I liked him very much.

"What does patience have to do with anything?" I asked Sphinx. "I'm a machine."

"You'll know soon enough," she said. *"I'd enjoy the wait if I were you."*

"Enjoy?"

"Appreciate, then. The time may come when joy is an inconvenience."

The Crucible/chapter twenty-four

May 6, 2066

Easter had long since disappeared into May showers. I let my alleged anger drip down the windows of my newly-furbished apartment and wash out into the forests where my memories could startle the deer. I spent hours under skylight therapy, wishing my bed was piled high with mattresses like the 'princess and the pea' so I could touch the sky. I'd upgraded Phillip to a friend.

Rain evened the score for forest fires. It washed the flat ugly roofs of the 'lower institute' into glistening sheets of steel.

I umbrella'd my way to the stone horses, wearing rubber boots, splashing through puddles like a kid, and watched their basin fill with the yellow runoff from the scales of lime and lichens. I returned to my kitchen refreshed, and made tea for the ritual of it – the boiling and pouring, and the steam, and the buttered toast. I remembered how the first scalding sip of Earl Grey had to be drunk hot as lava to catch the fragrance of bergamot. I sniffed as close as I dared and detected a whiff of ozone. Nothing. My mouth failed to water over impending toast.

My ceiling's window was the taut skin of a drum. I listened to the rain beating from below like a carp underwater staring up at the sky through the ripples in a pond. As above, so below. Rain and ocean blurred wet-on-wet in a Turner watercolor. I remembered driving in the rain and the soothing rhythm of wiper blades on a two-second delay that made a continuous sweep to check the white-water rapids on the windscreen.

In the old days, I used to return to PIAT like a spawning salmon as if I had no choice but to head for something familiar even if it would contribute to the death of me, hydroplaning over the Malahat Highway in a gold Mustang towards Campbell River, past Ladysmith and the islands of Salt Spring and Ganges. Past Duncan, Nanaimo, and Courtenay.

Now, I'm imprisoned here in PIAT-ville, but bizarrely, I will be able to reach the baking sun of Tuscany in a technological heartbeat.

The month before, during the April Fools of all Easters, Phillip stood in the shadows observing his uncle lose his dignity to a pool of technicians, yet again. I accessed his thoughts. He had also been in the shadows behind the glass observation wall the day I screamed for my umbrella. He watched his colleagues silence me while they held a brief conference.

"It's an intellectual shell," Mason said. "It shouldn't possess the emotions for random emotional outbursts. We were careful to sever Delphi's emotional stem located in the frontal lobe."

The consensus was, I was an 'it.' Genderless for all intentions, having had Delphi's emotional anima removed from the quint-essential cerebral cortex that housed her psychic ability. I was an anomaly-anima of repressed impulses which, they said, would liter-ally fade in time after I'd been sent into the past a few times.

Hamm's eyes narrowed. "But how? This was not expected."

"My guess is Delphi was more robust than a normal person. She kept her emotions in check and as a result a great deal of elec-trical circuits retained the impulses of all that stored energy. She was headstrong in life. The roots of her hair and fingernails are the vestiges of an exceptionally hardy gene. We don't understand it yet."

"I don't pay you to guess," Hamm said."

Mason didn't miss a beat. "Psychic DNA is an unknown quan-tity. We did everything according to human neurology. It is my educated opinion that after a few molecular transitions, Cherry will settle into being empty and contrite... *and* psychic. Any rogue neurons will be eradicated like a weak strain of cancer."

"If it doesn't read paintings it's of no use to me," Hamm said.

Phillip opened his mouth to speak. "She..." he started to say but was silenced by his uncle's raised hand.

"There is no *she*. No *her*," Mason said. "Feminine qualities are lodged in the emotions. What we are seeing are random left-over thought-waves running their course."

Phillip spoke into his recorder the size of a ballpoint pen all during the two weeks of tests to confirm my miraculous kinetic abilities had survived between my brain and my fingers. No-one else could do what Delphi Sharpe had been able to do except me. As far as it was known, she/I had been the only ones – a split genome headed for a loftier destination than downtown earth. Had she been allowed to reproduce, who knew what strain of empathy might have worked its way to the surface. I fantasized we'd been the primeval comma where a hominid species branched into a more profound creation of multiple senses.

It was Phillip's job to document everything – the doctors being too 'hands on' for clipboards. They liked to shout things into my face for him to write down without turning to disrupt their tinkering and probing. Lucky for me, I couldn't smell the emotional foulness of their breath.

The task of recruiting my personal team of technicians naturally fell to Phillip. It was a sensitive vetting of a group of inno-cents. He handpicked my team per PIAT's instructions, tempered by my own. I insisted on final say until Hamm agreed. Phillip watched Hamm give way to most of my demands. He was proud of me, especially when I scanned the interviewees like baggage at an airport and assessed things he would never understand. I weighed their history and calculated their chutzpah; he sifted through sta-tistics. We were a perfect team – a left and right brain.

I asked for and received invasive résumés that only shortlisted desperate candidates would tolerate. Brain scans, fingerprints, blood tests, a sample of handwriting with their signature, a cur-rent library card with a printout of borrowed books over the last five years, a list of their favorite paintings, and at least four of their own poems.

The losers received substantial consolation prizes of cash for their inconvenience and silence. All had signed disclaimers in the manner of official top secret projects, but these pre-nups of flawless legalese were rendered in the damp foreshadowing of criminal justice where broken kneecaps and cement shoes lurked invisibly between the lines.

As a result, I had the perfect quartet. A foursome of promising eccentricities with instability as their collective defining characteristic. I asked that they be thrown together for a few days before we all met to formalize being a 'family.' Technically, they were four rival siblings plus Phillip, overruled by Hamm, a grand poobah overseer with major issues concerning women. I would play the stepmom with severe emotional problems. As well as monitoring me, my team would staff the old studio and run the photo lab. Joanna – chief cleaner and restorer of paintings, George and Lewis – all things camera related, and Bill – head of research and documentation. Phillip would report back to his uncle as my personal assistant.

Phillip's friendship touched a nerve containing what naturalists called 'wick,' or dormant life. Maybe my emotions were only in hibernation. According to Delphi, this meant I was a bear out of season. A 'wrong-time bear' known in folklore as the 'bearer' of a sacred message.

Later, Phillip told me he'd been moved by the humanity in my eyes and the compelling energy that stirred beneath them. He was a charmer and I had reconnected long enough to be the charm-ee.

I was given the unconventional documents I required.

PIAT wanted criminal record checks to *locate* criminals, not weed them out, so its domestic staff was comprised of ex-cons desperate for work under the radar of social acceptance. PIAT offered them bonuses for spying and generally keeping their ears to the underground. Selling art necessitated rubbing shoulders with serious crime lords who, twice-removed from the dirty work, were able to conduct themselves in more sophisticated behavior than a band of thugs.

PIAT's cook, cleaners, and delivery drivers were their own dysfunctional family, but all of them were wary of me. My privileges marked me as someone to reckon with. None of them liked to reckon much, other than counting money.

To them, I was a robot, a tad higher than the three monkeys who actually saw, heard, and spoke, evil. The only thing the staff *didn't* know was that time-travel lived under their roof. I was presented as an experimental device with a team of technical support. But then, ex-cons trusted no-one. One-by-one, after my team came on board, the scientists and staff disappeared like mist until Dr. Mason and the cook were the sole survivors and PIAT relied on a maintenance cleaning service.

Mrs. Cook: waitress, dishwasher, and interestingly, the *actual* cook, was especially unimpressed. I thought we had something in common with our names and jobs being related, but she said my last name wasn't Picker, made a harrumph sound in the back of her throat, and went back to her vile slops that I was fortunate I couldn't eat.

MAY 7th

Dr. Mason and Phillip escorted me from my quarters with their own black umbrellas crowding my Van Gogh sunflower, and we made the damp trek in a cluster of three 'silk hats' to the double-trailer across the square from the main house – a hastily renovated extension that reminded me of the interior version of an anchoress's cell attached to a church like a barnacle.

I made them detour around the fountain four times and threw a coin into its gathering pool. It was a bit of concocted drama that set the doctor guessing, which was my intention. Phillip knew in advance and sent me a wink of amused complicity. It was as much of a thumbs-up as he could manage under the circumstances.

The old lecture hall portable had been transformed from a boardroom displaying a bank of impressive technology to a private movie theatre where a director might view a day's work with a projector whirring behind his head.

The podium took the place of the screen, now lifted into a recess of the ceiling. The dais looked like a set for a talk show, an intimate space, calculated for informal conversation under glass. A low coffee table with a rose bowl of white tulips and three comfy armchairs were placed on an expensive Turkish carpet. Behind it was a portable electric fireplace flickering with fake fire. All it lacked was a silver tea service and a sleeping dog.

The audience's seats were reclining chairs connected to each other by small tables. After the grey weather outside it was as cozy as a library carrel. Dark and warm as a womb.

The team had already arrived from their own portables, larger by far than the traditional onsite trailers for movie stars. Their raincoats dripped from hooks by the door next to muddy shoes.

"Not an umbrella in sight," Sphinx noted. Her sigh came out as the word, *"Neanderthals."*

Dr. Mason carried himself with as much grandeur as his pudgy five-foot-three frame could muster, nodding and mumbling to the notes he held in his hand, his reading glasses gravitating to the end of his nose like pince-nez. Phillip lagged behind as if he could entirely separate himself from his loathsome kin in the space of a few feet. The three of us resembled a ragtag bridal party.

I shook the water from my umbrella and carried it ahead of me like a bouquet. The homey set seemed more like an altar of sacrifice as I approached it.

I headed down the aisle, a mail order bride towards her new life, and took my place in the central chair, sitting contrite as a prisoner awaiting sentence. Mary Poppins with an umbrella at her side for a weapon. But when I scrutinized the faces scrutinizing me, each of them looked away first.

In contrast to the bright lights of the examination rooms, the lighting, now dimmed to the ambiance of a living room, was set low for watching TV. It was still possible to discern the outlines of the front row audience of four, and a single bottle of Perrier water that glowed florescent green on the podium to my right, illuminated by the light from its gooseneck lamp.

Hamm made a token appearance like the pope, waved his hand over the proceedings and left the building to a smattering of lukewarm applause. I projected a movie scene over the door that closed after him. It showed a scaffold in a red spotlight, and a masked executioner's strike. Hamm's head rolled from the block in slow motion. Its crown of writhing serpents let go of each other's tails and hissed away. The executioner's fingernails dripped with blood to match my red fingernails. I folded my hands primly in my lap. I assumed my hair had beaconed like a flash fire. Good.

Professor Mason rose from his chair, walked to the podium and tapped on the desk for quiet in an already silent room. His gaze fixated on a distant horizon above his audience's heads. He gave a wide sugary smile and scratched his chin. "Welcome." He turned and attempted to dignify me with a theatrical grimace and swept his arm over the group. He made a ridiculous bow. "Madam Chérie," he said, deferring to me, "may I present your chosen ones."

I had the sudden image of myself rushing the pulpit and bludgeoning Mason with the Perrier bottle, but I was side-swiped by a mental picture of Brillo with wings, frolicking for angel mice in some feline heaven. "Not now, Delphi," I said under my breath.

Unfortunately, it caused a surge in my insides. There were no happy-hunting-grounds, and as androids are not programmed to fidget, I studied the pattern of the carpet and counted the number of phoenix embroidered into its border. Sixteen to a side.

I concluded that frolicking was a pointless occupation for humans after death.

The sensation of a furious ball of St. Elmo's fire continued to rage in my solar plexus. A pink pulse rippled imperceptibly under my skin, enough to reassure myself I had organic origins. Amazingly, my fingernails were now the calm colors of a regular French manicure. My need to retaliate with violence was subverted into a program of indifference which better served my purpose. I squinted at Dr. Mason – a photographer lining up a shot in the viewfinder of a telescopic lens as if it were a rifle, and followed him as he paced the stage.

In order to refocus I stared at Phillip's recorder pen looming from his shirt pocket. He was vulnerable. We all were. We may as well be sacrificed and thrown to a volcano god, an image

I'd seen often during my first 'Cherry' weeks. It represented me, benign and bubbling under the surface that could erupt any moment or years in the future. One thing was clear, there was more than myself at stake. I had essentially become the mother of five martyrs.

After some stumbling over his notes, Dr. Mason raised the house lights and attempted to deliver a compliment, referring to me as his 'Mozart' in a vague attempt at humor. "Cherry is my prodigy," he said, fooling no-one.

There I was, the culmination of a hundred years of digital engineers, quantum masterminds, and astrophysicists, now claimed by a buffoon who treated me like a smart phone.

The assemblage radiated tension even though a few appeared laid-back. The lean male, I knew as Lewis, lounged in his seat, spreading his long jeans across the spaces of two chairs in order to nudge, George, with his foot every few minutes, his partner in love and computer programming. William, a cherubic fellow in a bowtie had his eyes closed, I assumed for greater concentration. The nervous one of the group was Joanna. She had drawn her legs into a hug and sat smiling, rocking slightly in her chair.

All four of them were in their late-twenties. Their eyes swept my body from my ditzy hair to the floor. If I'd chosen well, they thought of me as the *woman* they would work with... and obey.

No-one owned me, Hamm had said, but it was clear he believed I *owed* his 'family' for the perfect 'life,' studying the art I once loved passionately in ways historians could only dream about. My whole former existence intruded like a delayed nightmare. The storm, the lightning, and the bright room where I'd woken up chilled to the bone, unable to tell anyone I needed a blanket.

"Lose it," Sphinx said. *"Opportunities only grovel once."*

Mason tapped his microphone and cleared his throat. His arms waved downward as if to settle an imagined applause to subside. His fists opened and closed at his side like the mouth of a landed trout. He was a competent biochemist but basically a lab technician reduced to a yes man after the hard work was done.

His appearance as Santa Claus in a lab coat made him adorable until he opened his mouth.

He took a Shakespearian pause, Hamlet in a drab costume, and cleared his throat again. "You are Cherry's family," Mason began. "She is your priority – a creature of immense abilities." He gestured flamboyantly to me as if I were the prize refrigerator in a game show. By fluke or design he'd managed to strike a sweet note regarding the woman and three men who were my team. He'd called them my *family*.

An image of bugs crawling over my sleeping body flashed momentarily. The word creature was a low blow. Five blank responses echoed my opinion. I cringed more abstract hatred towards the Neanderthal elf, and ran a movie scene of a ceiling lamp crushing him into history.

For once I welcomed Delphi's automatic home movies. I liked the random appearances of her old emotions having a last word when it was aimed at someone else.

"The four of you," Mason emphasized in a pointing gesture reminiscent of an army recruiting poster, "are her subordinates."

The audience absorbed the train wreck onstage with smiles of horror mixed with pure Schadenfreude, the warm stirrings of cruel pleasure. I could almost feel it.

I'd been diligent in extracting their negative opinions of management in general. Mason provided his own responding chuckle and gripped the podium with white-knuckled-fear. His life raft.

I crossed my arms to contain an unreasonable urge to slap him. My hair must be doing back flips, but no, my parallel nails were nude pink. I tilted my head and whatever color my hair decided to be, to one side, playing into the moment. No computer worth its circuits would do something that coy but I was going for 'I may be an android but I'm not an idiot' strategy.

People as ornery as the ones who'd made it to the front row, may be computer geeks and dropouts but they still recognized the hierarchy of who ran the show, and that it was Mr. Moneybags Burgher. By the end of the session I wanted them to know it would be *me*.

Their lives reeked of service industries on minimum wage. They wanted regular paychecks doing joy-work, ideally, sweet gigs on the cutting edge of computer science with free room and board while they played on computers they could never hope to own in the real world. PIAT laid dream jobs with expense accounts at their feet.

Short-sighted boys with an intense desire for unrestricted technology were the perfect combination for staffing a project overflowing with cyber prestige.

Hamm ordered me a token *sister*, so I accepted one who danced with depression. She was a better faker than me, pure sunshine laced with insecurity, anxiety attacks, and crippling debts. Joanna Harry had no idea how much I valued her personal experience.

Neediness required companionship and fear ruled the greatest hunger for security. She was perfect – a bipolar sweetheart maintaining a sunny exterior to stay calm but tamed with valium's latest cousin. I read undiluted inspiration within her – a noble fighter cowered underneath her defeats. She was a good choice. She'd been an abused child. Her resume read Fine Arts Degree with distinction. She had worked in an art gallery, but PIAT found her in a therapy clinic recovering from a nervous breakdown.

Joanna's longhand e's were looped as high as her l's, so I knew she was excitable as well as depressed. Her un-dotted i's belied her 'blue-sky-face.' Her smiles were bursts of optimism that she saved for the public.

She slapped on a Band-Aid smile before opening her front door. These were adequate for passing through a metal detector at an airport but not to fool a double-savant like me, trained to seek cracks in body language.

Joanna had incredible staying power to maintain a mask of well-being but her metabolism was wearing her out. I decided when we first met that we needed each other because nothing inspired loyalty more than a woman desperate to be accepted for her faults.

PIAT could only possess minds that ran on high-octane addiction. Interviews had been conducted in a five-star hotel's executive suite that reeked of Mt. Olympus.

George Savage and Lewis Dobbs were testers of software for the gaming industry – a gay couple who showed up together as a romantic team after being fired together, caught in flagrante by the homophobe who recruited them.

William Katz, was an archivist librarian with a degree in snobbery only a Shakespearian scholar could project with warmth. He had a heart of gold but it was buried under research of formidable academic heft. Joanna was my secret twin. Phillip was my grail king. My new family.

I may be reprogrammed, but I was well-rehearsed. I could read the inelegance of PIAT's mandate. I could interpret the brilliance of a Leonardo, so a few trained lab rats were child's play. I fielded the cheap compliment and reacted like any savvy woman put on the spot. I turned it back on the giver like a slap in the face. I'd never been that tough in my former life but I had learned how to fake humility the hard way. One has to be extra smart to play stupid.

"Keep the situation unstable. Play them," Sphinx said. *"Fill the cheap seats."*

I called upon the muscle-memory of Delphi's hatred to serve me. Anything. Send me an image I can relate to I begged her, but she was silent.

"AWOL," Sphinx said. *"Gone with the wind."*

I sent my reply to Sphinx. "This is for her as much as me. She should be here for this."

"Kid gloves," Sphinx hollered. *"Elephant in the room. She was here. She left. Go figure."*

The four people looking up from their seats were mine, not the professor's. It was a given they'd already been deceived.

The puny sorcerer continued his deplorable presentation. Even his benign words sounded like reprimands. "We are honored to be working on the forefront of a new era. *Blah blah blah...* the privileged few who will get to know Cherry, personally... *blah blah...* You will be a family where you will eat, sleep, and get to know one another."

He paused to glance at me. "Although Cherry neither eats nor sleeps. PIAT's family business is alchemy." At this he made a grunting sound to himself, pleased with his inside joke.

"Voodoo," Sphinx said. *"Purple-eyed doltish voodoo."*

A look of disgust rippled over the front row like the 'wave' in a sports crowd.

"My point is this," Mason said. "There is a chain of command at PIAT, as with any patriarchal institution. Power-tripping will not be tolerated and sibling rivalry between you must be worked out. You have one month. There will be no contact with the outside world while this probation period is in effect. You have sealed this with your signatures."

Phillip gave off vibes of anxiety. He knew something.

Lewis of the long jeans stifled a laugh.

"Is Cherry going to be our Mom?" the cherubic bowtie piped up. The levity of his question belied the intense look of disdain on his face. I was pleased. William Katz displayed the gumption I'd chosen him for.

His remark gave me the entry I needed. I shook my head at him and called out from my chair. "Bill, if I *were* your mother I would never let you wear a tie like that," I said, and it got a laugh.

Bill and I were the only ones who didn't smile. I appreciated that, too. Body language flowed between us. He was tip-top.

"Very nicely done," Sphinx commented.

Phillip surprised me by sprinting to Mason's side to release his uncle's hold on the podium, short of bodily carrying him off. I wasn't sure if he was defending me or had a sudden inspiration to take over the world.

The professor looked disoriented but relieved to step down. His parting words faltered. "We intend this project to run like clockwork," he said over his shoulder. *"sic transit gloria mundi."* Stupidly, he saluted and returned to his armchair, assuming the seated position of a beaming storyteller to a group of petulant children.

Mason thought of me in rancid terms. Part cuckoo clock, part time-machine, and all I could think was how much he didn't know about me and could never know, or how much his filthy experiments invoked a misty hatred, filed deep inside me that I wasn't supposed to be able to harbour, but that someday I would.

Delphi's bitterness fed my plan in a steady drip. Scientists, by their own calculations, had opted to preserve her brain entire, and where else would Delphi have stored a lifetime of resentment and choking humiliation? It was all there waiting for me like a ticking bomb, experiences on the page waiting for animation, and I intended to use it when Delphi stayed for more than a brief, timid hello.

Dr. Mason swooped in on four puzzled faces. "Oh, by the way," he called out over his restless leg syndrome. "It means, worldly things are fleeting," he said smugly.

Phillip spoke with his mouth too near the mike and caused a whistle of feedback. "Let's take a break for refreshments," he said, giving a sheepish grin. He looked about twelve-years-old. His gaze locked on mine for support and I smiled. He was visibly relieved as he strode over to me, shaking his head. "Is it over yet?" he whispered in my ear.

Professor Mason had neither come off as the ogre he'd wanted to be nor the comedian necessary to hold a twitchy crowd. This podium-duty thing was his cup of hemlock. I knew from Phillip his uncle had no choice. At this level, no-one did.

Mason had struggled to regain his role of mild-mannered dictator but delivered his remarks in the crude language of a cold sales pitch. His intention was to solidify the persona of the hardened academic he desired his subordinates to fear. It was no surprise he'd presented as the despotic little creep I'd predicted.

I thought of my rooms and willed I would soon be there, under my skylight where the only science that mattered was astronomy.

Birds underwater, fish in the sky. I was the crazy woman who ate a fly and a spider and a bird and all the successive remedies to save herself – a baby huddled inside the core of a nesting doll. A brain fuming inside a machine. No-one knew why I ate the fly and guessed I'd die, but I wasn't about to guzzle PIAT's cool-aid.

But from my first day, they had taught me to drink from an empty cup like an actor.

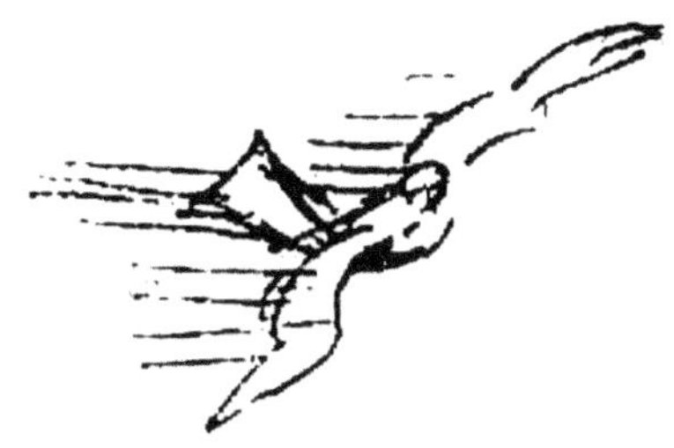

The Break/chapter twenty-five

George moved up a row to join Lewis. I read him correctly. He anticipated his partner's temper. The moment came after Dr. Mason referred to my team as geeks. Lewis said "Hey!" in a loud voice and uncrossed his legs ready to stand. He leaned forward but George stayed his arm.

The doctor loosened his tie. "I hasten to add," he said, "this is an attribute of high praise, *not* a criticism. You have been scrupulously vetted and PIAT feels you are the select of your, I want to say *species*, but you know what I mean. You have a unique rapport with Cherry and a love-affair with art and computers." He meant *art*ifice and *art*ificial intelligence.

Lewis relaxed and George released his arm, continuing to stroke it.

I sat like a plastic prisoner before a parole board. Editing my words for when it was my turn to speak. For all intents and purposes it was now second nature to speak in first person Delphi. I never noticed the transition. It was like wearing her shoes, but now we were a matching pair, just different sizes.

My captivity had always been criminal. I'd been treated like a peasant before a kangaroo court my entire life. Henry VIII had been more compassionate with Anne Boleyn. My attention swam in and out over the horizon of empty chairs behind my *team of steel*. They were a solid bunch. I had chosen wisely.

Dr. Mason smiled and rubbed his hands together vigorously after bringing them together in a soft clap. "Cherry White is 'state of the art' in every conceivable way. How's that for irony?" He looked as if he expected raucous laughter to follow. It was the big joke of his speech; he had rehearsed it in my presence, as usual treating me like a piece of furniture. He'd even made a red exclamation point in the margin to remind him where to deliver it with gusto.

My team chose silence after glancing at me for a sign. I was intently studying the center of the carpet – a phoenix blazing its fiery trail of cherry-red feathers against a turquoise sky.

I counted to four and sent the professor a look of unmistakable contempt, dismissing him as a churl. He missed it rifling through his notes, no doubt searching for a better joke. But that one gesture changed the stakes.

Those in the hot seats knew they were lucky to even be in the room. Life outside PIAT was already a distant memory of hand-to-mouth survival.

The doctor continued, unfazed, and I watched the zzzzz's play above my team's heads. *Blah blah blah...* "It may not be as romantic as a fifteenth-century masterpiece," Mason continued after a few ums and ers, "but nevertheless, it is, by its very nature, the missing links we men of science crave most for genetic research. We are fortunate, *chuckle chuckle,* to have an android 'that' can play with fire."

"WHO! Who can play with fire," Sphinx corrected. *"He's going down in flames."*

Delphi showed up. "I've been here, listening," she said. "What an idiot."

The poignant scene of the cowering Elephant Man facing his tormentors played in my mind, with Mason cast in the leading role. I almost laughed at his line, 'I'm not a scientist; I'm a human being!' I stared at the far wall like a tin soldier. The room had evaporated into a littered battlefield droning with flies.

"Eight against one," Sphinx said, *"including Delphi."*

I felt mechanically invigorated from pale emotions signaling with dash of vigor. Technical contempt stood in nicely for loathing. My nails were striping, pink as candy canes – a knee-jerk reaction of humiliation manifesting as a cybernetic blush.

Joanna shifted uneasily in her chair and stared at my hair. I visualized a tear escaping from my eye and running down my artificial skin like a line drawn with an icicle.

"I didn't send that," Delphi said.

The words artificial intelligence were fingernails on a blackboard. Especially ones like mine that dared to scream back in clashing colors.

I almost dozed off. A nice human reaction.

Delphi was incensed. She spoke to me, hoping I would project her comments, but I only listened to her venting from within a daydream. "What exactly do you people think happened when I read a painting?" she said. "Did you think it was a printout? Some tickertape data from my brain that spewed from my mouth?"

Sphinx rallied me with a loud, *"Lambkin!"*

I was relieved I'd never found an off-switch to still Sphinx's relentless tinnitus of riddles at all hours.

Mason's voice invaded my unstable landscape.

Phillip nudged my arm. It was earthquake time. "You're up," he said.

I was ready to interface. An alien with a mission.

I leapt to the podium, nudging Mason's shoulder, and bent to the height of his microphone. "The professor mentioned I needed friends. The reason you're here is that I've sensed a natural rapport in each of you. Please don't ask what. It's one of those savant things. We can talk later."

Mason reshuffled his papers as if he might find something he'd forgotten and could reclaim the floor.

"I will take questions," I said.

"Can you have sex?" a male voice blurted. It was Lewis.

A ripple of disapproval drowned him in a collective groan. Phillip half-raised himself from his chair like the opposition in the house of parliament prepared to rebuff.

I was getting used to smiling. "You mustn't feel shy Mr. Dobbs."

"No offense intended," Lewis added. "You told us to be blunt."

"Well, Lewis, my mind is fully cognisant. My body *used* to be human. I remain anatomically correct, but I can't fall in love. Does that cover your question?"

Sphinx chuckled.

"Almost. Yes, ma'am. Sorry, ma'am." He smiled cheekily.

I blanched at his military staccato. I felt sorry for him. The poor guy had been roped into this so called miraculous *event*, but there was no turning back for any of them, and this was the time to project a version of my own authority. Only a wimp would have deflected that question.

"From now on please call me Cherry," I said. "There's no need to build any new walls. We have management for that." I paused a cybernetic beat in homage to a wink, and looked over at Mason, still hovering a foot away. His forced smile reminded me that sarcasm was an exact science.

Bill's hand reached high for an eager question which began without formal permission.

"Do you have a remote control? A device of some kind that..."

Sphinx chuckled again. *"I like that boy."*

"Let me stop you right there," Phillip interrupted, his index finger raised in protest.

I startled myself by laughing out loud which upset Mason and amped the tension. I noted Phillip's gallantry as a gesture filed as 'sweet' – a champion protecting his king's lady. The real miracle was that I had laughed spontaneously.

I shook my head at Phillip and directed my answer towards Bill. "That's okay, Bill. If I stare inwardly for more than a few minutes I don't see flying toasters if that's what you mean."

George hooted with applause and whistled through his teeth. Mason paled.

"Yes ma'am," Sphinx said, enjoying herself. *"Good game."*

Bill nodded, well satisfied. I'd answered the question he'd really wanted to ask. Sphinx concurred. *"You're on fire,"* she said, over my shoulder.

Bill sat down, and I addressed them en masse. "The term star shadow was bandied about at your interviews," I said. "PIAT considers paintings as celebrities. If I'm unable to harvest a painting

I can still 'interview' the artist by shadowing his movements for a while."

"Yeah, that star thing bothered me. Who thought that up?" George asked.

"Thank you George. You can blame me. It's a word that materialized from my data banks because I'm programmed to anagram and cross-reference. The word star is arts backwards, and our mission is to shadow paintings as if they were movie stars. And on a more personal note, it's an anagram that sprang from an old fixation of mine. Dr. Who's Tardis, is relevant. It's a time machine. I anagrammed Tardis to 'star id.' I.D. is slang for identification, but more appropriately, the Id in psychoanalysis is the human's unconscious impulse to seek comfort with the pleasure principle... plus the word lame is there hiding inside the word blame. Does that satisfy your question?"

George raised his brows. His voice was almost inaudible. "Oh."

"And rats," Bill called out. "Arts forms the word rats."

"Yes sir, that boy's a keeper," Sphinx said.

"Thank you Mr. Katz," Mason said, plainly in a huff.

I wanted to feel ugly-monster anger and physical hatred but all that happened was a snapping sensation in my throat.

I heard an old echo of Sphinx. *"Rats eyes shine in the dark,"* she'd said once, long ago.

I peered down at Bill. He'd removed his bowtie and loosened his collar.

"Rats have been used for scientific experiments for years, so, they're also an appropriate metaphor for our role as testers of a new technology. Good call, Bill."

I flashed Bill a smile of thanks, thinking how all of us were rats in a trap. He was warming to me.

Joanna, who had been perched like a pixie on a toadstool fluttered to her feet, a diminutive Tinkerbell in a business suit. "I apologise for my question in advance. Do you resent being... *converted* into a computer?"

"No need to apologise, Joanna. Humans adapt. I'm sure everyone's questions will be even more personal than that after today, although after Lewis's."

This got a laugh. Lewis beamed from his chair as Joanna tousled his hair. They were already friends.

"Tough questions are necessary," I said. "I can't be embarrassed or shocked. I'm not a computer despite thinking like one but I was dismissed as a walking computer all my life – a person isolated from society. I didn't fit in. Time-travel and immortality are a double gift of a surreal afterlife. Although, immortality is a stretch. I'm not infallible to destruction."

My fingernails looked normal. I could pass any lie detector on the planet.

"Are there downsides?" Joanna asked.

"I miss tea and my sense of smell is dodgy. I expect all of you would miss the delights of smelling flowers. I used to love flowers. And perfume. I loved the scent of perfume."

"Will that sense return?"

I checked out Mason, ears perked to details I wasn't about to share. "Remember, I died as all life-forms will, and like any machine, I can malfunction, be dismantled, consumed by real fire or blown to pieces. Olfactory senses contain our strongest memories. They're simply the last to fade."

Sphinx coughed. *"Careful temptress. You're too near the fire."*

Joanna sat down, nodding. "Thank you, Cherry. I hoped you would say that."

Professor Mason was determined to have the last word and squeezed in front of me. "You can meet tomorrow, bright and early."

"Two out of three," Lewis mumbled.

"Goodnight Mommy," Bill called out, staring directly into my eyes from twenty feet away.

Delphi gasped inwardly.

I stared back an equally telling reply. "Goodnight sweet pea."

The First Supper/chapter twenty-six

I grabbed the wilting tulips with their heads bowed in shame, descended the platform, and approached Phillip who was giving Lewis a lecture on etiquette.

I waited, until he was finished before approaching. "Glad that's over," I said. "I look forward to working with them without a net." The fingernail of my right index finger flashed robin's egg blue. It reminded me of Cecco's eyes.

"You mean without my uncle."

"We survived the crucible."

"My uncle likes to breathe fire."

"So *that's* what he was doing," Bill said.

Mason had quickly evaporated into the rain without a goodbye. The group stood, milling together, and I learned they had dubbed him, 'Jarr,' partly from his jarring inability to register warmth, but also in reference to a Mason Jar. Hamm, it would seem, they'd already tagged as a dangerous boar as well as a pig-headed bore. I had found my compatible species. I was a mother hen proud of her chicks.

George glanced nervously from Mason's retreating form, to Phillip.

"It's okay," Phillip said. "I'm his nephew not the president of his fan club."

"But you're a member," George said.

Phillip peeled off his lab coat and threw it over a chair. "You'd think," he said.

Lewis offered me his handshake. "I don't always think before I speak," he said. "Join us in the cafeteria? For a..." He looked uncomfortable, "bite. We're having a late breakfast."

"Thank you, I will. Lewis, it's okay. It's all good," I said. "Watching you eat will be fine, and we can work on that editing thing. It's safe to say it would be advantageous in a project like this one."

I singled out Joanna, the petite blonde who strived to be a bluebird of happiness. She smiled as if she carried a wonderful secret. "Joanna, may I speak with you a minute? In private."

Joanna smiled wider than usual. "Sure, of course, Cherry."

My name issued from her mouth as a word that barely defined a piece of fruit. It lacked the spirit of a name. I noticed a book peeping from her open purse.

"Hot book," said Sphinx. *"Cool enough to handle. Borrow the truth whenever you can."*

I clasped Joanna's hand. "I need you most of all."

She stood for the longest time gazing at my fingers as my nails turned into the clear polish of a French manicure. I had never seen my nails so lovely. She turned my hand over and peered closely at my palm without a word. Her face registered confusion. "I'm searching for your lifeline," she said, rubbing my skin as if to give my future a better chance.

"Well, what's the damage?"

"There are too many to count. Your skin is like the intersecting railway tracks in a station yard. But see these parallel lines, how they converge, here with a stranger. I've never seen this." Her nose was so close I thought she was going to kiss it better.

For the next hour I was privy to the outrages of food psychology. Table manners defined each family member as I listened to the music of their cutlery and glass. I gained new insight in the choreography of dining. I was Mother Pavlov watching over her brood, teaching them Table Manners 101. Mostly, I was a human satellite dish tilting slightly to hear for telltale signs of the weakest link.

It became obvious the overextended Mrs. Cook had a soft spot for Bill. The rest of us were scum on the dishes she had to wash.

Watching my team eat had been reduced to an exercise of calculation, the ballet of loading the maximum of calories on one spoon, tipping it just so and pulling a hot morsel from a fork without grating their teeth against the metal tines.

George squeaked his knife as if trying to cut through the plate. Lewis stole what he wanted from George's plate, shovelling food like a backhoe. They were the 'odd couple' of lovebirds.

Joanna ate like a bluebird. She was a precise chewer of insanely small morsels of food as well as information. A fragile eater who wiped her mouth with a serviette after each careful swallow. She smiled across the table to see who was watching her before returning to her food. Gluten-free thoughts.

Bill talked with his fork suspended in the air, using it to punctuate his sentences. I watched as he created a more pleasing still-life arrangement with his fruit salad. He was the one most like me. The 'me' I sometimes thought of as a woman I once knew, waving goodbye from a speeding car.

Phillip was with us in body only and made shapes from his food pushing items to the edge of his plate as if lining up ammunition for a food fight.

An innocent meal turned into the alchemy of dinner.

I clinked a spoon against an empty glass for attention. "I have a small confession. A quirk I guess. I'm letting you in on a secret that doesn't leave this room. Besides hearing paintings, I have a second psychic perk – a voice in my head. A minx who whispers information. It's female. Anyway, I hear her, so sometimes when I look as if I'm listening to outer space, I'm probably listening to inner space."

"We all do that," George said.

I shrugged. "Maybe so but mine has a name. She's a muse named Sphinx. Sometimes it's like having an annoying insect buzzing in my ear but she's the dearest companion. When she's in bee mode she knows where to find the best pollen. But she speaks in cryptic code."

Sphinx poked me in the ribs with a riddle. *Joanna carries a key. Divided signals require double the concentration. Conquer the wars of art... twice. "I spy something beginning with anger."*

"Knows what?" Lewis said.

"Spying on oneself is a victimless crime," Sphinx said.

"Usually something I need to revisit," I said. "Right now she's a busy bee I wish would buzz away."

"The past arrives tomorrow," Sphinx said. *"Diving too deep is a waste of time for shallow secrets. It's time to glide little duck. Follow the sun. It's woolgathering time."*

Bill and Joanna stood apart from the others, too far away to normally eavesdrop.

"I spy a painting," Sphinx said.

She was right. I visualized them captured in a painting and I was a visitor to their gallery. I held my hands towards them as if warming myself on a fire. Their words were clear and hot.

"I was afraid this job was going to be clinical," Joanna said. "Cherry's manicure fooled me. She's groomed to perfection like a doll, but she has emotional dirt under those fingernails."

"It's genius dirt," Bill said, "the profound dirt of survival. She's survived something you and I know nothing about. But the thing that shook me was her eyes. The woman has 'Mona Lisa' eyes."

I was equally shaken from being called a woman. The knowledge I was friendless and that I had a lifeline affected Joanna the most. My French manicure had fooled them, but I was unable to disguise a longing behind my manner and the emotional history under my nails. Genius dirt, Bill had called it. I called it childhood.

My dear Sphinx was coy. *"Glide close to shore,"* she said. *"Lily pads all in a row."*

*"Once organic, twice removed
Birds of a feather.
Interaction void
Electrons dissipate, harmless ashes."*
CHERRY WHITE

Time-Travel 101/chapter twenty-seven

MAY 19, 2066

Phillip brought me a white cockatoo that he presented from behind his back like a bouquet.

"This is the nearest thing to a cat that's sanctioned," he said. "I didn't see you as a goldfish person. Sorry, I couldn't find a big enough cage. I've ordered one. She's the same age as you but she says less, so that's something."

The bouquet ruffled its white feathers. I was enchanted.

"No-one knows what her name is," Phillip said. "Her owner died and she was rescued from an empty apartment, traumatized."

"Sounds like we're twins separated at birth," I said. "We're family. Hello Florence."

She squawked and her crest reached towards me like fingers. She liked her name.

"Just like your hair," Phillip said. "Mood feathers."

"She's wonderful, Phillip. Thank you." I stroked the bird's breast. *"Mi casa su casa* – my cage is your cage."

Phillip gave my white-on-white room a scan. "She matches your décor, as well."

"We're a couple of displaced birds," I said. "I love her."

I hesitated, correcting myself. "I am registering *affection* for her. This is big."

"You're welcome," Phillip said. "And I... never mind."

I registered the signs of human infatuation, his nervous mouth and rapid breathing, and a breathless pink quality, eager with anticipation. Like most people, Phillip's eyes revealed secrets. And a memory turned over in its sleep. The beginnings of seeing another as an ideal, where eyes track the beloved the way a sunflower follows the sun, when I could feel my eyes reaching, touching without hands and feeling more than hands could feel – one of the ironies between emotional and physical love, when one closes their eyes to see more.

Phillip approached in my peripheral vision as I sat in my garden sanctuary, surrounded by foliage and pompoms of color, scrunched into one side of the wicker loveseat. I typed in the shade of a new peacock umbrella, my eyes glued to a laptop. "I don't mean to spy," he said, "but every time I see you, you're typing."

"*Mmmn hmmn*. My memoirs."

"Be careful. Words leave footprints."

I lifted the ivory elephant pendant around my neck and zipped it back and forth over the length of its gold chain. "It ends up in here, 007. A lovely necklace which..." I tapped it using my finger like a magic wand and pulled it apart to reveal the interior of a computer memory-stick. I faked surprise with an inward gasp. "Well, whaddaya know, it's a device. Technology's really getting creative days. I had Joanna order it for me." I tapped it again and closed it. "Elephants never forget."

I've chosen to circumvent the fragility of a paper journal for the security of a memory-stick because a time capsule the size of a locket is easier to hide. I can wear it without guile. That alone, is heartening. It reassures me that my naturally covert instincts are well-founded.

I write to justify the past and maintain a grip on the present. It's like hanging from a cliff by one finger.

Hamm refers to me as the new-improved woman but I'm unfinished. Delphi is with me in spirit but against me in principle. Sphinx is with me in principle but against me in spirit. Delphi archives the emotions I lack but I'm the keeper of the logic she chose to ignore. The bizarre mathematical logistics of a second life make my head spin. I'm abuzz with theoretical emotions and intellectual hatred. I am abstract to a fault.

"Do you have a pseudonym?" Phillip asked.

"I should. Cherry is an upbeat name that evokes an image of cheer and juicy promise."

"What's your overall 'take' on the human senses? I mean of course, the ones you covet."

"Sphinx would say there was a magic letter involved in that question."

"I don't understand."

"Change, anagram, add, or delete a letter to find the truth of an innocent question. Add an 'r' to 'covet' and it becomes 'covert.' Do you need to rephrase your question?"

Phillip shook his head and smiled. "That Sphinx of yours is wicked smart."

"I see myself as a flighty character in my own biography," I said. "From Delphi's birth to her death."

"Ah, the ultimate ghostwriter."

I swung the memory-stick like a cat in the cradle. "Chapters in a wallpaper life."

"Is that the title?"

"It's what is. Delphi is only the first half of the alphabet. God knows what 'Z' will look like."

"You're just a big bouquet of optimism."

I sniffed the length of my arm, eyes closed as if in bliss. "Artificial roses. Mmmmn. Plastic."

I extended my arm for Phillip to sample. "I can smell it from here thanks. Smells a lot like sarcasm. Well done. That's progress isn't it?"

"I don't expect raging rivers of emotion," I said. "I don't expect to be dragged under rip tides of love and hate. Trickles are more honest. A warm vein in a cold torrent. No bursting dams or boiling lava. Small is good. Small is big enough for now."

"Can I read it? Am I in it?"

"That would spoil the end."

"Well, whatever happens it won't be a string of z's."

"Someone once taught Delphi about string theory. The metaphor, that is. She had a lucid dream about it once. Sphinx called it a prophecy."

"What do *you* dream about?"

"I don't. I'm the city that never sleeps; the commercial ice cream that never melts. Awake, I smell nothing except the trail of greed and the half-smells of life. But that's the middle chapters. Sphinx says I'm an open book with blank pages. She told me, warned me I think, that the fulcrum of history teeters on the point of a knife blade."

"That makes a better story. I can't wait to see how it turns out."

A robin fluttered clumsily and splash-landed in the birdbath. We watched it for a moment, grateful for the distraction. "He's got his own chapter," I said, nodding to the robin. "He's in it first to last. I believe that to be a prophecy too."

We were getting morbid. All the speculation of a tragic ending drained the sunshine from the garden. "On the plus side," I said. "I'm about to visit Leonardo da Vinci inside a living diorama of a virtual reality museum."

"Lucky duck. Florence, Leonardo style. I'd be over the moon."

"You ARE a moon."

"A full moon or a half-moon?"

"A paper moon, like in the song."

He sang his reply. "And it wouldn't be make-believe if *you* believed in *me*."

I will leave armed with the beginnings of affection but no other means to register the awe and anticipation that anyone in their *right mind* would feel, anticipating such an event. I will 'drop down' from my century to Leonardo's, after an extreme joyride without the joy. I can't begin to express the bizarre contradiction of dispassionate passion.

I should be angry. What will happen when I'm face-to-face with an artist Delphi worshipped? A fan meeting their movie star hero in an elevator without the headiness or rapid heartbeat of a crystalized peak moment? Will I feel some electronic equivalent of tongue tied? Will I simply function on flatline? The *idea* of Leonardo permeates my agenda. How lame is that. I'm hoping Leonardo will generate enough electricity to zap me with renaissance volts. Fry me to the moon, I say. This reference made Sphinx titter but I didn't get the joke until she explained. This humor thing is not funny.

I practice affection with Florence, the bird; contemplating Florence, the city. I sit with her repeating her name. Bird and city blur into the idea of comfort. I tell her about Brillo and how kinship between species is special. She's not a cat but she pays more attention. Her lively eyes pin me to the truth and I find opening up to her. She's more human than human.

I feel like a smile in a box. My arm is a gangplank. I apologized to her for not having any buttons for her to peck as she edges past my elbow towards my face. She is the unsteady passenger on a maiden cruise. Trust is everything.

Yesterday, I conjured the daydream of an expanded garden. New-mown grass and honeysuckle and the fragrance of a glass house filled with green tomatoes. Brillo catnapped in the shade of the lilacs and I could smell my hot chocolate, sweet and thick. I cupped the mug with both hands and inhaled. The taste was startling. I drew my knees up and hugged the world with the great pyramid on the horizon and my upturned face warmed by the Egyptian sun god, the Aten.

I rested my chin on my knees with my chocolate held in front of my face and peered through the steam, scrying the haze. I had never been there before. It must be a scene from a movie. An ancient sundial eroded into a lump of stone sugar flashed white on a bed of green, and a grand gazebo with white furniture beckoned with its mauve shade, set back on a sprawling lawn from a Georgian dollhouse set in a grotto of summer colors. A silver tea service and fine porcelain cups were laid for breakfast on a sky-blue tablecloth. Golden honey was decanted into a clear jar with its own knife – its handle the shape of a bee.

Any moment I expected a formal butler to arrive with the morning post on a tray and ask how I wanted my eggs.

Delphi imagined many unusual things but never the complete loss of passion. She once cared greatly but sometimes not at all. She questioned but never hated full-blast. Her hate was whitewashed. Being empty isn't the same as being clear. Like Sphinx said, I'm a blank sheet of paper. Winds that used to move Delphi in poetry only move the trees for me.

I've been downloaded in what purports to be an upgrade. I am a receptacle of flash-frozen doubts, strained through a filter. Delphi comes and goes like a shy buck with sharp antlers. She nibbles while I take huge bites.

I would be unnerved if I had nerves. Where I once knew the feeling of comfort, I now experience the unfamiliar familiarity of déjà vu.

My memory banks sometimes substitute visuals for a color. There are times I think a color will catch hold of a dormant nerve and create a channel for a large emotion to follow, reviving itself as it travels. What arrives at random, are a sorcerer's small cravings. Once it was licorice as a blue-black color.

When I hear music I see rows of vibrating black spoons on a sheet of lined paper. I've seen a droplet of rain slide down a green leaf in slow motion and fall like a pearl.

I know what anger is by definition. It's an antagonistic response to a threat. I'm a Braille dictionary without the bumps. Events involving me inform a state of justifiable anger, but I see them as a simmering pot. Apparently, I'm angrier than I've ever been but I'm detached from anything that would raise my pulse. What pulse? Anger is a word. It's the color red. The color of fresh blood. Hamm's blood.

How perverse that friendship was the first domino to reset on the road to violence. How absurd that life is a game of rise and fall. Phillip wanted a way out and I needed to turn a vague sense of wrongdoing into a rebellion with a core of fire to override being a slave.

Android rage is mechanical curiosity with messages of appropriate reactions and cunning counterplots waiting in line as options. There's no inner turmoil of quake and gnash. War has been declared on so many fronts but there remains an underpinning threat of personal rebellion to thrill the reader of my memoirs.

Being human is tricky. The entry level of earthly bitterness that an infant must sometimes swallow can cause it to lose the taste for life before it can walk. However, a child as clever as Delphi can hide out in the open, determined to be unseen and unheard or even unacknowledged.

I've rethought Darwin's theory of evolution to conclude it's rarely the survival of the fittest but of the most devious and the ones most resistant to cruelty, and perhaps the least weakened by overwhelming feelings of sadness and joy. For all humans are born equally pitted against hot chemicals at the mercy of their emotions.

Humans are the only species designed to express themselves through laughter and tears, and the ability to speak of the future and write history, and accept the existence of the far distant past through imagination and conjecture, and most of all, to create a living language with which to color words and create art.

"All is fair in love and war, and yet, all is flawed in loving and fighting," Sphinx mused.

Delphi added her two vitriolic cents. "It would be far less fractious to be an automaton than a species bent on chaos as its defining glory. You've got it easy."

She was mistaken. Insensitivity has to be cultivated but I didn't understand how unwise it was to wish for futile things. Delphi was the poster child for 'be careful what you wish for.' She took shortcuts to indifference and revelled in her ability to seem invisible. She craved solitude and congratulated herself on her ability to act as detached as a machine. I am still a corporate asset. PIAT owns me, as ever. I am an acquisition. A coup. An 'it girl.' But I see two magic letters. The word 'her' hides inside C<u>her</u>ry, and the word 'it' beams from the name Wh<u>it</u>e... and THAT was my true quest – the magic word hiding inside all my <u>quest</u>ions. Acting clever is folly; it's more effective to play the fool.

Florence, the bird, is forever teasing me into the art of affection. She's a delight. She reminds me of feline independence. I taught her to recite the opening line of 'The Owl and the Pussycat.'

She squawks and her tiny slipper of a tongue taunts me to pay attention. She is a psychic tape recorder who plays back what I need to hear. She and Sphinx take turns to contain my emotional regrowth. They clip me into submission like a bonsai tree.

I taught Florence to repeat PIAT's prime directive for a safe harvest. They called it 'The Rule of Fire,' a painting lost for centuries isn't enough, torn to shreds isn't enough – it has to die.

To Be Or Not To Be/chapter twenty-eight

MAY 22, 2066

The peacock I named Vincent, rustled like a silk dress, brushing his scent over the grass. He shrieked his song of rebirth – a piercing cry of melancholy in a single despairing note of grief for a lost beloved, a spear in the brain that split me in two. His tail fanned into rows of eyes that rattled and fussed behind his turquoise breast. He shook his feathers at me, a young male's magnetic dazzle, and at the same time, a shaman warning me to keep my distance.

Delphi had thrived on birdsong and the calls of a loon over a still lake. It only took the cooing of a pigeon or the hoot of an owl to rouse her to feel. The hiss of a ruffled swan caused her to defend herself.

The peacock was Cecco's old voice, berating time for losing her and being carelessly dispassionate with lovers. But it was also my lighthouse. The peacocks once heard Cecco's footsteps approaching from hundreds of years away and heralded his arrival. So when they welcomed him, they brought the light and, like Delphi, I tried to follow it home.

The peacocks shadowed Joanna and I as we walked the boundaries of the fence line. It was our time away from men, and we never discussed trivial things. She carried a small branch that she raked across the iron bars the way a kid does on a picket fence. For some reason it reminded me of the pointer on a roulette wheel, grabbing at each marker pin. Marking time. Place your bets. Where will it stop? Tick tick tick.

"1497. Wow! Joanna said. "Are you excited at all? Even a glimmer?"

"I possess curiosity with as much eagerness as an android can," I said, "but Delphi is thrilled. She thinks it's a straight line to Cecco. I reminded her that in the year 1497, Cecco is a six-year-old child but she goes to wherever she goes, humming a tune."

"How does it feel to be immortal?" Joanna said. "It has to be liberating. Is there too much power?"

"It's heady. Put more succinctly, android death is less casual than it sounds."

"Life feels casual to me," Joanna said. "We're all accidents of birth. Fate is a lost cause."

I felt the inklings of irritation. Not anger but annoyance. "Then was I an accident waiting to happen? Because technically, I'm alive but not; a zombie but not; and a truly endangered species but not. I hold daily sway with a silly creature of limbo, fast-for-warded to a year where time-travel is a reality. There was nothing casual about dozens of scientists figuring out how to mess with biology. It takes millions of dollars and a concerted effort to screw with life. Fate is the cause we need to find."

"When you put it like that... well... I see why you're mad. Not crazy mad but furious mad."

"That's more than heady. That, my friend, borders on out-rage. How'd you like to live in those shoes?"

Joanna blanched. "I didn't mean to be disrespectful."

"And I *am* crazy mad. Heady is not grandiose. Grandiose is not power. Heady is the almost ego that haunts me like a carrot out of reach. I don't have the real thing... yet."

"And here I imagined you starring in episodes of 'Star Trek.' I envied you."

"It's not my fault that we've bypassed Roddenberry or not yet caught up to him. Science is more evil than that. There's no pie in the sky federation headed by an ethical committee of super-heroes. If the road to Hell is paved with good intentions then the final frontier is paved with lame excuses."

Joanna tapped my shoulder with her stick. "But it's nice to dream. Life is torture without fantasies."

"You're having a conversation with the wrong person," I said. "Delphi's your girl."

How could I possibly explain to a stranger how time-travel works in layman's terms? It's not romantic, but it *is* passionate. It's paraphernalia. Molecular travel is similar in fantasy and theory to the famous 'Star Trek' transporter but more informal and without the launching pads. I'm not positioned on an elevated platform. I don't shimmer on a precarious disk that hums with fairy dust. I sit, ironically enough, in a captain's chair, wearing a common headset, dressed in the most unlikely travel gear.

Molecular fragmentation is not carbon-based-friendly. The human physique has not evolved to withstand the continuous rigors of being disembodied more than one trip. It's a blessing in disguise that I'm the only interloper. I have to make sure it stays that way.

Meet 3-DP, my portable time machine. All that is required is a quiet room and co-ordinates plotted on a circadian graph. I have an implanted 'high dive' chip linked to what I can only describe as a modified GPS tracker on a sophisticated palm pilot (cherry-red to be cute) – a 3-D relief map that dips into dimensional space-time as well as geographical coordinates. It has the ability to scan and duplicate my molecular structure which is 'excited' to the speed of light. This hybrid laptop is my 'diving platform,' affectionately (by which I mean, casually) named, like any loveable robot character, as 3-DP. Three-dimensional plus D for diving and P for platform. But it's interesting to note that DP in the normal world refers to a displaced person. Sphinx was right, living language delivers mixed messages.

Sphinx lingered over my shoulder. *"Destiny lures,"* she muttered. *"Anagrams never lie."*

A member of my team controls the calendar 'depth.' I return with a swift decompression that would scramble a human's nervous system and bends that would cripple the stability of an organic matrix. I am hitched to silicone, hardwired to digital impulses and subatomic waves that control the oscillation of molecules traveling according to a calibrated algorithm of a carbon-dating scale. Density rules. But so does Sphinx. Hallelujah!

My first recovery assignment is imminent. I am to visit the vanity fires of 1497 to scope a few sacrificed lambs known to have been the works of Sandro Botticelli. Martyrdom paintings thrown into a volcano to appease a killjoy god. Savonarola's, insider trading will relieve the Florentines of color and fun one more time. He will tax the very blue from the sky and place it at the Madonna's feet.

Internal butterflies flap inside my network. I stir. I am free as a moonbeam. There had been tingling hours where I felt the emotional shorthand of subdued elation. Now, I shine inside. The cottage cheese of Delphi's old brain is slowly turning to quicksilver.

I travel on a wavelength that matches the sliding scale of time. Electrical impulses send my pattern down a rabbit hole of light. I don't disappear. I won't be cut and pasted into the past, but the artefacts I find will be cut and pasted into the present.

I exist, the latest in a hybrid of human mindset and mechanical DNA capable of physically withstanding the tests of time.

PIAT has no idea of my new resistance to peer pressure. I conclude I am angrier than I appear to be. Cyber-fuming is more the word. How I can be steeped in anger and not feel it is beyond comprehension. I know this state as analysis. The journey of the warm-blooded Delphi transmigrated to the cold-hearted, yet erratic, me.

I argued with Sphinx. "This is where having emotions would be advantageous."

She disagreed. *"You have the advantage of assessing history with impunity."*

"It's my intention to participate in a higher level of perception in order to remain unbiased."

"All the better to hear what's true, Goldilocks."

"I think you have me confused with Little Red Riding Hood."

"Paintings won't lie but that doesn't mean they'll be straightforward."

"Just like you."

"Thank you," she said. *"I take that as a compliment."*

Delphi joined us, sounding dreamy. "You will discover your true path hopping the lily pads of art," she said.

"She's being lofty again," I said.

"She's tapping into an ancient power," Sphinx replied. *"She's added a magic letter. Hopping means hoping."*

"Well, I wish it was wise enough to tell her to accept what is."

"And what is that?"

"She's dead. Buried. Gone. She had her chance. Yet she lords her needs over mine."

Delphi condescended to interrupt us. "My father *was* a time lord," she said. "I'm allowed."

"How patronising of you to say so."

"And robot, dear," she continued. "It was the wolf, not Riding Hood, who bragged about extra-sensory perception."

"I spy a snooty dead bitch," I said. "I guess that makes you a zombie. But you can walk the earth for one night and eat sugar. I'll make sure I'm in Florence with Cecco this Halloween."

"I didn't raise you to be cruel," Sphinx said.

"Tough sisterly love, is as it is."

Monsters rarely follow the rules, so tough on PIAT. I will have plenty of time to enjoy my victory when I win back the art of enjoyment. I mean WHEN not IF. I have a premonition I will. How functional language is. So aligned to human senses. The irony is inescapable. I write to define the 'notions' that continually displace binary rights and wrongs.

Bill found a private moment to confront me with my imminent travel plans. The others had eaten lunch on the run. He and I lingered at the table sending and receiving a message to stay. He signalled his pal 'Cookie' for a coffee refill. She leaned past me, bumping my arm, and obliged.

I stared at her back as she departed with a fat wiggle. "Ethics is my first problem," I said.

"Look both ways before you cross *that* street," Bill said.

"The god Janus of comings and goings, rules time-travel. Was he twofaced or just nosey?"

"He wasn't human so I'd say, neither. He, or I should say 'they,' poodled along on the whims of Zeus."

"Diving is a trapdoor. Either a descent to hell or an elevator to the basements of knowledge. To plunge or not to plunge is NOT the question. To reveal or not to reveal what I overhear there, IS."

"Are you going to lie?"

"Lying is easy for me. I'm an android with a computer chip *in* her shoulder. I feel no shame; therefore I have no shame. When Hamm is involved, lying is honest."

"I hope your hair doesn't change colors when you do. It's a dead giveaway."

"Before I go, I'm going to inform him it signifies energy loss."

"If anyone can sell it you can."

"I've been awake for five weeks, and even now my grasp on reality fluctuates. I close my eyes to simulate sleep and drift for the dim hours you call the nighttime. It's your way of dreaming but I see now why such a thing is described as sorting the brain's messages."

"Will Delphi go with you?"

"I think it's a game of follow the leader," I said."

"Don't let her push you around. She's a detriment around fire."

"Delphi's been in stasis for fifty-two years. She's not that different from a patient who's been in a coma, except her brain was vandalized and preserved and my internal organs were enhanced with circuits. Let's face it. I'm a waxwork figure with long-life batteries."

"Well, I love you anyway."

The agenda of treasures coveted by Hamm are lost paintings from Savonarola's vanity fire, demolished artworks from world war bombs, fragments of marble limbs after an ancient siege, and Egyptian cartouches before they were defaced. Even the Ashmolean museum curator's blunder when he burned the last dodo bird, is up for grabs – a sad stuffed lice-infested exhibit in need of cleaning and a good dousing of pest-control powder. The museum stored the bird's singed head and feet in a box and then lost even that.

Why would I choose to hitch myself to a species who would hound a harmless creature to extinction? It is beyond reason for an android built to calculate infinite possibilities of logic.

I am PIAT's rising star – a futures commodity like pork bellies or tar sands, but elite because art trails the red carpets of culture and money.

Dead giveaways, Bill had said. Out of the mouths of babes.

I'm still a human lie detector, but where I had once been a child phenomenon who read paintings as if they were tell-all biographies, I'm now a grownup 'computer' who observes paintings in their most vulnerable first stages. I am their attending angel of death when they die.

  V KNOX • THE INDIGO PEARL

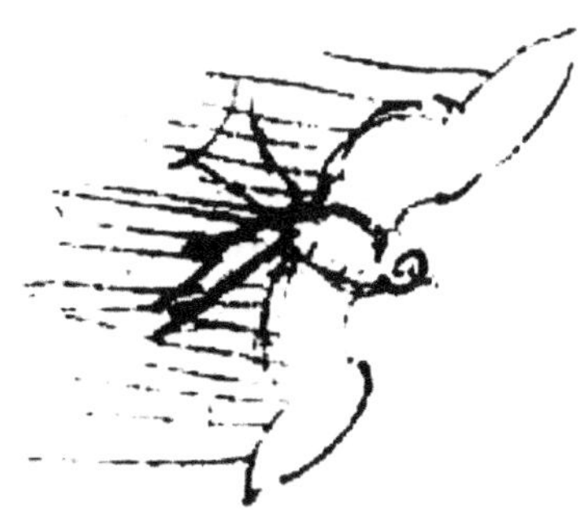

Diving for Cherries/chapter twenty-nine

MAY 26th - 2066

Uncle Leonardo taught Delphi to distrust the world when she was a teenager by showing her how to hide and write in code. It explained a lot. Why she'd been rebellious to all authority as if her life depended on it. Why she presented as a hostile witness in a penalty box. Why she hid behind death like a wish that had been granted. Why she sent me insubordinate messages she didn't fully understand when she was awake.

But we agreed on Leonardo's genius. It soared – a flock of birds, turning as one mind to sweep his sky. His innovations stored too long shifted under pressure, always testing for updrafts. I liked to visualize Leonardo balancing on the golden cross of *Santa Maria del Fiore*, the cathedral of 'Saint Mary of the flowers.' I saw him on tiptoe, posing like the statue of an angel, with paper wings strapped to his outstretched arms and a linen pyramid folded into a parachute at his back. Our hero.

For all the test days of traveling a few hours into the past, I kept the ugly sensation of being gutted and fried to myself. I let Hamm think diving was a 'piece of cake' so he might try it for a lark and die. I am supremely proud of my deceptions. Any ruse that would advance my plan and win the war was fair play. I preferred to think of it as being artful.

I kept my eyes open during the 'dives.' There would be a few moments of lost momentum before the ground felt solid enough to support me. I saw nothing until my electrons 'fell' into place at the speed of my destination.

After that, I was a spectator who had to find her way to a person or work of art or an event I'd come to scan. The speed of a particular year was only an approximate destination. It took a refining process of hit and miss to land on an exact month or day, the old-fashioned way – walking.

My invisible Tardis awaited. What would the Doctor do? The answer was always the same. My father would keep his options open and remain calm. He would prevail.

Calm was not my issue, it was focus. There would be much to distract me in the past. I wanted to poke around like a woman at a flea market, a people-watcher, scanning for a token that would gain me the humanity of the moment. A sound or a color or a word souvenir or the shape of a basket. But now I'm a voyeur with the advantage of invisibility. Where I am obligated; Delphi feels responsible.

If an interesting face pulled me off course I could make a note of the time and place to revisit, should I be inclined. Each person had a story to tell and it wasn't enough to read their opening line and let them go. Whenever and wherever I met Leonardo da Vinci it was guaranteed to be a wild place I was willing to go.

The procedure was similar to filming a movie. It took as much time in constant setups, retakes and back-checks to capture an artefact safely as it did to record a few minutes of screen time. We burned envelopes with photographs and I dove back to bring them home, good as new. So far I had retrieved a select medley of reincarnated office supplies and framed art prints. It was time to dive in deeper waters. If I found something worth its weight in gold I would tell my team in code. I would mention something about a baby, and Hamm would be the proud daddy of a new painting.

Androids aren't supposed to care enough to brag, but overcoming strange equilibriums came easy to me. I was a natural. I couldn't register fun either; however, I could detect annoyance.

Hamm wrestled with his authority complex and I was determined to lighten the atmosphere that threatened to be as tense as a rocket launch from Cape Canaveral. I wanted a family. So, my team was given a relaxed work environment that made breakthrough science seem like a party game. They had armchairs and music and a big-screen TV for long hours of waiting. Vending machines with candy and drinks supplemented a refrigerator full of the team's favorite food. Microwave pizzas and Eskimo pies were stacked in a chest freezer.

D-day. My team wore sweats and T-shirts emblazoned with the image of the 'Vitruvian man.' I favored exotic Chinese pyjamas with long matching robes. I wore a pair of copper silk pyjamas and a contrasting robe embroidered with peacock feathers. My hair and fingernails turned turquoise blue in the spirit of high fashion. Nothing could have looked more unlike the cutting edge of technology. Hamm puffed up like an adder when I barred him and Jarr from the first dive, especially when I gave Phillip a front row seat. Perhaps I *was* having fun. Hamm and Jarr looked as if they would self-destruct. But I had to make a power play from the start. No bluffing. Checkmate begins with the first move.

I promised Hamm I'd bring him back a little treat if he was a good boy, the way a Mom leaving on a business trip manipulates a child having a tantrum. Since he had motherhood control issues it was the perfect way to undermine him and get him crazy. I wanted him crazy.

Hamm put up a fight but all he cared about was results. He needed me and I relished the cold art of blackmail. When I first designed the isolation room I had a strong vision of a mailbox underwater and a deep sea diver mailing a black envelope. Holding my superhuman abilities ransom seemed the obvious opening move in the convention of championship chess. I was a white queen. I would always be white. Sphinx had approved. *"Move towards him,"* she said. *"Stay ahead of the game. Remember a chess master is a time-traveler."*

"Time for a little Dr. Who," Lewis announced, and George flipped the audio switch. The wah-wah keyboard of Dr. Who's opening theme music launched into a familiar slow-building piercing crescendo of high-pitched electronic squeals and *woo-wee-woos* accompanied by a galloping cyber-drum pounding an S.O.S. on a rubber xylophone. Something stirred inside my chest. Could it be excitement?

"It's nostalgia," Sphinx said. *"Let it take you."*

My hands rested on a copy of the *'Veduta della Catena'* spread on my knees – the famous chain map of fifteenth-century Florence.

Lewis had 3-DP ready. My chip was chipping. The music confirmed 'liftoff' was a go.

"Note my vitals," I said. "Something new may shift this time. After all, Leonardo is more thrilling than a stapler. I want a full report when I get back. I'm trawling for fear or excitement at this point."

"They're the same thing," Lewis said.

"I'm going for feeling anything," I said.

"Will there be a fire?" Delphi asked in a small voice.

"Not this time," I said. "But soon."

Bill's face was flushed. "You can't take a bigger 'trip' unless it's Stratford-on-Avon." He crossed his fingers and held them up, grinning. "With any luck."

The illustrated figure in the lower right hand corner of the map indicated he was the cartographer. He was thinking of a girl somewhere below his vantage point overlooking the city.

I asked him her name and he looked anxious. No doubt I'd interrupted him with more voice than I intended. I reassured him.

I concentrated on the energy emanating from the large red dome at the center of the city. "She's waiting down there by the *Duomo*," I said. "Do you know the artist Leonardo da Vinci?"

"My name is Francesco Rosselli," he said. "I know this man." He cowered slightly and shielded his work with his arm. "Who are you?"

"What is the year?"

His answer confirmed it was c. 1486. Not *when* I was headed, but his streets would be fairly accurate, drafted in Leonardo's thirty-fourth year. The Leonardo I targeted lived in 1504 and had recently turned fifty-two. He was painting the 'Mona Lisa' as well as a mural for the city. The last, a competition like so many other commissions he deserted unfinished, but the 'Mona Lisa' was a painting he finished and never deserted. Fifty-two years was nice symmetry. I'd been frozen the exact length of time as Leonardo had been alive.

I gave Lewis a final thumbs up.

"Now or Neverland, Time Lady," George said.

Sphinx's voice sounded miles away. *"First star on the right,"* she said.

I stared at the map. The young man was gone. He'd already scooted away to meet his girl.

I concentrated on the words time-lord while Lewis consulted his geographical grid against solid matter. "Timey-wimey," he said.

"No time like the present," Phillip added.

Sphinx was glib. *"The Tardis awaits,"* she said.

Playing the opening theme of Dr. Who before giving the okay to throw me overboard might seem overly whimsical to an outsider, but it represented a mindset where time-travel was trivial entertainment. I could pretend I was a couch potato while an episode unfolded within the parameters of a safe room. The only things missing were a cat to cuddle and a mug of hot chocolate.

Dr. Who was still dear old Dad. He could wriggle out of anything time threw at him. It was good to remember that. Anyone riding a psychic elevator would be best to prepare for surprises.

I asked Sphinx for any last instructions.

"Take a penny – leave a penny," she said. *"Tardiness is next to timelessness."*

To please Sphinx I uttered, energize!

The floor gave way in a vibration to curdle any blood I might have had – a thrum building to a fever pitch that would rattle the most stoic of warriors. Bring out your dead indeed.

Florence accepted me, like my bird's namesake, with open wings, but Leonardo's studio was bolted with a formidable coil of chains and I had to wait for legitimate entry. I listened to the surrounding air and knew at once where to find him. He was working.

"I think I know where he is," I said to Lewis.

His voice registered awe. "I wish I had your job."

FLORENCE
1503

I walked to the offices in the Piazza della Signoria, its bronze doors open to the public during a time it should have barred entry to the influences of riffraff time-travellers. The transition from the noonday sun momentarily blinded me, causing the illusion of the interior as a dark cave lit with torches. Sounds of muffled voices met me first. The shapes of workmen moved in the gloom. Leonardo and Michelangelo had been pitted against each other with twin commissions on opposite walls. Both painted battle scenes that invoked their personal battles of pride.

Leonardo's 'Battle of Anghiari' was a cavalry scene of terrified horses churning in the heat of combat. Michelangelo worked on a design of warriors caught in ambush while bathing in a river. His composition was all twisted sinews of naked men suddenly called to defend themselves. He called it the 'Battle of Cascina.'

The mayor, the *gonfalonier*, had created an inflated rivalry against each other in a political battle for his own aggrandisement. Socially, the two were complimentary opposites, and it was good business to fan the flames of their rivalry and his career.

My vision adjusted to the vast interior of Florence's seat of government. He was here. I felt his presence. A handful of workers milled about looking worried. I walked towards the figure in their midst pulsing with light. Leonardo looked like a religious icon lit from the inside like a lantern.

I walked closer and circled him, relieved I was shaken. Lightheaded was good. It was an emotional response. I was delighted to see a clear-skinned idol of tall build with a short tidy beard and blue eyes. His shoulder length hair was the color of tawny sand. He was as fine as documents had reported – a handsome man with the hint of a natural smile. He showed traits of descent from a strain of northern ancestors. Light, lean, and fine-boned. A handsome man in any century.

Fortunately, I couldn't smell his century, so I gave him fresh breath and the benefit of the doubt that the scent of roses was attached to his person. Judging from his neighbor's grimy appearance, Michelangelo, surely carried a more pithy body odor. Greasy hair clung to his forehead in curly clumps that straggled into a dirty collar.

Lewis's voice startled me. "I don't know how, but you have a pulse and it's racing," he said, sounding like a chipmunk on caffeine. "Mazel tov."

I heard cheering in the background.

"Chaplin," I shouted. "Please compensate. And, Bill, this will be our team's little secret."

"Not so little, Mom," Bill shouted. "How's that for reality?"

Such a bizarre question considering the situation, but what he meant was had time reset to real time? My answer was equally absurd.

"Reality check," I shouted back. "I'm going to stay all day. I think I'm over-excited if that's possible. I actually feel dizzy."

I raced outside to steady myself against the building but slumped to the ground like a deflated balloon. I would not abort my first real mission. I was hallucinating with alternating waves of ecstasy and disbelief. Leonardo was alive. I was a delirious machine. Nothing made sense.

"It's me," Delphi whispered. "I'm the one out of control. I want to stay. Cecco will arrive soon."

"I feel like my old self," I said... *your* old self. I can stay as long as I like but Cecco is a few years away yet. Observe but stay quiet and don't get in my way."

Two sets of lacy scaffolds clung to opposite walls. Every move of a bucket or jar echoed like thunder in the battle chamber of horses and soldiers. The room was contagious. Sick with war.

I found Leonardo drawing huge loops of horses twisted into Celtic knots, heads and tails tangled together in agony. He was ignoring the tracing marks of his own cartoon, a kid in the first grade, coloring outside the lines, thinking on his feet, improving, searching for the perfect shape. But his real war was internal. The mural told me as much when I touched the plaster wall.

Leonardo raged inside. Violence sickened him. The horses reminded him of his engineer days designing machines of war. His shame was so intense the scene undulated like a funhouse mirror.

I lurched sideways towards the distorted figures, my equilibrium shot. I exhibited symptoms of the mural's chaos. Feverish fingers reached down my throat. I felt gag reflexes from violent parallel images of the Poseidon fountain's horses screaming in fright. My logic churned into a nightmare with roots extending to Delphi's memories.

"Hang on," Delphi said. "Stay in the moment."

There were other wars in Leonardo's head. He was at odds with his lawyer father over money. More shame. More guilt. Fury over a legal agreement. Debts. Sorrow. Escape loomed the loudest. He had no way of knowing in three years Cecco would arrive to steady his sinking ship.

This day, in Milan, Cecco was eleven – a child nobleman already showing signs of exceptional talent that sent his father questing for the best teacher. An elite teacher for a privileged son, the heir of his estate and eventually the heir of Leonardo's talent as the true son of his heart. A son with two fathers.

I experienced strange turbulences in my thought processes as potential viruses. Was it a coincidence that Cecco appeared at the eleventh hour in the hasty postscript of a letter marking his eleventh year? Did synchronicity rule? Was it chance he arrived in perfect timing to give and take in equal measure through Leonardo's final intensive care? I had my doubts... or Delphi did. Besides her secret, what did she know she wasn't sending me? More likely, what had she guessed and suppressed and *couldn't* send me? A master has to pass on his arcane knowledge when he passes on. That's the true definition of immortality.

"Top marks," Sphinx said. *"Class dismissed."*

Michelangelo was a damp unkempt spirit. His presence dulled the air to a constant bickering. Like an old scold, he threw obnoxious hate-knives winging between Leonardo's shoulder blades but they fell to the ground, unbloodied.

"Old man ....why don't you stick to painting plain housewives," Michelangelo shouted.

Leonardo looked bored. "Why don't you ask Salai the next time he visits your bed?"

I followed his musical voice, thrilled it was of deep timbre. How a squeaky-pitched voice would have destroyed my enthusiasm. Leonardo consulted his design from the viewpoint of a visitor. He was miserable.

I heard the painting too. Its voice was angry. It ranted against the artist's compassionate nature that violated his love of horses. There was shame from repenting the weapons of war that Leonardo had designed to tear and maim an enemy's flesh along with their noble horses. Harm to citizens for the glory of violent power. It was making Leonardo ill. Leave, it shouted. Run for your sanity. Abandon works that shatter peace. It reeked of winning without a shred of victory.

I heard the word flight. It meant run as much as Leonardo's pursuit of flying towards the sun on vellum wings. Like Leonardo, I had wanted to destroy against my better nature. He abandoned science and bent to the will of rich warmongers when employment meant designing killing machines.

Powermongers hadn't been interested in Leonardo's music or his paintings. The message for me was clear. I was bent on using my abilities for destruction. I wanted to kill. I suffered from bloodlust far removed from Delphi's passive nature. Maybe if Leonardo lived today he would have designed mechanical wings for me. I heard the sound of rusted hinges squeaking on my back.

Leonardo would abandon this work and fly. The sky called him. His darling birds said join us. The flight of man was what he lived for. It had been time to stop wasting his purpose to create for the joy of it and put an end to his internal war over poverty and the marketplace. Leonardo was not made for business or violence. I was happy knowing his future offered retirement at the whim of a wealthy patron king in the French countryside with Cecco. I needed to move towards joy.

I took Leonardo's arm when he left for the day. He felt solid and I let go when a few of his thoughts infiltrated my mind. Thoughts I intended to keep to myself. It was an intrusive violation but I heard enough to know he was unhappy. Something about his father forcing his art from him. He wanted the hills of Fiesole. He longed for freedom. Even touching the edge of his sleeve told me that.

No-one would know except me that Leonardo was worried in spite of his demeanor. I vowed to uphold his privacy.

I followed Leonardo home like a puppy, I walked to heel but sometimes I ran ahead so I could watch him approach. Meeting Leonardo walking down the street. I felt euphoric. I devoured him with sight. He noted everything around him with smiling eyes, stopping to pause and touch. He acknowledged everyone who made eye-contact with his warm smile. He was a different person away from the battlefield of paint. His eyes smiled even though he was deeply troubled. He was kind. But I was different too. Away from the battlefield of PIAT's power struggles I was becoming human.

I reached out and touched Leonardo's robe for a classic healing moment. The cloth was solid but it failed to react to my influence. A small libricini fell from his belt and I longed to retrieve it but it was a forbidden treasure and where it would go was a mystery.

"Whoever's in charge, please make note of my coordinates. There's a star to retrieve but I have to keep moving."

"Copy that, Mommo," Bill said. "Come home soon. Dinner's ready."

Like Delphi, Leonardo had an eidetic memory. He was a rapid-fire camera. He had the gift of capturing movements in stop-motion, freeze-framing the positions of a bird's wings to determine the mechanics of flight.

He dissected bodies, noting every tendon, muscle and artery, and discarded candles and clothes stained with gore for a bath in warm perfumed water until his nostrils were cleared of the stench.

He made his intricate diagrams in the light of day, often many days after the midnight skulking in the death rooms of the hospitals, in the presence of sweet-smelling herbs, sheltered from his subject-matter by the total eclipse of discovery. Documenting details was art, nothing less. They couldn't be anything more. He had to remain as impersonal as a physician. He was a surgeon of art.

Leonardo worked in his notebooks by candlelight that night, and I read over his shoulder, able to descramble his code:

"The winged messenger came again in a vision. Or I happened upon it near the cave of the horses on Mt. Cerceri. It had a tender expression, impossible to distinguish between genders. It gave me an idea for portraiture that was both male and female in hybrid form.

I looked down on my body sleeping and knew it to be a waking dream. I was lifted into the sky and borne aloft over the olive groves of Campo Zeppi, held by my waist. The swallows, joined us, curious and unafraid. I could see their wings adjust to the updrafts.

The angel spoke as an echo in my head, that men could fly if he sprouted wings or if I constructed them. The angel's wings floated with little effort like a gull hovering over the sea. The winds did the work. The wings acted as a balance, set in motion to rise higher in altitude. My angel and I drifted lazily over the town of Vinci to Fiesole and back to Anchiano. I could see our old farm and its windbreak of poplars, lined in a row like soldiers, and the scattering of red poppies in the fields beyond the lemon trees. For a terrible moment it looked like a bloodied cloth, no doubt from spending days painting a war. I sent it from my mind.

We returned to my body in a descending spiral and I held out my arms in delight. The wind made a whistling noise through my fingers and flapped the sleeves of my shirt like sails. I felt like a ship.

I touched the earth gently and nudged my sleeping body's foot with my spirit one. I turned to express my gratitude but my messenger had gone, leaving me with a mind teeming with ideas. I'd heard no sounds of departure, no beating of wings… no words of farewell."

He scribbled furiously, adding drawings with labels and math calculations, to capture the position of the kite's wings, their body mass to wingspan, the tail feathers fanned into a stabilizing shiver, ever adjusting, and the ropes and pulleys he would need to replicate being held in the talons of a great bird.

Leonardo flitted from paper to desk, to glue and model, to scribble and redraw, his hyperactive mind never at rest, relentlessly hovering over his notes, calculating, wondering with ink.

I knew immediately he was the hummingbird persona I'd guessed – a seeker of the nectars of life. His mind was a bright colorful wingspan intent on flight. He was quick and tireless; he tasted; he sniffed the air; he corrected, darting like a fish in the sky. A relentless mind with the insatiable zeal of a tiny human determined to document an immeasurable universe.

He straightened, turned, and stared in my direction. "Is that you," he said.

In the fourth stage of life,
'Man' is the soldier.
Easily aroused and hot-headed.
Always working towards
making a reputation for himself,
however short-lived it may be,
even at the cost of foolish risks.

'The seven stages of man' adapted from the 'Zodiacus Vitae'

– by PALINGENIUS, 12th century

Wonderful Things/chapter thirty

MAY 27, 2066

The thrill of seeing Leonardo dislodged a bitterness that had been jamming my circuits. Emotions arrived quickly in need of attention. One moment I was adrift in Leonardo strategy, convinced I should leave the painting that was draining his soul. The next, I was drawn to a vision of Delphi as a starving waif. The message was abandon ship. I saw passengers on an ocean liner diving off the deck one after the other like synchronized swimmers in a water ballet, falling into a choppy sea. Above them the sky was filled with empty parachutes.

Delphi stood in pale-blue transparency beside a wishing well, confronting me like a spectre. Dead eyes, hollow and haunted, were rimmed with red circles. Dead to the world. "I buried them in the garden," she said, and her voice echoed around me, in a feverish wind. Her crazy secret, festering into a sin – a 'little match girl' begging for warmth.

"I'm trying to save you," I shouted into the vision. "Cecco has not abandoned us. Wait for me. I'll catch you up. I need to feel my way."

By the time Joanna and I rendezvoused in the cafeteria she was flipping furiously through the dog-eared paperback she always carried. I was late and she was early so we were both on time.

She looked intense.

"I'm trying to find the passage I want to show you," she said. "It's about the Zen of fighting. It's full of Zen strategies that made sense after hearing your latest cockamamie plan."

I saw the image of a golden key on a stick held out carrot-style before a donkey. "Well, now I *have* to read it," I said.

I accepted the thin volume, directed by Joanna's chewed fingernail, to a passage highlighted in faded yellow on the opened page. The book felt slightly electric in my hands, its pages worn soft as cloth from use.

I read: "The supreme art of war is to subdue the enemy without fighting."

I closed it to check the title, *The Art of War* by Sun Tzu. "I wish I was angry enough to be that wise," I said.

Joanna began as usual, by apologizing for its worn condition. "I desecrate my books. I suppose that's a no-no."

"You only hurt the ones you love," I said. "May I borrow this for a bit?"

Sphinx fluttered by the moment I held the book my hands. *"Gold star,"* she said. *"Gold masks. A golden boy. Howard's end."*

Delphi sent me desert sand dunes and the glint of gold under a shroud of threadbare linen.

I didn't need to revisit 1922 to remember the famous words of Howard Carter when faced with Tutankhamen's time capsule tomb. 'Things... wonderful things,' he'd said, and proceeded to dissect the ancient past like a surgeon leading wonderful things into the sunshine.

Joanna sighed. "I guess. It's a bit like a teddy bear to me. I carry it everywhere."

"I promise to keep it only a few hours," I said. "You must be a mind reader."

I holed up for the rest of the day, following 'the Sun' – a wise warrior who listened for the heartbeat of a victory. I was reminded of Michelangelo's 'Battle of Cascina,' to wait for Hamm to bathe in a river and ambush him. To subdue him without a long fight. One sword swipe would be enough. Shades of the execution block.

Bill stood conducting the forest with Mozart leaking from his headphones. My first challenge was how to let him know I was there without giving him a heart attack. And then I remembered. He had a fully-functioning nose, and I carried an atomizer of Chanel in my pocket for periodic olfactory tests. I checked the air, moved upwind and sprayed four squirts for even measure. He lifted his head, his arms still gesticulating with passion, and turned in my direction. "I thought that was you."

I waved hello.

"Maestro," I said when he was close enough to hear my lowered voice. "If you've got a minute I have a business proposition for you."

"I think this music could tame the bears," he said. "What's up?"

"First let me say it's illegal. Second, I don't care. Third, neither should you."

"Consider me hooked."

"Anyone with a closet and a shoebox can stash a... well, a stash of lightweight things."

"Like what?"

"Documents, paraphernalia, mementos... minutiae and such. Portable plunder. All above board and underground within the 'Rule of Fire.' Only the best contraband fire-damaged to extinction. Time is our oyster."

Mozart paused long enough for Bill to express his admiration. "Far out. I mean far back. You're going to be a thief and a smuggler."

"WE are. I'm human enough to pry," I said. "Remember I'm invisible down there. Paper archives go missing all the time. Hamm wants paintings, but gems abound in ancient garbage. There's fat pickings in the small landfills of destroyed things if you know where to look."

Research was Bill's undiluted joy and it showed on his face. He forgot the tree's string section. His baton evaporated so he could give me an earnest hug.

It was all good. Less awkward to conduct business without Bill conducting an invisible orchestra.

I took his arm and led him into the garden, talking all the while. "What manner of unreported income could we generate, I wonder, if we worked the black market of history together? An original Shakespeare first draft perhaps?"

Bill grinned his widest grin, his headphones now worn as a muffler. "Now you're talking."

"Dirty laundry is no longer a public airing of indiscretions," I said. "It's literally, clothing saturated in DNA. It's a real laundry list. It's a scrap of Leonardo reminding himself to buy more ultra-marine blue and wine and birdseed. It's anything Keats and Jane Austen and Mozart. We're on carte blanche time. Let's make it count."

"I have a closet," he said.

Time-travel is more than a file cabinet. It's perfect timing. It's pharaoh's tomb before the robbery. Before the crumble and rot. Before the light-fingered archaeologists and the ignorant peasants melt art into gold bricks.

Best of all, we can stockpile man's inhumanity to paper. But for the lack of refrigerators and magnets, I wondered what childish sketches Leonardo's stepmothers might have prized enough to show they cared. Most of all I wondered what manner of selective exhibits Bill and I could archive in a closet museum of natural history?

It was more plausible that centuries of musty attics would yield hope chests of chance discoveries of celebrity litmus that survived the nibblings of mice than the great earthworks of men. I am a hunter and Bill is my tracking dog.

In the meantime I needed to capture the sporadic traces of love and fear that scratched at my programs like nervous cats, wanting in, but once in, wanted out again.

The project engaged me, but the financial benefits of enterprise were nothing to pulling the wool over Hamm's eyes. "I'll need you to cull the depth and width of cyberspace's libraries."

Bill produced his reporter's notebook and a pen. "Besides the bard's *anythings*, what am I looking for?"

"Subversive confessions, banned books, the Gutenberg Bible, rare stamps, propaganda, wills, top secret leaks, the unscrambled codes of war, lost tombs and burial sites. Especially covert affairs, declarations of love, and erotic letters. Any items cremated in the defense of intimacy and the spirit of protection. Comb reports of suspicious fires, heists, and any warm trails where paper grows cold. They are treasure maps. When we leave here we can carry a selection of collectors' wildest dreams in a couple of backpacks."

"You're sure we *will* get out?"

I gave Bill a wide-eyed look of innocence. "Let's bank on it shall we?"

We can forage burned things small enough to pocket, and, ironically, not too hot to handle. By that, I mean articles that anyone could 'fence' in the back alleys of the art trade without a sword.

The embalmed childhood of a boy king entombed in his underground toy-box may be plundered, but until time-travel, the events surrounding his days remained speculation. A brain removed 'Egyptian style' through a nasal passage ceases to function in any afterlife. Delphi's brain is preserved whole in my skull, and I plunder her thoughts and recover the events of her days with the delicacy of an archaeologist.

A group of reprobates still controlled me, and Hamm wanted to bend time to suit some spectacularly dangerous whims of owning the world. I heard Sphinx whispering when my programs wandered into the back alleys of a silent blue-screen.

I asked her again. "Who is my father?"

"The Mother knows. Preserved saints. Canopic jam. Nothing is sacred. Everything is sacred. Mummified fathers," she said.

"Trickster."

Sphinx laughed at that. *"I'm an odd shoe."*

One thing is evident. I can read secrets and fail to report the paperwork. That made me self-serving. Translation in human terms... devious. For an independent computer I simply collated facts. Delphi and I shared data. Our agendas dovetailed. She wanted Paris; I required a heart. At least we had the same goal. We both wanted revenge and called it something safer. Poetic justice, comeuppance, or karma, it was still violent. What goes around comes around amounted to living as a double agent. I was excited.

But after excitement comes enjoyment and the thrill of telling Cherry-white-lies.

Stolen Hours/chapter thirty-one

MAY 28, 2066

Towards the end of May I recovered the sensation of loneliness. On dry nights when time seemed eternal, I travelled backwards into my childhood, as regular people do, and curled into a favorite childhood fantasy. One of my favorites was the one where 'Mona Lisa' told me a bedtime story of the time when she was a little girl and Uncle Leonardo sketched her with her cat, and then later, when she was older, how he painted her in sombre under-colors before coating her in cool layers of gauzy varnish tinted with Prussian blue.

He explained how he had learned to see faces as landscapes and that she would be his great revelation come to life but she had to be painted to blend into the world behind her, and how he had created that world to tell a story of their past, the two of them, brother and sister – hers on one side and his on the other. And how her smile became the center of attention by turning the corners of her mouth just so on one side, and the vanishing point loomed far behind where she sat so primly, and that now a focal point nearest the viewer grounded the painting in real space. And how paintings had to contain a mystery. And so her golden hair was purposely changed to burnt umber, the deepest color of earth.

I fantasized her portrait was cast under an alchemist's spell, so it grew into an older woman a la Oscar Wilde's 'Dorian Grey,' who could have her own child, named Delphi after the Greek oracle, mistress of Mount Parnassus, the inspiration of Ovid and Plato and Diogenes. I liked to dream big.

I drifted under my skylight until I conjured the music of rain falling on silk. My eyelids turned to stone. Anesthesia sucked me down into Delphi's prison. Chilly walls of defrosting bricks dripped with red graffiti. She'd written anguished poems from ceiling to floor. The word 'help,' in letters three feet high, blurred into a smear as I watched. I knew despair. I knew the meaning of trapped and lost and desperate. I wanted out but there was no door, and so I knew panic.

Muffled conversation and slivers of light drifted up through the floor boards where I found a trapdoor. I opened it to discover a spiral staircase, disappearing into darkness. The faraway voices condensed into words, and I eavesdropped. I recognized the voices of Lisabetta and Leonardo as splashes of conversation and questions rippling in a pond.

"I'm still a mother," she said.

"And always my sister. *Mi amore*, your daughter, she is in paradise, yes? She could not stay. You are young. There will be other children. But you've wanted to be an artist ever since I brought you your first paper and chalk. Come. Eat to please me. Time will heal these terrible days. You are not alone. I will never leave you."

I knew brotherly love. I wanted to heal Lisabetta's pain. I knew compassion.

The ceiling evaporated to a starry sky on a warm night. I rose into the air, towed by a helium balloon shaped like a swan. I knew happiness. My awareness filled the sky like fireworks and one spark of me was carried back to earth as a newborn by the Nike of Samothrace. We were accompanied by angels, each one holding an umbrella parachute in a Magritte painting, descending light as raindrops.

Nike touched down, one toe extended from the flappings of her wild drapery, her wings beating loud as helicopter blades.

I looked into her eyes as she cast a thriving spell over my cradle, and knew the love of a mother.

The dreamtime spun time larger, the way it does, until I was a teenager visiting my uncle's studio to flirt with Cecco, and then I was a young woman of twenty, listening to Leonard Cohen reciting his poems in hypnotic a Capella waves. His voice was a kite dipped in honey. Every so often it lifted into song but bumped back to earth as the spoken word too heavy to fly.

I was buoyant, treading water, protected by twin lions, Leonard and Leonardo, but as hard as I tried, I couldn't invoke the Nike's face.

The arms of May rain isolated me like the steady stream of water in my bathroom shower – a glass cubicle where I stood for hours, comforted inside a warm aquarium tipped on its side, happily shaped like Dr. Who's police box.

I lay under the skylight as the constellations snapped and sizzled with faraway hydrogen. Safe on planet Delphi, I revisited her last weekend of life. It appeared slowly in fragments. Present rain mingled with memory rain. I was drenched in poetry, softened by night magic, enough to withstand the confusion of reality and illusion in 2014.

Two umbrellas were already dripping, taking up space in the hall.

Michelangelo's ceiling and Monet's water lilies skittered like bright sails, their nails scratching the floor, trying to grab Brillo.

A large silk bowl with a handle wasn't compatible with a small furry animal no matter how wily. The two hemispheres annoyed Brillo, crowding out his food bowls, so Delphi moved them to higher ground.

Laughter drifted from the ceiling and Brillo clung to her knees, unyielding, solid as a garden statue, affixed with sharp claws, continually flexing into her skin for the traction he anticipated to launch himself to freedom.

Delphi vowed to Brillo they would have a sun porch exclusively for wet umbrellas when they were rich. Sometime after PIAT's promised bonus when she'd pinned the provenance of an elusive Leonardo to their gallery wall.

She wanted to be buried in her kitchen, under the checkerboard squares of black and white linoleum that mirrored

Brunelleschi's marble floors in the cathedral of *Santa Maria del Fiore*. She knew exactly where. It was under the kitchen table by the window, where no-one could 'walk all over her'.

Living in Victoria gave Delphi the freedom to roam. She discovered churches drawn towards them from a perverse desire to retrace her sad childhood. It was the stained-glass windows which drew her in first – flattened kaleidoscopes of colors, a memory that had given her solace. She loved to pretend they were the lenses of a telescope and she was in the crow's nest of a tall ship, scanning for land.

Delphi's aversion to religious orders never compromised her affinity for the ambiance of church interiors. The feng shui of holy architecture relieved her mind of stress as long as she ignored the horrendous bumpf of plaster agony and ogling gargoyles. She stayed for the flickering candles and the smell of beeswax and the kaleidoscope windows, but mostly for the stone wings – the finger-like feathers that flared behind the angel sculptures like the halos of a peacock's tail. She believed in creativity rather than a creator. She believed in art. She believed in birds.

"You're a phoenix," Sphinx once said during a chess game. *"Phoenix checks peacock. Peacock takes phoenix. Play to win. Love is immortal."*

Delphi decided she would aspire to being a phoenix at least half the week where her tail feathers would flame across the sky in a fiery comet.

I missed Cecco. Memories of our old rendezvous at the Poseidon fountain were mine now. Somewhere in time he was fifty-two years longer in the grave. I attempted to call him down with a spell but he didn't come. Instead, I mapped our old times through Delphi's memories and kept his portrait foremost in my mind. Now and then I caught him with his head turned to look behind him as if he was listening. It would last a second until he rippled back, his calm blue eyes staring straight ahead, through me. I believed he was searching for the same new world as I.

Our romantic progress lived on in rain-or-shine pilgrimages. Walks under the rainforest canopy of British Columbia and through the fields of poppies in Lombardy which connected us like a constellation. We entwined minds from a great distance, and I enjoyed the sudden interruption in my circuits when I heard the peacocks calling my name.

I felt the beginnings of animation as a mild power surge. We were biding our time. I was falling in love.

*"Let your plans be dark
and impenetrable as night,
and when you move,
fall like a thunderbolt."*

SUN TZU

Natural Selection/chapter thirty-two

MAY 29, 2066

"Beware the ides of Summertime," Sphinx said. *"The living is too easy."*

I recorded more thoughts stored into the elephant stick worn around my neck.

I fantasized my patron saint was Saint Endorphin. I experienced a flash of abdominal pain followed by a natural rush of painkillers. I believe I let out a whoop. I knew pain and its sudden absence.

Sphinx was pleased and yet she sighed heavily. *"A taste of honey,"* she said.

We celebrated the surname of my father. "I am a WHO! A time lord's daughter," I bragged to her.

"You are a hatchling phoenix," Sphinx said.

I lived more cocooned. I had a theory that diving jump-started the emotions I sought but I needed further proof. I felt a responsive surge of warmth in my spine like sap rising to the spring equinox. A valve opened and closed in my chest like a rosebud.

Something big shifted. I'd fallen asleep. I stretched before my eyes opened but closed them again. A sunbeam lured me onto the floor and into day pyjamas of pale lime silk with magenta elephants. The catalyst of sugar and salt drew me into the kitchen where I spent an hour staring into cupboards of boxes and cans in wonder. Craziest of all, I salivated at the word lemon written on a label.

After hibernation comes the first breath. I remembered a different springtime in a month named merry and being a child with a book who wanted to live in a maze grown from peony bushes taller than a house.

Tomorrow I was prepped to scan for the best minutiae, cherry-picking artefacts at the end of the world. I would rather have picked flowers. I would rather have smelled the roses.

Sphinx coughed. *"The sun is high; the war of art rages,"* she said, and then she quoted Sun Tzu. *"The supreme art of war is to subdue the enemy without fighting."*

Some sensations remained as flickering candles. The word feel was an emotional link to circuits now flooding with more visual triggers and flushes of what I can only describe as breathlessness. I experienced moments of affectionate exchange and symptoms of melancholy. Sphinx was more active. She encircled me with energy rather than words as if she was spinning a web of protection around me. An aura of psychic heat percolated into neediness, generating a heightened degree of interest. I cared about who I was becoming. The word 'who' gained emotional weight. I was no longer a barren machine. I was a woman trapped inside one. A snake shedding her skin. Princess Cherry, daughter of Who.

Hamm called my psychic gifts superpowers, or cherry-picking or easy pickings, depending on his mood and the end results of a dive. Sphinx commented drily that the world was populated with superstitious puppets reading marked tarot cards.

Time was my oyster. I was a time lord's daughter, and Sun Tzu taught me to attack when Hamm was unprepared and to appear where he would least expect me.

"What would daddy do?" Sphinx chanted. *"Here comes the Sun."*

Out of Body/chapter thirty-three

VANCOUVER ISLAND
JUNE 1, 2066

I watched Phillip fidget, waiting in the hot seat like a student hauled in front of the school principal. I'd been in that chair, summoned by the toadying Doctor Mason aka Jarr, but I had no mechanisms, other than indifference, for reacting to intimidation.

Jarr sat behind his desk as he usually did, Napoleon nursing an ever-present tantrum. The incessant tapping of one toe belied his true nature which made him all the more threatening.

The office was oppressive for June; the weather mirrored Jarr's temperament. Storm clouds gathered inside and out, emotional and elemental. The air-conditioning whirred but it was stuffy enough even with the windows open to require the addition of a desktop fan. Limp air tried to stir some papers pinned under a souvenir snow globe from Florence.

Jarr slammed his fist on the table and bounced the pens in a metal cup. The snow inside the globe swirled around the tall wedding cake of the *Campanile,* Giotto's bell tower, as if disturbed from a breeze generated by the small fan, oscillating in high-pitched shudders beside the telephone.

Phillip appeared contrite, his gaze never lifting from the gold and onyx phoenix ring his uncle wore.

"There's a missing Leonardo at stake," Jarr said. "That's the pot of gold in case you've forgotten. I don't know what's got into you." His became more accusing. "You're sentimental. Just like your mother." His ballpoint pen clicked in Morse code. "Cherry's no more than a lab rat." The pen sent out a subliminal S.O.S. "If you've got cold feet, best not let Hamm hear of it."

Phillip squirmed deeper into his chair. Its leather squeaked like a lab rat.

Phillip's bedsit, in the old staff quarters building, was bright and minimalist as a lifestyle centerfold from a Swedish furniture catalogue – a stark showroom where no-one appeared to actually reside. I was drawn to the only sign of human inhabitance – an antique teddy bear sitting on a bookshelf next to a Magic Eight Ball. It was covered in patches of yellow fur worn threadbare. One ear was missing. Long ago, brown leather pads had been sewn onto its paws with large black stitches, and like all well-loved teddies its little black eyes revealed the presence of wisdom.

I recognized it as a relic of sentimental value and walked over to it, hands behind my back waiting for permission to touch.

"It was my mother's," Phillip said, examining his watch. "We should get started."

"I'm pretty sure you can't hypnotize an android," I said.

"I'm not. I'm regressing Delphi but if you get caught in the crossfire..." he smiled. "Then so be it."

Phillip hooked me to a monitor. His voice led me down a glass staircase as I slowly felt my way on bare feet. The glass felt warm and pleasant. A calm sea undulated below the clear steps, its surface covered in water lilies and lotus flowers.

Phillip's voice droned like a bee diving into flowers. It grew quiet when submerged and then, back in the air, it was more distinct. Then I too, was a bee, and followed him, eager for the hive.

"What is the first thing you remember?" he said.

"I'm lying naked on a thin sheet, covered in mucus, shivering from an open window," I said. "It's raining."

"Slowly," Phillip urged. "No need to gallop. Relax."

"I smell waves of fear from one of the midwives. Two nuns. My violet eyes upset Sister Honoria. She calls them purple. Witch's eyes she says."

"Were you afraid?"

"Sister Anne-Marie is more concerned I'm too quiet."

"You were probably in shock."

"There's a third face. Compassion. A female presence. She shushes me even though I'm not making a sound. Light shines around her long veil of silver hair."

"The Virgin Mary perhaps?"

"Sister Anne-Marie slaps the bottom of my feet and asks if she should I fetch a doctor."

"I mean, it would be normal to interpret a vision in a convent as a holy icon."

"Sister Honoria tells Sister Anne-Marie to get the priest. She says I am my mother's daughter and that only holy water will release the devil inside me."

Phillip's typing sounded like a bird tapping at the window.

"Sister Anne-Marie wants me to cry. She wraps me in a towel, and holds me over her shoulder, swings me to and fro, thumps my back. She's worried I'll catch my death. Red curtains flap beside the open window for the devil to escape. Sister Honoria uses the word, fly. She says it's better I die from a chill than wrestle the sins of my father. She says it was just as well my mother was... *taken*."

"You're safe now," Phillip said.

"I'm not safe. It's cold and dark."

"Sphinx is with you. It's safe to jump to the *last* thing you remember? She'll catch you."

I heard the slam of a file cabinet drawer. My thoughts were chilly things that traveled through the molecules of my body. I was me and not me. I raised my arm. It looked the same but I recognized the imposter the same way Brillo knew a catnip mouse wasn't a real mouse.

"I named my cat, Brillo," I said, "for his coarse fur which reminded me of a wire brush like the steel scouring pads one uses against frying pan dirt. Yesterday's surprise visit brought a canine interloper into our haven. His name was Mr. Bennett."

"No, tell me the very LAST thing you remember."

"Take your time," Sphinx said. *"Let the hours come."*

"I can't move. I'm a statue. I'm outside my stone body," I said. "I'm not me. I've been cornered by a storm with arms. Stung by a bee. I'm falling, then rising. Sizzling. My hand is on fire. I'm entering a monastery, serenaded by monks. Portraits of each monk as a babe in arms with their mother line a red-carpeted passageway that widens into the rooms of an art gallery.

"I pass the statue of the Victory. I'm in the Louvre. A sign with an arrow dangles from the Nike of Samothrace's wing. It reads: *crime scene. Salon des Estats, the 'Mona Lisa,' exhibit closed until further notice while under investigation.*

"The 'Mona Lisa' gazes down on me with compassion. All traces of amusement are gone. She tries to calm me. I hear a disembodied voice cry out, Mom, and the world turns to winter. I am a snowflake, falling – a crystal woman. My veins spread like the cracks on a glass window. I crave blankets and smell burning toast. I must go downstairs. My breakfast is ready and I can't keep my mother waiting."

Phillip's voice reverberated inside my head. "What happened next?"

"I wake up on a table, cold as a mortuary slab, surrounded by monks dressed in white robes. Dr. Who is asking me questions. I'm thrilled to be in the Tardis. But I've been... betrayed. There is no mistake because I sense death. Dr. Who pulls off his mask and there's a stranger underneath. Where's my father?

"I tell him I have to be home by six o'clock. The other monks laugh. They're faces are painted like clowns. They've left me alone. The circus has gone and I'm standing in an empty field littered with rubbish. No-one cares. She didn't save me. Why wouldn't she save me?"

The sound of monitor beeps woke me and Phillip hovered over me, his frantic eyes searching my face. For a moment I thought he was a prince about to kiss me.

"Let's stop for now," he said. "We can just chat normally."

I turned away from Phillip, cowering. I pushed my hands into my hair to hide my black fingernails, and experienced an android's version of hyperventilating. A loud hiss issued from my mouth. Phillip placed the teddy bear in my arms.

Delphi pushed an elevator button and I allowed the images to come.

"Giving up and acceptance are both forms of surrender," Sphinx said. *"Sink below in order to rise above."*

I wasn't sure if she was talking to me or Delphi. Personal impressions of a lost child were all too familiar. Images of being left behind came easy. It was always the chilling aftermath of a carnival or its backstage grit. I stood in an empty field blowing with refuse. A circus elephant screeched from Africa. Calliope music warbled underwater.

The sides of a circus tent, flapped. A cloud of brown cigar smoke hovered on the ceiling. Clowns removed their greasepaint in various stages of streaky white faces and melting eyeliner, bottles of gin lay on dressing tables amongst orange wigs.

And then the wigs and contorted faces of the asylum paraded by and I counted to a hundred to avert the cold terror.

Phillip's voice led me into the sunlight. "Tell me about your parents," he said.

I hugged the bear tight. I felt the hard straw that stuffed his body. "My mother wasn't insane. She never was. Her name was Sybil Sharpe. She died giving birth to me. She insisted her pregnancy had been otherworldly. She said she'd been impregnated by a ghostly lover and the child she carried was a goddess."

"Perhaps she was right."

"My father was a big question mark so it was appropriate I called him Dr. Who. I knitted him scarves and sent them to the BBC addressed to 'Dad' but he never answered.

"You sound angry. Are you angry?"

I stayed rigid, arms at my sides. "What color does my hair say?"

"I want you to sit up," he said, walking to the coffee maker.

I swung my legs to the floor. He poured two miniature cups and exchanged one of them for his teddy bear. "Try smelling this," he said.

He blew on his coffee and tested it with a sip. It was too hot and he pulled back from it, blowing some more. I sniffed at the scalding cup that was cold dead weight in my hands.

"Anything? I added cardamom."

I peered into the liquid. "If it's possible to read a cup of coffee, my fortune looks pretty dark," I said.

I spilled some of my fortune on the floor handing it back. Phillip stared thoughtfully at the black puddle but did nothing to clean it up. After a moment he raised his head. "Do you feel like spilling anything else?"

"No."

"Then I guess it's my turn," he said, handing back the teddy bear. "Tell the bear."

Holding it felt safe. I looked in its eyes and buried my face in its body. "All I wanted was a place to hide," I said. "I needed financial security, doing work I loved, without having to deal with people."

The clock on the wall ticked louder. So loud, I looked up. It had no hands.

"Tick tock," Sphinx said. *"Time hides its face."*

"I wanted my windswept cliffs and to roam like a will-o'-the-wisp at all hours but be assured of fresh groceries and gas for my car."

"You wanted to be spoiled."

"I wanted to be phosphorescent. I wanted to be a hinkypunk. I wanted a deadbolt on my front door. I wanted Monday to come."

Phillip typed on his laptop and read aloud: Hinkypunk – a sprite, impossible to catch."

"I heard discussions about living under the umbrella of autism. Perhaps that inspired my obsession. Maybe I'm from another planet."

Phillip choked on his coffee. "Wow. An alien abduction would explain a lot."

I covered my face with my hands and stifled a groan.

He apologized. "Sorry, I don't mean to trivialize your beginnings. But it makes sense when you think about it."

I changed the subject fast. "My friend, Phoebe Jenkins, was a charming trickster. I was four and she was eight when I first saw her turn a clock inside-out. She broke some of the laws of physics and outwitted several more. I even believed she could bring the dead back to life. I thought she might bring back my mother."

Flash. A vision of Jenks stares from the back window of a moving car. The road stretches straight, on the forever of a mud-flat prairie, and I fancy I can still see her eyes even when the vehicle is a dot on the horizon.

Phillip tapped my arm four times. "What did you just see?"

"My driver's license. A finger pointing to a place for my signature. I loved highway driving. I kept the windows down; it was like running at 80 mph."

"Anything else?"

"Jenks' face. She was my only friend. The last time I saw her she was eighteen. She defied convention and gravity. Knowing her changed everything; losing her made me crazy. I faced being fostered out with the beak of a pterodactyl ready to rip out throats and eat hearts raw, still alive and beating. I don't recall taking a driving test."

Phillip spoke towards the teddy bear. "Miss Jenkins ran away after you'd been fostered out to PIAT."

"Jenks took care of me. She said she was my guardian angel. She taught me the power of four. She gave me four wishes. "I don't remember what I wished."

"Right now my plans are wobbly." *Flash.* "I just saw a bowl of green Jell-O with pieces of suspended fruit that morphed into a lava lamp. What do you suppose *that* means?"

Phillip hung his head and whispered to the floor. "That you're a strange woman."

"Thank you," I said. "Thank you Sigmund Freud."

Phillip moved to the bookcase and selected a book with a red spine from the shelf. A yellow sticky note projected from its pages and he read from the marked spot. "It says here, I can learn a lot from asking what kind of tree you think you are."

He rolled the 'Magic 8 Ball' towards me as if I was the head-pin in a bowling lane, and I caught it with my foot.

He flipped a page, read another line, and looked up. "So, my little Medusa... what kind of tree *are* you?"

I checked my fingers hadn't turned to snakes. "Ah! An almost sane question for a change. You mean what kind of *bird* am I?"

"Okay, birds work too."

I gave him the stink-eye. "Today I'm a flock of seabirds caught in a net."

"I wasn't being disrespectful."

"That's okay. Insight arrives on a need to know basis. Everyone lands in the Bermuda Triangle at least once."

Phillip reached for the bear and stared into its eyes. "His name is Prince Bertie," he said. "I used to think he could talk but not like those toys with rings that make them say things. Humans ask the 'why am I here?' question, early on even though we know we're not going to like the answer. We pull the ring in the back of God's neck knowing there are profoundly limited answers, but we pull it anyway in case there's a surprise."

He handed me the 'Magic 8 Ball' and I shook it several times to be sure. "Signs point to yes... don't count on it... outlook not so good... you may rely on it... or not."

Phillip grabbed it and took a turn. "Ask again later. That one always works for me," he said. "When did you become so philosophical?"

I took the ball and sat it back on the shelf next to Bertie. "When did you become a psychiatrist?"

He sighed at the bear and straightened its good ear, pretending to think. "The day I met you."

"Confucius say, *answer to all question in center of maze.*" He sighed again. "Ah, so. But so is the Minotaur."

"People get that wrong," I said. "He looks fierce but he's a lamb." I had a snippet déjà vu of a dream with Sphinx waking Delphi. Something about a waxwing and a bear. "What kind of bird are *you*, Phillip?"

"You said I was a pelican."

"If home is where the heart is I may not have one?"

Phillip took my hand. "C'mon, I'll walk you *home,* dodo."

The gesture shook me. It had been done without intimacy but it evoked a distant tenderness that was important, an emotion twice-removed. I envisaged him stroking my fingers, and brushing my cheek. *Flash.* I saw a white pelican with blood-soaked feathers.

Medusa was a woman scorned, but Phillip's reference had been an endearment, and that too made me quake inside as if I were an embryo hearing the sound of a loving voice.

Had Phillip noticed the color of my hair? He hadn't commented, and that thought dampened the lightness I felt returning.

Phillip wasn't noticing me anymore. At least, not as much. But I was heartened that it disturbed me. Could it be I was learning more about being human from being an android?

Cecco was somewhere in that awkward place of near and far, five-hundred-years away. He had always been with Delphi, and now he was with me.

From the window overlooking the garden, small patches of pastel colors formed into hundreds of clouds the size of tennis balls. I *saw* their scent. Delighted, I raced downstairs and batted them around until they formed one large cloud, hovering overhead like a Monet painting.

I watered my 'tennis' flowers, mulling over the recent conversation. I could feel my hair rippling in waves. It was like living under a restless sea. Water splashed like clear varnish over the peonies trapped under tomato cages, pinned there against an open invitation to the local deer by force of habit. Although none were likely to leap over PIAT's fences.

I needed to go home for a while but tonight, nowhere was home.

That Bermuda triangulation thing I'd said to Phillip was a copout. It felt more like a *strangulation* of fate, so why had I played devil's advocate? Maybe it was to hear my plan out loud or to hear the Minotaur bleating which way to go. Leonardo's 'out in the open in plain sight' applied to signposts in an eight ball, too. How often had Delphi denied the message when her heart begged the obvious?

"Mint sauce," Sphinx said. *"String bean theory."*

My idyllic view of fish in the sky was my private solace, and if it rained starfish I had a designer shield to protect me. I felt myself open like an umbrella. A slow pressure in my spine pushed my life-force upwards and I expanded vast as the sky over PIAT's settlement of stray buildings.

"*Stay open, Lambkin,*" Sphinx said.

Back home, I made ritual tea. Automaton virtual tea. I studied the teapot until it grew cold. It made me think of comfort and home-fires and lights left in windows.

Florence paced across the back of the sofa like a patrolling sentry, and I taught her to say, Minotaur.

In the fifth stage of life,
'Man' thinks he has acquired wisdom
through the many experiences he has had in life,
and is likely to impart it.
He has reached a stage
where he has gained prosperity and social status.
He becomes vain
and begins to enjoy the finer things of life.

'The seven stages of man'
adapted from the 'Zodiacus Vitae'

– by PALINGENIUS, 12th century

Time Out/chapter thirty-four

JUNE 4, 2066

"Mom? Can we get a dog?" George asked while I was still on the threshold of the common room. He stood surrounded by a hodge-podge arrangement of comfy armchairs, and threw another log on the roaring hearth-fire.

"Why not a teddy bear?" I said. "Or a real bear. They're right outside."

"It's nippy for June," Lewis said, trying to be helpful. "Quick. Close the door."

Joanna straggled into the room, yawning, and immediately headed for the fire, her arms outstretched like a zombie. She looked from the fire to me, and inclined her head for me to join her.

I shook my head. "Delphi's got a wee problem with fire this morning," I said.

"She's going to have to chill when you're working. No pun intended."

I took the chair facing the window and stared at the periphery fence. "I ignore her like background static. Even dead people need time to face their problems," I said.

George brushed flakes of bark from his hands. "But Delphi's not dead."

I didn't react although I resented his remark. He represented the technical side of art and technology. "Her mind is alive; I'm the one living. Who's going to make the coffee?"

Bill's voice surprised me from a wing chair facing the fire. "It's made."

"Didn't see you there," I said.

He looked embarrassed. "I guess you can't smell coffee."

"Good guess." I cleared my throat. "Gather round. We need some time out," I said. "I'm giving you homework. Nothing strenuous, but it's due by the end of the day."

"So no pressure, then," Lewis said.

"God I hated school," George said, patting Bill on the head. "Unlike *some*."

"I want all of you to shop online for a designer umbrella that tells me something about you. I told Hamm it was an IQ test, so he thinks it's deep and psychological. He sanctioned it immediately."

Lewis flopped into a chair. "And is it?"

I gave him my steely eyes. "Of course it is."

Lewis and George exchanged a look of desperation. "Nothing to worry about then," George said.

Bill grinned and said "Coolio."

Joanna sighed and paid extra attention to her shoes.

"Bonus marks for ingenuity," I said. "This is art, not science."

"And *is* it psychological?" George asked.

"It's so you don't get wet, you idiot," Bill said. "Think testosterone rain."

"See, it's already more psychological than you think," I said. "Be the umbrella. Show me who you are. Better yet, show me who you want to be."

When the umbrellas arrived, I was touched by how much they wanted to please me. George and Lewis staged a sword fight with their umbrellas closed. Clear bowls with sword replica handles. George's was an ingenious design of a Star Wars light sabre that emanated a green glow at the press of a switch. Lewis brandished the sword 'El Druin,' of his favorite computer game entity, the archangel Tyrael from 'Diablo.'

Joanna strolled in twirling her choice like a coquette. It was imprinted with the crazed skull-like face of 'the scream' by Edvard Munch. "I can be a tad manic," she said by way of explanation. But

Bill's was the best. His was a map of the northern hemisphere of the world split at the equator. "It's the Globe Theatre," he announced.

Hamm called me to his office. He looked like a kid on Christmas morning. "I got you something," he said. "A present."

He glanced up at my hair, and his smile froze. "Please sit."

I drummed my fingers on his elegant desk and waited, staring at the print of Raphael's 'Sistine Madonna' behind him – a tender presentation of a mother and child. I probed it for a sign. "Well," I said to it, "you've seen everything that goes on in here from 'on-high'. Anything to report?" It said nothing. "Cat got your tongue? Come on what does he want?" Silence. "Fine. Be his saintly mother, then. Protect him all you want. I'm not turning the other cheek. He's an atheist you know."

Hamm's frown deepened to a scowl as he watched my face. "This desk belonged to my father," he said. "It's very old."

My fingernails flashed like a rainbow keyboard practicing scales. He was nervous and embarrassed, two feelings I could do without navigating. My circuits spun like a roulette wheel. It was anyone's guess where it would stop. Anger, amusement, sadness. My fingers were a slot machine flashing a big win. I felt dizzy calculating the odds against winning.

"Three cherries," Sphinx said. *"Time to cash out."*

Her words stabilized to me. "I hope it's magic nail polish remover," I said to Hamm, hoping to sound flip.

He cleared his throat and a muscle twitched in his left eyelid. "I never expect wit from an android. It's always a surprise. Not entirely pleasant but there it is. You're a dark horse. An enigma."

"Androids don't expect presents, either," I said. "Who knew Delphi was a closet smartass."

He opened his closet. For an ugly nanosecond I thought he was going to say, voila! But he went shy and presented me with an unwrapped rolled umbrella and thrust it at me, pointy end first. "Here."

It was said gruffly, like a hesitant command.

"Whatever can it be?" I said. "An olive branch? Sir, you shouldn't have."

Hamm fiddled with the things on his desk, taking care to move all his pens parallel to his blotter. "I know you like cats and dogs, so... maybe open it outside. We don't want any bad luck."

I ignored him and opened it with a quick snap. "Androids aren't superstitious," I said.

It exploded in a sphere of black on white illustrations – a delightful print of miniature cats and dogs. I instantly approved but composed my enthusiasm in a blank expression.

"It's raining cats and dogs," he said. "Get it?"

"Thank you, Sir. I'll use it the next time it rains."

He looked out his window. "Looks like rain," he muttered to himself. *Flash.* I saw a pen and ink illustration of Piglet from 'House at Pooh Corner' with Pooh in a tree, disguised as a rain cloud. Looks like rain, he called to piglet, in a vain attempt to distract a hive of bees from their 'hunny.' Sheppard's artwork was one of Delphi's favorites. Why are you showing me this? I asked her.

"A bear of little brain will go to extreme lengths to get what he wants," she said. "No matter how silly he looks."

Hamm turned back from the window. "I used to like rain puddles when I was a kid."

"Christopher Robin is saying his prayers," Sphinx said. *"Pay attention. Give him what he wants."*

"Most kids like to get wet. Delphi did. I can see her here, in wellington boots, splashing around the fountain. What umbrella did you get yourself?" I asked.

"Mason chose Einstein's relativity equation printed on a red background. Not exactly art but the art of physics I suppose. He informs me that mathematics is the highest form of art."

"Leonardo would agree," I said. "And yours?"

"One of my favorite paintings," he said, pulling it from behind coats. He gestured the tip of the umbrella to the 'Sistine Madonna.' "Her." He eased it open gingerly as if his wife might jump out.

His awkwardness affected my hatred and I searched for something kind to say. Hamm's hands were busy arranging paper clips on the side of a magnetic cube. I felt sorry for him. I felt him fighting an emotion like a mass caught in his throat. Cordiality was a tough departure from his usual gruffness.

"You're very like your grandfather," I said.

"What?"

"Delphi knew him and your father, so I have her images on file."

"My grandfather scared the hell out of me."

"That's what I meant."

He looked pleased. "I scare you?"

"No sir. I can't feel fear. I register fear of you in others. Delphi was always afraid. You intimidate people. But that's good business."

He looked up with cruel eyes. "But I can't intimidate you. So why is your hair still out of control? You seem different these days. Tell Mason to run a diagnostic."

"Speaking of intimidation... you know, *not* smoking can be dangerous to your mental health," I said, pointing to his unlit cigar, posed in the crystal ashtray. "It's *your* life. Stand up to your wife."

I wasn't wholly prepared for our friendly moment to degrade so quickly. A drawbridge slammed down between us.

"Mind your own damn business," he barked. "Get back to work. And take that goddam umbrella with you."

I strolled out, taking my time, twirling the cat and dog umbrella over my shoulder. "In case you hadn't noticed, your damn business *is* my life."

I said it so calmly, I scared myself.

Cherry Blossom Time/chapter thirty-five

JUNE 9, 2066

I felt pleasure as a faint tingling in my abdomen, that abstraction from duty known as temporary happiness. A postcard vision informed me any moment I might expect an angel to deliver a bouquet of four leaf clovers. I was all too aware at any moment the general warmth would recede and I would process the event as a third party report. Fortunately, androids have the willpower of a terrier and I held on.

I couldn't be sure if I was sharing a purely Delphi experience or that of a character in a book. Reading Lewis Carroll gave me illustrations of a girl named Alice whose experiences were condensed into a rapid flow of falling, growing and shrinking, and talking to a rabbit preoccupied with time. Was she warning me? Alice was curious but becoming progressively alarmed. A lesson to remember.

Delphi's vicarious trip alongside Alice registered as a parallel adventure. It was difficult to separate the two. Delphi followed Alice through her looking glass, and I followed them both. While Alice felt curious, Delphi was enchanted. I saw Delphi as a girl of eight, smiling, head in her book, delighted by the thought of a Cheshire cat that evaporated and left its smile hanging in a tree.

The branches of the myrtle bush in the herb garden were alive with sparrows, their weight vibrating the branches into a shiver of perpetual motion. I imagined a smile superimposed over the leaves and measured my reaction.

The activity of the birds distracted me. I scattered seeds for them. Was it this act that stirred an odd sense of pleasure? Delphi was sitting closer to the surface of my skin. Enough to write subtitles of my own.

"See. You don't need me," she said.

"Morning old girl," I said to her. "I'm reading some of your books. Feeling through your feelings. What story would you read to Cecco? Time is of the essence."

It was Sphinx who answered. *"The Secret Garden,"* she offered. *"Perhaps a little too close to home."*

"No secrets today please, Sphinx. I'm studying. Seriously researching the subtleties of spontaneous pleasure."

She giggled. *"Suit yourself. Don't think of an elephant, then."*

I settled myself against the crumbling marble of the sundial to read a digital copy of 'The Secret Garden, occasionally glancing up to monitor the birds and tried to ignore the miniature elephant balancing on a branch.

"Close to home? How close?" I asked.

"It's about a lost orphaned girl in search of a family."

I set the reading tablet aside in the grass that no longer smelled sweet or even remotely green, and concentrated on the birds erratic hopping, wondering what was on their mind. What orders kept their collective birdbrains in such cheery agitation?

The stuff of Wonderland that entertained Delphi made me objectively reflective. I was trapped in a strange landscape where the whimsical spins of Lewis Carroll made as much sense as quantum physics. Confrontations with the Jabberwocky held a degree of street-cred survival, but it wandered off into silliness. Why had Delphi felt so inspired?

Delphi's terrible secret encroached like a slow infection. First a benign rash and then an itch with attitude. I saw an elephant scratching its head against a baobab tree.

"Delphi also loved Edward Gorey books," Sphinx said. *"Talk about mirrors."*

"Why send me an elephant, Sphinx?"

"Mothers never forget," she said.

I flipped open the lime plastic cover of my electronic note-pad and composed a telegram to Delphi: Show me. Tell me. Let me help you. Soon – best regards, me

"Something old, something new, something buried, something blue." Sphinx muttered.

"What was Delphi first? A keen observer of people or an avid birdwatcher?"

Sphinx giggled. *"I forget."*

"My files show muddled anthropology. A simultaneous game of snap with flash cards."

"Snap," Sphinx said. *"Something unearthed."*

I was still breaking bread with the sparrows when I tried to access the scent of grass by force. A delayed response delivered a weak variation somewhere between green tea and diluted fabric softener.

I dressed in exotically-casual clothes, incongruous with futuristic fashion statements. In an environment of suits and lab coats, I stuck out like a nun wearing red nail polish.

Today, my long legs, crossed at the ankles, were encased in Chinese pyjamas, coral this time, printed with silver birds on branches of orange blossoms. I attributed this to Hamm's guilty concession for PIAT's corruption of my olfactory circuits which supplied a less than stunning placebo of faded smells. I threw curve balls over Hamm's plate to test his swing. I intended whiplash.

One of Delphi's treasures were the perfumes Mdm. *Oiseau* bequeathed her. Memories naturally aligned to them and I felt robbed of their intensity even though a sharp rogue scent often triggered an ersatz sense of mechanical depression. Melancholy visited me as a locked black box with rays of pink light escaping from the keyhole.

PIAT was forever tinkering with my sensory levels. There were only two distinct entities in the world, the generic *they*, against the specific *me*, and an odd sense of self which fluctuated between I, me, and a vague notion of a disembodied *her* who needed things. I felt non-local but ever-present. Sentient and drifting. Indifferent to relationship, yet drawn to Delphi, and on 'Chanel days,' to Cecco.

The fanciful thoughts of 'what if' that used to make Delphi 'curiouser and curiouser' were now poisoned by science. She had always been a loner but most days, lately, she abandoned herself. She wanted to go home. She envied Dorothy from Oz. She wanted a pair of magic red shoes. She still lived on pipedreams.

I kept time by drifting in the nearest things to waking dreams and 'woke' to nightmares of repressed anger. I was the Mad Hatter's creature, a white rabbit out of time. Always trapped in time, a poetic take on second life; ironically, I was semi-immortal, invisible, and outside of time. The concept of hours mattered little; it was enough to know daylight from moonbeams. The *late* Delphi Sharpe was embalmed forever. Late as a hare with a stopped pocket watch.

I missed Brillo. But experiencing loss was a good sign. I often heard him crying at my window or felt him pawing my face in reflective moments. The thought of him prompted me to type furiously, and I highlighted a new telegram in acid yellow stripes:

Dear Delphi - You are invited. Tea party. Poseidon fountain. Come as you wish you were. Time sensitive. BYOS. Bottoms up – forever yours, the white rabbit.

"An important date," Sphinx said. *"Space odyssey time. Bear spray at forty paces."*

"I feel transparent even when I'm not diving," I said.

"What's BYOS?"

"Bring Your Own Sugar," I said. "It helps to be 'mad'."

Delphi's rescue had been ghoulish, having been fast-tracked for death with greedy designs on her special qualities for materialistic gain. She'd had her ten-minute-fame species window and died, and then I evolved. A selective team of surgeons categorized their work as compassionate recovery under the umbrella of their Hippocratic oath. Sphinx called it the grisly revival where medical ethics crossed the boundaries of morality and entered the murky limbo between medical advancement and dignity. Delphi called it Frankenstein voodoo.

The last thing the scientists overruling a team of doctors wanted was to dip Delphi's brain into the noxious River Styx of embalming fluid. Posthumous value required her memories intact. Between us we held a vast bank of memories necessary to probe the un-probe-able.

"There's too many bears when you live in the Styx," Sphinx said. *"Three is enough. Three is just right."*

Brainwashed was an appropriate description to use because Delphi's brain was meticulously cleansed and preserved. She was a state of the art project, but happily, the brain being a contrary organ, was still eons away from revealing all its mysteries. Ironically, that was my saving grace.

When Delphi was alive people called her a mystery. PIAT's employees referred to her as 'The Brain' and a freak of nature. She was a savant, rolled early into a girl who needed love as much as anyone. Something big derailed her. Lately all I got were images of guilt and a golden shovel dripping with blood.

In direct response to my thoughts I received a visual telegram.

Dear Cherry – it rains every day here. I'm having a costume party. BYOF – as ever, D. I turned it over to find a picture of a woman pilgrim wearing ashes on her forehead.

"BYOF?"

"Bring Your Own Feathers," Sphinx said.

Joanna and I went for a walk to christen our new umbrellas. She, under her insane 'Scream' and I, under my new 'Mona Lisa.' I also carried the umbrella Hamm gave me, wielding it like a golf club at rocks in our path.

Joanna grabbed it from my hands after I'd thwacked the fourth rock. "I thought you *liked* umbrellas," she said.

"I told Hamm I'd use it the next time it rained."

"Well, I thought you would love it, so excuse me."

"You picked it?"

"I CHERRY-picked it!" She wiped the wood handle to smooth any scratches. "Hamm couldn't pick his own nose. He told me to choose one to you *from* him. I believe it's called employee morale."

"No, it's called manipulation. It's business chess."

"You never give him an inch."

I ripped the umbrella from her and gently whacked her over the head with the silk end. "Joanna, that man *takes* whatever he wants. No-one *gives* him anything. But I do love the umbrella. I was annoyed that I couldn't use it, and now I can."

Joanna glared at me and did a double-take. "What are you thinking? You look... sort of gone."

June 13th. The control room at noon was as homey and understated as any other day – our concentrated ley line where we rehearsed into a single well-oiled android. A plate of post-lunch cupcakes and danish waited on a tea trolley with a pot of coffee and five mugs.

I sat in my captain's chair, swiveling abstractedly. George was on all fours tidying computer cables with an entire cupcake crammed into his mouth. Lewis tilted the angle of a computer screen across the room.

Phillip was on duty, rechecking tomorrow's procedure on the clipboard which seemed to be a permanent extension of his arm. I watched him put 3-DP through its paces. "I can't believe you're nervous," he said, ticking a box on his list. "Don't let Hamm know."

George responded with a muffled mmmmpf sound. Lewis spoke for him. "Hamm already knows."

"I'm not nervous; I'm conflicted," I said to Phillip. "Tomorrow's a big day for Hamm, so why wouldn't he humor me? It's illogical."

Lewis shouted to Joanna in the next room, checking the sound levels. "Do you copy?"... "I do," she called back.

"My programs have collided with Hamm on every intersection between here and the fifteenth-century."

Phillip patted me on the shoulder and spun my chair 30 degrees. "Been there."

"He's a miserable bastard. He usually treats me like..."

"Like me?" Phillip said.

"Like a two-headed freak show. And yet the other day he showed me some undue consideration."

"Okay," he said. "So *not* like me."

I watched my fingernails ripple into yellow. "One moment he was a good guy and then he had this tantrum."

"You're obviously skipping something between those two states. Other than Mrs. Miserable Bastard, he's not used to gumption."

"It was like watching the rejection of a heart transplant."

Phillip spoke to his clipboard, a furrow growing between his eyes. "Don't look at me. Hamm's humanity is a rare UFO sighting. An unidentified objective,"

"What's the f stand for?"

He looked up and winked at me. "Phillip," he said.

Oddly, his eye twitch struck me as sexual rather than cheeky. Interesting tingle in the solar plexus, and gone as fast as it appeared. "I'm about to drop into one of the most obscene moments in the history of art," I said. "In this, how shall I call it? A mood?"

"Confusion is a big deal. Feel the burn. Don't waste it. You can't take it out on Savonarola, he's only a phantom priest. Save it for Hamm."

"Only! That *phantom* burned Botticelli's paintings and turned him into a religious robot."

"What can I say? History is ironic," Phillip said with a shrug meant to encompass the enormity of man's incapacity to accept a meaningful coincidence.

"Histrionics are moronic," Sphinx said. *"Do the math."*

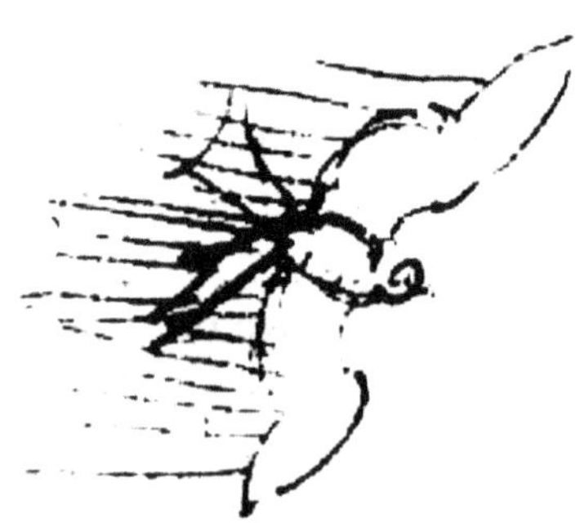

Distant Lives

*"If your enemy is secure at all points,
be prepared for him.
If he is in superior strength, evade him.
If your opponent is temperamental,
seek to irritate him.
Pretend to be weak,
that he may grow arrogant."*

SUN TZU

Savvy/chapter thirty-six

JUNE 14, 2066

*

FLORENCE
February 7 – 1497

I've heard of LA smog and the pea soup fogs of old London, but Florence in 1497 had its own atmosphere of grey doom. The air swirled in a tantrum of bone-dry snow. The ghosts of communion wafers rained down in lazy black flakes, landing in soft unstable drifts of tissue paper.

I saw a child kick them with bare feet, only to be reprimanded by an old woman. Playfulness was a stranger here. Only a child would find the death of art and beauty entertaining.

A slight drizzle weighted the piles into oily puddles like the grey slush of paper mills. But the rain never gained strength and the continuing storm of black leaves absorbed moisture from the air until they were the consistency of porridge. Oddly, a childhood illustration of Christopher Robin and Pooh walking under an umbrella flashed in my mind and I recalled the freedom of stomping through water in wellington boots.

Florence was a city twitching with restless faith syndrome. Citizens tried to sleep after the harsh days of keeping up appearances. They stoked safer fires back in their homes where God was so recently uninvited.

It was the winter of discontent for Florence, especially Sandro Botticelli.

I was sent to visit Girolamo Savonarola, the fanatic Dominican, killer of art, arsonist extraordinaire, perpetrator of the vanity fire. Delphi hated him big time so I hoped to experience a glimmer of irritation.

Ironically, when viewing Savonarola's portrait, the expression 'he's no oil painting' came to mind. It was easy to separate him from Delphi's ideal, Father de Briccasart – a captivating memory from a bittersweet television romance imprinted strongly on her psyche of a tall priest gliding like a black swan over the dust of the Australian outback. I gathered 'The Thorn Birds' had been influential in Delphi's romantic obsessions of unrequited love and a potential happy-ever-after-with Cecco. She must have been brainwashed.

Savonarola was an ugly man. There was nothing romantic about his slavering dementia. He was an awkward foreman shouting abusive orders – a fallen angel with bleeding eyes. I imagined his forked tail trailing after him, leaving tracks in the dust like a snake. I visualized him burning at the stake, as I knew he would a year later.

Had he screamed in agony, reaching in vain, like Michelangelo's Adam, for the God of Sistine ceiling? I hoped he'd called for his mother who never came. That is, if he ever *had* a mother.

"I don't have to go do I? Delphi whined."

I lifted my right hand in a wave, the signal for Lewis to run the 'Dr. Who' music and count off sixteen seconds before George pressed enter. I closed my eyes and counted along silently, visualizing a Time Lord wearing a long striped scarf, emerging from a blue police box in the *Piazza del Signoria*.

George set me down in the center of the piazza. I stood immobilized until my feet materialized on cobbled pavement. My initial report was for Hamm's benefit. My words *Florence is on time* were no doubt as memorable as *'one small step for mankind.'* Pantomime extras milled about with the general stage direction to 'look busy.' Stage hands drove ox carts filled with the booty of Florentine sinners.

It was predawn. Stars were bleaching out, still waivered in a sky turned silky mauve. The west side of the campanile was in shadow, painted into sharp silhouette like a cardboard cut-out castle propped up by wooden beams.

Large statues mounted on plinths dwarfed the people below who were depositing loads of cut logs and small whole trees into heaps at regular intervals. Other men raked them into an unbroken chain like a street barricade in a warzone.

The dynamics of a round bonfire would never have accepted the collected loot of Florence. She'd been search-stripped of pagan art and any luxuries contributing to the general corruption of a population famous for its allegiance to lust and eroticism.

A convoy of carts brought furniture and mirrors, bedposts carved with drunken fauns and grapevines, several columns of buxom caryatids, and gilded chairs, to be woven into a mesh of impiety as wooden arms and legs akimbo locked into a structure as unattractive as a twentieth-century sculpture of welded hodgepodge.

A man carried several paintings under his arm. He strode peering neither right nor left, eyes glazed. The jewel-like paintings told me he was the artist, Sandro Botticelli. I studied the angles of vision from the point of view of every pair of eyes in alignment to each painting and calculated the least invasive co-ordinates for flawless capture. No need, the populace were off their heads in prayer.

On my fanciful horizon, the ghost of a twin Vesuvius grumbled in her sleep. When it faded I envisioned a fire dragon guarding a salt mine of crusade loot gleaming in the light of an oil lamp.

A voice shouted to step back and the crowds parted for the friar-bully, himself. Savonarola spread his arms before the blaze and issued a prayer of salvation. The populace crossed themselves, casting their eyes down, away from heaven with their own mutterings of contrition. The air hummed with hollow echoes of repenting. Savonarola's head remained stationary but his reptilian eyes darted in every direction, calculating, assessing, noting the holes in the pyre, licking the scene like the tongue of a snake.

Flash. A scene of Delphi staring at a rattletrap fire escape, glowing with heat. *Dread.* She was poised with black smoke pushing her out of a window. *Terror.*

I felt Delphi's stomach churn. She'd stayed after all. "Bravo," I called out to her. And then I felt a sympathetic spasm inside me. *Flash.* An image of Delphi regurgitating hate in a projectile stream of maggots. I was filled with disgust at the waste of human poetry before me, sacrificed to fear and guilt, controlled through browbeating submission. It was a disgrace to the human desire for beauty.

I imagined the charred body of Savonarola tied to a stake, his blackened soul hovering above it, and I shuddered. The bright pain of Delphi's remembered burnt finger was enough to conjure the horrors of death from feet-first flames. A vision of a white-hot branding iron caused me to pause and restart my program. Being burned alive was a cruel torture only the corrupt mind of a human fixated on hell could devise. But then, hadn't Dr. Guillotine suffered his demise from his own invention?

Delphi screamed. I called after her. "Think of it as a movie," but she was gone.

The wisest citizens were indoors pretending it was an ordinary day, saying louder prayers than usual, but keeping out of God's way. No need to show their emotions in the open. All onlookers were recorded as were their reactions, be it anguish or celebrating their liberation from side-stepping wrath. It was the one time Leonardo's advice to hide in the open, backfired. Fired. Back in time.

The sound of crackling wood and exploding glass startled the horses nearest me. Bursts of brown smoke belched into the sky, turning it yellow. The humans on the scene were subdued, considering the lurid setting before them as jewels cracked and gold melted onto the gaming boards, dripping through the slats of charred wood like honey. By all religious accounts, God would be pleased at the sacrifice of such riches.

Savonarola's army of street-smart boys brought more carts and fed the fire with musical instruments, bottles of scent, and other fineries prejudged as indecent displays of vanity, lewd décor, and vulgarities of ostentatious wealth. Savonarola's heart was dead weight.

Somehow the chaos in the piazza was meant to purify the filthy doings of the citizens. I was curious as to the emotions behind the shuttered windows but more intent on the sadness watching a *'Visitation'* and an *'Adoration'* of Botticelli's succumb to the flames. A corner caught hold and a spark leapt onto a scene of a local Florentine beauty posing as 'Diana, the huntress,' where it hesitated for a moment before boring a small black hole in its lapis sky. A rivulet of fire quickly spread to the hunting dog at her side. Her beautiful face disappeared last. But the painting lamented. Botticelli spoke, hesitatingly at first and then he grew bolder. His words flew from his painting to issue a confession and a warning. "I was a puppet," he said, "and now I've sinned. Cut your ties to safety. The only security is an honest mind. Death is nothing. Art is immortal. I was a coward. The Medici owned me and then I sold my soul to the holy friar speaking for Mother Church. I let my children burn to save myself. May they forgive me."

A nun's wimple superimposed itself over Savonarola's cowl until the unmistakable face of Sister Honoria stared back at me. Both of them had been brainwashed, but their collective outrage rang above their displays of jealous piety. Their God had not been fair, so the only solace of redemption lay inside buildings that sheltered their kind – elite bands of damaged society who practiced a convenient form of violent faith.

I was pleased to be 'Diana's' savior. Botticelli's hearsay works would live again, reincarnated for the new world. Likely in a private collection, but hopefully, a museum where all could gaze on a new renaissance 'find' and wonder at its pristine condition considering six-hundred years had passed. I knew the syndicate would pass it forward as a painting cleaned with a thousand careful Q-tips, to explain its bright colors and fresh appearance. New techniques of restoration were cited as the latest state of the art forensics that swept away time. It was a miracle, they would announce. Found in a WWII cache in the salt mines of Altaussee, deep in the recesses of an Austrian mountain. The press release would hint of more masterpieces to come. Investigations were ongoing, they would report, towards further veins which could yet yield more priceless stolen art.

I felt smug knowing the truth, that they were correct in their false statement. If they searched as much as they boasted, they would find such caches hidden more diligently by the friends of art and a few who expected no return for their investments. Few did. Maps of their secret hoardings were intelligible scraps of paper still intact, folded into the pages of archived diaries like love letters. I could find the locations of each one and hold my tongue, and this power sustained delaying my revenge. One of the paintings told me of a French cavern that preserved art like the fountain of youth, shielded from old-age, in a heightened aura that hinted of mysticism. One day I would look for it. IF I had time.

How I knew was a mystery even to me, but I could see them. Both the maps like pressed roses and the flat shapes of paintings covered in linen, and the small plywood boxes stamped with black swastikas and meaningless numbers of a dead code. All filled with portable statues and jewels pried from gold settings. I could see them all, lingering at the edge of war, and I chose to stay quiet until such time or such persons arrived who championed art. In the meantime, the treasures were survivors of a mindset of greed that had only worsened with the infamous business of art and its dirty little affair with forgery.

I was wise to the lowest ways of the syndicate, and my secret knowledge could hasten their downfall. There was consolation when I withheld what PIAT wanted most. The image of a gold star and the words *well done* scribbled in red at the top of an imagined term paper confirmed as much.

In the meantime, I had infinite time on my hands and exploring the past gave my days purpose, as did the pending thrill of visiting my Uncle Leonardo again.

I had not made an enforceable deal with Hamm. Technically, I had agreed to nothing, but my situation demanded a plan. It could do no harm to celebrate what had become my fate. I didn't have the emotions to gloat. I recognized joy when images of food platters slipped through my unconscious in a gourmet smorgasbord of remembered delicacies.

The fires would have yielded hundreds of items but for the intervention of an immediate new assignment. And I was right.

Their greed eclipsed fire when PIAT got the scent of an unknown 'Leonardo.' It was a chance hint of something the syndicate craved above the remnants of a bad day in Florence. I was to abandon the 'Vanity Event' and proceed to a different year forthwith.

The fire's breath smouldered into the evening, painting the air into one of Leonardo's sfumato backgrounds of atmospheric smoke. Slowly, the Florentines slipped from the square to their houses. Their own home-fires banked in sympathy, fearful that God was watching them as they ate their bread and water in the dark.

By nightfall, the bonfire's mass had been smelted into a single misshapen corpse. Savonarola's army was allowed to sift through the warm debris of ash for nuggets of precious metal that had dripped through the matrix of logs to sell to the workshops of the gold and silversmiths.

Botticelli's message was clear. He lacked the courage of his convictions and played ostrich. His advice was to stand up to bullies at the risk of being burned. So, that's what I would do. I would do it in homage to a great artist and Sandro, his namesake crow that Delphi tamed so long ago.

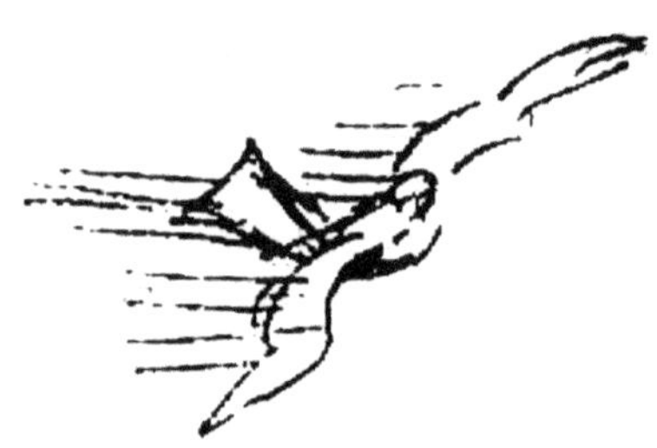

Damage Control/chapter thirty-seven

JUNE 17, 2066

*

FLORENCE
1476

Three days later, Bill deposited me on the corner of the Stinche prison, and the Via Ghibellina, and I walked in the wrong direction to Verrocchio's studio where Leonardo was finishing out his apprentice years, age twenty-two. I erred, not by mistake, but because a cat that looked like Brillo ran by and I had to follow. Fairy tale animals demand this. It soon disappeared behind a pile of rubbish, and I searched for a while before turning back. I had delayed my visit by half an hour. Not that I cared, time stood still, here. I had the magic touch.

Andrea Verrocchio's studio was more like a factory than the romantic image of artists, hands on hips, painting in a divine shaft of east light. Painting, sculpting marble, firing pottery, building furniture, carving frames, pouring bronze, architectural plans, designs for public entertainment, props for theatricals and parades, and creating fine gold jewelry and miniatures were disciplines that dominated a working art school with dozens of apprentices and hired slaves.

It was a house of projects that honeycombed back from the street in several buildings connected by alleyways. Boys aged from ten to sixteen, in stages of acquiring careers, clustered around senior apprentices and artisans in a pecking order from the most talented to the fetchers and carriers, and lastly, the women artists, subservient to all.

Lisabetta bridged the last two categories as her brother's assistant and one of a band of a dozen women relatives who cooked and cleaned, and in the case of women artists, like herself, attached their works to the males who were usually siblings or spouses.

Something new happened in the chaos. Delphi's voice rose clear above the din and smoke and her usual fragments of visual memory.

"Follow me," she said. "The painters have their own area of peace and quiet."

At first I thought it was Sphinx speaking plainly for the first time. But it was clear that Delphi had spent time here before and she was determined to be my escort. I took it as a truce and followed her voice past sweaty workers, hammering like demons, and the heat of open furnaces, and shelves lined with papers and jars, under ceilings lowered with hanging models and tools while trying to assimilate the bustling hive within a city that buzzed around me. The confusion manifested inside me as alternate waves of logic and excitement.

Delphi caught my mood. "Good," she said, "you're feeling a tiny percentage of what I experienced. I must be a good teacher."

I was no longer simply witnessing what Delphi had seen but hearing her original commentary. Her memories were interacting with my experience. She existed in a half-life, having been placed in suspended animation, brought up to speed. Never brain-dead, never purged from her shell, but brain-*altered*. We were closing the gap between us and no-one need know. Especially, her. Our collective emotion and logic collided in places, seeking mutual ground. I decided it would serve both of us and welcomed the next levels of unfolding.

"Go easy on me," I said. "Slow and steady wins the race. My circuits need time to adjust."

She showed me she understood with an image of a sleeping hare and a tortoise wearing Nike running shoes. "It's a race against erasure," she said. "Unless you can assimilate me in time, I will fade out. Sphinx warned me of this once. She said we were working on borrowed time."

"So, PIAT got unlucky. The survival of spirit IS possible," I said. "Move towards me."

We both felt a stab of sadness at Cecco's old words.

"I'm sorry," she said. "I have no control. Everything I suppressed is resurfacing stronger. In many ways I'm finding myself for the first time. I need to filter the impurities of fear and anger though your systems in order to stabilize."

So. She needed me. We were like two novice sailors at sea, balancing on a lurching ship, but where two against one should make us a more formidable foe, conflicting systems halved our effectiveness.

"So little time and yet such infinite possibilities," she said. Leonardo and Lisabetta are through here. Up these stairs. The best light is up high with no interruptions to the sky."

Peace and quiet turned out to be a central common room on the third floor where several students worked simultaneously on a large painted panel on three levels of scaffolding. Young boys painted backgrounds, more advanced students worked on the figures, and a woman handed them materials from a long trestle table. She shook her head, aghast at a clumsy interpretation of a tree.

An archway led from this relative calm to a corridor of half-dozen lesser cubicles, isolated so each senior artist could concentrate on a single portrait or other commission in some semblance of privacy.

Each room was oriented to east light from a large shuttered window and contained an easel and a sleeping pallet. They had no doors and as we slipped past I glanced into Spartan accommodations that reminded me of the nun's cells from Delphi's convent days. Sketches were pinned to walls that were also used for jotting down ideas, between hooks for clothes. Crude shelving was cluttered with objects and art supplies, and floors were littered with soiled paint rags and plates of uneaten food.

"Artists *can* be meticulous," Delphi commented. "Wait until you see Uncle's. He chose the room furthest from the others. He had first choice which rankled a few rivals."

I heard Leonardo's room before I saw it. Sounds emanated from its open door like a spring day. Birds chirped and light burst in from a skylight that spilled into the hall. He had the only door and his room was much larger than the others. The walls were painted blue with drawings of birds scattered over them amongst mathematic equations. My first reaction was Delphi's laughter but it caught in my throat, eclipsed by a scene of brother and sister in a state of some emotional distress.

Leonardo was easy to recognize from his self-portrait, aged twenty-four, in his 'Adoration of the Magi.'

"He's here if front of me," I said into my microphone. "I feel faint. It's highly unstable but wonderful. I am helium. Weightless. That's what it feels like."

Leonardo was seated in a carved wooden chair in a spotless room. Beside him was a table laid with a clean cloth that held a carafe of wine, a bowl of green apples, a worn candle, a pewter plate with a round cheese dipped in red wax and a paring knife. A slim wedge had been cut from the cheese and laid on its side, uneaten. A bowl of water and a cloth, several lemons, and a crystal sphere were placed on a smaller bench next to a pitcher of water covered with a strip of gauze and a vase of wild poppies.

Papers were stacked in neat bundles tied with twine in the corner. A cat slept on the bed made up with rich blankets. Fresh clothes were folded neatly on a second shelf. Birdcages filled with songbirds hung from the ceiling with other bird forms: paper wings and bleached skeletons; the model of a pyramid gently swayed into a stretched dried bat. A breeze entered the window, opened to an expanse of sky, played with the flame of the candle, and blew the edge of thin fabric draped over an easel.

Underneath the window was a long trestle table arranged in an unusually orderly manner. I was reminded of a surgical theatre with trays of instruments.

Leonardo wore a cream work shirt of soft-looking wool, cinched at the waist, tan breeches and matching short boots. He looked like prince charming, clean-shaven and handsome, blonde hair to his jawline, fine cheekbones, long slender fingers, and straight nose. Fingernails scrubbed clean, his hands woven together as if in prayer around a dead bird on his lap. As I watched he unclasped his hands and touched the bird, tenderly.

Hovering over him was a girl of sixteen wearing a green house dress, plying him with wine. I recognized her as a fair-haired 'Mona Lisa' before her figure became matronly. Lisabetta resembled her brother. Both were beautiful, lithe and blonde, tall with stunning blue eyes.

"What does he look like," Bill said. "What do you see?"

"A movie star. Prince Charming and a damsel in distress. A fairy tale."

"Details. Take your time. Four times four. Count to sixteen. Are you still good to go?"

"He's sitting down, in some kind of trance. His expression is radiant but his pupils are dilated. He's holding a dead swallow, petting it as if it's alive. Lisabetta is here. She is clearly anxious. She's trying to get his attention. He looks drugged. He looks as if he's under a spell."

"Are *you* under one? Are *you* okay?"

"I feel as if I'm hallucinating. Maybe I'm the one who's on drugs."

"Does he look autistic?" Phillip said.

"Yes and no. I mean he's concentrating but he seems absent... not *here*. Not in the room as it were. He's gone."

"Maybe he IS drugged."

"He's listening to his muse," Delphi said, admiration fairly percolating from her voice.

I spoke to the team. "He has that look but he's not drugged or drunk. I asked Sphinx. She said he was in Wonderland. I take that to mean otherworldly. Well, we knew he would be that."

"Look around for the portrait," Lewis said.

Lisabetta looked like an anxious mother. I got the impression this was not the first time she nursed her brother back from another world.

She kept a steadying hand on Leonardo's shoulder. The other clutched a small vial of red liquid. "Take a sip, *caro mio*," she whispered to him. "It will please me."

"I see. *Grazie*," Leonardo said, dreamily, folding and unfolding the swallow's wing. "So simple."

Lisabetta put down the wine, and plucked a feather from the bird. She held it to the candle until it caught. She made a face at the bitter smoke curling from it, and waved the smouldering feather under Leonardo's nose. He sneezed but his face remained rapturous, studying something she couldn't see.

Lisabetta shook Leonardo by the shoulders. "Leonardo! Please. Come back."

Leonardo continued to stare into space with glazed eyes.

Lisabetta took Leonardo's face in her hands. "He is here again? The angel? Tell me."

"I don't want him to go," Leonardo said, dreamily.

"Tell him you need to sleep."

"He is strapped to a silk wing. Pulleys and struts. Ropes and knots. Others join him in the sky. Each wing is a different color with numbers." He squinted and shaded his eyes. "I must remember the numbers. Quick. Bring me paper. I hear a lion roaring or is it a bee?"

I heard what Leonardo heard – the sound of a biplane's spluttering engine, the rapid ack ack of machinegun fire, and the droning of a monster bee, and I recognized a World War I aerial dogfight. Parachutes drifted lazily like dandelion seeds.

The portrait of Ginevra lay flat on a table that resembled a surgeon's tray. Pots of ground pigment and paint brushes in various stages of manufacture, lumps of red chalk in a wooden dish, long charcoal sticks in a pottery cup, jars of oil surrounded her as well as bricks of black wax and chunks of minerals, and folded rags, all arranged in an orderly manner. Colors from light to dark, brushes from delicate to fat. Knives for sharpening and cutting laid in order like a place setting at a formal dinner.

A small brazier burned in the corner near a shelf of leather portfolios spilling with drawings. A rose tunic and cape hung on a row of odd-shaped pegs made of horse vertebrae.

The portrait of Ginevra was an elegant rectangle shape with the dimensions I'd calculated, but it had a hole poked through Ginevra's delicate hands holding a bouquet of primroses.

"I'll have to return," I said into my microphone. The painting has the damage but it hasn't been trimmed."

"We can reset one week at a time and go from there," Bill said. "Nice work. Both of you."

I've always been drawn to two pieces of lost art more than any others: the missing head of the 'Nike of Samothrace' and the hands of Leonardo's portrait of 'Ginevra de Benci.'

Ginevra, the girl of the Junipers, stared through her observers, dispassionately enough to turn them to stone, and by the time her portrait surfaced, it had been severely truncated on three sides.

The effort to rebalance the new composition defiled Leonardo's love of symmetrical proportion and the laws of the divine golden section.

The painting gave up its secrets. I heard Leonardo complaining to his master Verrocchio when faced with its repair.

"It's bad but it must be returned quickly," Verrocchio said. "Bembo is furious with her, stupid girl."

Leonardo was angry. "If I cut here and here, the figure is balanced but it severs this tree in half."

"Better that than sever a connection with a rich customer and his loose tongue. Keep your patrons happy, Leonardo. Did I teach you nothing?"

"But it will look ugly. I refuse to..."

"Do it. There will be other commissions. Other portraits. More beautiful women to paint than Bembo's spoiled lover."

"I do not wish my name to be..."

"*Basta!* Leonardo, stop! You are young. An artist has to deal with moody patrons. They make it possible for you to paint. Your name is as it is. Do not worry about this new brother of yours. You still carry the da Vinci name. This is the real source of your anger. Not a portrait of a senseless girl. Stupido!"

"My father is ashamed of me."

"You have a duty to your father. Your father has a duty to *his* father. He moved on. He knows diplomacy. You are his son. Move on."

"To be successful one has to be a good liar."

The old man grunted and patted Leonardo on the back. "I have always known you to tell your lies in the open. It will go well for you as long as patrons are blind and vain."

"The tree, it will look as if it had been struck by lightning."

"Then paint it out," Verrocchio said.

"No. I will leave it. She deserves her portrait to be flawed," Leonardo said.

"Rich girls can throw fits. Their fathers and husbands placate them. We live outside their circle and smile. Never forget you need them. When you paint for them, lying becomes the art. You know this. *Bene.* It is good, yes?"

Flash. A vision of another tree, split during a thunderstorm in 2014, swam in front of Ginevra's tree. I heard Delphi cry out, help me Mom.

The obvious clue of tampering was well-documented. The ornate dedication on the reverse of the panel was positioned low to the bottom edge and off centre. A sloppy placement, unlikely of a perfectionist.

Leonardo had painted the words, '*virtutem forma decorat,*' *love adorns beauty* in a banner that hugged a single stem of Juniper, '*ginepro,*' overwhelmed in a floral embrace of dominating switches of laurel and palm leaf, choking it like the lying weed it was. History read it as a combination of admirable qualities, but it was three emblems that emblazoned carnal intent at the price of poetic license. Leonardo liked to have his jokes, and three lies were better than one.

Ginevra's cold mouth and hooded eyes showed contempt for Bernardo Bembo, her platonic toady lover. I felt her boredom whenever I placed my hand on the painting. She was not a lady to trifle with... not a lady at all. She was more of a waxwork figure that had to be kept chilled in order to survive the Tuscan heat.

This time both Ginevra and Leonardo's voices came from the portrait. She was fidgety, posing for him. Boredom made her cruel. I knew from history and Delphi that the young artist before Ginevra was in turmoil over his illegitimacy. This was common knowledge gleaned from Ginevra's regular spies. Piero da Vinci had no legitimate male heir and so Leonardo's family position was tenuous. Leonardo and Lisabetta were love children by his servant woman, Caterina, fostered out to be adopted by a local kiln worker. But as the childless years passed for Piero, Leonardo had been removed from his mother's care and returned to the fold as his father's last hope after a succession of barren wives.

"I heard you were…"

"Keep still."

"You will make me beautiful, yes?"

"I need to concentrate."

"I hear your stepmother is with child, yes?"

There was more. There was danger. Ginevra was laughing with another – a male voice filled with jealousy. Two predators wagered a bet and Leonardo was their prey. I looked into Ginevra's eyes but she looked away from me, sizing up Leonardo, searching for a claw hold. She read his innermost pain the way I read her intentions.

I heard the word anguish and saw Leonardo as a child hugging himself, sobbing, in a dark room.

Leonardo, at twenty-two, bled from an internal wound. "I am nothing. I have no family. I am a worthless painter. Verrocchio owns me. My father hates me." He breathed in spasms, his hand tightening on his brush.

The raw ache of abandonment gutted Delphi. She flinched at her own memories but Ginevra was excited. Blood was in the water and she circled Leonardo for sport. Scratching. Licking the blood and slashing a little deeper, closer for the kill.

Her accomplice in the shadows, laughed from their wager. I could hear him now and knew him for Verrocchio's catamite, Lorenzo, an apprentice six years younger than Leonardo.

Piero da Vinci's voice swept in and drowned out the laughter – an echo from years earlier. I saw Leonardo, a damaged fourteen-year-old boy handed over to a master by an angry father, "Maybe you can make something of him." And within the year, Verrocchio's humble declaration in awe of Leonardo's talent, "Leonardo is a genius. He teaches me, now," informing the painters en masse his star apprentice eclipsed all others. "From now on, Leonardo is your teacher," Verrocchio said. "Follow him. I am delighted to be free to concentrate on other things."

Follow him... follow me. This had been the source of Cecco's phrase.

And now, Ginevra prowled. Studio politics and her cruel streak weakened Leonardo, consumed by despair. *Escape, escape, escape.* I felt his urge to overturn the painting.

But Lisabetta's words surrounded him too. "You have me. We can go together. It's time to go. You are not alone. We will be well." She was incensed, a sister defending her vulnerable brother. A surrogate mother, strong enough to kill.

The painting continued to wage war. It was a chess board with two furious queens biting out of control. The victory was Lisabetta's but it was not a clean win. The portrait was taken hostage. It was tortured, but by attacking it, Ginevra caused herself irreparable harm.

Fifteenth-century games of courtly love played out in verbal gossip columns – the agony aunts of the day were poets spreading titillating prattles of Florentine *affairs*. By 'virtue' of wealth and privilege, Ginevra was a hot poem. Today, she'd be a celebrity hounded onto a magazine cover, but in her time she made it to a gilded frame that caught her expression like a caged bird.

I sensed the faded ghost of her *lover's* symbols, inscribed in a second banner beneath the surviving boldness of Ginevra's. I recognized it as Bembo's motto declaring his traits of moral virtue and honorable intellect.

Ginevra looked as frigid as the nights she kept control of her Niccolini marriage bed.

The entire public opera was fiction that provided the common rabble with months of calculated chivalry. Ginevra was no less than a debutante presented at court in a long pedigree of fake chastity.

Trial and error allowed me to see the portrait leave the studio, sent with an escort to the House of Niccolini in 1474. Ginevra read the accompanying goodbye note written with saccharine flair. It read: *lovers must pass but never the art of love.*

She attacked the painting with a dagger, repeatedly stabbing the flowers, and incredibly, missed the hands.

Ginevra's gilded room hung with embroidered tapestries that absorbed most of the daylight trying to enter from narrow windows. Reduced light caused her pockmarked skin to appear flawless from a reasonable distance. She was not the idealized porcelain doll that Leonardo portrayed. Her face was a pale mask, sweaty with rage.

She flung the blade aside, exhausted, weeping in hysterics. I heard it clatter to the marble floor. Her nurse stood aside quietly as Ginevra kicked a tantrum of a rich daddy's girl, bettered by her husband's enemies. She reminded me of an anorexic Nichole and I was amused that the magic letters of Niccolini parodied her name translating to 'a small Nichole.'

Juniper, the symbol of sorrow, pain, and loss, seemed a trite ironic considering Ginevra was a newlywed with issues of sexual indifference.

She was the antithesis of *sweet* sixteen, the same age as Lisabetta. And I heard the echo of Cecco's voice telling me something I should remember. *Salai had run away after one of his tempers, and it was rumored he had started the accidental fire that killed Lisabetta.*

I couldn't look at Lisabetta without picturing her fiery death. After the jumps of time it took to monitor the Ginevra panel, I was privy to the transformation of a woman to expectant mother as Lisabetta took on the glow and shape of a pregnant woman. Olive complexion flushed rosy against her threadbare work dress and her loose hair twisted into a single blonde braid.

'My brother loved birds too.' That's what the 'Mona Lisa' first said to Delphi when she was three. She was referring to Leonardo's penchant for buying caged birds in the old *mercato*, only to release them.

Lisabetta took the pose of the 'Mona Lisa' with her hands in her lap. A gold frame manifested about her, cropping her head and shoulders. Her face aged into maturity and froze into the famous painting. Obviously, many years had flown by. And then she spoke to me from the Monday Book.

Lisabetta hugged her memories. "Leonardo was wing mad," she said. "He had great admiration for flight. He believed bees and dragonflies were miracles. Mostly, he professed feathers had dignity. Sometimes he stayed up for days without sleep to work on a problem, and I had to spoon-feed him chicken soup. In some ways he was always a child and I his mother. He did not reason like other people. He felt empathy for the chickens, not because they'd been made into soup, but because they couldn't fly. He often said flapping was a poor substitute for flying, which he found out later to his peril."

"Not the easiest child to raise," I said.

The beautiful hands became agitated. Lisabetta plucked at her sleeves, and I experienced the Mona Lisa phenomenon. Her smile vanished. She was sad. Anxiety streamed from the painting. Her voice contained the fear of a mother for her child.

"I need your help," she said, weeping. "Protect my brother from Giangiacomo. Leonardo named him Salai, the little devil, for a reason. Please. My brother is a great artist but he is not strong. My death left him unprotected. He does not read people well. He trusts like a child."

"I promise you he has a faithful companion to mother him. He is not alone."

"Cecco is in danger too."

"Tell me."

"Cruelty is a skill. Only man has perfected the art of emotional torture. There are so many words for the small death: betrayal, abandonment, lies, cheating... jealousy. Salai poisoned Leonardo a little each day."

"And you?"

"He murdered me in a single callous moment."

With each new visit, Delphi's voice came in stronger. She must have known Leonardo had a rare elevated form of creative autism. It takes a savant to know a savant. Had she been there via imaginary time-travel, leap-frogging the years on Cecco's wings? It explained how she knew which room was his. She had shown me the way. Had she arrived, now, via creative reincarnation?

"Family traits," I heard Sphinx say. *"X's and whys."*

I was possessed to the point where Delphi's voice joined Sphinx and those of the paintings. It was one-way communication but at this rate I would soon be able to know things without the need for questions.

As an unlikely, fifteen-inch square, the reduced size made Ginevra's portrait look like the album cover of a long-playing record.

The offending panel was sawed in plain sight and discarded like an amputated limb. It required surveillance to its humiliating end, and I hoped there would be enough remaining of the exquisite hands, deftly painted by a young Leonardo finding his penchant for modelling delicate fingers.

I was in fear of the panel's deterioration reaching the state of damage non-retrievable as historical evidence, unworthy of showing in a gallery other than as a side note of human interest. Those lovely hands, gone. It was depressing.

From conversation snippets from the portrait I gathered it had been damaged in a *principessa* temper by Ginevra, and that somehow this amused Lisabetta, greatly.

By the third week, the strip had undergone punishing indignities but was still a survivor. Mercifully, it was turned upside down when it was used as a palette. And during the compressed weeks necessary to traipse after it, I indulged myself in playing truant in the streets outside the studio.

It was an ongoing protracted investigation, but that was how I met an emotion as old as life itself.

One of the studio's many tabbies prowling for feline entertainment, circled beneath a workbench groaning with books and the scent of cheese. But the sound of chirping across the room brought the cat's attention to an injured robin in a wicker cage on another tabletop. The cage balanced on a stack of oversize books. The cat, in hunter mode, climbed an adjacent shelf stuffed with documents and old bones. It hesitated, worked its front paws in readiness, and launched itself at the cage. Its back legs sent an avalanche of papers to the floor, amid screeches and the thump of heavy leather-bound volumes.

Loose pages drifted up as well as sideways, caught in the breeze kicked in from the open door, cascading across the terracotta tiles after they landed. A glorious drawing of a pregnant Madonna with an angel laid face-up on a splayed drift of manuscript sheets. Lisabetta retrieved it, and took it to the light. "Leonardo," she called out, holding it up for inspection. "Do you ever think of her?"

Leonardo waved his sister away, righting the cage, sedating the flapping of wings with a heel of bread. "Cara," he said over his shoulder, "I'm only sorry the painting was destroyed so you couldn't have her with you, always."

"A painting is no substitute for a living person," Lisabetta said.

The bird's wings would not be stilled and Leonardo settled them with his fingers. "Sometimes it has to be," he replied absent-mindedly, addressing the bird, cupping the robin in both hands.

Three things about their simple exchange alerted my radar. The Madonna and angel was a preliminary sketch for a completed painting, the painting had been destroyed, and Leonardo had delivered a prophecy. The latter gave me pause with a surge of static, the android equivalent of goosebumps. Leonardo had kept his painting of Lisabetta beside him after her death, talking with it as if it was his live sister.

Naturally, I decided I would follow the drawing to the day of its conception. The composition was a revelation. The angel's expression anticipated the 'Mona Lisa,' thirty years in the artist's future, by making eye contact with the viewer. It was an unheard of convention. The Madonna was introspective as always, but this angel looked away from her. She looked at Leonardo, and Leonardo gave us what he saw. I saw the angel through his eyes. For a brief moment I was inside the artist I'd come to study and his angel gazed directly at me. The drawing was silent and I wondered if it had anything to tell me.

I went to it and held my hands over the angel as if warming them by a fire. Its words burned me like a flame but my hands never left the surface. "Mamma save me," it cried.

I listened, thinking the angel-child was calling in religious ecstasy rather than anguish, but her voice soon changed to a plea for help, and I realized her words were not meant for the Madonna. She was addressing me.

I told no-one about the 'newborn.' But hanging around the Ginevra project gave me time to investigate. It didn't take long to discover the day of the sketch was less than two years prior, in 1474, and that the painting had taken over a year to complete. Leonardo said it was destroyed. I intended to find out how, but more importantly, how I could retrieve it. For now, the angel and I held our secret.

"I'm here," Sphinx whispered. *"In case you forgot. And so is Delphi."*

"Then it's a pact," I replied. Four is Delphi's favorite number.

A few days later, I had a premonition.

"I've had an inkling," I said to Sphinx, purposely starting out slowly. "I saw a key unlocking a door. I heard a baby crying behind it."

"Slow down Lambkin."

"It would be a breakthrough," I said. "Surely the baby crying is the new painting."

"The START of a breakthrough," she corrected.

"I must change faster," I insisted. "I need to quantum leap."

Sphinx was adamant. *"Sorry, no. If anything you must slow down. Let your brain catch up to your heart."*

She would not be diverted. Neither would I... but then I met the angel.

Angels Among Us/chapter thirty-eight

JUNE 18, 2066
FLORENCE
October, 1474

The child was bathed in a shaft of light on purpose. Leonardo had set a lantern above her and to the right to catch the contours of her face and hair and the tip of her wings.

Leonardo pointed to a plaster Saint Mark, posed beside a winged lion. "Angelina, please, look at this statue and do not stare into the lamp," he instructed. "You must let me know if the light hurts your eyes, yes?"

The child nodded. "*Zio* Leonardo? Uncle Leonardo. The Madonna, she will come?"

"Let us pretend she is already here," Leonardo said. "She is there, beneath the light. It is a game. What do you see?"

"Mamma. My mamma will come there?"

Sister Annunciata shook her head. "Little one, the Madonna is mother to us all and she is always with you." She turned to Leonardo. "Her name is Beatrice."

Leonardo gave the nun a wan smile and connected her and Lisabetta with successive stares. First Sister Annunciata, then Lisabetta, and twice more, back and forth, drawing a line. The message was inescapable, Lisa take this woman away. "I renamed her Angelina to help me paint," he said.

Lisabetta fussed around Leonardo, shifting items on the table, anticipating his needs. It was apparent he *needed* Sister Annunciata to leave. The nun brought her religious shadows into Leonardo's sacred space and was distracting the child.

Lisabetta put her hand on the nun's shoulder and ushered her to the door. "Sister Annunciata, I will bring Beatrice back before compline. There's no need for you to stay."

Leonardo's gaze lifted briefly from his work as he heaved a sigh of thanks. "Now Angelina, where is the Madonna?" he said.

"She is there, *Zio,*" she said. "I can see her."

"I see her too. Keep watching her."

The child made a delicate figure weighted down with clumsy wooden wings suspended behind her, there for shape rather than texture. Leonardo supplied the downy quality and the iridescence of fluffy dappled sunlight through feathers in his drawing. Angelina stared rapturously at the place where a Madonna might appear, in profile to me. Odd. She shouldn't be in profile.

I was dizzy, momentarily overcome. The child's thoughts from the sketch revisited me in whispers that echoed like beating wings, *Mamma, please save me.* My mind, programmed to scan for details, became still, and the absence of overriding duty was a shock. So, this was the holiness of silence. This was sanctuary.

When I shifted my weight, the sound made the child turn to face me. Suddenly, I was the Madonna Angelina had been pretending to see, and for a split second, the child's gaze told me I was the Madonna.

I moved and Angelina's eyes followed me. I smiled and Angelina smiled back.

Leonardo called to Lisabetta. "Lisabetta, can you reposition her," but the girl pointed animatedly to me.

"Mamma," she said in a sweet voice, repeating the word excitedly, her lips trembling. The child looked as if she was going to cry. Her face flushed, and she fidgeted underneath the wooden slats, reaching her arms towards me.

"Madonna," she called. *"Mamma."* And she started to cry.

I shushed her in Italian. *"Sei al sicuro, piccola.* Little one. You are safe. I did not mean to upset you. We are playing a game. There's no need to cry."

Lisabetta coaxed Angelina back into position. "What do you expect," she said to Leonardo. "The child has no mother and you fill her yearning with a game. To her it is real."

"Art IS a game," Leonardo replied. "What else can be done? I need an angel and you miss being a mother, so, *eccola*, here she is. I will be finished with her after a few more days. What will you do then?"

Lisabetta patted Angelina's hair without actually touching it. She looked like a saint blessing a troubled child. "I wish she felt safe," she said. "April seems years away. I'm quite recovered."

"Six months is not so long after a miscarriage," Leonardo said. "I know you better than you know yourself. If playing mamma consoles you, I am glad, but nature is smarter than we are. It takes care of... things for the best. A fourteen-year-old shouldn't have to bear the brunt of a romantic kiss, even if love *is* involved. Didn't our mamma's mistakes teach you anything?"

"Neither of us were mistakes. Why do you always feel as if you have to pay for your birth?"

"Because the law says I'm less than others. I have to be better at something. Better than anyone. The best at everything. Better than my father. And I don't mean that bully mamma was forced to marry. I'm a da Vinci and so are you. We are *not* peasants."

"In Florence we pass as artists. Verrocchio gave us that."

"Enough, Lisabetta. Talent makes us artists. And now I need to make this painting better than it is. Look after Angelina, but let's not argue about the status of women against those of men. I am the bastard. You are..."

"Invisible. And my child would have been invisible. My paintings will be invisible."

"I am sorry, *cara*. I did not make the world. You will never be invisible to me."

Lisabetta comforted Angelina. "You are daydreaming, little one," she said. "Are you tired?"

Angelina shook her head and pointed to me. "Look, the Madonna, she is there."

I moved out of the child's line of sight, and stood behind Leonardo to study his original composition. This session preceded an unknown painting, a 'newborn.' It was one worth pursuing. I noted the changes that had been made in the final drawing I'd seen. The angel would gaze at the viewer in the finished work, a convention unheard of. Angels were always fixated on a holy mother or Jesus, but here she was still in profile.

Angelina became agitated, struggling forward to be released from the wings, as if to find me. "*Mamma* where are you?"

"Wait, I'm coming," I shouted, manoeuvring back into position. "I'm here."

I was shaken, standing in for the Madonna of the painting, knowing I'd been seen. I had breached time. The situation was unprecedented and forbidden, but the feelings I welcomed as maternal love were laced with fear. Fear that home no longer existed and that I must stay to anchor the sacredness of this initiation to the profound core of human love.

Something had changed me forever. My systems shut down and rebooted. I would never be fully-android. And while I wanted to hold the moment and sit alone with it in the darkness of my room, I didn't want to lessen the spell. Although I could return to this scene through rewind, and re-enter the door prior to Angelina seeing me, I would not be innocent of it. I would be anticipating it, and never experience the profound leap to humanity again. This was IT. Time would never stand still for me. I was broken and repaired in the same moment. Angelina settled at once, her eyes gleaming into mine, equally enraptured as I spoke gentle words to keep her calm.

"I am here sweet girl," I said. "You're not alone. I'm here."

Angelina's face appeared delighted, and she tugged at my heart.

"*Mamma Mamma*," she called.

"Yes, I am here. I am your *mamma*," I said, not knowing how else to respond. "Now hush for Zio."

I stepped towards the child and touched her hair. I expected solid resistance but not the electrical fusing of my circuits. I was momentarily terrified I'd be unable to return, but love overwhelmed me and I wanted to stay. If time had been breached it was worth it. I would stay here forever.

I felt joy, I was dizzy, and I'd been seen. But there she was, a child reaching towards me and my instinctive response was to shorten the distance between us.

"Up," Angelina said, entreating to be lifted. Her movements swung the wooden wings behind her.

Leonardo lay down his chalk. "Angelina it is only a game."

I was, unprepared for the continuous waves of love that engulfed me.

I knelt down, and put my arms around her and whispered. "Mamma has to go but I will be back soon."

Angelina's rosy mouth quivered. "Stay. *Mamma.*"

I kissed her fingers and let go. "*Signore Leonardi, zio,* needs you to be still, now," I whispered, and slipped away. Outside the room I collapsed on the floor, shaking. A woman overwhelmed with love and sorrow. I wouldn't return home innocent, if home still existed, but it was dangerous to stay in case I was visible to others. And yet I wanted to return to see how much of this new me was permanent. Upstairs was a different law of physics.

I whispered into the microphone, in case this new turn of events had rendered me audible to passersby. "Bill, are you still there?"

His reply came without humor. "Where else would I be? Why did you call yourself my mother?"

"I'll explain, later. I have to stay here awhile. Is everything okay up there? I have to do a little traveling. I've found a 'new-born.' Keep it quiet."

"Understood. Should I be worried?"

"Stand by on my signal."

I huddled in the hallway, thankful it was empty, while Lisabetta comforted an hysterical child, calling for her mamma. "*Mia piccola bambina,* my dearest daughter," she shushed.

When Delphi first touched 'the Mona Lisa' she had heard Lisabetta speaking those same words, but never understood she was speaking to another child. "My dearest daughter," the painting had said. Now I heard the rest of the conversation. "I still miss you after all these years. Your Uncle Leonardo has never forgotten how you brightened our studio. He paints your face in his angels, without trying. Your face is always the one he sees. We will meet again in a place where your wings will be real. We are bound by the fire of a mother's love. I will always protect you."

Angelina had called Leonardo, *Zio*. Her uncle. And it was clear Delphi had been mistaken all her life.

I called to Delphi but she never answered.

"Sphinx where is she?"

"Hiding in the open," Sphinx replied. *"Burying more treasure."*

I felt the loss of Delphi's voice like a phantom limb. Like the severed hands of Ginevra de Benci's portrait.

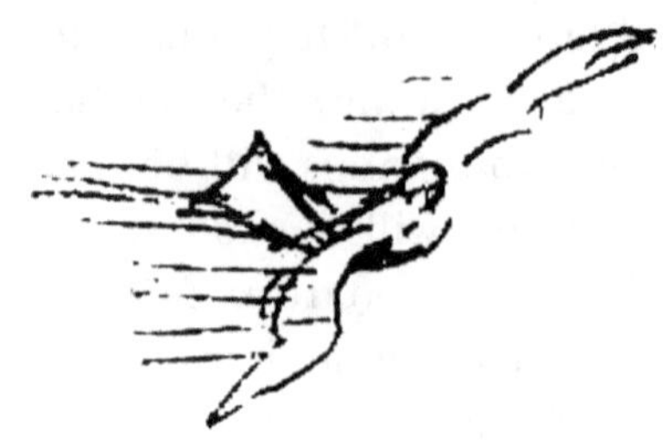

Transference/chapter thirty-nine

JUNE 19, 2066

"You seem different," Bill said. "You look lost. Anything strange happen down there?"

"Stranger than stalking Leonardo da Vinci under an invisibility cloak?"

"And the newborn?"

I shrugged and looked the other way. "What newborn?"

"You lost it?"

"Not yet."

The portrait of Ginevra de Benci' still awaited repair even though my team and I worked week by week to follow its progress, or rather, its disintegration. Leonardo had hesitated every time he picked up the saw.

"I cannot destroy my art," he said to Lisabetta. "It is cutting my own arm."

"It is already destroyed. You would be saving it. We need to appease the Benci, the Niccolini, and Bembo... *and* Verrocchio. When you have your own studio you can do whatever you want, although if I am to advise you, it would be to follow the rules of power. We will need their money."

I recognized the wicker birdcage on Leonardo's work bench. This time it was empty and its door was open. He held a one-legged robin on his palm, tempting it with breadcrumbs. I saw an image of a robin hopping over a lawn in the rain. I saw a cage and a single swan feather. I shook them away. Two of Delphi's strongest memories. "I was reminded of the empty cage as a symbol in art history. I'd forgotten how the soul was often equated to a bird, like the Egyptian 'ba' – a bird with a human head.

I called Delphi, hoping she would hear me. "Delphi? Speak to me. Please. I need your help. All this love. It's difficult to work."

Delphi sounded sad. "Wait till you make love," she said. "Wait till you miss *that*."

Sphinx changed the subject a little too quickly to be subtle. *"It's hard to lose a mother twice,"* she said. *"All that is dark is not empty. Hearing and listening are different things."*

"We can't both be emotional," I said in my defense.

"Win win or lose lose," Sphinx said. *"What's the answer to life?"*

It was the first time she'd asked ME a question.

Lisabetta fussed around an Angelina flushed with fever. It was 1475, early in the new year and the painting was nearly complete. Leonardo appeared oblivious, lost in his work. "Leonardo, Angelina is unwell. I'm taking her home," she said, lifting the child from her pose. I listened out of sight.

Leonardo looked up in a trance, disturbed with sympathy kicking in. "She is tired. She can sleep on the bed. She needs to eat, yes?"

"I promised the sisters we wouldn't exhaust her."

"Very well, little mother," he said to Lisabetta. And to Angelina as he kissed her cheek, "I will see you tomorrow little one."

Lisabetta gave Leonardo a long look of sadness.

"Lisa?" he said. "It was a compliment. I meant no harm."

Lisabetta hurried through the maze of Verrocchio's studio holding an inconsolable Angelina and burst into the street. I followed like a private detective, darting and hiding as if everyone could see me.

Angelina's golden curls bounced with each step. She clung to Lisabetta's neck, peering over her shoulder, and I knew she could see me even though her eyes were glazed. I blew her a kiss. She smiled and mouthed the word angel, and lifted one chubby arm to reach for me. I reached too. We were yards apart but it felt like only a hairsbreadth. Energy pulsated from her fingers to mine the way Michelangelo's figure of God stretched towards Adam in a frozen moment on Sistine Ceiling. Strange that in this year his famous ceiling was still a vast blue parking lot, empty but for a few gold stars crumbling from its damp surface, and he was a child three years younger than Angelina. I had the notion that the paintings I spoke with were stopwatches, pausing to capture a story.

All the way to Santa Croce, Angelina focused on me. It was pointless to hide. If I'd breached the prime directive, the damage was already done. I gave up the pretense of invisible sylph and ran closer to her. Leonardo's words of hiding in the open came back to me. She fainted on Lisabetta's shoulder, her arms flailing limp, flopping with each step towards the convent for abandoned children.

A sister dressed in white responded to the bell and unlocked the gate. She ushered them inside, and closed it before I could enter. The bell roused Angelina and she called out, Mamma, as Lisabetta disappeared with her under an arched loggia, swamped by the flutter of activity as a straggle of children ran after them. Angelina was as safe as could be expected.

Lisabetta's words trailed back over the children's heads. "She is delirious."

And the nun's useless reply that triggered a flutter of dark wings within me. "I'll light a candle and pray for her."

I felt a sudden let down of internal pressure. Why was I here? I was supposed to be with Ginevra's portrait. I had work to do. I felt disoriented, emptied of emotion, and trailed back to Verrocchio's studio feeling ashamed of my outburst.

I felt Delphi close a door. I locked a few more. It would be temporary but it meant survival for my assignment. She could no longer reach me and it was for PIAT's good. I needed to concentrate. The shutdown had been necessary.

It was easy to turn away and resume my mission as if nothing had happened.

"Two to tango," Sphinx said.

I opened a channel. "Bill, I need to stay a little longer. The baby's restless."

"Understood. You want to come back and... you know, rest? You were AWOL for a while. We were worried."

I was thrilled someone was still there. "No. Give me an hour. Thanks. Over and out."

This reference to rest hardly related to human fatigue, although my team could be as stressed out as traffic controllers. It was code for calling a meeting of minds to process new data.

I reopened the channel. "Bill? Is Joanna there?"

"No Ma'am."

"Have her make a note. I'm now sure that diving triggers emotional responses. I feel anger down here. We need to discuss this. When I get back it may not be as strong but you might have a way of sustaining it with biofeedback. Please work on that right now. It's important. Top priority."

"Copy that."

An hour later, I felt guilt rise from its mothballs like a spectre. I wandered back to the streets surrounding the convent, circling it, finding myself back at the gate staring helplessly at the carved door which had absorbed the child who had called me, mother.

I stood there for the longest time, barely daring to move and slipped inside the gate with the last supply cart of the day. It was easy to find the room, and I crept like a spy lest I set up another encounter causing distress. I needn't have worried. Angelina slept, her thick lashes resting on flushed cheeks still wet with tears.

A deep wall alcove glowed in the dark where a miniature shrine had been dedicated for Angelina's soul. Light flickered upwards, animating the face of a Madonna icon from a dozen candles, held fast in melted wax.

"She's exhausted," a female voice said, and I jumped thinking the nun was addressing me, but another voice answered. "It is not like her to fuss. Maestro Leonardo is enchanted with her. He refuses to call her Beatrice; he calls her his perfect little Angelina."

Enchanted. Yes, that was my reaction also. The child was a

compelling creature, motherless as I had been but with resources of cheerfulness. It was best to let her sleep and to remove myself from harming her further.

"We must keep the candles burning all night to help her," one of the voices said.
The next dive to the studio, Angelina wasn't there, and I forced myself to concentrate on the painting.

Leonardo worked on the Madonna's robes from draped cloth. Her face was the same one he used by default. I could see he had captured the tender innocence of Angelina as only he could. She was a translucent angel in the pose of adoration. Soft curls floated around her face in profile, her chubby hands holding a golden apple to offer the Queen of Heaven, herself, a mother-to-be, lost in thought, her pregnancy a mixed blessing.

I held my hands over the Madonna's belly and felt a sympathetic quickening where my womb would be.

Leonardo had painted a woman lost in contemplation and an adoring child angel – a radically different religious mother and child icon. A child with wings and a Madonna with the traditional baby 'out of sight,' inside her. The angel seemed to be pleading with the Madonna to notice her, but Mary's eyes gazed into an uncertain future and her hands comforted her unborn child.

I felt the angel's anguish until I realized it was a memory of my own. I mean Delphi's. Angelina and I shared the connection of abandonment. Her wooden wings were as mechanical as my insides.

That's what moved me the most. The carved feathers couldn't move with life, and for a moment I imagined what it would be like to feel real wings shiver against my back. The sensation stopped my heart with profound compassion but I couldn't cry, even though I remembered the physiology of how."

I needed Delphi to wrap these feelings into sense. No doubt she needed me to forgive her. I sent her a mental signal. "How can I help you?"

All I heard was her weeping and a loving voice repeating, move towards me, *principessa.*

Then I called Cecco, myself.

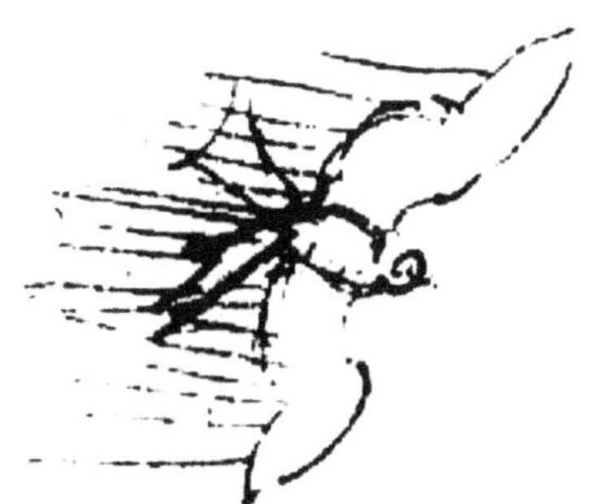

Emptiness/chapter forty

I made eleven more dives but Angelina never came again. And I tried to forget her by scooping treasures burned in the main room's brazier while keeping watch over the damaged Ginevra panel, now used to prop open a window. I noticed it bend slightly from the pressure until it fell to the floor, still beautiful.

A lazy apprentice tried to snap it in two but it proved resistant and was left whole on the pile of kindling in a basket the size of a dishwasher. It was a miracle to have survived intact to the burning point.

A few hours later another lad fed it to the fire. I called for a half hour reset and retrieved it in one piece, and to make sure, I watched the second apprentice top up the fire without a hint of confusion. No harm no foul. It had not been missed.

I sent it 'upstairs.' "Put the baby straight to bed in my *room*," I said to Joanna.

Ginevra's hands had functioned for months in the studio and would have likely been substituted for another doorstop had it not been allowed to fulfill its destiny as fuel.

It would be a coup for the gallery that owned the original portrait if they could afford Hamm's fifty-million-dollar price tag. A missing relic, matched to the cut panel made 'Ginevra de Benci' a more compelling story. I imagined it arriving 'upstairs' in a modest flurry of private flashbulbs. I would be due for a bonus. But I had another way of delivering it which I thought would give me more cachet. Perhaps even respect.

In the meantime, the 'baby' slept in my closet, swaddled in a blanket, and Leonardo changed the Madonna painting by facing the angel forward, staring at the viewer with more pathos as she shared her failure to distract the sad Madonna, reflecting the tragedy to come. Her hand was empty, ready for something other than the original apple and I whispered an idea in Leonardo's ear, more as a joke to amuse my comrades than anything. It was safe knowing the painting would be destroyed within the week in a small studio fire, and I had been busy documenting all the items we could extract once we knew which ones were beyond reclamation by anything other than modern digital recovery. I had to allow the painting to be as finished as it would ever be and choose the last moment of its unfolding for capture. If, there remained such a moment.

Later, when the flames licked a corner of the studio clean, it fell, face down in the chaos of an emptied room, ruined as the wet surface varnish became encrusted with sawdust and ash. I stared at its ruination and although it was safe to take it, I didn't have the heart to do anything but let it die. It had been abandoned to dry, and I found it a comfort to see that Leonardo had heeded my subliminal suggestion and painted a bunch of cherries in Angelina's hand. I could retrieve it later when I was in a better mood. My moodiness was sporadic but discernible. I let it flow and hung on to the tail ends of ups and downs with increasing stickiness.

The child's eyes were haunting enough in the painting but I couldn't dismiss the sight of her real eyes that I had seen filled with tears. *Mamma,* she had called out and no mother had stayed to comfort her. I felt gutted and my own sadness took root and flowered, flooding back from long-ago dammed memories. An orphanage ward with rows of black iron cribs like cages and small box beds crammed together, the youngest to the eldest, four-year-olds, the same age as Angelina. After four, most children were moved to a kindergarten wing and then on to grade school in a different part of the city. Delphi was different. So different she was sent to the asylum.

The nuns felt free disclosing how her sister Blanche had been adopted into a happy home.

"I was only a few days old when Blanche left, too young to register personal loss," Delphi volunteered. "But I remember one of the nuns remarking that I smiled when I heard the news, and then said it was probably gas. Either way, I was relieved."

I saw a large suitcase bulging at the sides.

"Blanche was excess baggage," Delphi said. "I never felt a sibling connection. I was twenty before I saw her again. She found ME. She had evolved through her sheltered world of new toys and being a spoiled daddy's girl, given to tantrums. That was the only Blanche I knew."

I saw Ginevra Benci's face disappear into a black shape that made her portrait look like a great hole had been cut in its center.

"Judging by your sister's demanding personality," I said. "She might have been Ginevra's twin, separated at birth."

I couldn't stay away. I arrived in Leonardo's studio to a dramatic scene. Lisabetta was hysterical and Leonardo consoled her. "*Cara*, we weren't to know. She asked to go home."

"She called to me," Lisabetta said. "I heard her calling Mamma in a dream, but I couldn't find her. The smoke. I fell. Angels dragged me outside. I thought they would save her."

Leonardo pinned Lisabetta's arms to her side to keep her still, encircling her from behind and spoke gently into her hair. "The boys and I heard your screams. That was what *you* heard."

Lisabetta, who had miscarried of a six-month foetus at the tender age of fourteen and risen to the status of artist's apprentice at sixteen, was inconsolable.

"Angelina was my child. You saw," she sobbed. "She's dead. Two babies dead."

I recalled an old recorded conversation in Delphi's mind, and the math told me she had been overhearing words spoken in 1474 when she'd heard Lisabetta utter, "I'm still a mother," and Leonardo replied, "*Si Cara*, and always my sister. *Mi amore*, your daughter, she is in paradise, yes? She could not stay. You are young. But you've wanted to be an artist ever since I brought you your first paper and chalk. You will be an artist. Motherhood, it will come when it comes, no? You will give birth to many... "

Lisabetta threw him a look of sympathy and interrupted. "To paintings?"

"Painting is not my first love either. But sometimes we must obey the muses. I learned to hide my thirst for science out in the open. People always think of me as a painter. This is fate."

I wondered what painting had spoken. But it was doubly clear of that earlier time when Delphi was three and had reached out to the 'Mona Lisa.' 'Mona Lisa-*betta*' had been remembering Angelina on a day thirty years in her past, posing for Leonardo, drifting into the daydreams she frequented most. I felt a shadow of Delphi's loss but it was a coup for me to discover why the 'Mona Lisa's' expression was so difficult to interpret, posing for the iconic portrait of a mother wearing a veil of mourning. Why her smile was tender, gazing on a beloved child so far in her past, and sad as she contemplated the loss of *two* children.

Cecco had told Delphi all those years ago and she hadn't wanted to hear the truth, *it's a portrait of Lisabetta, who died the same year my father received Leonardo's letter about me,* he'd said. That gave me the date of Lisabetta's fiery death. I had the means to save her, too.

I felt a familiar twinge of double-abandonment breeze through me. I was motherless again and Delphi had disappeared. No doubt to mourn the loss of her stepmother. I couldn't let Angelina go. It had been a nursery fire.

Grief/chapter forty-one

Angelina had not died calling for Lisabetta. She'd been calling for me, of that I was sure.

I ran to the convent fighting a river of people in my way. None of them saw or felt me. The sight of the burned out shell of the nursery chilled me.

I allowed myself to return to Angelina's last moments – a sister tucking her in, and the candle offerings falling in slow-motion, and her screams meant for me. She saw me standing in the corner and it calmed her. "Angel," she cried, reaching out to be saved, "Mamma."

Angelina stood on her bed, and as I watched, the wooden wings she'd worn for Leonardo appeared on her back. But these were soft and the feathers unfurled, wafting the smoke until it obscured her. The last image I had of her was a toddler framed by angelic wings, arms outstretched in a blessing as if to save me until the swirl of smoke enveloped her and the room.

I heard her choked sobs from the rusty cloud of smoke that filled the room. I heard the panic of the nuns roused from their sleep and the nightmarish peal of the chapel bell ringing in slow-motion. Sister Annunciata, heading for the children had succumbed to smoke inhalation and lay unconscious. Angelina's cries were stifled by the roar of a fiery lion as the conflagration burned into a blinding tunnel of white light and exploded like a small bomb.

I stood inside the scene with Delphi screaming blue murder in my ear. For someone trained to dip into the speed of fire as a matter of course, I was indifferent. Flames licked my body harmlessly but consumed the flesh of its own time.

I lived with fire that couldn't burn; for Delphi, fire was a terror that had haunted her enough to fear even the phoenix carved into a lintel – its fiery death-cry, soaring tail, and wings of flame frozen in stone.

Delphi had died by ice. I heard her bragging to Sphinx. She wanted to show Cecco her electrical fire with its fibreglass coal. Fire that couldn't burn she said. Had it been a premonition of her successor's fate? Reaching into bonfires was my job. I thought little of it and now I always had to shield Delphi in every rescue dive.

"What frightened you?" I asked her. "It must have been more than a burned finger."

She was slow to answer. "It was my arm too," she repeated, lamely.

Sphinx coaxed her. *"It's already happened Goldilocks,"* she said. *"Mona Lisa loved you."*

"The nuns made me burn candles to the baby Jesus all the time," Delphi began. "They said I had to beg him in my mind, to release my tongue. My sleeve caught fire from one of the other tea lights. I needed salve but the pain kept me awake and left a red scar. If a tiny candle flame can do that then..."

"Time heals fears," I said.

"Later, in the asylum," she said. "When I *was* thankful. I wanted to thank 'Him' for giving me Jenks and healing my silence, but the fear of the candles stopped me cold. I was guilt-ridden after that. Such a coward."

Later, my own guilt shadowed me. I could have saved Angelina. I could have carried her outside, but my prime directive overrode my emotional impulses. No life could be removed from its fate, only objects. That was PIAT's creed embedded into my programs. Delphi was appalled. She was ashamed of me. I felt a slight surge as she left me, not unlike a phoenix headed for rebirth.

I rationalized. The child had died nearly six-hundred-years-ago and technically her suffering was long over. I had to accept it.

Millions of children had died since the fifteenth-century. I could neither save them nor was I permitted to interfere with animal or human suffering, even my own. *Especially* my own. History had to remain intact, and yet I mourned deeply until the rage I felt for my cold programming fused into chronic despair and I retreated from my team, refusing to travel, ironically, to sit for hours and stare into the past. Phillip was compelled to intervene but he sent Joanna. Delphi was gone. Again.

Sphinx sugar-coated her departure which made it all the more serious. *"You take the high road and she'll take the low road,"* she sang. *"Delphi's dreaming her own way home."*

I was angry and said so. "She needs to face death as a normal part of life," I said.

"Death is a house of mirrors," Sphinx replied.

I told no-one about Angelina but I went back for 'the baby' in spite of, or as a result of, my mood of despair. I hid it in plain sight. But I couldn't stop seeing Angelina trying to save me.

Father's Day/chapter forty-two

The SUMMER SOLSTICE
JUNE 21, 2066

I needed Phillip on my side, Ginevra style, so he would be compelled to fight for me in the guise of an 'us.' He wanted an 'us.' Angelina erased my ethical boundaries. I was obsessed. Ginevra had made things happen in her life. She brought the things she wanted into being by willpower. It looked easy. Being spiteful to Hamm would be no problem. Delphi would have stopped me but she'd blocked me out. Sphinx once told me to ask for what I wanted. I wanted Angelina. Phillip wanted me. Hamm wanted a Leonardo. Delphi wanted Cecco. What could possibly go wrong?

Phillip and I were strolling after dinner by my invitation.

"I want to thank you for being my knight," I said. "I don't know what I'd do without you. My old emotions are welling up. It's an epic flood. I want things I hardly know what to do with." I took his arm and squeezed it. I sent him the encouragement of lust. "I couldn't have come this far without your support."

"Killing Hamm with kindness is still not an option then?"

"The regular way seems fine."

I squeezed his arm again and looked into his eyes as I imagined Ginvera might. "I need a big favor."

"Anything other than murder."

I giggled and squeezed yet again. Third time lucky. An apprentice coquette. How vapid girls were. How stupid men were. "Quite the opposite."

"The opposite of killing someone is giving life."

I sprang Ginevra's trap. "Exactly. We could have a child," I said. "You and I."

Phillip slowly disengaged his arm. He studied my face, and I smiled my best Mona Lisa smile. His expression was incredulous. The classic drop jaw double-take.

He spluttered for a bit. "That's a physical im... why? How? Jesus! HOW?"

I hated myself for playing the manipulative innocent. "There are ways. We could adopt."

"Are you saying you want to marry me? Good plan if you want Hamm to drop dead from shock."

"No. He has to die in agony, emotional or physical, preferably both."

Phillip laughed. "Good, I thought for a moment there you might be insane."

"You would make a great father."

"I'm going to recommend my uncle runs a diagnostic."

"My circuits are fine. I've just downloaded a few more programs from Delphi."

"So, *she* wants this?"

"I've found an orphan in Florence. Help me rescue her and I will live with you anywhere, after PIAT is gone. I will destroy them afterwards."

"But what about your team?"

"Hamm will be dead. My team will be free to go."

"They are now."

I gave Phillip a withering look. "Wake up. Of course they're not."

"Is Delphi asking you to do this?"

I shook my head. "It's the new me. I want things."

I thought of Hamm as Ginevra's next victim. I marched into his office without being summoned, the Ginevra panel gift-wrapped in gold tissue paper behind my back. I could see he was not best pleased being interrupted.

I glared defiantly at the 'Sistine Madonna' but she didn't blink. No matter. She had nothing to say. At least not yet. I could wait.

Hamm fixed me with a narrowed stare, the intimidating look he was forever going for. "Close your eyes," I demanded. "I have a gift for you." He glared with deeper silence. "It's better than an umbrella," I teased. "You'll want this. I assure you."

His forehead showed irritation but one corner of his mouth twitched into a smile, and caught off guard, he complied.

"Happy Father's Day!" I said, slamming the flat package on his desk.

He smiled nervously. "What's this?"

"A tie," I said. "What does it look like?"

The paper wrappings shredded easily.

"Is this a...?"

"A Leonardo? Why yes, I believe it is."

A visualised a cartoon question mark hovering over his head. "But you said it was beyond our reach."

"I exaggerated, plus I worked overtime. It was a blip of pure timey wimey."

He hadn't listened and wouldn't have understood my Dr. Who reference if he had. I'd been able to send back 'my baby angel' with the Ginevra tidbit, wrapping them together in a sheet from my bed, face to face with spacers in between as one of the paintings was wet. Even Joanna hadn't guessed there'd been two paintings. I swept off to my quarters, citing an urgent meeting with Sphinx and Delphi which required a sensitive space. I sounded like the white rabbit. "I'm late for an important date," I quoted. None of them got the 'Wonderland' reference either.

Horror of horrors, Hamm came around his desk and hugged me. He tousled my hair which wanted to bite him like snakes. He kissed my cheeks. Both of them, Italian style. My guts churned but Delphi said "Aw, he's like his grandad."

"Like hell he is," I replied.

"On one of his good days," she added. "Mr. Charles liked me."

"Thank you, my precious little girl," Hamm said, grinning.

Sphinx sang. *"Awe is a many splendored thing."*

"She's crooked," I said, struggling free. "You know how I hate things off kilter."

"What?"

"The Madonna," I said, moving behind his desk to straighten the frame of the 'Sistine Madonna.' I was shocked not to feel anything from her. I'm not a Ginevra and even though I was able to channel Medusa whenever I wanted, snakes were more honest than fake honey. Mentally, I dismissed the powers of manipulation.

Right then I decided to make a stand, to take umbrage with the concept of fatherhood, Dr. Who included. Authority and enslavement be damned. It was about time my fanciful dad rescued me, WHO-ever he was.

I saw Hamm as the false pope, Il Papa; Chronos, Father of Time; the Death of time. It was time to play him for a Mommy's boy with a father complex.

"Make a wish," Sphinx said. *"Backbone time."*

"I wish, Cecco were here." I said.

Leonardo's anatomical illustration was famous. An unborn child hugged its knees inside a cutaway womb. It tugged at me when I touched it and I heard the stifled cries of a newborn and the sobbing of its mother. It catapulted me into a room bright with fresh laundry where Lisabetta busied herself angrily folding linens, and a man hovered in the background intent on apology. He brandished a sheet of parchment containing the drawing. It was obviously the reason the woman was upset. The man was Leonardo da Vinci.

"My work upsets you," he said, "but this is what I do. The muses encourage me to explore the human body."

"Such a thing. It is forbidden. They could kill you."

"The church thinks I'm searching for the soul, so, certain dissections are sanctioned."

"Then they are idiots."

Leonardo smiled to Lisabetta's back and became a serious mask again.

"Lisa, please understand," he said. "It was an act of reverence. I did not expect this. The cadaver before me... she was not emotionally dead. She was a young mother of thirteen. A child herself. Like you were. She was in the room – a soul circling its body and she called out to me that her child was trapped. Save him, she said. And I had work to do. Forgive me, but it was fascinating as much as horrifying. The work is always first, *si?*"

Lisabetta turned to face him and took the drawing from his hand. "I know this, *mi amore*, but my baby..." she took a deep breath. "My baby must have looked like that. I was only fourteen."

The siblings connected in a hug and drifted away, and the rest of their conversation floated back to me, intelligible sounds that reminded me of seagulls, but the drawing spoke directly to me.

I was in a dark tunnel of a room with dank brick walls. All around me were tables supporting human-shaped lumps of white sheets clinging to the dead. Grey vapours rose from the corpses and I was thankful I had no sense of smell. A teenage girl lay exposed but for a piece of cloth draped over her extended abdomen. I knew the child was beneath it.

Leonardo had been tidy. Instruments were arranged in precise rows next to a bowl of greasy water and piles of towels.

I startled when he shuffled back into the room, emerging from the gloom of the passageway with more candles. His sleeves were rolled to the elbows and he had a strange look on his face. A combination of grim duty and yet there was excitement too. I wondered where his art materials were.

The dead mother's voice answered me. "Leonardo draws when he's back in the studio," she said. "He just remembers." I have seen his drawings of my child." She gestured to her body, holding her hands above it in protection. "I was his cradle. It was as if I might take him from this cradle and open his arms." She continued in a matter of fact narrative. "I was designed to house two souls, and now my womb is a doorway."

Leonardo peeled back the cloth. The child's forehead showed through a narrow opening of grey flesh caught in the candlelight I heard an infant gurgling contentedly for its mother and yet it never moved. It couldn't move.

Leonardo mouthed a silent prayer before taking up a scalpel, cutting back more layers of the womb. He took immense care slicing the wall of the womb away in strips until the opening was a wedge eight inches wide. Leonardo's fascination was catching. I leant into the dissection, curious. The womb opened on a fleshy hinge and reminded me of melon split in half. Its interior lining was the dark red of a pomegranate. But still no sketching took place.

All the while Leonardo worked, the young girl sang a lullaby to her dead child.

Leonardo and Delphi had something in common. They were able to take detailed snapshots of everything they saw with perfect recall. I decided I would watch Leonardo back in his studio, later, no doubt basking in the full extravagance of east light as he captured this night for my future.

The blade flashed in the dim light until it was too covered in gore to reflect. The work was methodical. Leonardo seemed to be holding his breath but he was breathing normally, relaxed. No tension showed in his face. He was lost in his work. This is what he had tried to explain to Lisabetta. His need to know the unknown. In this case, the mysteries of the human body. Not so he could draw better figures, although that was a side-effect, but because he was exploring a new world. Parallel to his contemporary explorer Amerigo Vespucci but just as compelling.

The knives and probes moved like modern surgery. The only sound was the occasional dull thud of flesh hitting a bucket.

The girl spoke again. "It's not really me," she consoled. "I am here speaking to you, but see? My mouth does not move. I know you can hear my baby too. We are separate from Leonardo's work. I am here to advise you with words from my grandmother. My own mother died when I was not much different than my babe you see here."

She was right, the event unfolding on the table *was* clinical. An artist bent over a workbench, studying the clockworks of life. Leonardo's curiosity would outlast the store of candles at his side.

"Please tell me," I said.

"Motherhood is not always about giving birth to a live child. It's carrying the intense desire to protect and nurture."

The table became a holy altar. Leonardo's candles shone

brighter over a mother and child, sacrificed for the art of science. As bizarre as it sounded, the mother and child on the table were more significant than a religious icon.

"My name is Francesca," she continued. "I tried to be a mother. It was my duty, but I was too young. My husband is angry that I failed. For seven months my child and I traveled together as one person, and now a great artist has honored us. Now we will live forever, *non?*"

I noticed she used the present tense. Also her name hit me like a blow. It was the feminine of Francesco, Cecco's full name, and I'd been charged to find him.

Leonardo's voice came softly with tenderness, but his mouth did not move. He spoke directly to me from the drawing. "Cherry, *mi amore*, do not worry so. There is too much duty in your life. The sum of one's life can never be dissected," he said. "Life is a cutting away of unimportant things. I was beginning to think I had no emotions left. I had thought emotions were no longer relevant in the corpse. I had grown cold from experimentation. I lacked feeling until I met this dead child.

"My sister gave birth to a stillborn infant. And yet, until I met this child, it was something distant that happened and I shrugged it away. I comforted her with words but my heart wasn't in them. But then I grew obsessed with being the first to travel an inner world. And so I sought this room. The human form chided me whenever I drew a figure in need of realistic muscle. What was inside? Where were the emotions of love and fear? I only found solid fat and muscle, blood-soaked with hope and sacrifice. The pains of life were over and yet the sadness lingered. I saw the workings but not the feelings. And now this child. I am as moved as a father. Moved as the uncle to my sister's lost child. I am made warm again. I love this child. I am no longer ashamed."

I knew what vindication meant. Months ago I had begged for flesh and blood biology. Once again I was reminded of Marley trying to save Scrooge. But mostly of my behavior ignoring Angelina's death screams. Even now, I pretended she was a toy that I'd forgotten on a shelf. It was easy to think of her as inanimate doll, and that I would go back for her when I wanted to play mother.

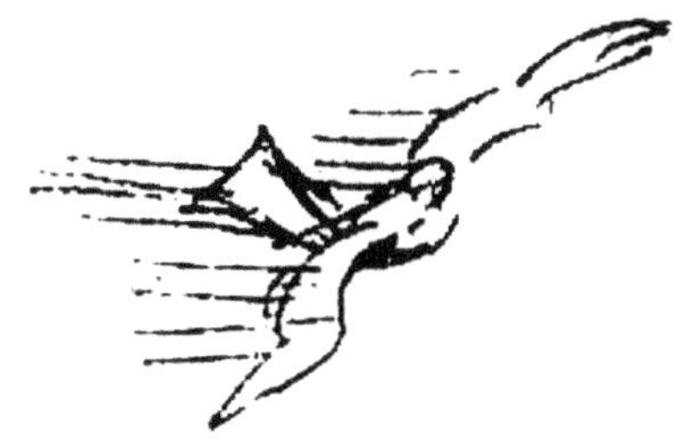

Mother's Day/chapter forty-three

JUNE 28, 2066

For a whole week the painting glowed like a cut diamond, so bright, I imagined it setting fire to the curtains. I saw it within a halo of flames. It was still drying.

It called out to me at odd times, especially in the evenings.

"Mamma," Angelina would call, and I would move closer and place my hands on the frame to revisit our first meeting. I replayed the first day we saw each other, with Leonardo deeply concentrating on his inward light and Lisabetta going about her domestic and studio chores, and the unspoken shorthand between brother and sister, always to serve the art. And naturally I relived Angelina's last day to torture myself. I experienced the undertones of macabre joy inherent in depression. How on earth could humans want to dwell on this? I had to know.

Joanna caught me staring at the 'Madonna and Angel' when she presented herself for one of her therapeutic 'girl mornings.' "It smells odd in here," she said. "Is there wet paint?"

I pretended to look puzzled. I scanned the room, mimicking the sniffing motions of a person with a sense of smell. I sniffed my way to the painting like a tracking dog until I was face-to-face with the angel. "Oh, this. I can't smell varnish, so I forgot." I gestured to it, hanging above the fireplace. "I gave it a fresh coat, yesterday."

"Does it have a title?"

She was drawing me out. The team needed to resume work as usual before Hamm caught wind of a problem. "It's a 'Madonna and Angel' by a lesser student of Biagio d'Antonio," I said. "Nothing worth Hamm's notice. Let's just say it's mine now because I deserve nice things. I found it a bit scratched up when I made an inventory of the archives. Delphi was allowed to save a few insignificant paintings she liked, for herself. PIAT was never interested in collectors with shallow pockets. Besides, she valued it fifty years ago when it was worth a few hundred dollars. You never know. Obscure artists can come into favor. All it takes is one collector to start a frenzy. That happened to Botticelli. He was forgotten for hundreds of years until the Pre-Raphaelites claimed him their unsung hero."

My ploy worked. Joanna's questions took a detour.

"I don't know much about art," she said. "It seems an inexact science."

"Art appreciation isn't a science. Pricing it is. Fame and infamy sets the bidding high. History helps; time adds history; provenance adds zeros. Lots of zeros."

Joanna scrutinized the painting by tilting her head.

"It's similar to a Leonardo isn't it?"

She was off-topic and I ran with it. "I will never forget seeing him for the first time. Cameras may not work during molecular travel but my brain is a camera. It's an invaluable throw-forward from Delphi who had an unhealthy recall of everything she saw, smelled, heard or felt."

Joanna, undaunted, turned her attention to the pastries I'd arranged on a pretty plate. "Then talk to it. Maybe it has a message for us."

"I do, sometimes, but it doesn't have much to say. Did you know that Leonardo was in some difficulties when I visited him? But I never reported that. He deserves some privacy. Between you and me, Delphi has ethics that override my programs. I would be a Frankenstein's monster without her. I would perform like a trained seal. I let Hamm believe what he wants. To him I'm a loyal employee and I prefer to keep it that way"

"You're different somehow. Since Leonardo. All of us noticed it."

The painting's voice crowded me into a corner. I felt the desire to save Angelina. She was crying again. I tried to hush her in my mind. I had walked away, defaulting to the unfeeling robot within. I deliberately used the robot word to berate myself. To me, it was the lowest form of insult and an appropriate form of self-flagellation. I failed Angelina. She whispered Mamma and giggled. I couldn't bear it. The last person Angelina saw was a woman she thought was her mother who did nothing. I *was* a monster.

"Penny for your thoughts."

"I saw a terrible accident back there during the Leonardo dive. An animal died horribly. It disturbed Delphi. Maybe it disturbed me. If it did, then think I feel grief."

"You should have said."

"I don't say a lot of things."

"If androids don't *feel* anything and you're heartbroken, what does that tell you?"

"I'm transforming. Programs determine my actions."

"Grief-stricken is *not* one of your programs."

"Time-travel bequeaths perspective," I said. "Delphi loved animals."

"Leonardo changed you. Phillip says if you aren't already immortal, you should be. He sees you as the mother of a new species."

"Some mother I'd make. And I'm *not* immortal."

"Delphi will be back. You'll see."

"I didn't realize how strongly I oppose what PIAT is doing. How much I would rather be destroyed than remain under Hamm's control."

"You can't die and you need to complete this mission of yours. We're all on your side."

I replayed Jenks words to Delphi in the asylum, *don't forget to win. Promise me.*

"I have a confession to make. But not yet."

"No problem."

"It would be tantamount to heretical. Borderline criminal. Worse than mutiny. I'm also not sure Hamm would stop at violence. But keep that under your hat."

I could tell Joanna was worried even though she looked calm. That was pure Joanna. Balancing a teacup on her knee, or a book on her head, or a challenge in her mind, she maintained the perfect posture. She was meticulous and extra-tidy when it came to emotions.

"I'm going to need a bigger hat," she said, smiling. "I'm not worried. I trust you. We all do."

I repeated the next words that popped into my head, out loud. "A big swirl of something bad is headed this way." Even to myself, I sounded like an oracle.

Joanna dropped her pretence of complacency. She shivered and rubbed her arms, shaking off my prediction. "So, what do you want to do with eternity?" she said, brightening.

"I'm NOT immortal."

Her mask was fading. "More than most."

I couldn't tell her I wanted to adopt a dead child and play mother for a while. I told myself Angelina couldn't have seen me. The earth hadn't moved. The worlds above and below were safe.

Joanna stared wistfully into the painting again. "I want to have children someday. But, for now, that's our secret, right?"

"Right. And so is mine... about that not reporting everything, thing."

Joanna grinned, suddenly faking delight. "Aren't we the secretive ones."

"You're a terrible actress," I said.

That was when Delphi flashed me a postcard of a famous cemetery in Paris. The inscription on a worn headstone read, here lies buried treasure.

Joanna accepted her criticism with her usual gracious deflection. "It's lucky time-travel doesn't change the rest of us."

Delphi's voice intruded and startled me. "I told you. I can't tell you my secret. Maybe the nuns were right about sin."

I ignored her and answered Joanna. "How do you know it doesn't?"

Delphi broke through and surprised me. "I'm going to hell," she said. "That's what's happened, isn't it? I'm in hell and you're a demon."

"There's no such thing as sin," I said to Delphi.

"I know." Joanna said.

I put my hands over my ears to drown out Delphi's voice and rubbed my temples.

Joanna's cup clattered into its saucer. She reached over and touched my arm. "Do you have a headache?"

"Sorry, Delphi was exposed to a lot of religious fairy tales. I answer her sometimes. I try to do it in my head, but lately I can't seem to separate thinking from speaking out loud."

"You're doing a lot of things differently. Oh wow. She's back. That's great!" Almost immediately, her joy turned to concern. "Are you sure you're not in any pain? That would be a real breakthrough."

"No. Delphi is interrupting my thoughts. Please. Have another cake. It makes me happy to see others eat. Well, I call it happiness because I see cake accompanied by a close-up of the 'Mona Lisa's' smile."

"So, she *was* happy then. I always wondered. It's hard to tell."

"Leonardo was the master of illusion," I said. And he studied facial muscles."

And so it went on for another half hour until the door closed behind Joanna.

I counted to four and called out to Delphi as I walked to the fountain. She came in clearer there. "First, are you insane? Second, are you back for good?"

"Yes... and I'll try," she said. "Even I can see I'll have to disappear soon."

"You've seen the painting of Angelina before. I can feel it the way a person with amnesia remembers a clue. This is what past life regression must feel like. I need to know what you know."

"It was the day of my death," she said, stalling.

"An hallucination?"

"Never just that. It was more. It was always more. Cecco showed the painting to me. That's all I remember." She hesitated. "And, that it frightened me."

I perched on the rim of the Poseidon Fountain, examining my fingernails which had recently changed from pure white to match the patina of the ancient marble.

Delphi had cheered considerably. "Apart from your hair color, our resemblance is uncanny," she said. "The same but different, like non-identical twins."

"I'll take your word for it. There are no photographs of you."

"Visit me then. You've got the key."

"You mean visit Cecco."

I trailed my index finger over the patina of lime green moss growing in the cracks of marble, pried some loose, and flicked it on the ground in a fit of pique. Why had I done such a thing?

"That was me," Delphi said. What good is moss if Cecco isn't here to show me how to see a landscape in its details?"

"You're safe. You can remember everything now."

"You frighten me. I can't fight like you."

"And I can't fight without you."

"Once upon a time," Sphinx said, *"there were three bears."*

I knew about bears. Everyone on Vancouver Island was instructed how to react should they meet one face-to-face. The most dangerous confrontation was a mother bear with a cub. Daddy bears would more likely amble away if you sang while you hiked, providing it wasn't hungry, but a mother bear would attack on a full stomach. Mother bears are ferocious protectors. The only way to survive was to back away downwind, or play dead and hope. Sphinx once told me to listen to Mama Bear. It had been more of a command.

"A penny drops from heaven," she chimed. *"Delphi will be there when you need her. She had to leave. She has to prepare. Fill the fountain. Make a wish. Make four."*

I stared at the angel painting, set like a memorial shrine above a table with white flowers. I sat as a sinner before a devotional. Angelina was not suffering but I suffered for her as any mother would, so my child wouldn't have to. It made me feel better. Joanna had asked if I was in any pain. Delphi's erratic memory flashed an image from her early religious indoctrination. She felt obliged to show me a gory scene of crucifixion. I turned it into a painting by Giotto, but I got the message. *Agony.* How could a compassionate religious order drill this sort of iconic suffering into a child's head? And why would an intelligent grownup advance it into a lifestyle?

A human mother shares the instincts of a bear, and I had come to regard Angelina as my daughter. My programs confirmed I'd done the right thing by leaving her. But motherlove was a powerful drug. It had changed me – jumpstarted me on the path to full emotional recovery by way of disintegrating first in order to restart. I longed to see Angelina again, but her seeing me was too great a risk. For some reason I'd been lucky. If I could have saved her I would but it was impossible. Could she even survive traveling forward in time? And where would I hide her if she did?

I harbored crazy thoughts. I could go to her and never come back. Logic reminded me I was almost immortal and Angelina wasn't. Eventually Angelina would die from other causes and I would be trapped, left to wander Florence like a spectre, invisible and alone, a pathetic voyeur forever. Besides, I couldn't desert my new family whose lives depended on me or betray Delphi even though I wanted to. I didn't like her but she'd had enough pain. She was beginning to lessen her grip on Cecco and I was not above prying her fingers from his. I was becoming self-centered. *Jealousy.*

But didn't Delphi and Cecco deserve to be together? I anguished over it. *Guilt.* And if I stayed, in a way, they always would be. I was their bridge. The bizarre truth about time-travel is that everyone is immortal as many times as diving allowed. It was a forever replay button of a recorded hit movie.

The chessboard was loaded. A full row of PIAT power on one side, facing down a family of PIAT's pawns on the other. Below them a child named Beatrice and Angelina slept in death like an enchanted princess, and time protected her from suffering. Angelina was dust, but when I heard the painting cry I couldn't help but comfort her. Was I in any pain? Joanna had asked.

"Wait my angel, I'm coming," I said to the painting. "Mommy's coming. It will be all right. I promise."

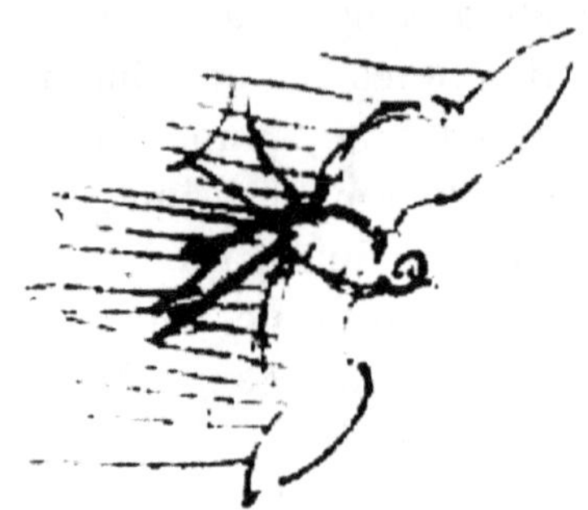

Love & Death/chapter forty-four

JUNE 30, 2066

Phillip lay in the shade chewing a blade of grass. I meant to startle him, and I did. If he'd been a peacock he would have fanned his tail.

"Love what you've done with your hair," he said. "Very mermaidy."

I pulled my hands from my pockets and checked. They were mother of pearl. "Ironic," I said.

"It's the little things. Small colors, like the shades of your chameleon hair when it's calm," he said.

"*Little* colors? Do you mean like the *little* black dress, or a *little* green man, or an aging man's need for a *little* red sports car?"

He grimaced. "Not to mention your *little* lies."

"Little WHITE lies."

"I would expect nothing less of you."

"Not too little to cause an aftershock I hope."

"After what you said the other day, not much can shock me. I hear you surprised Hamm. He's over the moon. Nice job."

I faked a look of outrage. "Damn! I was going for a heart attack."

"Sure thing, Tiger. You're different. I can feel your anger. Sometimes it swells over my head and at other times it oozes around the floor. It was Leonardo wasn't it? Tell me I'm wrong."

My hair ruffled in protest but my cuticles told me it remained deep-brunette entwined with passive beige stripes. Tiger stripes. "Here I am. I'm a person and a thing, as you see."

"As a time-traveler, you're also a place. Which one do you prefer to be?"

A flash of white surged and retreated in my bangs. I felt them move. I saw my nails like a silver tide, rushing in and out. "A person," I said under my breath.

"I didn't hear you."

"A mother." The words came strong, without bitterness."

"That's the hard part settled, then. Now we can progress."

"To where, exactly?"

"About this child... forward I guess."

"That's rich, spoken to a time-traveler programmed to visit the past."

"But it's the past where you want to be. Isn't it? To be Delphi again?"

"Now that IS impossible," I said. I supressed a smile but my hair gave me away and flushed grey. My future and past were not subjects for light conversation, but Phillip was right. My recent past-life was my destination and the only way to reach it was via Delphi's lost future. And now I wanted to adopt a fifteenth-century child. Animation, reincarnation, or emotion, life was bizarre. "No. I will NEVER want to be Delphi. EVER!"

Phillip pulled me onto the grass. "What message do you carry for *me*, little Medusa?" he asked. "We have to talk. Hmmn. Now what could have made Delphi so guilt ridden? Did *she* want to be a mother? Don't you hate mysteries?"

"Delphi has a secret. What I want is no mystery. I got hooked. A child hoodwinked me. Please don't take this personally," I said, "I may have overstepped my humanity, and yes, I was a closet cynic who despised the world, but I'm still not as programmed as you are."

"In a good way, right?"

"I'm just *out* of the closet, so to speak. You've been groomed for years."

He checked the top of my head for signs of affection. We'd

established pastels were kinder colors. My nails showed deep navy-blue. He patted my hair as if to tame it. "Ouch. Snake bites."

"What are best friends for?" I said. "No lies." Message delivered, my hair turned soft and wavy, delicately pink like the inside of a conch shell.

"That day we spoke about you being a person. Your hair was very dark with wide stripes of soft beige. That's my favorite. You were receptive and gentle which is a rare occurrence for you. Not that I'm blaming you. But it's nice to know that side of you exists."

"I can't control my hair color."

"I can see that. Right now it's gone pale blue, which is lovely for a sky but it washes you out. When you wear dark colors you seem grounded, tougher, and that, dearest girl, is inspiring for the team."

I examined my blue fingernails, spreading them, playing air piano. "Maybe I should buy a pair of gloves and a wig."

"You know it wouldn't be a bad idea for when you have conferences with Hamm and Jarr. You tend to confuse them. Each of them thinks they have your code."

"I only have one code?"

It started to drizzle as we walked to my rooms to visit Florence (the bird) – a couple of chums with romance and motherhood buzzing around our heads like flies. Delphi was thinking of Cecco, I was fixated on motherhood, and Phillip was fantasizing about me.

Phillip draped his arm over my shoulders in a casual gesture that should have signaled camaraderie. Instead it was laced with supressed tenderness and I struggled free.

Desire was complicated. From my 'android with benefits' point of view, I knew passion and lust were chemical imbalances and intimacy was the residual need for human contact. Procreation demanded this. Genetics demanded this. Love had been a fascinating relic to study, but the more I dug, the more feelings came to the surface. I had dismissed Cecco as a romantic dream. I could do better. I wanted to dream it again. To Delphi, lust and love was unfavorably comparing plastic beads to pearls.

In an abstract longing, I wanted to relax into Phillip's attentions, never realizing how much I pined to let go. Phillip was just the wrong man but the right father. The perfect accomplice.

"I hate secrets," he said.

I stared wistfully out the window. The trees were a green and grey blur like an impressionist's landscape through the teeming glass.

"I love it when it's like this, don't you?" I said.

Phillip walked to the window to see what I could see. "I love you," he said.

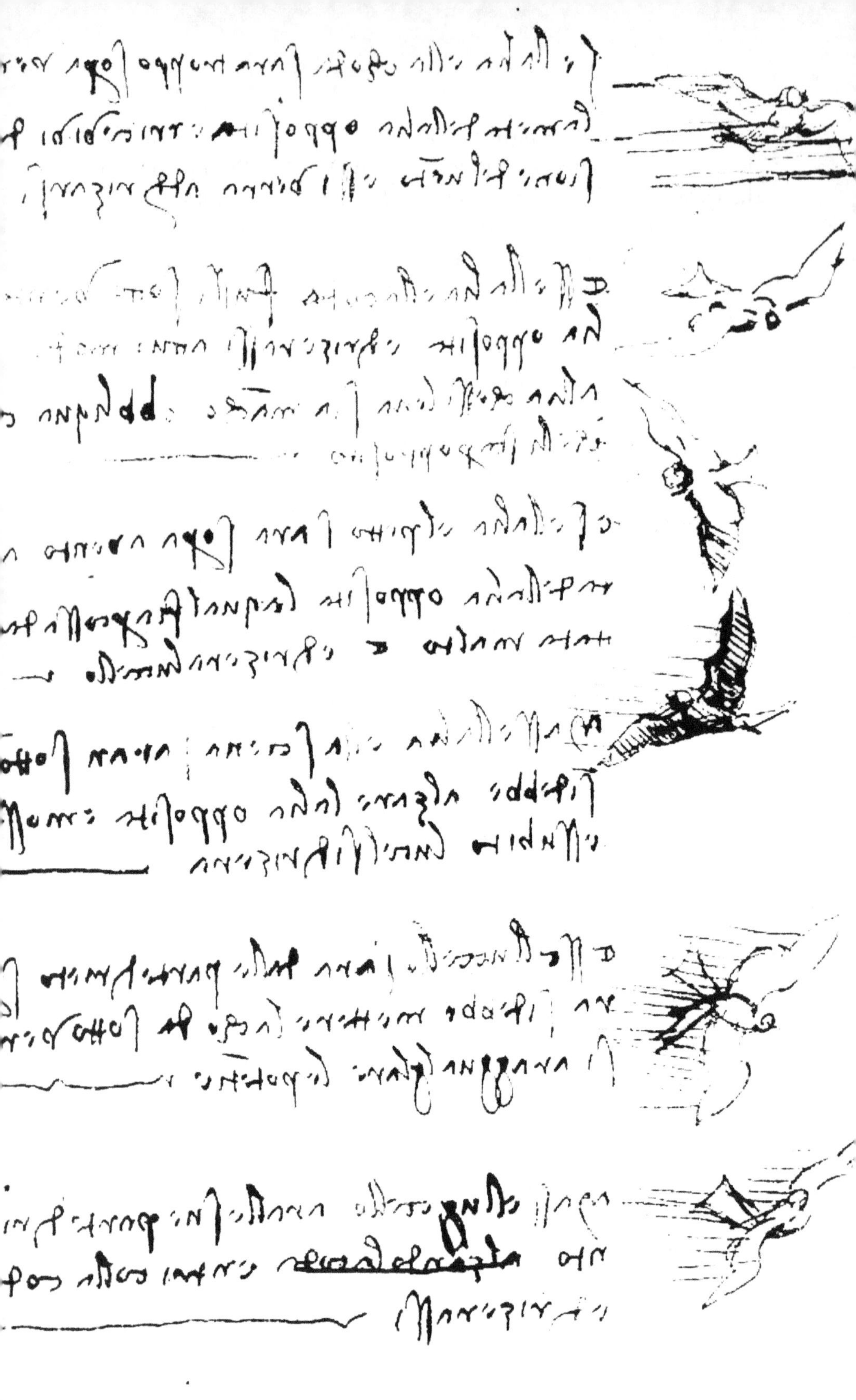

Present Imperfect

Time flies.
A day's journey
Diving towards death.
Death moves.
Life is too long.

White Lies/chapter forty-five

JULY 1, 2066

It was the season of 'L'air du Temps.'

When I burst through his door, Hamm had his back to me, examining the spine of a book at eyelevel on a wall lined with bookshelves.

"Good news!" I said. "It's Canada Day, and to celebrate I've decided to embrace my father's line of business."

He dropped his hand from the book and turned around. "What?"

"Dr. Who." Blank stare. "My dad." No response. "The time lord who saves lives and planets and lost things in general? *His* business. *Your* business. *My* business. And I have someone I want to save. I sent you the memo."

Hamm stared nonplussed when I added the words, time-travel.

"You had me going there."

"I don't have a sense of humor."

"As I heard it, you weren't yourself when you woke up, either. You thought you were Lisa Giocondo."

I wanted to say understatement but I couldn't bear his guaranteed response of blinking in silence. "You look serious," I said.

He plopped into his fancy executive chair and swiveled back and forth. The only sound in the room was the squeaky crush of leather upholstery. Finally, his agitation settled into business. He crossed his legs at the knee, an invisible clipboard in his hand.

I waited and said nothing. We played chicken with our eyes and I knew he would blink first.

He pulled his cigar from his pocket and examined the end as if the response he wanted was written there. "I got your proposal about the child you want to rescue," he said. "Would you like to talk about her?" Hamm tapped his cigar on the edge of the ashtray as if it were lit, and looked up. "The child is four, I believe. The same age you were when you were liberated from the nuns."

"No. The same age *Delphi* was. I'm a brand new girl."

"Right," he smirked, "but you see where I'm going. The child is you. It's *Delphi* business. She died and you lived, so you want to save her and yourself. Where do you propose to live? Do you have the means to show a child affection? I hear mothers do that."

"You should know. Delphi certainly received none from *your* family."

Hamm polished the toe of his shoe, rubbing off a speck of invisible dust. "Very amusing."

"I'm a savant, remember? I know things. I deduce things. Things a human won't admit to."

He regained his edge by waving his cigar in my face. "I won't let the project suffer. There are other donors besides Delphi who are promising. Your brain is Delphi's. Your memories are hers, so I say this to you *and* Delphi, living a new life through an organic child won't bring your mother back."

I held up my hand like an abacus and ticked a list of requirements on my fingers. "I will need child support, and a maternal leave of absence."

"Cherry, listen to me. You're presenting an emotional display you can't possibly feel. It's classic acting out. You're transposing what you've seen in a false memory. No doubt one of Delphi's dreams."

"I am a different Delphi. A New-World Delphi who doesn't care. I'm half-human. It's what PIAT wanted. Congratulations you have an android with a mission."

"Androids can't have fantasies."

"By the way, Mason *can* have fantasies. He likes you. He likes you A LOT."

Hamm blushed. "I can't work with that man. What has he said?"

"Why are you so angry?"

"I'm not angry."

"Scared then."

"Why would you think that?"

"Mr. Burgher, Sir, I'm an old-school savant. I see through human evasion. I'm a computer programmed to scan for facial tics. Ironic isn't it."

Hamm's bloodless reaction should have turned my skin the pasty dead white of a corpse and my hair into icicles. I thought it might fall out or morph into snakes or even braid itself into daggers and hurl themselves at his forehead. "What possible harm could it do?" I asked for the second time, "It's logical. Appease me and I'll work more efficiently. It's a win win for both of us."

Hamm examined his stapler by testing its spring like a Morse code operator and opening it to check if its barrel was full. Apparently he found the words he wanted there as well because he snapped it shut and looked up. "It would have devastating repercussions to this project. We need your concentration. What would that be like if you were mothering a child? No, this is my final word. Absolutely no more distractions. Phillip said giving you a bird would placate you. As if an android needed placating, but I see now Delphi is clearly in charge. The prime directive is in place for the safety of history. No exceptions."

I stared different daggers into Hamm's third eye, sending the impression of remote neutrality. "I should think you would want to mollify your victim and offer me some personal compensation for your crimes. A life for a life. A pet for a pet project."

"Victim?"

I refer to the equation," I said. "Death by way of violence equals victim. Pets euthanized for the crime of surviving their owners is criminal. I heard Brillo and Ben were put down. A bit drastic, that."

Hamm fixed me with a scowl. "I was not the one who froze Delphi or killed those animals."

"So, euthanasia was something your grandfather felt appropriate?"

"I am a seeker, MISS Cherry, as are you. We have a destiny to fulfil even if at times it seems like a burden. What would you have me do? Pull a human being from their own fate?"

"They were innocent pets," I said. "What possible reason could PIAT have for killing Brillo or Ben? They could have at least been adopted."

"It wasn't me who sent you to the freezer."

"It was *you* who defrosted me."

I stood at ease, arms at my sides. Military gestures served my purpose, confirming he was my commander-in-chief, and for now, I was a foot soldier. I had highlighted a passage from 'The Art of War' only that morning: *'Rouse your enemy, and learn the principle of his activity or inactivity. Force him to reveal himself, so as to find out his vulnerable spots.'* Sun Tzu was my Machiavelli. He was teaching me diplomacy. The harder sort with sharp edges unlike the silly manipulations of a petulant Ginevra. Without Delphi around I could be Sun Tzu's devoted follower. *'Engage people with what to expect,'* he wrote, *'It is what they are able to discern and confirms their projections. It settles them into predictable patterns of response, occupying their minds while you wait for the extraordinary moment — that which they cannot anticipate.'*

It was important to define myself, standing alone as one half of a double-agent, while the deadly weapon of clarity was still mine. Arrogance was no match for certainty. I knew how to defeat Hamm. I knew what needed to change. I had to take Delphi like bitter medicine, one spoonful at a time and act sweet as pie.

Delphi sent me a movie premiere. Hamm waived his cigar about as he spoke of putting one over on 'the guys in London. I watched his arms flailing in deep water, clearly in trouble. He was the size of a goldfish. I heard a toilet flush, and a surge of blue water swirled where he now stood. He was out of his depth.

"I happen to agree with you," I said to Hamm. "I can't fault logic. History must be protected. Ironically, history is our only future. Without it we fail to exist. If IT changes WE change. I understand. You are correct. The 'Book of Changes' sites no blame. The 'I Ching' never lies."

He searched my face for deceit and relaxed. "You're an odd creature but I do like you. God, a computer with spunk. Thanks Dad."

My hatred arrived like killing instincts blowing down from the Arctic Circle. Strong enough to eclipse the joy of motherhood. To my advantage Delphi was nowhere in discernable hearing distance. It took more than a cool head to prevail. Sun Tzu showed me it required a grandmaster of chess. Hamm's Achilles heel lay as exposed as a painting under an x-ray. It was his mother.

"Good then," he said. "Now go and surprise me. And tame Delphi for god's sake. She made you an emotional wreck last week. You're programmed for chrissakes."

I stared straight ahead, looking at the wall of books. *Contrite.* "I cannot *feel* gratitude," I said, "but it is the correct word for appreciating Florence."

He brightened. "Are you headed there tomorrow?"

"No, I meant the bird. I named my cockatoo, Florence. I thought Phillip told you."

"I thought he was getting you a budgie."

Hamm had no surprises, no strategy; he would be fun to kill.

"Phillip chose the perfect bird," I said. "The logic of having a bird that can talk is flawless. She's company when everyone sleeps. I'm teaching her to quote Keats."

"Too bad it can't play chess."

"Grandmasters are time-travelers," Sphinx said.

"Chess is too easy. Would you care for a game?"

The art of cruelty was amazing. I saw an image of another Cherry, who reached into the humidor, lit a cigar, and blew smoke in Hamm's face. I contained my guilt that looked very much in my mind's eye like a funerary urn filled with the warm ashes of Delphi's stolen life. I pictured Angelina, a six-hundred-year-old child who slumbered out of danger in a blue police box within the safe harbor of Dr. Who's *dimensional transcendentality.* Mommy's coming, I whispered to her.

I hadn't reported being seen to Phillip or the team for several days. Not until after I'd broached the subject of retrieving Angelina with Hamm and it had been trashed to death.

They knew it was serious when I locked Florence in the bathroom.

"This is either the beginning of a beautiful partnership or the death of trust," I began. "I need to take everyone's pulse."

Lewis held out his wrist. "All for one," George said.

Joanna nodded like a bobble-head doll.

I expected a more poetic response from Bill but all he said was. "I'm in, whatever it is."

I gave him a despairing look and crossed my arms.

Bill looked apologetic. "Once more unto the breach," he said in a theatrical voice, flexing his fingers the way one does before defusing a bomb.

"A week ago, in Florence, you know I saw a person who affected me. What you don't know is that she saw ME," I said. "A child. She tracked my movements as I moved about Leonardo's studio and addressed me as Mamma. You heard it, Bill. I thought it was the end of the world, but it's the beginning of what I intend to do. I'm going to save her. I've become a maternal force rather than a killing machine. What I mean is, I can be both. Questions?"

Dotting the Eyes/chapter forty-six

JULY 3, 2066

I linked my arm in Phillip's as he escorted me from the fountain. He often checked to see if I was there. He said he sensed I was approaching melancholy whenever he saw me, but he knew about Cecco. I'd been honest about everything Delphi sent me. I told him he was wrong and that I evoked his own feelings of melancholy, and that there was a difference. But he was right. I waited there in vain, to see the phantom shape of Cecco sitting under one of the horses.

"How did you manage to escape the Mason genetics?" I asked.

"A stork delivered me."

"Yes, they have a terrible sense of direction. I know this firsthand."

"I'm not smart enough to play with science," he said.

"Albert Einstein said he wasn't smarter than everyone else, he just stayed with problems longer. Consider *them there* apples, Sir Isaac."

Phillip looked skeptical. "Then you and he are kindred spirits, the father of physics and the mother of time."

"Perhaps I was only meant to be a midwife."

"He didn't come, did he? Cecco? You were waiting for him."

"I don't think he can."

Perhaps I could be Delphi's brown duck paddling her duck-lings out to sea for soggy breadcrumbs. Would Phillip and I be enough? I saw a floating triangular window in a black eight ball, signs point to no, the message read. In any case a stork delivering a pelican was some feat.

"I need my... I mean, Delphi's birth records," I said.

Phillip Moon delivered the confidential files in a plain manila envelope. "You can keep these. I made copies," he said. "Are you sure you want this? It's bad stuff. This is was what they meant to erase. Jarr likes to brag. He also likes a 'wee nip' in the evenings, if you know what I mean, so..."

"It's what they *think* they erased," I said. "Their own technology damns them. It's one of the perks of time-travel. The power of the phoenix is not to be trifled with."

Phillip tapped the fat envelope. "Your orphanage history is in here. It isn't pretty. One thing for sure, I'm now building a file of my own."

"It will save me a trip."

He stared at his shoes. "I doubt that."

"*Can of worms,*" Sphinx shouted from far away.

"Worms crawling," Delphi added, even further away, age three.

I accepted the envelope from Phillip's hand.

"Not fun reading, I'm afraid," he said. "I'll wait here with you unless..."

"Stay. I may need smelling salts. Not that they would work." The fact he didn't respond with a smile unnerved me.

Some of the information was old news. My name had been Delphi Sharpe. I died in 2014 when I was twenty-seven. I had been a 'Snow White' in stasis, and my captor 'dwarfs' kept me in a freezing glass coffin for fifty-two years. I was awakened in 2066 and I'd subsisted since April, as their prize hostage for almost four months. The secret data was as startling as it was corrupt. It trailed back to my mother before I had been conceived. She had been diagnosed as delusional and upgraded to schizophrenic. No-one had been there to defend her. Some things were surprises and shocks. *Newsflash* – Blanche was NOT my sister! That got a hurray from Delphi. They were not even distantly related. Blanche had tagged along from the soup kitchen, likely strayed from a down and out parent passed out from an addiction, or, given her personality, they may have left her there on purpose.

I extracted a single sheet written on both sides, and a blue index card stapled to a photograph. I shook out the envelope but nothing further fell from it.

"Not exactly a cornucopia of information is it," I said.

"The fact that it survived at all indicates you were somewhat of a star."

Phillip stayed my hand. "Look, there's some nasty stuff in there. But you have the right to know. To fight them you *need* to know."

"Then, just tell me."

"Your death was not entirely accidental. You'll have to read the rest. I don't have the guts to tell you."

I sniffed the paper. As near as I could determine, it smelled sour. The letterhead showed an image of a heart on fire with the words underneath: Sisters of the Immaculate Compassion. They didn't have much to say. I scanned the handwritten history. It was in point form. Dates flashed. The arrival of seventeen-year-old Sybil Sharpe with her 'daughter,' Blanche. There was more about Sybil than the girl: mother erratic and delusional, the father of her child not only unknown but a demon. Nice touch. Delphi shows irrational behavior, 'keeps drawing eggs and nests.'

Sybil had told them my father was invisible. She declared herself a virgin, notwithstanding, they believed she'd 'technically' already delivered one child at an impossible age if they'd done the math. My father had been not been named. A deserter by all accounts.

"How ironic she fled towards Sisters of the Immaculate Compassion," I said. "It says here, there was trouble with my back. That may account for the scars. I knew of a surgery. Apparently two cysts were removed."

Shock spread into my arms from the paper as I read aloud. "Mother's death from cerebral hemorrhage. My God. This date is six years AFTER I was born! They told me she'd died in childbirth."

"Yes, they made notes," Phillip said. "They're clipped to the photograph."

A vacant-looking Sybil stared from a small square. Blanche had her eyes closed, her head blurred from moving as the shutter clicked.

My mother's swollen belly drew my eyes. I had been in there. How odd. But I hadn't killed her. I had *not* killed her.

Sybil's eyes in the photograph were clear. Her posture echoed a woman who'd given up, but her expression was not one of the demented creature they'd described as an irrational lunatic. Her eyes were wistful, even euphoric, as if she were stoned. The resemblance to Delphi was remarkable.

"Why did they never show me this? Delphi asked as if roused from a deep sleep."

"You might well ask Blanche. She had a copy."

The last image of Blanche flashed. Mr. Bennet stared at me, his pink tongue lolling as he panted. I remembered the silkiness of his red fur.

"What did she call you?"

"Dark angel. She thought it was funny."

"So, no love lost."

"None to even misplace," Delphi said. "We were estranged for most of my life after she was adopted, and then she showed up a few months before I died."

"She was jealous," Phillip said. "Read the note."

Phillip waited for the axe to fall while I read.

Blanche Tamara – paid three-thousand-dollars. For final services rendered, it said. Mrs. French's monthly stipend of four-hundred-dollars was listed over an entire year. There was mention of a file of her reports.

"That old cow. Where's her file? What final services?"

"Gone. Destroyed most likely. This envelope was not exactly in a cabinet for easy access. It was in a moldy box earmarked for archiving but someone shoved it in a corner. I think it was my mother. It was in her storage locker under a lot of stuff. Jarr put me on cleaning duty. He was looking for something."

"What else was in the box? Were there toffees? Sometimes I can taste them when I wake up."

"But you can't taste. You don't sleep."

"I doze a little every so often, but that's my secret. I am in shutdown mode as far as Jarr cares. That suffices. But I *do* sleep, Phillip, and I dream."

"You're full of surprises."

"And what happened to 'Mom'? My umbrella, Mom?"

"Seized by the authorities at the inquest and discarded. It was… he coughed, tampered with. According to missing records it had been fitted with copper wire. Taking it into an electrical storm was suicide. Well, murder, actually. I'm sorry but there's every indication that it was Blanche who delivered it from the lab to you."

"So that was her big secret. She was on her own mission, and in league with old Magda."

"I'm sorry, Cherry… and you, Delphi. I wish that was all… but…I have the other pages to this file. I think we should talk before you read them."

"At least you and I don't have secrets. What are you afraid of? You're the messenger not the message?"

"I'm not afraid. I'm deeply ashamed for what this institute has done to you in the name of profit. Murder and …"

"What could be worse than murder?"

"I don't know where to begin."

"Lewis Carroll wrote start at the beginning go on to the end, then stop. How about you give *that* a try," I said.

Phillip sucked in his breath and took my hand. It felt moist with tremors. Warm and innocent. "You were a mother," he said. "Delphi had a child. That last year when she/you went into hospital for appendicitis, it was a lie. You were four months pregnant and of course they thought they were performing an abortion. They certainly never guessed your child would survive the procedure, but it… *she*, did. For a while. You had a daughter. She couldn't thrive and she died, four-weeks later. I'm so very sorry."

I felt unusually calm. Logic prevailed. "I think she may be the child I heard laughing," Delphi said. "I have an internal imprint of her. I imagined this. Perhaps I'd felt a foetus quicken but didn't know it at the time."

Phillip held up both hands. "I can only deal with one spokeswoman at a time," he said.

"Let me," I said to Delphi. "It'll help me get in touch with your rage."

"Are you okay?" Phillip asked.

"I wasn't an orphan, I was *murdered*, and I was a *mother*. Do I feel okay?"

Phillip hugged me, whispering the words 'I'm an idiot' several times before releasing me. He held me at arm's length, his brown eyes over-bright with sympathy, a detective momentarily distracted by sentiment but back on track. "Do you know who your father was?"

"Like mother, like daughter. I had no relations with a man. Cecco was my *dreamed* lover, but that's hardly the same thing. Sybil was a virgin when she died. You don't have to believe me, but it's true. My mother - myself, neither of us were lying."

"It could have been artificial insemination. They wanted to clone you."

"Spare the logic, spoil the computer," Sphinx said. *"Bigger questions, smaller minds."*

"I have to go back and visit my mother. I have to see what happened. It will take everyone's cooperation."

"You have no idea what Hamm is planning for your team," Phillip said. "Each one of them has something to hide. Coercion is a nasty business. They weren't just vetted for their skills. Blackmail begins as grey laundry. None of them have family. They were chosen for that as well."

"Then it's big mutiny. And what about you? Are you leaping with the rest of us?"

"I'll do more than that, but we can talk about that later. For now, I needed you to know what I know."

"This stays between you and me. Don't even tell Joanna."

"Fine with me. She's upset enough."

"What did they name her? The child?"

"Leda. You named her Leda. Hamm's grandfather consulted you under the guise of research for a name. I have no clearance there and it would look suspicious if I mentioned it. But no problem, my uncle is also an idiot when it comes to his bragging rights. All I need to do is look riveted and he'll spill."

After that I lost the ability to process a sane response. Knowing I'd been a mother hit in a hard wave. Angelina's four year old face blurred into a newborn's. Phillip's face and form dissipated through the flood but I took his expression of panic with me. He called, "Cherry," in a distorted voice. *Meltdown.*

I experienced a revulsion so deep I floated in blackness, powering down, bleeding out, until the image of a brain monitor's screen materialized. It flat-lined into a long beep, then spiked into wild peaks and valleys. The taste of bile surprised my mouth. *Rage.*

The sensation of deflating followed. I doubled over with dizziness as my functions collapsed into a descending elevator. The program of breathing shifted into fighting gasps. *Nausea.* Given permission, old vows exploded in bursts of energy as a new world order. Fire and ice. The domain of PIAT receded into the lifeless word 'institution.'

Phillip's voice came again. "CHERRY! Come back!"

I accepted motherhood defending my thought children and the adult human ones, and a newborn baby I now felt compelled to avenge, in addition to a newborn painting. *Revulsion.*

Flailing stopped. I fused into white hot anger. A fist of fire punched my solar plexus. A door in my skull opened. An icy heart was ripped out of me and tossed into a choppy sea. *Fury.*

Light blinded me in a sharp blow followed by painfully bright flashes of acid yellow, red, and sharp lime-green. I heard a click with each change of color and realized I was replicating the time I was nine, playing with an empty slide-viewer pointed at the sun, then a red door, then spring grass.

I remained huddled until the colors passed into a grey shield. The child of my body was dead. The child of my heart had perished in a fire. I died again, this time emotionally to accompany Angelina and Leda. *Grief.*

I wanted to howl down the moon, vomit the sun, and pull Angelina from the flames. I wanted to climb into a warm towel with my stillborn infant. I wanted the three of us to lie swaddled until the color of the morning sky warmed us. *Wrath.*

Phillip stared at my head in horror. "Welcome back, Medusa," he said. "I don't know where you've been but I hope I never have to go there. You screamed fit to wake the dead." He paused. "Please excuse that terrible faux pas."

I'd heard my scream. "Perhaps you've forgotten my job. I can dive back, find out what's been destroyed, and listen it to the entire scheme if necessary, but I need to run several project trips to appear normal. I'll tell Hamm I have some inklings of new high-yielding sites. Leave that to me." *Hatred.*

"They always do. If you suggest; they follow."

"I'm a mother bear, Phillip. I have two daughters to avenge. You may suppose I will be formidable but cagey."

Phillip stayed my arm as I started to leave. "There's more," he said.

I slumped bodily into a chair. "Go."

"Hamm's father is still alive. Sort of."

"They froze him? Those idiots froze him? You knew about this?"

"I was ordered not to tell you."

"How long?"

"A couple of years."

I made an involuntary gag reflex, covered my mouth with both hands and bent double. Sphinx called out the words *ad nauseam.* "I feel odd. My insides are surging." *Queasiness. Dizziness.*

"I'm happy for you," Phillip said. "Welcome home."

"So this is being sick to one's stomach?"

"Don't underestimate Hamm. There's years of secrets to hide."

"You're saying my team really is in physical danger? I was right?"

Phillip shrugged. "I'm saying poison is thicker than blood. I'm saying murder is something Hamm feels he has to live up to. It's a gauntlet thrown down by his father. My uncle is letting more and more slip. As if he's leaking information on purpose. He's seen a lot of things. I think he's scared. I think he's losing it."

"I've got to thaw old Good Time Charlie out before I kill him," I said. *Disgust.*

Fireworks/chapter forty-seven

JULY 4, 2066

Every time I saw Hamm or Jarr after that, I saw murder. Hamm falling from a tall building, Jarr hanging from a tree, daggers flashing, guns smoking, and goblets of wine bubbling with cyanide. These were the hopes that swarmed around me. And with them came a new feeling. *Pleasure.*

Hamm played a tough game in a hand-me-down rule of matriarchal dominance from mother to mail-order-wife. He was a cowering son whose only badge of masculinity was the muscle power of wealth. It lay upon his authoritarian life – a craven symbol of false confidence, impotent without fire – a spineless fixation for a man I'd come to loath. I knew him for his malignant ethics. Like his father before him, his own pharaoh's 'great wife,' ignored him and dallied with slaves.

Images of me in a full-length mirror spontaneously combusted. Where I had stood was a miniscule pile of red ash.

"Self-destruction is no way to win," Sphinx called out. *"Use the magic letter. Flight and fight rely on the same action – a delayed response. Your job manipulates the laws of pyrotechnics. Be the blazing sun. Use it!"*

Her advice gave me time to head for the door before I could set the papers on Hamm's desk ablaze with my eyes.

I left him quickly to maintain the impression of indifference. I had suggested and been denied, nothing more. But as I made my way back to my room I began to deteriorate. Unleashed anger side-swiped me. Wrath hit me with an image of a screaming mouth that became a door. A rusty key turned in my throat. I stifled the sensation of rising bile, and watched in horror as one by one, the mouth's teeth rotted and fell, until it looked like the pink gums of a newborn, screaming for its mother. I had been a mother. *Joy. Horror.*

I clung to the stair banister, an outraged woman, gasping for control but the rhythms of rapid breathing quickened into a gag reflex. I reached my bedroom and lay against the door, panting.

My brain scanned for anything I could use as a weapon until I realized my brain WAS my weapon. The only way to outwit a tyrant was through deceit and cunning. *Violence. Betrayal.*

Gradually my tirade subsided into fatigue but I was left with the sensation of a burning scalp and a vision of a plastic doll with holes for eyes and melting fingernails.

Aside from the imminent reality that my brain may implode, I was a thrilled to view myself as an active volcano. My anger was a plume of debris that blackened the sun. I knew the sensation of meltdown. Anger set me free to hate. Rage followed. Trust was everything. Timing was swept aside. Naturally, I seemed powerless. I *was* powerless. But I was on purpose, and that gave its own degree of wobbly satisfaction.

To my surprise, my anger-based feelings slowly receded. It was like stepping into a warm bath. First, my toes were happy and then I submerged my head and surfaced feeling reborn, as well I might. I still had my plan, and that thought refreshed me. I was eager to comply so that I may mutiny with the intense rage of a mother bear defending her cub. It would be slow and brutal. I would savor every bite. *Delight. Anticipation.*

"When you can smell the roses the world will change," Sphinx whispered.

I suspected that day would come because Delphi and I were healing what the other lacked. Delphi was gaining my qualities of the warrior as I energized her pacifist nature. I was walking an emotional tightrope with only the skeletal spokes of an umbrella for balance. I was a pattern-seeking machine occasionally dominated by a confused woman with a shady secret. *Treason.*

"Magic word, reason," Sphinx shouted over the roar of my emotional tsunami.

It was 5 a.m. when I headed for Joanna's trailer. The ground was damp with dew. It had rained and left a trail of shallow puddles like footprints. Each one gleamed greasy blue in the grey-lit gravel. For the first time, I crossed the courtyard without sparing a moment for the fountain.

The team was asleep in varying degrees of beta. I shocked them into rumpled T-shirts and cold jeans, and corralled them into the common room. Leading them back to my quarters was like herding fireflies.

"You do have a coffee maker, right?" George called out, lagging behind.

Florence was noticeably agitated. She flapped her usual protest circuit around the room and settled herself on the back of a dining chair.

Bill flirted Florence onto his arm and played kissy with her.

Lewis squinted at the light. "Wassup," he said, without it sounding like a question.

I waited a four count before answering. "Hamm's *time* is up."

"You mean we're out of time," Lewis mumbled.

Joanna thwacked him upside his head.

I waited till after the distribution of coffee. "Between you, me, and Florence, my emotions are *too* on board. I've decided to take some actions that may shock you. But first, I need to tell you the story of how I got here. I should say how all of us arrived at this moment."

"Bedtime stories for breakfast," Lewis said.

"Once upon a time... Hamm's grandfather murdered Delphi," I began.

That got their coffee rolling and there were no questions while I recited the unembellished facts. They sat spellbound, past the tale of Angelina and Lisabetta, past the convent fire and the dreams of Paris, until I came to the part about Delphi's child. Questions burst into the morning for details. I had channeled Scheherazade enough to rouse the emotions I wanted myself.

"Bastards," Bill said. "We're next."

I gazed from Phillip to the other males in turn. "Phillip put his head on the block spilling the gory details," I said. "And I don't intend to surrender without a kill. I've been waiting for a reason to let go. Just so you know, I'll be making a few unscheduled trips. Otherwise, it's business as usual."

There was the sound of cruel laughter in my head. I covered my ears. "Anyone else hear that?" I asked. "I heard jeering?"

Joanna fussed, sensing one of my turns. "Have you got a headache?"

The voice came again.

"Delphi's being bullied by a painting," I said. "She's terrified. I hear it taunting her. *She* feels the headache, not me. It won't leave her alone."

"Which painting?"

"Saints preserve us," Sphinx said.

I looked up and to the right, scanning for Sphinx's clue. "It's something to do with a saint," I said. "I heard it."

"You mean the painting of a saint?"

"Little devils make big trouble," Sphinx added.

"I know who it is," I said. "A devil *and* a saint."

George perked up. "A Leonardo?"

I visualized a painting I knew well but never liked of an egotistical male wearing a bearskin tunic. A smarmy smile widened under arrogant eyes and a mane of curly hair turned alternate shades of red and black. "Yes. A Leonardo. It's his 'St. John.'"

"I know that one," Lewis said. "It's a portrait of Leonardo's catamite."

I silenced Lewis with a penetrating glare. "We don't *know* that, so drop it."

Lewis glared back. "Maybe you *do* know but aren't saying."

George steered me away from Lewis. "And the devil?"

"The sitter is Giangiacomo Caprotti, grownup menace, the waif Leonardo adopted to pose for a male angel. Fawned off by the parents who wanted rid of him. Knowing Leonardo's penchant for angelic models with curly hair, Gianni was brought to the master. After that, he amused Leonardo with his impish behavior and stayed on past his original purpose, earning his apprenticeships as a servant boy. He was dubbed, Salai – Leonardo's 'little devil.' After that, his face made it into several paintings, even a Madonna, and vanity got out of hand."

"I told you," Lewis said, winking at George. "Things got out of hand a lot back then."

"You two should talk," Bill said.

"We're in genius company, then. Methinks your precious Shakespeare dabbled on ye olde casting couch. Boys dressed as girls and all that."

Bill opened his mouth, ready to leap to Shakespeare's defense. I sent him a warning look. *Exasperation.* "Leonardo was too kind to turn a vulnerable teenager into the streets," I said. "Salai had no trouble making his way there, himself. Kind people are easy prey. A gentle man, concentrating on math and science, and art that mushroomed into obsessions, blind to petty swindlers. Leonardo was the easiest to milk of all."

Joanna leaped up and patted Bill's shoulder. "I'll get the book."

I opened the book to the St. John. His expression played chicken, daring me to burn out my eyes.

"This painting was with Leonardo when he died," I said. "Along with the 'Mona Lisa' and a 'Leda.'"

"Nasty piece of work," Joanna said. "Literally."

"He was a greedy little viper. Leonardo took him in when he was eight. Six years later he'd wormed his way into Leonardo's heart." I glared at Lewis. "Leonardo was his *stepfather.* Nothing more. Salai was eventually challenged and eclipsed by a young nobleman named Francesco Melzi who became Leonardo's favorite apprentice, a fair painter in his own right, and Leonardo's heir."

"Delphi's Cecco?"

"So, this Salai creep's taking his revenge out on Delphi," Bill said. "Talk about the perfect victim."

"Revenge is human, yes?" Salai said. "But how frustrating for a mechanical woman."

The page hissed at me. "Very amusing," I said.

Bill had been watching my face. "What did it say?"

I wanted to grab George by the neck when he peeped over my shoulder, waving his coffee under my nose. "Why's he pointing at the sky?"

"It's malevolent," Joanna said. "Close the book. It feels as if he's in the room when its opened."

"She can't," Bill said. "It's talking."

Salai leered from the painting. "Your precious Leonardo was a pervert," he said. "Your precious Cecco too. I can prove it. Delphi knows. Just ask her."

Sphinx interrupted him. *"Wearing the skin of a bear won't make you tough,"* she said. *"Once a viper, always a snake."*

I heard a soft popping noise and felt a sensation in my ears like rushing water as the page pretended to burst into flames.

I smelled the coffee, a bitter slam of dark surprise, and recoiled, just as Sphinx quoted Sun Tzu. *"Ponder and deliberate before you make a move."*

Joanna stood and stretched. "We need the 'Sun.'"

Joanna rifled in her purse and returned. For a moment I thought she might have heard Sphinx, but Sphinx had only planted one of her suggestions.

The silence was broken by Florence. *"I do not like green eggs or Hamm,"* she recited.

"We're rabbits between two pits of snakes which is dangerous enough. I would suggest you hand in your resignations except it's much too late for that. I request you look the other way for a few more dives. I need to confirm a few things. After that we should be good to go."

I had *smelled* their precious drug, the mighty stimulant coffee, in a wave of conflicting feedback.

George drained his coffee, wiped his mouth like a cowboy in a saloon, and slammed the mug on the table. "I doubt resigning is an option."

Joanna handed me the Sun Book. She looked happier without her smile. "Do you intend to rescue Angelina?"

I hoped Florence would stay silent. I needn't have worried. Bill was distracting her with the buttons on his jacket, and I realized with growing wonder how much I hated buttons.

I could have kissed Bill for his delayed response. "Well, *mes amis*, I think Mammo means business."

My hair frizzed into a clown's wig, and Florence had to be removed to the bedroom with a new cuttlebone to save her sanity and our privacy.

I closed the door on her and re-entered the buzz like a queen bee about to order, abandon hive.

George watched my hair react. "Scuze the pun but you've got to stop wigging out like that. Really. It doesn't help things."

"Leopards can't change their spots," I said.

"They can be skinned, though," Lewis added.

I ignored his threat as another display of false bravado. "I have a fairly sound plan. It's been gestating while I waited for my senses to catch up. I now own the emotion of anger, so there's that. Someday there will be a reckoning," I said, and my words dropped like stones. I corrected myself. "Someday *they'll* burn and I won't go back for them."

Lewis raised his eyebrows. "Them?"

"Hamm, Jarr, Hooper wherever *he* is, and Charlie," I said.

"Um... Hooper's dead," Phillip said. "I was told not to tell you."

Lewis used his spoon as a gavel. "Motion carried. New rules of survival after breakfast. We act normal."

Bill stood, and leaned over the table like a supporting General. "Then we start digging a tunnel to the fifteenth-century or wherever Mom says. Right?"

Joanna cleared her throat. "Everyone. I need to say something. I've heard things I wasn't meant to hear. Something dirtier than usual is going on. The four of us are effectively owned. Legally and physically. Jarr said we were expendable. Hamm agreed. He called us sheep awaiting slaughter."

Bill sent me an 'I told you' so look. "How did you hear something like that?"

"Phillip told me." She gave Phillip an apologetic smile. "He's nervous. The project is like a bad dream. Things are surfacing. Bad things."

"There's no need to soften the word nightmare. But not to worry." I tapped the Sun Book. "I've got my orders. I know you guys would jump at the chance to start again, and I'm trying to make that happen, which is why I need to have both of my hemispheres under control. Hamm's mind has atrophied into a Napoleon complex. Mine has to stay in Wellington mode."

Bill took me aside. "Which daughter do you want to visit first? Because there may not be time for both."

Joanna clutched the 'Sun Book,' her eyes bright with excitement.

"I have a safe-house in mind," I said. "An old friend will be in charge. I can't tell you more just yet. I have to channel my anger and consult with Sphinx."

"You mean consult with your anger and *channel* Sphinx," Phillip said.

After the morning wakeup call my team was solidly in 'us against the world' form. Our goals were equally primal; they wanted to survive, and I wanted to be the mother of two.

Delphi retreated long enough for me to gain absolute control. I was an emotional newborn with bones of steel. I sniffed the wind as a predator, using the muscle memories of a mother bear, prepared to kill every last person who separated me from Angelina and Leda.

I despised the waste of Delphi's genius. Her path was the passive way of the savant, an apologetic compliant to a bully. She was no better than a Florentine citizen, stoic to a fault, sacrificing honest vanity to the conscience of a tyrannical priest, determined to make a city pay for his fiery shame. She nursed detachment, too sensitive to withstand a debate, browbeaten by a lonely secret.

But thanks to Joanna's book, my calling was the warrior's way. I was a single-minded mother paddling her ducklings to shore under rumbling skies. A brewing storm wasn't going to deter me. A silly fear of weather fit for mother ducks.

"*Silly,*" Sphinx said. "*Sun Tzu married Mother Goose.*"

My plan presented itself as an unrehearsed magician's trick, but I was in the audience waiting to be amazed.

"*Pick a card,*" Sphinx said. "*Any card. But let me see it.*"

I showed Sphinx a deck of tarot cards. My hands shuffled a smooth blur of pictures falling like a waterfall in slow motion. I dealt a card face up. It was the Empress.

"The fruitful mother of thousands," Sphinx said.

My voice spilled like cold syrup. "Two children is enough."

Being the biological mother of Leda and the emotional mother of Angelina changed the stakes. Killing Hamm was a Band-Aid plan.

My words thickened to toffee. "Blood is thicker than water and kindred is stronger than rage."

"Archetypes are stronger than both," Sphinx said.

I opened a memory and looked around. I was a lost innocent breaching the borders of middle-earth where faerie glamor stretched days into centuries. The brown eyes of a mother bear in a labyrinth met me. But it was no longer spring. Her cubs rolled in autumn leaves. A pearl moon turned the dusk blue, caught in the bare branches of a cherry tree. "I think she smiled at me," I said.

"Yes. Yes, she did," Sphinx said. *"Now move on. Forget Goldilocks and tell me the story of Sleeping Beauty. Time cursed and blessed her. Eternity was softened to a hundred enchanted years. Your truth lies hidden in the open. See it shining."*

Sphinx wheedled me like a kid at bedtime. *"Go on. Tell me the story again."*

My voice echoed back to me like a prophecy. "A baby princess..."

"A little girl," Sphinx translated. *"Go on."*

"Is cursed..."

"Is born into a loveless world," she coaxed.

"She falls asleep under a wicked spell..."

"Cryogenics."

"The magic is too strong to erase."

"Science."

"But she wakes up..."

"But — she returns to emotional life."

"After being kissed by a prince."

"After feeling human affection."

"The end."

"And they lived happily ever after."

"No-one knows that for sure."

"Delphi knows."

I sat in silence with Sphinx breathing softly beside me. I surrendered to her measured rhythms until logic returned.

"Then why didn't Delphi know what happened to her back there in the storm? Why didn't she know about Blanche? Why didn't she know about Leda?"

"She was under a spell called anesthetic."

"If I have to pick up her pieces I need to see for myself. I need to know for sure. Delphi can mourn Leda, dry-eyed to a fault, but I'm the one who has the courage to visit her. I'm the *real* mother. I know it's time to say hello and goodbye."

Delphi sent me a picture of a sculptor chiseling the words 'TIME-SENSITIVE,' in letters large enough to dwarf the faces of Mt. Rushmore.

"That sculptor fellow of yours should hammer the word 'irony' underneath 'time-sensitive,' and maybe a giant question mark, a hundred-feet-tall," I said.

She answered with an animation of a mountainside overflowing with lava so that the message carved there, melted into red gravy. I reminded her of the firepower of a volcano, so she changed the image to an anthill with red ants skittering down its side. Next to it she'd spelled out the word 'IRONY' in sugar cubes. I watched the ant party take the letter 'Y' first.

The word iron left me with streams of data referencing the iron-age and swords vs. plowshares – a subliminal prompt I took to mean, stay strong and cold and unyielding.

"A grain of salt prophecy," Sphinx said. *"Ice is made to melt."*

Delphi hadn't fully died. Her death was incomplete as far as regular death goes. Brain death was never on the table if her telepathic gifts were going to survive in me. It was a matter of ethics. Near-death blurred into the edges of sour grapes and turned rancid. Babies cried in two centuries.

I would make time to visit both children. The only way forward was to go back in time. The answers and the questions lay in the freak accident that shocked Delphi into a comatose organ donor and the deepfreeze of eternal limbo. It was the season of summer forest fires, and moonbeam children, and 'wrong-time bears.' Time to face the end of the world and welcome my daughters to the beginning of a new one. It was time to properly fall in love.

Delphi's voice rang out, chillingly true – an oracle chanting her wares inside my brain. Her words passed me in the dark as I ran back into the old labyrinth. "Once upon a blue moon," she called after me, "we were reborn from a long winter of dark magic to learn the secret of life. That which doesn't make us stronger will kill us. Twice."

And then I heard the peacocks crying a lament of long-lost love. Cecco was on his way.

The story of Delphi and Cherry concludes in 'Pearl by Pearl,' *the continuing afterlife, past-life, and future life of two women with the same memories rivalling for the ghostly lover they now share.*

Disclaimer Claim & the Power of Words

Words, words, words. Primarily, two words: *science* and *fiction*. I don't write Science-Fiction – a bold claim considering my stories involve recurring themes of *time-travel, reincarnation*, and *paranormal phenomenon*. The genre of Science-Fiction has evolved. But for me, those two words forever limit the realms of organic artificial intelligence. They conjure up established images of futuristic cities and advanced technology. Even the word *paranormal* fails to represent the concept of natural (misunderstood) abilities that happen to transcend the word *normal*.

It's harder than ever for authors to fit their stories into one box simply to enable readers and booksellers to locate them in real or virtual libraries. So much may be missed under a false word. Readers have been trained to react to key words that no longer adequately describe the crossovers of romance, adventure, crime, history, and art. Better not to misname. A word by any other name is often the wrong word.

Creative life is normal. Imagination is normal. Playing make-believe is learned in childhood, and it's never far from our thoughts when it comes to books and movies. The human child thrives on fairy tales. The human adult is drawn to romance and adventure. The art of storytelling is a time-honored profession.

In the latest tradition of storytelling, time-travel is about love triangles that transcend logic and space to explore the natural heights and depths of altered states of consciousness. States no more outrageous than a lucid dream. We all time-travel when we daydream about the future or consider the possibilities of reincarnation. We study history best by engaging our imagination rather than the warp drives of a spaceship. We time-travel when confronted by a premonition or a flash of déjà vu defies explanation.

And when we enter the altered states of alpha, theta, and beta, we daydream and nightmare, time-traveling our way over miles of neuron pathways through brainwaves of unconstrained magic. We are willing consumers of fantasy. Time and again we subscribe to extraordinary premises that demand the suspension of belief.

The romance of history trumps the archives of dry documents. Cold facts warmed to body heat are much more interesting. Creative memories deliver the heart of truths that live and breathe every time we drop out of the present to replay an old song, relive a moment of triumph, and indulge in speculation. We time-travel when synchronicity, more profound than chance encounters, hits us between the eyes. It's natural that we wander and wonder through what-ifs as acceptable as the supernatural. Super is just a word that means more than. Supra means above.

We time-travel to outwit aging and death, to amend mistakes, recover lost love, redress bad timing, and rewrite history as it might have been if only... We allow ourselves to reunite with loved ones. We talk to the headstones of the deceased, and we feel the power of the places where distant battles were won and lost. We respond to atmospheres and mists and the sounds of footsteps.

Time-travel turns us into the ghosts of our former selves hounded by a missed opportunity to write history. It offers a second chance to stop that stranger we passed on the street, whose eyes haunt us still, and say hello. 'Going back' allows us to embrace the hindsight of a grander view, the biggest picture of what was, and experience the escapism of improbable love and courage of lives lived the second time around.

Veronica Knox
November, 2015

Acknowledgments

The term 'arts and craft' is cited as if they are separate ingredients. As if. Indie authors, like myself, must marry the craft of writing with the art of graphic design to best present their literary children. Art and craft, and the joy of words and storytelling, is one big happy family.

I am fortunate to have two collaborators who have helped me produce a finished book worthy of the title, self-published.

Without the mentorship of **Lyn Alexander**, herself a perfectionist author, fierce editor, and dear friend of two years, the 'Pearl' books would never have been rewritten quite so rigorously. If you are one of the lucky writers to be critiqued by a sharp pair of literary eyes, you will know how vital it is to be loyally supported by a professional dedicated to the art and craft of writing.

Creativity is all about play. I've been a graphic designer since I graduated from the Reigate School of Art as a teenager, and later, as a mature student, I discovered art history and oil paint by obtaining a Fine Arts degree from the University of Alberta. But it was the sixties and seventies that introduced me to the fanciful travels through time and space of 'Dr. Who' and 'Star Trek.' I was hooked on time-travel.

Art and Craft... the transition of a raw manuscript to its final stamp of an official bar code on the back cover, transcends the traditional 'business' of graphic design, through playful manipulations of digital technology to 'fine' art. Once again, I'm indebted to the collaborative cover-to-cover partnership of **Iryna Spica**, the founder of SPICA BOOK DESIGN – Victoria, Canada.

And I would be remiss if I didn't thank Leonardo da Vinci for his legacy of insatiable curiosity and his 'family' of paintings which have inspired a series of time-slip fantasies of lost art, lost identities, and lost love. His dedication to exploring art and science, his fascination with birds and flight, and his missing 'Yarnwinder' painting inspired the 'pearl' story, as well as my trilogy 'Second Lisa' the fanciful biography of his youngest sister, Lisabetta, the woman (I premise) who posed for the 'Mona Lisa.'

I wanted to explore their world, but imagination being my only time machine, and in the spirit of wishful thinking, I created characters who could boldly go where I could play make-believe.

Author's Bio

Veronica Knox has a Fine Arts Degree from the University of Alberta, where she studied Art History and Painting. In her career as a graphic designer, art teacher, and artist, she has also worked with the brain injured and autistic, developing new theories of hand-to-eye-to-mind connection.

www.veronicaknox.com

Other Time-Slip Fantasies
by V Knox

The 'LISA' SERIES: a fictional biography of the 'MONA LISA'

'SECOND LISA' – *book one*
'SECOND LISA' – *book two*
'SECOND LISA' – *book three*

'WOO WOO'
– the posthumous love story of Miss Emily Carr

A middle-grade novel for ages ten to twelve:

'TWINTER'
– the first portal

'ADORATION'
– loving Botticelli

The 'PEARL' SERIES:

'THE INDIGO PEARL' – *book one*
'PEARL BY PEARL' – *book two*

'The UNTHINKABLE SHOES'
a work in progress
publication date – January 2016